all because of you

Melissa Hill is originally from Cahir in Co. Tipperary, and now lives with her husband Kevin and their dog Homer in Co. Dublin. She is also the author of *Not What You Think* and *Never Say Never*.

Praise for Melissa Hill

'Laugh-out-loud humour and a thrill to read' *B*

'A very warm, good-hearted story' *OK!*

'Be warned – you won't put down' *Sunday World*

'The literary equivalent of *Thelma & Louise* – feel-good and bittersweet . . . feels as good as a gossip with your mates!' *New Woman*

'Compelling, gripping, a real page-turner' *Irish Examiner*

'She writes wonderfully life-like characters, whose negotiations of the trials of life are easy to identify with. Her writing is natural and effortless – her stories cannot fail but to be satisfyingly consumed in a matter of hours' *Irish Independent*

'A gem!' *Evening Herald*

'A warm and engaging read – perfect for the beach!' Colette Caddle

'One to read' *U Magazine*

Also by Melissa Hill

Something You Should Know
Not What You Think*
Never Say Never*
Wishful Thinking
The Last to Know

* Published by Arrow Books

Melissa Hill

all because of you

arrow books

Published by Arrow Books 2007

7 9 10 8

First published in 2006 by Poolbeg Press Ltd

Arrow Books
Random House, 20 Vauxhall Bridge Road,
London, SW1V 2SA

www.rbooks.co.uk

Addresses for companies within The Random House Group Limited can be found at www.randomhouse.co.uk/offices.htm

The Random House Group Limited Reg. No. 954009

A CIP catalogue record for this book is available from the British Library

ISBN 9780099499695

The Random House Group Limited supports The Forest Stewardship Council (FSC), the leading international forest certification organisation. All our titles that are printed on Greenpeace approved FSC certified paper carry the FSC logo. Our paper procurement policy can be found at www.rbooks.co.uk/environment

Typeset by Palimpsest Book Production Limited,
Grangemouth, Stirlingshire
Printed in the UK by CPI Bookmarque, Croydon, CR0 4TD

Acknowledgements

Huge thanks yet again to the following people:

As always, lots of love and thanks to Kevin. In more ways than one, I couldn't do this without you.

My family – Mam, Dad, Amanda and Sharon – and all my friends, who continue to be supportive and excited for me, despite trying to keep their eyes from glazing over whenever I mention the word 'book'. And to Homer, who always manages to cheer me up if my writing happens to hit a tight spot.

To Poolbeg – Kieran, Claire, Lynda, Conor and Niamh – who continue to do Trojan work on my behalf: thank you. To my editor Gaye, who somehow always manages to 'get' what I'm trying to do and (most of the time!) lets me. And huge thanks to Paula, who has championed my work from day one and to whom this book is dedicated.

To the Arrow team – thanks to Kate and Georgina

for being so enthusiastic about my writing, Faye, Rob and Trish for working so hard on my behalf (Rob, thanks again for bringing me along to Parky to see George M!). To Rina Gill for Herculean publicity efforts, and to everyone at Random House for making my visits to London so enjoyable. Also huge thanks to those at Random House Australia for such a lovely welcome in Sydney last December.

To my brilliant agent Sheila Crowley (and her seemingly never-ending supply of bubbly!) and all at AP Watt who look after me so well.

To all the booksellers in Ireland and the UK who give my books terrific support, and who are always so welcoming whenever I pop in for a visit. Thanks in particular to Hilary at Bridge St Books in Wicklow, also Eason in Clonmel and Pat in Chapter One in Cahir for supporting me so well back home in Tipp.

Finally, a special thanks to all who buy and read my books, and allow me to continue living my dream. I'm so very grateful. Thanks too for your lovely messages of support through my website **www.melissahill.info**.

I very much hope you enjoy *All Because of You.*

To Paula Campbell –
thanks for everything

all because
of you

Prologue

So this was how real love felt, she thought happily, her body humming with joy as she lay back and closed her eyes. This was what she'd waited all this time for. *He* was what she'd waited all this time for.

And it was just as wonderful as she'd imagined.

She turned her head sideways and in the darkness watched him sleeping peacefully alongside her – watched the way his long eyelashes looked strangely feminine against such a masculine face. God, he was gorgeous, she thought, reaching out and gently stroking his cheek.

And, after tonight, he was hers at last.

She still couldn't believe that it had finally happened, that after all this time he had finally admitted that he was in love with her too, that she was the one – had always been the one – for him. OK, so he hadn't said those exact words out loud, but he'd said them in other ways, hadn't he?

She sighed as she recalled the feel of him, the taste of him, the softness of his skin . . . She shook her head, amazed at the immense effect he had on her. But what would happen to them now, she wondered, her initial euphoria about the wonderful evening they'd just spent together slowly being replaced by a creeping trepidation and a growing sense of guilt. She bit her lip.

There would be problems to overcome, certainly, and yes, people might get hurt, but this was meant to be, wasn't it? *They* were meant to be.

She hadn't really given it much thought earlier on. She'd been aware of the fact that they shouldn't be doing it, of course, it was difficult not to be, but the few drinks she'd had beforehand had thrown any restraint she might have had out the window.

And how could she not be with him, this amazing guy she'd adored almost on sight, who was the first person she thought of in the mornings and the last at night? Who made her feel like she was the most beautiful woman in the world; who made her think she could achieve anything? Who had kissed her so passionately and when making love had instinctively known his way around her body? All of which convinced her more than ever that the two of them were soul mates.

And that was all that mattered at the end of the day, wasn't it?

After all, if they were really in love, what else could they do? They couldn't help how they felt about one another, could they? And it had all felt so right – so it seemed inconceivable that they wouldn't be together properly after this. OK, so there were lots of things to sort out, but whatever happened, they'd face it together. And eventually, everything would work out fine.

Just then, the sleeping figure beside her stirred and opened his eyes.

"Hello there," she smiled leaning forward, and kissing him on the lips. "You nodded off for a good while there." Although she had dozed a little herself immediately afterwards, there had certainly been no question of her falling asleep – not after such an amazing night and certainly not here. There was way too much to think about. But of course men were different, she thought affectionately.

But instead of returning her kiss, he quickly sat up and stared wildly around him, as if trying to remember exactly where he was.

"What's going on? What are you . . .?" Running a hand through his hair, he turned back to look at her properly and, taking in her still-dishevelled dress as well as his own, evidently began to recall what had happened. "Oh, God."

This was inevitable, she told herself calmly. It was only natural he'd be a bit bewildered by the whole thing. It was all right for her – she'd already spent the last while lying awake thinking about it all, while he'd slept things off. So, once he'd woken up properly, and they'd had a chance to talk about what had happened between them, and where things would go from here . . .

Then, catching sight of his expression, her heart sank.

This wasn't just disorientation, she thought, gathering her clothing protectively around her – he was already having second thoughts. Oh no, please don't, she said silently. Not after the wonderful time we've just spent together. Please don't ruin it.

"What is it?" she said, longing to touch him but sensing that she shouldn't.

"What is it?" he repeated, his voice shaking. "What do you think it is? We didn't . . . I didn't use anything. Jesus, how could we have been so stupid?"

She gulped. She was well aware of that too, and doubly aware of how stupid she'd been for allowing it to happen. But she'd been drunk – not only on alcohol – but on her love for him and, at the time, everything else just seemed unimportant. But it would be OK; she knew her cycle well and she'd just had her period the week before so everything should be fine.

"I can't believe it," he was saying. "Of all the stupid . . ."

He seemed different now, jumpy, irritable. She didn't like it.

"Look, it'll be OK," she said, trying to convince herself as much as him. She didn't know if it *would* be OK, but she didn't want their special night together ruined by worrying about it.

He turned to face her.

"Look," he began, his tone now considerably calmer and sounding much gentler, much more like the real him. "I'm sure you know as well as I do that all of this was a mistake – a huge mistake."

She didn't know how she found the strength to nod, never mind speak. "A mistake?"

"Look, you know I care for you a lot, but this should never have happened. We'd both had a few drinks and . . . well, I really should have known better." Then he stood up and ran a hand through his dark hair. "God, you have to know that I don't make a habit of this kind of thing, I've never . . . well, we both did something very stupid and if anything were to happen or if anyone were to find out –"

"It's OK," she told him gently. "Nobody will find out. I won't say a word."

A look of relief crossed his face, and then he reached over and kissed her chastely on the cheek.

Instantly her heart plummeted in her chest. Why was he acting like this – so cold and distant and so utterly different from last night?

"Thank you," he said, as he turned away and began putting on his shoes. "You don't know how much I appreciate that. And please don't think badly of me – as I said, I've never done anything like this before, and the last thing I want is to hurt anyone." He sighed.

"It's OK." She tried not to let her disappointment and utter humiliation show. How could he change so suddenly from the wonderful gentle guy she knew to this . . . this aloof and almost detached one? What had gone wrong? Surely it couldn't have been just the drink? In order for them to be in this situation in the first place, it had to have been more than that. Or was it that he just didn't want to admit it? Was he afraid that, because of their circumstances, it would all be just too difficult?

"Look, I'm sorry if I sounded a bit . . . weird there," he said then, as if reading her thoughts. "Last night was great – it's just . . . you know," he shrugged, "obviously, it shouldn't have happened – and especially not like this. But please don't think badly of me. You're great, and the last thing I want to do is hurt you."

"You haven't," she said, trying now to harden her heart, trying to pretend this wasn't really happening. "You're right – it should never have happened and, to be honest, I'm as much to blame as you are." She shook her head. "And I feel as guilty as you do too." She did feel guilty, but right then the overpowering emotion she felt was regret. Regret that their wonderful night together was ending like this.

"God, if you were to get pregnant or something –"

"I won't," she assured him once more, hoping she sounded convincing. "I promise you, everything will be all right."

Chapter 1

"Before you ask, no, I haven't."

"You haven't what?"

"I haven't lost any weight since the last time I was here." Her stance was resistant, almost hostile, Tara Harrington thought, as she surveyed the woman sitting across from her. "I know I should have but –"

"Mary, wasn't achieving fitness your primary goal the last time you were here?"

"Well, yes, but . . . I haven't done it anyway," she replied quickly. "I know I should join a gym or something but . . ."

Lots of "buts" and "shoulds" in this conversation, Tara noted.

"You spoke about joining a gym last time we met, didn't you?" Tara said, trying to keep her tone non-judgemental. "I take it you haven't yet done that?"

"Well, I really didn't have the time," Mary replied defensively.

Tara immediately changed tack. The gym was clearly a non-runner here.

"OK, well, besides the gym, what other everyday things could you do to increase your fitness levels? Simple things that don't take up too much time?"

Mary shrugged. "I suppose I could use the stairs at work instead of the lift."

"Good." Tara nodded approvingly. "What else?"

"Em . . . I suppose I could walk to the corner shop when I need milk or a newspaper instead of taking the car?"

"Very good." Then, as Mary obviously wasn't about to come up with any more ideas, Tara continued, "Are there any other forms of exercise that you used to like doing, or would possibly do if you had more time?"

After a beat Mary replied, "I suppose I like swimming on holiday. I was in the pool every day during our last holiday in Spain so I suppose I should do it at home. That's a form of exercise, isn't it?"

Mary's use of the expression "should" yet again put Tara on alert. The woman wouldn't get results if she had to force herself to achieve them, and it was up to Tara to ensure she didn't see it that way.

"OK, well, what would you need to do to enjoy swimming at home here in Ireland?" she asked her, using a slight inflection on "enjoy".

Mary looked thoughtful. "I'm not sure really."

"Perhaps you could arrange to go swimming with a friend, or a work colleague, even?"

Mary didn't look too thrilled about the prospect. "Maybe."

Tara put down her pen and looked the other woman directly in the eye. "Mary, on a scale of one to ten, ten being fully committed to becoming fit, where are you?"

The other woman sighed and looked away. "About a five or six."

Tara's tone immediately became firmer. "Then, do *right now* what you need to take your commitment to preventing heart disease to a ten."

Mary looked up, a little taken aback at this. She thought for a moment before answering. "Well, now that you mention the reason I'm doing this in the first place, it's a ten, definitely a ten."

"So, on a scale of one to ten, how committed are you to becoming healthy?"

"Definitely ten." She was now nodding vigorously.

"So, if your commitment to becoming healthy is a ten, what is your commitment to walking up the stairs instead of taking the lift? Or walking instead of driving to the shop?"

"Ten." Mary was speaking with much more conviction now, exactly the response that Tara wanted.

"Are you sure? Because I don't want to find out at our next session that you've taken the lift instead of walking."

"Yes, I'm absolutely sure."

"Great," Tara said, before asking casually, "So, on

the subject of swimming, how committed are you?"

Mary took a deep breath. "I suppose about an eight or nine."

"OK, and how are you going to ensure that you enjoy swimming here instead of just on holiday?"

Mary brightened a little. "Well, I've always thought I might like to try an aqua-aerobics class or something like that."

"Why an aqua-aerobics class?"

"My friend Sinéad goes, and she enjoys it. I suppose I could go along with her."

"Would going with Sinéad help you keep to your commitment to increasing your fitness levels?"

Mary nodded, now at last getting the idea. "Yes, it would."

"So, on a scale of one to ten, how committed are you to joining Sinéad at the aqua-aerobics class?"

"Ten," Mary replied proudly.

"Are you sure?"

"Yes."

"So what do you need to do today to ensure that you attend the next aqua-aerobics class?"

"I need to ring Sinéad and arrange it."

"What time will you ring her?"

"Well, she gets back from the school run around four. I might ring her then."

"So you're committed to ringing Sinéad this afternoon between four and five o'clock to arrange to go the next aqua-aerobics class, yes?"

Mary nodded once more. "Definitely yes."

"Great, Mary. I look forward to hearing all about it at our next session." Tara was feeling a little drained by the repetitive and rather patronising process of getting Mary some way committed to attaining fitness. But she'd achieved it (for the moment at least) and that, after all, was what any life coach worth her salt wanted.

Poor Mary was a good three stone overweight and, if she wasn't careful, was heading for chronic obesity. Having tried every fad diet under the sun, she'd eventually contacted Tara to see if there was anything she could do to help her lose the weight. From the outset, Tara was careful to distinguish between "becoming healthy" which had positive connotations, and "losing weight" which had negative connotations, and (as every woman who'd ever tried to lose a few pounds knew) naturally fostered mental resistance. And in Tara's view, the only way clients could achieve their goals was to feel that responsibility for that success lay with them, rather than her.

But today, at least, she'd helped get Mary back on track.

Mary stood up and picked up her jacket. "So, I'll see you when you get back, then. Enjoy your holiday." Then she added, winking, "I'd say it'll be relief to get away from all of us whingers for a while!"

"Don't be silly, Mary, I love my job," Tara said good-humouredly as she saw her out the door of her office. "It's very fulfilling. As I told you the very first day I met you, I'm in show business and –"

"I know," Mary repeated, grinning, her earlier bad

humour now well evaporated. "You *show* people how to achieve the life they want!"

Tara waved goodbye to Mary – her final appointment for the evening – then closed the door of her office and went into the main house. Although "office" was a bit of an overstatement, as it was actually the converted front room of her own house (yet another overstatement as the house was rented – there wasn't a hope of her and Glenn being able to afford exorbitant office rates). But the room was quiet, restful and its homely qualities actually seemed to put clients at ease. People often mentioned that they felt as though they'd just popped over to a friend's house for a cup of tea and a chat, which was exactly the cosy atmosphere Tara had been aiming for, rather than the stuffy and sometimes overwhelming surroundings often associated with counselling or therapy.

While there were links between therapy and life coaching, the latter had very different techniques and methodologies. Unlike psychology or psychiatry, coaching did not deal with diseases of body and mind – instead it helped with issues of self-esteem or inability to achieve desired goals. And today, in post-Celtic Tiger Ireland, it seemed there was no shortage of dissatisfied individuals seeking assistance in finding what they really wanted out of life.

Although admittedly, she thought, going upstairs to change, it had taken Irish people some time to get used to the idea of using life coaches, and because the profession was largely new, she knew there were still many who viewed it with suspicion. But life coaching was ultimately all about results and, in this regard, Tara's track record spoke for itself.

When she first set up the consultancy three years back, business had been slow, but following some aggressive marketing and a series of talks at local business groups, women's clubs and organisations, she began to pick up clients here and there, and after a year to eighteen months, began to get many, many more through referrals. These days, her services were in so much demand that new clients could be waiting up to three or four weeks for an appointment. Also, in addition to individual face-to-face appointments, Tara also ran face*less* coaching sessions and, sometimes, after finishing a long day seeing clients either in the office or out of it, she spent a further few hours holding online or telephone sessions for people who were uncomfortable with meeting her face to face or who lived too far away to do so.

So, after spending three solid years building the consultancy to such a level (with darling Glenn supporting her massively from the sidelines), she felt that this year they just might be justified in taking a well-earned break, and the following Wednesday they were heading off for a ten-night holiday in Sharm El Sheikh on the Red Sea.

"Egypt?" he'd moaned when Tara had announced she'd booked their first holiday abroad in years. "Does this mean you'll be dragging me around the place looking at dead mummies and ancient tombs?"

"No, it means that we'll be sunning ourselves under blue skies and in thirty-five-degree sun, instead of facing the autumn wind and rain here," Tara had explained. And when she'd pointed out in the brochure the glorious five-star hotel she'd chosen, there hadn't been another word out of him.

They both really needed this holiday. Glenn had been working like a demon lately; in fact, he'd had to beg for the time off from Pixels, the computer firm in which he worked. Unlike him, Tara didn't have to beg for time off from anyone. Anyone other than her own conscience anyway, she thought ruefully.

Having changed out of the skirt and blouse she wore for seeing clients into a more comfortable sweatshirt and a pair of jeans, Tara went back downstairs and into the kitchen.

When she came in, she found Glenn sitting at the counter eating takeaway pizza and looking so utterly handsome that her heart skipped a beat. With his almost jet-black hair, liquid brown eyes and naturally sallow skin, Glenn was the kind of guy that always turned heads and, not for the first time, Tara couldn't quite get her head around the fact that he was really hers.

"I thought you were making dinner?" she said, referring acidly to the pizza. Although she loved the stuff, she knew it wouldn't do her figure any good to be munching on cheese and pepperoni stodge after a day's work.

"I did – well, Four Star Pizza did," he replied, shrugging. "I didn't have time to make anything else,

Tara. I'm due at work in an hour." Glenn had recently begun working overtime at Pixels in the run up to their holiday.

Tara looked at the clock. It was almost six and she'd promised her mum she'd be at her place soon after seven. Blast it – she didn't really have time to make anything else either – the Friday evening traffic out of the city was bound to be mental!

"Just don't make a habit of this, OK?" she said, picking up a slice of pizza and taking a huge, satisfying bite of it. "Otherwise, we'll both end up looking like the Michelin Man."

"No worries. From now on, I solemnly swear to make the boring chicken and vegetable pasta we usually have."

"It's not boring, Glenn, it's *healthy*, and you could do with keeping an eye on what you eat now and again," she said, conscious that she was still in life-coaching mode but unable to switch off. "All that Red Bull rubbish you drink is not good for you. It's full of caffeine."

"Tools of the trade," he said, his mouth open as he ate, and Tara elbowed him.

"Were you brought up or dragged up?" she teased, shaking her head in exasperation. His job as a system's analyst necessitated working long hours in front of a PC and, like many other habitual computer users, he relied on caffeine to keep him going.

His choice of career seemed inevitable, given that he'd had an irreversible bond with computers since his first Atari and, even when not at work, could barely stay out of cyberspace for more than a couple of hours. Tara had long since got used to the clattering of the keyboard from his study which, depending on whatever system he was trying to hack into, could often be heard till the early hours of the morning.

"Are you finished for the day then?" he asked, eyeing her casual clothes.

"Finished for two long weeks, you mean," she replied with a self-satisfied sigh. "I can't wait for this, Glenn, I really can't. Imagine, two whole blissful weeks without work."

"Hmm, it remains to be seen how blissful it'll be." He was still convinced he'd be roped into discovering the more "cultural" side of Egypt. "Knowing you, we mightn't even get a chance to relax."

"Love, believe me, we'll be doing lots of relaxing! And I'm going to make the most of being off-duty for a change. But speaking of duty," she looked up again at the clock, "I'd better get a move on. I told Mum I'd be down soon after seven." She grabbed a napkin and began to wipe her sticky fingers.

"Oh, I forgot you were heading down to Castlegate for the night," Glenn said, scooping up another slice. "Say hi to them all for me."

"I will." Then, catching sight of the pile of rubbish for recycling in the corner of the kitchen by the back door, Tara sighed. "Damn! I meant to drop all that off to the centre today," she said, eyeing the tidily bound newspapers, crushed aluminium cans and washed glass bottles. "I'll hardly have time to do it now, and the stuff is really piling up."

"I'll look after it. Although I still can't understand why you don't just throw the whole lot in the wheelie bin and be done with it, instead of all these treks to and from the recycling centre."

Tara fixed him with a look. "Because, unlike you, Glenn, I'm quite happy to do every little bit I can to help clean up our environment – while we're here it's the very least we can do and –"

"I know, I know," he interjected wearily, having heard the same argument many times before. "It's the least we can do, and future generations will thank us for it. And how will they do that, incidentally? Send us a postcard or something?"

When Tara didn't seem to find this funny, he raised his hands in the air in a gesture of defeat. "OK, OK, I said I'd do it, didn't I? Anything to make you happy."

"Anything to stop me nagging you, maybe," Tara said with a grin. "And you might as well get rid of that pizza box while you're at it – don't forget to clean it off first though."

"Yes, master, whatever you say, master!" Glenn replied, bowing his head exaggeratedly at her bossy tone.

"Oh, give over!"

Leaving him to finish the last of the pizza, Tara went to check her appearance in the hallway mirror. She wiped a very obvious splodge of tomato sauce from her face and quickly applied a coat of lipstick before running a brush through her fair hair.

Then she went back into the kitchen and gave Glenn – who had another huge slice of pizza in his mouth mid-bite – a quick kiss on the cheek, before picking up her jacket and bag and heading for the front door. "See you tomorrow night, darling – don't work too hard!"

"I won't . . . oh and be sure to let me know what they think of the car!" he shouted to her retreating back. "I bet that'll get some reaction!"

Tara grimaced as she closed the front door behind her. She'd forgotten all about the fact her parents hadn't yet seen the new car.

Well, it would get a reaction all right, she thought, as she reversed out of the driveway and drove off in the direction of North County Dublin, although hardly the one that Glenn anticipated.

Chapter 2

She smiled to herself as she drove along the dual carriageway, enjoying the feel of the wind on her face. Despite the late hour, the sun was still shining, the sky was blue; everything was so perfect, you'd think whoever was in charge of the weather had given her this fabulous evening on purpose.

Of course, she always looked forward to returning home to Castlegate, a small, picturesque and hugely popular tourist village some twenty miles outside of Dublin city, and again she wondered if she and Glenn should think seriously about moving back to live there. But Glenn loved living in the city and, with the majority of Tara's clientele to be found in the capital, it wouldn't be practical just yet. But it was certainly something to think about for the future.

She put the convertible into fifth gear and deftly moved into the fast lane, only remembering to check her rear-view mirror at the very last minute. *Eeek!* Her heart lurched, but luckily there was nothing behind her. She exhaled deeply and shook her head from side to side. It was all very well being in a good mood, but she really should be more careful – especially when driving this bloody thing!

Approaching a set of traffic lights on red further down the road, Tara eased off on the accelerator. Typical – once you got stopped at the first set, you got stopped at them all, she groaned, tapping her nails against the steering wheel impatiently. Then, vaguely sensing she was being watched, she looked to her left and spotted the driver of the car alongside flash her an appreciative smile.

Tara reddened and looked away, desperately willing the lights to change. She supposed she should be used to the attention by now, the sporty Renault cabriolet turning heads wherever they went – much to Glenn's delight – but Tara always felt like such a bloody poser in this thing.

Then again, a blonde in a convertible always got attention, didn't she? Never mind that the blonde in question was really a *strawberry*-blonde who badly needed her roots done, wore very little make-up and was today dressed in decidedly unglamorous sportswear – totally undeserving of such attention. If anything she looked like some cheeky gurrier who'd hot-wired the thing!

She stared straight ahead, trying to ignore the other driver. Why on earth she had let Glenn talk her into buying this she'd never know.

But wasn't it a blessing twice over that the weather was fine? Because even though she'd been driving the car a few weeks now, she still couldn't for the life of her figure out how to put the top back up. She had meant to ask Glenn for another demonstration before she left but had forgotten.

Glenn, as always, was horrified at Tara's lack of appreciation of auto-excellence.

"What's the point in having a class machine like that if you don't appreciate it?" he'd say, while Tara would roll her eyes and point out that she'd have been much happier in an ordinary, run-of-the-mill Golf or something, rather than this snazzy, attention-seeking number he'd insisted they get.

She eventually spied the turn-off for her parents' place, which was situated in a small mews just outside Castlegate village. She made her way tentatively towards their house, hoping that no one she knew would see her driving this pretentious car. She could almost imagine the comments. "Did you see that Harrington one in her fancy car? Who does she think she is coming down from Dublin and lording it over us all? Next, she'll be telling us all how to live our lives like she does with all those snobs up in the city!"

Tara's career as a life coach was something she knew her poor mother had a terrible time trying to explain to the neighbours and couldn't quite get to grips with herself.

"Surely people don't need to be told how to live their lives, Tara?" Isobel would say, when Tara had first set up her consultancy. "Surely they have enough common sense to be able to work things out for themselves?"

Tara had given up trying to convince her mother that there were people out there who needed some form of direction in their lives, who needed somebody objective to help them get to grips with things like time management, relationship issues and – more often than not – boost their self-confidence. And most importantly, there were people out there who were willing to pay good money to do so.

"It's perfect for you," her best friend Liz had said, when Tara originally broached the idea of life coaching. "You have a natural empathy with people and, unlike lots of people I know, you have a terrific ability to see things objectively – not to mention that you've got a lot of common sense about things – well, your love life aside," she added sardonically.

Tara ignored the jibe. It was all right for Liz; for as long as she'd known her friend, she'd wanted marriage and babies and happy families and all that. Tara, on the other hand, had no interest in marriage whatsoever, and she and Glenn were perfectly happy the way they were. Tara spent most of her time trying to help people decide what it was they wanted from life and how to get it, but despite what Liz thought, she herself didn't have that problem.

Reaching her parents' house she parked outside and prayed inwardly that the rain would hold off for the rest of the evening. Despite the earlier sunshine, there were by now a few dark clouds gathering overhead, so fingers crossed. Glenn would not be best pleased if the car's lovely leather interior got drenched! On second thoughts, she rooted in the glove compartment and pulled the instructions handbook out. She'd get her dad to have a look at it – maybe he could figure out the mysteries of raising and lowering the top.

She rang the doorbell and cast a nostalgic glance around her dad's well-tended garden. Her parents had lived in the same estate since Tara was born and through all of her subsequent thirty-four years.

Thinking of her and Glenn's rented house in Dublin, and their polite but rather detached neighbours, Tara now felt a brief loneliness for the sense of community always present here. Most of the families in this estate had lived here just as long as her parents and knew each other well. Now, while it had of course been a right pain in the backside getting caught sneaking out of the front window at night to go to the disco when she was a teenager, Tara thought it was nice to know that there was someone you could trust with a set of spare keys, or someone to call in to for a chat whenever you felt a bit lonely. Tara had nobody like that, really, not since Liz had almost a year earlier moved here with her husband Eric (who was a childhood friend of Tara's from Castlegate) and young son. And single-handedly running a one-to-one life-coaching consultancy wasn't exactly conducive to gossipy chats!

But she was calling over to Liz's house later and was planning to spend the night, so no doubt they'd have a good chat then.

Tara smiled warmly when her mother opened the door.

"I thought you'd be here earlier," Isobel said by way of greeting, her face impassive as she regarded her eldest daughter. "Too busy telling people how to live their lives, I suppose."

"Hi, Mum!" Ignoring the remark, Tara stepped forward and gave her mother an enthusiastic hug. Isobel had never taken what her daughter did for a living seriously, and Tara didn't expect that to change now. "I thought I'd be earlier too, but the traffic was heavy, and I got stuck at every single red light on the way."

"Is Glenn not with you?" her mother asked, looking behind Tara, and her eyes widened as her gaze rested on the car. "Is that *thing* yours?"

Tara shrugged. "Yep. Glenn's wanted one for ages. As long as it's got four wheels and a steering wheel, I don't care what I drive." She wasn't sure why she felt she had to be dismissive of the car, particularly as the money to buy it had been hard-earned and, as Glenn had insisted, "totally well-deserved". Perhaps she felt it would be better if she herself got the jibe in before her mother had the chance.

"I see. A bit fancy, isn't it?"

"It's just a car, Mum. And no, as you can see, Glenn's not with me. He had to work up some extra hours in order to get time off for the holiday. I thought I told you that?"

"Right. Well, it's probably just as well he isn't," Isobel replied cryptically as she closed the door behind them, but Tara hardly heard her.

"Is Dad here? The garden looks great – and I can't believe how much the clematis has spread since last year . . ." She rambled happily on, all the way in from the hallway to the back of the house and out to the kitchen. Then she stopped short.

Tara's younger sister Emma was sitting at the kitchen table alongside their father, her face solemn and mournful, and instantly Tara knew that something was up.

While talking to her mother on the phone a few days back about her impending visit, Isobel had briefly mentioned something about Emma being a bit off form.

"Why, what's wrong with her?" Tara asked, before adding silently – *this time.*

"Ah, she's very down in the dumps," Isobel replied. "She came down from Dublin last weekend and was going around with a face on her like a wet week."

Man trouble no doubt, Tara thought, and smiled indulgently. At thirty-one, Emma was three years younger than Tara and, in more ways than one, very definitely the baby of the Harrington family. Emma had probably got a bee in her bonnet over some guy she was seeing in Dublin and had come home to Castlegate for some attention and sympathy. Which, of course, was something she'd get from Isobel in spades. Emma was the baby, the pet and the one who over the years had always needed a lot of mothering, much more than Tara who, from a very early age, had sought independence and was very self-reliant.

For this reason, and the fact that she was usually

man-less, often jobless and habitually gave off a general air of misfortune, Emma was very much the favourite in the household – something Tara had long since come to terms with and wasn't at all bothered by. Still, despite their different personalities, she and Emma had always got on reasonably well, although at times Tara did find the "poor me" aspect of her sister's behaviour a little irritating.

So, what was the problem this time? Emma was always experiencing some kind of drama, and if it wasn't trouble with a man, or trouble with one of her friends, it was trouble with work. Despite the fact that there were "Staff Wanted" signs everywhere Tara looked and companies seemed to be crying out for employees, for some reason Emma couldn't seem to hold down a job either in the village or in Dublin. Laziness being the obvious reason, Tara mused, but quickly stopped in mid-thought and urged herself to snap out of judgemental-older-sister mode.

"Emma, hi – how are things?" she asked easily.

"Hi," Emma responded with one of her trademark mournful looks – the one that implied that the world and his mother were conspiring against her.

Tara groaned inwardly.

"Maybe you could use your life-coaching skills on your sister, Tara," her mother said, her voice tinged with annoyance. "After what she's just told us, she certainly needs them."

"What do you mean?" Tara looked curiously at Emma.

"I'm pregnant," her sister replied in a small voice.

Tara's eyes widened. Oh dear, this *was* a problem.

"I just told them the news before you arrived. I'm three months gone." Emma glanced away, refusing to look any of them in the eye.

"But . . . but how?" Tara spluttered, shaking her head in bewilderment. "I mean . . . I didn't know you were seeing anyone or –"

"Neither did we," her mother interjected, her voice laden with disapproval.

"I'm not . . . I wasn't seeing anyone," Emma confirmed quietly. "It was a mistake . . . an accident."

"An accident? You mean a one-night stand?" Tara persisted, while her father looked away, clearly uncomfortable with the whole scenario.

Emma nodded, her huge blue eyes filling with tears.

"Oh, Emma!" Her heart instantly going out to her sister, Tara took a seat alongside her at the table. "I know there's no point in saying it now, but you really should have been more careful –"

"Er, I'd better go back out to the garden." Evidently feeling awkward with the conversation, and the direction it seemed to be taking, Bill stood up. "I'll be back in later on," he told Isobel, who remained stony-faced as he went out and closed the door behind him.

"I know I should have been more careful, and I didn't mean for it to happen," Emma said, her eyes shining with tears. "Believe me, it was the last thing I expected –"

Tara shook her head. This was awful. Though, at thirty-one years of age, at least Emma was old enough to cope with an unplanned pregnancy and was a million miles away from the state of some unmarried teenager.

"So, have you told the father?" she asked.

Emma shook her head vehemently. "No, and I'm not planning to tell him either."

"What? What do mean you're not planning to tell him?" Isobel's eyes flashed with annoyance.

This was a shock for every parent, but perhaps even more of a shock for their mother, Tara supposed. Coming from a small village like Castlegate, Isobel's initial concern would undoubtedly be about what the neighbours would say.

"Why *wouldn't* you tell him?" Isobel demanded.

"It's complicated, Mum," Emma replied, her face going even paler, and Tara wondered why she looked so uncomfortable.

"Complicated? What could be complicated about it? Call me old-fashioned but the two of you were there, so the two of you should be responsible. Or is it that you don't even know who he is?"

Tara sighed inwardly. When upset, Isobel could be unnecessarily vindictive, although not usually where Emma was concerned.

"Mum, I . . ." Emma seemed lost for words, obviously taken aback by her mother's chastisement of her.

"Look, it'll be OK," Tara interjected softly, hoping to defuse the situation. "Everything will be OK."

"It certainly *will* be OK," Isobel remarked, her tone brooking no nonsense. "As long as the fellow in question, whoever he is, admits his responsibility and stands by you."

Tara looked questioningly at Emma.

"That's not going to happen, Mum," Emma stated, her chin lifting in determination. "The father of this baby will have nothing to do with it."

Tara's heart sank even further in her chest.

"Emma –" said Isobel.

"Mum, as I said before, it's complicated and I don't want to hear any more about it!" Emma's voice was raised. "I'm sorry that this has happened – I didn't want it to happen, and I certainly don't need you making me feel any worse than I already do about it, OK?"

Isobel pursed her lips but said nothing more.

For a little while, the three women sat in the sun-filled kitchen, each lost in her own thoughts, Tara deciding that you didn't need to be a life coach to figure out that something was very wrong here, and that Emma wasn't giving them the entire picture.

Why was she so insistent that the pregnancy be kept a secret from the father? Granted, if it was simply a one-night stand and she didn't know the guy that well, fair enough, but didn't she realise how difficult this was going to be without his help, financial or otherwise?

"You're certain you don't want to tell him?" Tara asked gently. "It'll be tough bringing up a baby on your own and –"

"I'm positive," Emma replied firmly, looking her sister straight in the eye. "I don't want to tell him and, before you ask, I'm not going to tell you either. This is all my own fault – I did something very, very, stupid, and now it seems I'm going to have to pay the price."

Later that evening, Emma lay on her bed and stared at the ceiling. She still couldn't believe this was happening to her.

How could it have happened? Why had it happened? Well, she knew exactly how and why, but why did it have to happen to her?

She couldn't tell him – not now. Emma's heart tightened as she thought about their night together, how great it had been at the time and then afterwards how abruptly her happiness had come to an end. How could she have been so stupid? He didn't care about her, had never cared about her, and now here she was alone and carrying his baby.

And to think that Tara had been trying to get her to approach him, at least for support – how ironic was that? No, this would be her burden, and hers alone. Well, her mum and dad would probably have to shoulder some of that burden too, and Emma felt a bit guilty about that. Just when she was getting her life back on track too. Just when she'd found a job and career that really fulfilled her, that got her excited about getting up in the morning and going to work, got her excited about the future. She'd really enjoyed living in Dublin these last few months, but all that was at an end now, wasn't it? She'd have to move back home again.

She knew people thought her lazy and selfish at her

age to be always relying on her parents and moving from job to job. But her mum didn't mind having her living at home with them and, anyway, her mum understood that her youngest child didn't have the drive or ambition or pure *confidenc*e of her eldest.

No, Tara was the high achiever in the Harrington family – her with the nice new car, own business and optimistic outlook. But it was easy for her big sister to be optimistic, because everything had gone right for Tara since she'd first come into the world, healthy and happy, whereas Emma had nearly died at birth and had spent her first few months riddled with coughs and infections and every kind of baby illness you could think of.

And whereas Tara had excelled at school, Emma had been bored senseless. She couldn't give a damn about dull things like maths and history and stupid bloody Irish. What help were these things to you in life at the end of the day?

No, at school she much preferred messing about with her friends and trying to get the boys to notice her – she couldn't give a damn about V-shaped valleys and stupid glaciation. Of course, if the teachers were any good they would have realised she wasn't learning anything and would have worked extra hard to ensure she "got" it – but no, in class they were too busy fawning over the lick-arses to pay attention to the likes of her.

So it wasn't really her fault that she hadn't got a good result in her school exams and therefore not enough points to go to university. Just as it wasn't her fault that she could never find a job she liked or one she was any good at. It wasn't her fault at all. All she had ever wanted was to be a model, but at five-foot three she wasn't tall enough and, of course, that wasn't her fault either. Maybe if she hadn't been so sick as a child she might have grown that little bit more, but there was nothing she could have done about that either. No, for Emma life so far had turned out to be a series of disappointments.

And now this pregnancy was another in a long line of problems Emma had to surmount, although at least her mother, despite her initial annoyance, had agreed to give her as much help as she could.

As had Tara, although clearly she would have preferred Emma to seek help from the father. But, of course, that was Tara – trying to find solutions all the time. Emma sniffed. Didn't she know that sometimes there were just no solutions to be found? That life didn't always turn out rosy, like it seemed to for her?

A stray tear escaped from one eye and traced a line down Emma's cheek. Nothing ever seemed to go right for her – ever. Whereas everyone else seemed to sail through life without a care in the world. And she often wondered why that was. What had she done to deserve this – why should *she* be the one alone and pregnant while he could go back to his happy little life and all the rest of it, without giving her a second thought?

Emma wiped her eyes and lifted up her chin.

Maybe she shouldn't make things so easy for him after all. Maybe Tara was right; maybe he *did* deserve to know. Deserved to know that he couldn't let her think they had a future and then just discard her like a piece of filth, leaving her to pick up the pieces of the mess he'd made.

No, Emma thought determinedly, he should *not* be allowed to get away with it. And now, all she had to do was find some way of making sure he didn't.

Chapter 3

On Saturday afternoon, Liz McGrath had just put her eighteen-month-old son down for a short nap when she heard the familiar cacophony of agitated barks and yelps outside signalling the arrival of her latest house-guest.

She ran her fingers through her cropped dark hair and briefly wiped the front of her top, hoping that her Toby's latest exploits with his *Petit Filous* might not be so noticeable. Dried strawberry fromage frais on a blue cotton T-shirt was not a good look, and while she'd normally never greet a customer looking like this, today her son had been acting up so much she'd had no time to change. Still, this particular guest wouldn't care less, she thought, smiling. In fact, there was a really good chance that he'd be thrilled to see her covered in goo – tasty, slimy goo that he would only be too delighted to lick off. Bruno was like that.

"Hello there!" Liz waved a greeting at the woman coming through her front gateway, and her heart lifted at the sight of one of her favourite customers, who at that very moment was straining on his leash excitedly, eager to get to her. "Hey, Bruno!" Liz bent down, and tickled the dog behind the ears. The German shepherd responded by licking her chin enthusiastically.

"Will you stop that?" Bruno's owner, a stern woman of about fifty, quickly jerked him back on his leash. Liz had been looking after Bruno since he was a three-month-old puppy, yet she'd never quite been able to take to Jill Walsh (unlike her skittish, adorable pet who, in fairness, was extremely well-cared for).

Still, in the boarding-kennels business, it didn't matter what you thought of the owners – the most important thing was what they in turn thought of *you*. And with previous "guests" returning on a regular basis since she'd first opened six months back, Liz was very well liked amongst the cat and dog owners in the region. In fact, most of her customers were not from Castlegate village itself, but from the bigger town a few miles further down the road.

"Oh, he's OK, Mrs Walsh, aren't you, Bruno?" Liz stood up and wiped her hands on her jeans before taking the leash from Mrs Walsh as was their routine. Some dog owners liked to see their pets settled in their accommodation before leaving, whereas others, like Jill Walsh, preferred to just drop them off and leave.

"I'll be back in the country on the twenty-fifth," Jill

told Liz, her tone businesslike. "But I'll give you a call before I come to collect him."

"That's no problem – one of us will be here anyway," Liz told her pleasantly.

And one of them would be. Since Liz and her husband Eric's decision to move to his home village of Castlegate and subsequently start the boarding kennels, she'd been tied to the place almost every day, what with trying to get the house decorated and getting the kennels set up. She and Eric had been living here almost a year now and, although she was a Dublin girl by birth, Liz was loving it, especially as the move out of the city had given her the freedom (and the space) to set up her precious kennels business in the first place.

But what Liz was enjoying most about her life now was finally having a family of her own. When growing up, she had always been shunted from family to family, her own parents having died when she was twelve years old. As the youngest in the family, her older married brothers had done what was necessary, and over the years took turns looking after their teenage sister and raising her along with their own children. While she adored each of her brothers, and now as an adult could truly appreciate the sacrifice their respective wives had made in taking her in, all the chopping and changing meant that Liz had always been on the periphery of their families and had never truly been part of any of them. Nor had their houses ever really been home and, for as long as she could remember, it had always been her dream to have a family and home that she could call her own. Now, in Castlegate, with Eric, baby Toby and their lovely (although still-dilapidated) home, complete with dogs Ben and Jerry, the dream had finally come true.

The lack of rigid working hours that went hand in hand with the kennels occasionally got to Eric, but knowing how much his animal-mad wife loved what she did, he didn't complain too much. In truth, he loved having the dogs around too, and although he worked hard during the week at his security officer's job, which was based in Dublin, he was usually willing and eager to help Liz out at the weekends.

But the real reason they'd made the move to Castlegate was for Toby. Here there was so much more room for a young child to explore outdoors and enjoy the fresh air – which would have been almost impossible had they stayed living in the city. In Dublin, Liz and Eric might have taken him to the park the odd time; in Castlegate their long back garden was practically a park in itself!

She'd loved Castlegate since she'd first visited the place with Eric towards the beginning of their relationship, and long before they married. The popular tourist village – in the centre of which sat a perfectly preserved Norman castle, itself surrounded by a wide river moat – was absolutely stunning. The river, its bank lined with low-hanging beech and willow trees, wound its way through the centre of the village and a trio of small hump-back stone bridges spaced out at intervals joined all sides of the township together. But it was the cobbled streets and ornate lanterns, as well as the beautiful one-hundred-year-old artisan cottages decorated with hanging floral baskets, that really made Liz fall head over heels in love with the place. Because of its beauty, the village had long ago been granted heritage status by the Tourist Board, so the chocolate-box look and feel of the place was intentionally well preserved. Having grown up in and around suburban Dublin, Liz had been blown away by the romantic little village and thought that Castlegate would undoubtedly be a fabulous place to bring up a family.

And when, shortly after Toby was born, she and Eric first set eyes upon their little two-bed pre-war bungalow a short walk from the pretty village – complete with one-acre field behind it – she couldn't imagine herself living anywhere else.

Of course, the beauty of the kennels business meant that Liz could be a working mum with the all the benefits of a stay-at-home one too. It had taken a while to get into a routine, and was getting trickier as Toby got older and was starting to walk a little, but so far it was working out OK. But it would be even better if Eric could find work in the village here, instead of having to commute to and from Dublin, but she was sure that would happen in time.

Not long after she'd said goodbye to Jill Walsh and settled Bruno into his lodgings, Liz had another visitor – the caller's approaching car again setting off a chorus of yaps and barks from the dogs, while the cats just yawned, pretending to be bored but, Liz knew, interested all the same.

Unfortunately, all this recent activity had in the meantime woken Toby, and by the time Tara appeared on her doorstep, it was a weary but excited Liz who came to greet her at the front door.

"Oh, I'm sorry!" said Tara, taking in Toby's red-rimmed eyes and mussed-up hair. "Was he asleep?"

"For about all of ten minutes," Liz replied, rolling her eyes. "But don't worry about it – he doesn't stay down for long these days, and I've just taken another dog in so . . ." She shrugged, then beckoned Tara inside the small cottage. "Great to see you! And I *love* the new car – when did you get that? Come in for a cuppa first, and afterwards we'll go out for a good look." Going through to the kitchen, she set Toby down on the floor amongst his toys, hoping that watching *SpongeBob SquarePants* on TV would keep him occupied for a little while, and hopefully tire him out once and for all.

"Mmm, I'm still not too sure about the car yet," Tara said, taking a seat at Liz's kitchen table. "It's more Glenn's choice than mine."

"Typical!" Liz laughed. "And where is Glenn? Did he come with you? Oh no, you said he's working overtime this week, didn't you?"

Tara nodded.

"Well, I know Eric's eyes will pop out of his head when he sees that car. He's in bed sleeping off the night-shift, by the way," she informed Tara.

"Pity – it seems like ages since I've seen you both," Tara replied, automatically lowering her voice so as not to be responsible for waking yet another McGrath male.

The two girls had been friends for a long time, having worked side by side in the same Dublin telesales company for many years, and Liz was really looking forward to a good chat with Tara. In fact, it had been Tara who'd first introduced Liz to her old friend and fellow Castlegate native Eric McGrath.

But since Liz and Eric had moved away from the city, the two girls didn't see one another as often as they'd like, usually only when Tara came home to visit her parents.

"So, how come you couldn't come over last night?" Liz queried, throwing an eye towards Toby. "Are your mum and dad OK?"

Tara had been due to call over after visiting her parents the previous day, but had phoned later in the evening to tell Liz she'd be staying the night at their house, instead of having a night in at Liz's as they'd planned. She would explain later, she said.

"They're fine but . . ." Tara hesitated. "I probably shouldn't be telling you this yet," she bit her lip, "but no doubt you'll find out soon enough anyway. Especially in this town."

"Telling me what?" Liz put two mugs of coffee on the table and took a seat beside Tara.

"Emma's pregnant."

Liz didn't think she could be more surprised even if someone had told her they didn't like dogs. *"What?"*

"I know," Tara nodded and picked up a Jaffa Cake.

"But . . . but who? What?"

"That's exactly what *I* said."

"But she's not seeing anyone, is she?"

"She's not seeing anyone – and she's not saying who the father is either."

"What? Why not?" Liz had no time for Emma's theatrics and even less time for Emma herself.

"I'm not sure. But she's pretty determined all the same. I tried to convince her that the father has a right to know, but she's determined to keep it all a secret from him – God knows why. Although reading between the lines, she must have been with someone she shouldn't have been."

"So what does your mother think? I'll bet she isn't too happy about it."

"That's an understatement," Tara said dryly.

"I can imagine. But look, Emma's old enough to –"

"Old enough to know better? You'd think so, wouldn't you?"

"That's not what I was going to say. I meant she's not a teenager, and she should be well able to cope as a single mother. It's not as hard for people these days, is it? What with all the help they get from the state and everything?"

Tara nodded. "I know, but it still won't be easy. I know Mum will help, but she's getting on herself now and wouldn't be able to handle a young baby. Not to mention that she shouldn't have to."

Liz swallowed, wondering what to say. "I'm sure it'll all be fine, Tara – and I'm sure Emma knows you'll do your best to help out too."

Tara groaned. "The last person Emma needs giving her advice is someone like me."

"She'd be afraid you'd start using your 'mind-warping' tricks on her!" Liz joked, knowing full well how poorly Tara's family viewed her profession. Then her tone grew serious. "Look, Tara, there's very little you can do for her other than be there to help out if she needs you."

"I just can't believe it's happened – and at her age. And then all this fuss about who the father is . . ."

"She really won't say who he is?"

Tara shook her head. "She's adamant about it."

"But why all the mystery?" Liz asked, shaking her head. "I mean, these days, getting pregnant outside of marriage is hardly a big deal, is it?"

Tara took another sip from her coffee but said nothing.

"Well, I really hope she hasn't got herself involved with somebody she shouldn't have – a married man or something," said Liz, finally vocalising what both had been thinking.

Tara rolled her eyes. "Unfortunately, where Emma's concerned, that's a distinct possibility."

There had never been any great love lost between Liz McGrath and Emma Harrington. Unfortunately, much of Liz's reservations about the girl stemmed from the fact that Tara's sister and Eric had once been an item.

When they had first started seeing one another in Dublin, Liz wasn't too bothered about Eric's relationship history; by this stage she'd fallen madly in love with Tara's childhood friend and that was all that mattered. She'd heard that he'd been a bit "wild" in his younger days and that there had been more than a few old flames, but at the time she didn't pay much heed. And when shortly after they'd started going out she learned from Tara that Eric and her sister had once been a couple, she didn't bat an eyelid. The past was the past, and it wasn't as if Liz hadn't left a few broken hearts in her wake too.

But when, a few months into the relationship, she eventually came face to face with Emma, all Liz's nonchalance went straight out the window. There were no two ways about it: this girl was stunning. Long flaxen blonde hair, huge blue eyes and a beautifully structured face – your average nightmare.

The first time Liz met Emma was when she had come to visit Tara in Dublin, at the flat she shared with Glenn, and Tara had brought her along on one of their nights out. From the outset, Emma let it be known very clearly to Liz that she and Eric had been an item. According to Eric, the relationship had been brief and ended not long after he left Castlegate to go and work in Dublin. But he and Tara were closer in age and had been friends when they were younger, and so they stayed in close contact and met up in Dublin frequently, which is how Liz and Eric had first been introduced.

But while neither Tara nor Eric had made too much of his relationship with Emma, throughout the course of that visit Emma used every possible opportunity to let Liz know that she and Eric had been much more than good friends.

"Does Eric still snore like a train then?" she'd asked Liz within two minutes of meeting her. Then she added with a beatific smile, "I could never get a wink of sleep with him!"

Her tone left Liz in no doubt that she wasn't just referring to Eric's snoring. She'd been so taken aback by the comment that she hadn't been able to think of a decent reply, something that would sort the girl out once and for all. Not to mention that she was doubly surprised that she could be so unlike her genial, good-natured sister.

Anyway, there was no point in rising to the bait; any fool could see that Emma was an immature and attention-seeking little madam and, anyway, so what if she and Eric had been together? They weren't together any more, were they?

And she might have been a little madam but at the same time she was Tara's sister, so Liz decided that there was no point in causing trouble.

"Tell me how long you two were together again?" she'd asked Eric, not long after Emma's first visit.

"Not sure to be honest. About a year on and off, I suppose," he'd replied off-handedly.

"Really?" Liz wrinkled her nose. "I don't mean to sound nasty, but what on earth did you see in her? I couldn't take to her at all – she's so different to Tara in every way."

Eric shrugged. "Yeah, she can come across a bit standoffish, but she's alright when you get to know her."

Which you obviously did, Liz wanted to say, but decided against it. There was no point in causing trouble between them. Emma would probably love that and Liz wasn't going to let the little witch have her way. And, in all honesty, she didn't really know what to make of her. Did Emma still have residual feelings for Eric, or was she simply one of those immature women who got an idiotic thrill out of staking a past claim on another's boyfriend? Liz didn't know and, for the most part, she didn't care. Emma would soon toddle off back home and Liz wouldn't have too much to do with her.

But when, a few years after they married, she and Eric began to think seriously about moving to Castlegate, where Tara's sister still lived with her parents, Liz was no longer so sure.

She was furious with herself for letting the girl mentally inveigle herself into their relationship like that – despite the fact that it had been years since Emma's relationship with Eric. She and Eric were married, had a gorgeous son and their relationship was as good as it could possibly get. They'd barely spent a day apart since they'd first got together and deep down Liz knew that their relationship was as ideal as anyone could hope for. Yet there was something about Emma that unsettled her, that had always unsettled her, though she wished with all her heart that she didn't feel this way. She tried to tell herself that there was no real reason to feel threatened by the girl or her previous association with Eric, yet she had to think very seriously about going to live in close proximity to her husband's ex.

Despite the fact that she was now thirty-one years of age, Emma still lived at home with her parents, the reason being, according to Tara, that she found it difficult to hold down a job.

"In this country?" Liz had said, surprised, as the news reports never seemed to stop going on about the jobs boom the country was supposedly experiencing. But it seemed Emma's employment requirements were very specific. She'd left school without proper qualifications, hated office work, refused to work in retail and, following a brief stint in the village café, would "never again lower herself" to serving tables. So instead, Mammy and Daddy looked after her while she sat on her pert backside waiting for the perfect job to come to her.

"Which is?" Liz had asked Tara.

"Last I heard, she's hoping for something in fashion or beauty."

"And, of course, Castlegate is the right place to be for that," Liz drawled, decidedly unimpressed. "Sure, wasn't it only the other day that I bumped into Vivienne Westwood in Ryan's supermarket – or no, now that I think of it, was it Stella McCartney?"

Tara laughed. "Stop it! No, apparently she's doing some kind of correspondence course – something to get her started."

"And a job in a boutique wouldn't help at all, I suppose?" Liz retorted, shaking her head in dismay at the girl's laziness and apparent lack of ambition.

Her own family had been very different. Liz and her

brothers had each left home at seventeen and had worked hard and made their own way in the world. She couldn't understand how an intelligent grown woman like Emma could sit at home and expect her parents to look after her. Again, she was so different to her sister. Tara had gone through years of hard study in order to work in her preferred career of social services, and had then eventually decided to retrain as a life coach. Such a shame she couldn't coach her own sister.

So, despite her misgivings about Emma and the fact that she downright disliked her, Liz eventually agreed to move away from Dublin and relocate the family in Castlegate, the fact that she adored the village and knew it would be a wonderful place in which to raise Toby having everything to do with the decision.

And in truth, she'd worried for nothing. She hadn't seen much of Emma at all other than the few times they might bump into one another in the pub (whenever she and Eric managed a rare night out) or briefly when she worked at the café. And recently Emma had secured a job in Dublin and gone to live there, so they crossed paths even less.

And now Emma was pregnant, and by a man who was, and would for the near future, remain nameless. Despite herself, Liz was curious, very curious, as to why Emma was being so reticent. That certainly wasn't the girl she knew; if anything she'd have thought Emma would be only too eager to boast to all and sundry about her relationship. Although in truth, she hadn't had too many in the space of time that Liz had known her. In fact, Liz couldn't recall Emma ever going out with anyone for a sustained period. It seemed Eric had been her longest relationship, something else that had always troubled Liz.

So who was this mystery man now? And why did the whole notion of Emma being pregnant send an inexplicable shiver up Liz's spine?

Later that evening while she prepared dinner, Tara having returned to Dublin, Liz found herself still pondering on Emma's mystery sexual partner. Why was it such a secret? Surely she was only making things harder for herself by refusing to reveal her condition to the father, whoever he might be.

Or was that it, she wondered, smiling absently at the sound of Eric's woeful singing floating in from the bathroom. Was Emma's reticence to say anything to the father more to do with *who* he was than anything else? Maybe he was a bit of a brute and she wanted nothing to do with him and was simply protecting herself or the baby, rather than protecting him? It was a possibility, she supposed. According to Tara, Emma seemed to have a knack for picking troublesome or unavailable men, so it could very well be that this time she'd chosen particularly badly, and as a result was adamant about not telling the man in question.

Just then, Toby gave a loud wail, temporarily putting a stop to his mother's musings. Liz whirled around, wondering what the problem was this time. Since starting to stand up on his own a while back, Toby had become a right handful and lately was getting himself into to all sorts of trouble. The other day, he'd almost pulled a bookcase down on top of him, so anxious was he to try and climb up on top of it. These days, Liz only had to turn her back and Toby was into cupboards, pulling down curtains and grabbing at everything he set his sights on.

"Oh, Toby!" This time, it seemed, her son had had a run-in with a drum of talcum powder and had emptied the contents on top of his head and shoulders, and all over much of her newly polished kitchen floor. Blast it! She was sure she'd put that out of sight earlier.

"What are you up to now, you divil!" As if on cue, Eric walked in and promptly swept his errant son into his arms, getting the front of his T-shirt covered in fragrant talc for his troubles.

"I don't know how he does it," Liz said, shaking her head in exasperation as she went to clean up the mess. "One minute he's playing quietly under the kitchen table, the next he's on the way to causing World War Three!"

"Ah, he's just trying to make sense of the place, aren't you, Tobes?" His dark hair still wet from his shower, Eric kissed Toby on the head. Seeing father and son together like that – both so alike – made Liz's stomach give a little flip.

Four years on, and still Eric McGrath had the power to make his wife go weak at the knees. Back then, when she'd first met him, Liz had been powerless to resist

Eric's lively green eyes, his hearty laugh and his infectious lust for life. Her husband hadn't changed that much since and was still a very attractive man – possessing the same lean build and chiselled good looks he'd had when they first met. Liz, on the other hand, had unfortunately changed quite a bit and had put on a few pounds over the years, especially after the pregnancy. And now, with the kennels business, Eric was coming home to find his wife in a pair of wellies and baggy jeans instead of the short dresses and sexy heels she used to wear before they married. Sometimes, Liz wondered what on earth she'd done to deserve such happiness. Eric was her confidante, her lover and her best friend all rolled into one and she knew that she would fall to pieces should anything ever happen to him.

Now he was expertly manoeuvring Toby into his highchair, something that Toby usually point-blank refused to let her do, but now with his dad he was laughing and cooing as if this was all a great adventure. Typical, she thought, smiling as Eric patiently brushed the powder out of Toby's hair and clothes – he's like a raging bull for most of the day and then as soon as Daddy appears . . .

"So how are things?" Eric asked, once Toby had quietened down and they were eating dinner. "How's Eminem getting on? Has he settled down yet?"

One of the dogs they had staying with them – a fabulous St Bernard who'd been unfortunately burdened with the moniker of a famous white rapper – was a first-time boarder and finding it difficult to come to terms with the change in routine.

"He's much better today," Liz replied. "He's stopped pacing and I think he and Bruno took a bit of a shine to one another, actually."

"Good old Bruno – is he back again? Your woman takes some amount of holidays, doesn't she?"

Liz smiled, recalling Jill Walsh's curt manner when she dropped Bruno off. Some pet owners were only too delighted to chat about their upcoming holiday and often left a contact number should anything happen to their pet in the meantime. But Jill Walsh definitely wasn't one of those.

"I don't know that she does take holidays – she never says a word about where she's going. For all we know, she could be travelling with work. Now, Mel Flanagan – you know, the girl who owns little Jasper?"

"Yes," Eric nodded.

"She was telling me today she's off to the Caribbean for two weeks at the end of the month."

"Sounds fantastic," her husband replied, looking genuinely wistful as he tucked into his tomato and basil penne.

"Doesn't it? And Tara was saying earlier that she and Glenn are going to –"

"Oh, Tara was down for a visit?"

"Yes, she popped in for an hour this afternoon. She was home visiting her mum and dad before she and Glenn go on holiday to Egypt next week. Lucky things."

"I haven't seen either of them in ages."

"Well, she hasn't been home in ages. She's really made a go of that life-coaching business, fair play to her."

Eric wrinkled his nose. "A load of old codswallop if you ask me. Surely people have more cop-on than to pay good money for someone to tell them what any eejit could. But that's women for you – more money than sense."

Liz gave him a withering look. "That's not how it works, Eric, and according to Tara it's not all women either. Besides, she's obviously good at what she does if she can afford trendy sports cars and holidays in Egypt." She went on to tell Eric all about Tara's gorgeous new car, which was a million miles away from the ancient embattled Peugeot Liz used to get around the place.

"Well, maybe we should think about doing a spot of coaching ourselves then," Eric suggested. "We could get the house done up properly and sort out all the Castlegate quarehawks at the same time! Hold on – forget dog kennels, what about *dog* coaching? I know a few mutts who badly need help in finding their way in life. John Kavanagh's useless bloodhound for one."

"Stop it!" Liz laughed.

Eric had been working additional shifts at the security company to raise the extra cash for redecorating (and, in the case of the dining room, *restoring*) the house. So, while the old cottage was without doubt their dream home, it hadn't fulfilled its true potential just yet.

Liz had hoped that the kennels would generate some

additional income for them, so that Eric didn't have to work so many long hours up in Dublin and away from her and Toby. When they moved here originally, the plan had been for him to look for some form of alternative work in the village, but so far he'd had no luck. And Liz hadn't had too much luck in securing customers from the villagers either. It was disappointing because she'd also seen the kennels service as an ideal way to interact with the community and get to know people.

But as Castlegate was a satellite village, the residents were no doubt used to "Dubs" coming to live there and spending their days commuting to and from the capital, and consequently being completely uninvolved in village life. So it was entirely possible that most of the residents viewed her and Eric as "blow-ins" – despite the fact that her husband was one of their own. Also, with Toby being so young, and Liz tied to the house with the animals for much of the time, she didn't get too many opportunities to get out and meet people during the day. Oh well, they'd barely been here a year; things were bound to improve. And she did know some people – Eric's friend Colm, who ran the village café, and Tara's family. And of course, Liz remembered wryly, there was also Eric's mother, Maeve.

"So anything else strange with Tara?" Eric asked, taking a forkful of pasta.

"Well, now that you say it . . ." Liz paused slightly before going on, "apparently Emma is pregnant."

Eric's fork stopped halfway to his mouth. "Oh? I didn't know she was seeing anyone."

And how *would* you know something like that? Liz thought nervously. "Well, that's the thing – apparently she wasn't seeing anyone, which is why it's so terrible for her to get caught – especially at her age." She was trying to keep her voice casual but feeling a little disconcerted at Eric's reaction or, even worse, his interest.

Eric continued eating. "I see. And who's the lucky dad?"

"Nobody knows," Liz said, shrugging. "According to Tara, she's refusing to tell the guy – whoever he is – that she's expecting in the first place and reckons that she can go it alone. In the meantime, she won't spill the beans on who he might be, even to her family."

"Right?"

Liz pushed the remainder of her food around the plate. "Tara reckons she got involved with someone she shouldn't have – hence all the mystery."

"Really?"

"But she also says that Emma can be a bit overdramatic at times so it could very well be a big deal over nothing. She might just have got caught out on a one-night stand."

Eric nodded. "Could be."

Liz stood up and began to clear the table. "Anyway, I suppose it's nothing to do with us. Of course I feel sorry for anyone having to deal with something like that, but . . ." she shrugged as she went to the sink, "as they say, she's made her bed and now the poor thing has to lie in it."

She sounded nonchalant but, as she rinsed off dinner

plates under the tap, Liz couldn't help but notice how strangely silent her husband had become and just how hard her own heart was beating in her chest.

Chapter 4

It was Monday and Natalie Webb was having a very bad morning. "What do you mean he's at it again?" she cried into her mobile. "Bloody hell, can't he keep it in his pants for more than two minutes? And who is she this time?"

She locked eyes with the cabbie in his rear-view mirror and he quickly glanced away. Natalie was aware that he was straining to hear every word. He'd have been straining even more if he realised who she was discussing – not some errant boyfriend but long-time England football international Michael Sharpe. Sharpe by name, not so sharp by nature, Natalie thought, staring out the window at the London traffic, incensed that the player had landed them in it yet again.

She cursed the day Blue Moon PR had agreed to take Sharpe on as a client. A single PR agency wasn't enough to manage the amount of scandal this guy generated from week to week. If it wasn't lap-dancers and football groupies, it was drinking and drunken public bust-ups with his team-mates. And the closer he was getting to the end of his playing career, the more reckless he seemed to become.

"The *Sun* are planning to break the story some time this week," Natalie's assistant Danni informed her. "Apparently they've got photos of Michael and this girl coming out of the nightclub together last Saturday night and –"

"What? The idiot! How many times have we warned him?" Natalie shook her head, trying to think straight. There was no bloody point. No matter how often they tried to drill into their clients the importance of being discreet, the message rarely got through.

Blue Moon PR's client list consisted primarily of successful, and in turn incredibly high-profile, individuals: sportsmen and women, singers and TV actors and actresses, the kind of public profiles on which the UK media thrived.

For this reason, Natalie and her colleagues at the agency were on permanent alert, ready and waiting to skilfully control their clients' public profiles by putting out fires here and there. But they'd need to employ a full-time fire brigade to handle Michael Sharpe!

"Right." Glancing surreptitiously at the cab driver, who now seemed to have lost interest, Natalie spoke low into the phone. "Tell him I want him and the missus at the weekend do," she said, knowing that Danni would understand she was referring to the Player of the Year

Awards on Saturday night. It didn't matter that he wasn't up for nomination – she wanted them there anyway, on the red carpet, posing lovingly for the cameras and acting the happily married couple. "Send her over –" she hesitated, glancing again at the cabbie, aware that the *Sun* or their rivals would just lap up an inside story from a London cabbie, "something spectacular . . ."

Danni, as ever, was on the ball. "A new Julien MacDonald number? Something that'll really wow the cameras?"

"Exactly. In the meantime, we'll see if we can come to some agreement with the . . . um . . . the *others* about his latest indiscretion." She glanced again at the driver, who still seemed to be concentrating on the heavy traffic.

"OK, I'll talk to Michael and see what I can do about getting his wife a designer dress, but with the amount of weight she's put on recently, that might be difficult," Danni said dryly. "Anyway, do you think you'll be back to the office later?"

Natalie sighed. "I hope so. Depends on how long this lunch takes, really."

"Try and nab them while they're young and innocent, eh?" Danni joked, referring to the prospective client Natalie was on her way to meet.

"Savour it while it lasts, you mean," she replied, before ringing off and replacing her mobile in her bag.

"Everything all right, love?" the cabbie enquired, his eyes in the rear-view mirror again fixed on her troubled face.

"Yes, everything's fine," Natalie replied shortly.

Realising that they were now nearing the Embankment Gardens, she took out her compact and quickly checked her appearance in the tiny mirror. Her hair could do with a bit of a trim; her wavy and usually shiny dark mane looked a bit dull, but what the hell, it would pass for today. And the make-up she'd carefully applied earlier that morning was still quite fresh, although her lipstick could certainly do with some touching up. She hastily applied her favourite Bobbi Brown lip-colour. Angelina Jolie eat your heart out, she mouthed silently, before tucking everything back into her bag and then fanning her hair attractively around her shoulders.

The lunchtime traffic was typically manic and, glancing at her watch, Natalie realised it was now close to one o'clock. No time to hang around sitting in traffic, not when English football's hottest rising star was meeting her for lunch.

"I'm going to just pop out here," she told the cab driver, and by his blatantly appreciative glance at her generous breasts, Natalie suspected he was thinking something quite different. This was something she was well used to, her curvaceous body having always appealed to the opposite sex. Such attention occasionally came in handy in her profession, but in truth she hated looking like a busty barmaid from *Corrie*.

Having paid the cabbie, she nipped quickly through the Embankment Gardens and out to the Savoy Hotel, where seventeen-year-old Jordan King and his father

Joseph were already awaiting her arrival in the foyer.

A young black footballer of immense talent and skill, Jordan had just signed a lucrative contract with one of the country's top Premiership clubs and had recently made his debut for England. Within minutes of coming onto the pitch, he had changed the game and sent the team three-two up, scoring a hat-trick in the most spectacular circumstances. Since then, the newest England wunderkind was in high demand, and for this reason, he and his family had been advised to employ someone to help deal with the ever-growing media appetite and to manage his public profile.

"Jordan, Mr King – so lovely to meet you." Natalie shook their hands. She knew instinctively that Joseph King would be a tough nut to crack. The man seemed suspicious and ill at ease in the hotel's sumptuous surrounding, as though he'd rather be anywhere else but there.

It was understandable. The Kings hailed from a working-class background in Birmingham, where Jordan had begun his footballing career with a lower-league club, and Natalie wouldn't have been at all surprised if this were the first time Joseph King had been to the capital.

This made her even more determined to secure Jordan as a client; he and his family were so obviously guileless that they would need all the help they could get when thrust into the relentless and often unforgiving spotlight.

"Let's go in to eat." Natalie led them towards the restaurant. She smiled at Jordan. "You're a wonderful player, Jordan," she said, "although I suspect you're used to hearing that by now."

"Um, thanks." Jordan blushed a little and grinned sheepishly.

Natalie sorely wished that the kid could remain like that, so innocent and so obviously unaffected by his superstar quality. But she knew such ingenuousness wouldn't last long. The huge adoration and, concurrently, the vast amounts of money these young teenagers earned tended to quickly put a stop to that. Thinking of the train-wreck that was now Michael Sharpe, Natalie hoped that Jordan would not follow his England team-mate down the same path.

"And you must be very proud of him," she said to Joseph King, as the waiter led them to their table.

"I am," Jordan's father replied, smiling indulgently at his son as they all sat down. "But obviously, I want to make sure his career is handled properly. Since the new signing, and especially after the England game, his mother and I haven't been able to deal with all the calls we've been getting. Newspapers wanting interviews, TV companies wanting appearances, all that stuff. And now all these companies are wanting to use him in their advertising."

"I presume you have a sports agency looking after your financial interests, club contracts etc.?" Natalie enquired. It was important to explain that managing Jordan's career as a footballer wasn't what Blue Moon PR did. Instead they'd look after the valuable currency that was Jordan King's public image.

His father nodded. "Chris Billingham. Do you know him?"

"Not personally, but he's got a good reputation." If there was such a thing, she thought inwardly, but at least some of the other vultures hadn't managed to get their claws into him. "Shall we order drinks? Wine or perhaps a Coke for Jordan?" With potential clients of this importance, she'd normally break out the Cristal, but something told her that this would not be appreciated by the father of a seventeen-year-old.

"A Coke would be great," Jordan replied cheerily, while his father ran a brief eye over the lunch menu.

"Something for you, Mr King?"

"Yes, a Coke would be fine for me too."

Yikes! So much for a liquid lunch, Natalie thought, eventually deciding on a sparkling Perrier for herself, although she could have killed for bubbles of the other kind. Oh, well, maybe later . . .

"So," she began, when the waiter had finished taking their lunch and drinks order, "I suppose I might as well start by filling you in on what it is we at Blue Moon PR do and, perhaps more importantly, on what we don't do."

"Jordan's been offered a contract from MagicBurger," Joseph King said, before Natalie had a chance to speak further. "It's great money and the agency thinks we should jump at it. I'd like to know what you think."

Aha, Natalie thought, the first test.

She sat back in her chair. "Well, as I said before, Blue Moon are not a sports agency in the sense that we don't secure endorsement contracts for you. However, what we *will* do is give advice as to how the endorsements you choose can affect your long-term career." She paused as their drinks arrived, then continued. "Now, if I were managing your image, Jordan, under no circumstances would I recommend that you endorse products from a fast-food company. You're young, talented and athletic and an inspiration to millions of young people out there. You don't want to give out the wrong impression."

"But the money is unbelievable," Joseph told her. "The agency reckons that no one in their right mind would turn down a contract like this. And it's a five-year commitment –"

"Of course it is," Natalie replied brusquely. "The company are simply making sure they're tying up England's hottest young footballer for the long term, because they know that if they don't, someonc else will. I wouldn't recommend it, Mr King, not in the long run. In the current healthy-eating climate and with the huge backlash against junk food, the media would have a field day with Jordan endorsing MagicBurger. We'd much prefer he be involved in promoting healthy products, sportswear, energy drinks – items like that. We don't want him peddling heart-attack food to teenagers."

Joseph looked thoughtful. "Still, the agency fought hard to get this contract for us – they must see it as beneficial to his career."

"The agency is there to manage the business and

financial side of Jordan's career, Mr King – a PR agency has to see beyond the money and look to managing Jordan's public profile long-term. As you know, footballers are valuable currency these days when it comes to the media. And you don't want your son being dragged into everything that's being offered to him. A clean-cut, respectable image is what I'd be looking at for Jordan if he were a client of our agency. Limited media appearances, very few TV interviews other than a couple of minutes post-match and negligible contact with the newspapers and magazines. The lower the profile, the more Jordan can concentrate on what's important – his football. Think Michael Owen or Jamie Carragher. How often do you see those guys in the papers falling out of nightclubs or details of their love lives splashed across the Sunday papers?"

At the mention of those names, Jordan's eyes brightened. Thank goodness for that, Natalie thought, breathing an inward sigh of relief. Thank goodness this kid saw balanced and upstanding footballers like that as role models and not imbecile piss-heads like Michael Sharpe or arrogant coke-heads like Nathan Corrigan.

"Michael Owen's the greatest," he said, sounding like any other teenage school-kid and nothing like the world-class superstar he'd undoubtedly turn out to be.

Natalie was more determined than ever to work on this kid's behalf, not because she thought she'd get an easier time of it than she did with some of her more problematic clients, but because deep down she wanted to help shield him against the ugly side of professional football. The side of fast cars, booze and blonde bimbos who one night treated players like gods and the next were gone running to the papers with stories of wild sex. The side that tore families apart, the immense success and pressure of the spotlight turning the game the players adored into a noose around their necks. No, it might be idealistic, but Natalie wanted to help Jordan King avoid all this. Keeping this kid's feet on the ground would do no harm to her beloved England's chances in the long run either, she thought wryly.

Their food arrived at this point and, when the waiter had departed, Natalie took the plunge.

"So what do you think?" she said, addressing the boy but really asking his father. "Do you think you'd like to have the public side of your career managed by Blue Moon PR?"

"I think we'd certainly like to hear more," Joseph King replied, his manner relaxing considerably as he and his gifted son sampled the menu of one of London's finest establishments.

Three hours later, Natalie arrived back at Blue Moon HQ, still buzzing, despite the lack of lunchtime bubbly.

Jack Moon, the company's fifty-something MD, accosted her on her way upstairs to her office.

"Well," he queried, his curiosity almost palpable, "how did we do?"

Despite her optimism, Natalie was non-committal. "Well, it's not official, but I did get the handshake."

"Oh, well done, you!" he replied effusively. "Securing someone like King is a massive coup for the agency, Natalie. I knew I could rely on you."

"No problem, Jack."

"Did I hear you correctly?" Danni squealed as Natalie approached her desk. "Did you just tell Jack that we're representing Jordan King?"

"Yep," she replied proudly. "The father was a tough nut to crack but I think I impressed them both in the end." They wouldn't officially be representing Jordan until the contracts were signed, but after this afternoon's lunch things were definitely looking good.

"Oh, my God, I can't wait to tell Lee! He's such a Reds fan and –"

"Don't go shouting about it to your hubby too soon, Danni – not until we get the signature," Natalie warned.

"Oh, all right, I suppose I'd better keep my mouth shut." Danni slumped glumly back in her seat. "So what's he like?"

"Jordan? A nice kid – a little bit naïve, but that's probably a good thing."

Danni sniffed. "A full season in the Premiership will soon knock that out of him."

"True, but it makes a nice change from the usual prima donnas we get here. Any calls while I was out?"

Her colleague grinned wickedly. "Plenty, now that you ask." She flicked through a list of messages. "Dean Phillips wants to know if you can arrange to get him tickets for The Murderers concert on Saturday night, *Heat* magazine want to know if Melanie Adams is available to talk about her divorce, Ken Forde wants to go over publicity plans for Blast's new single and –"

"OK, OK, just give me the bloody list," Natalie said, groaning. She still had to try and sweet-talk the *Sun* over the Michael Sharpe scandal, never mind arranging concert tickets for a fussy MD, interviews for a soap star and media appearances for a teenage boy band. But that was the job and, despite her apparent exasperation, Natalie loved every second of it and on any normal day would approach each task with gusto. But not today. Today – or more accurately *tonight* – could very well be the most important night of Natalie's thirty-two years, and as the evening drew ever closer it was difficult to concentrate on anything else.

"Just one more thing," Danni added, her voice dropping to a whisper. "The clinic phoned to confirm your next appointment for . . ." she trailed off and cast a furtive glance around the office, "you know."

"For my lipo?" Natalie finished out loud, and Danni's eyes widened. Natalie didn't care if the entire world knew she was having lipo-dissolve injections – everyone over twenty-five was at it anyway. Natalie dealt with excess flab as she did with most things in life: if you didn't like it, do something about it. Not for her the furtive sneaking in and out of clinics for lipo or botox. How different was it than going to the gym? The end result was the same (and admittedly a lot faster) so what was the big bloody deal? "Great, I'll phone them later. Did you manage to speak to Michael, Danni?"

"Yeah."

"So how did he react to my suggestion about the awards ceremony?"

"He said he'll do it because he trusts you, but if the press start giving Clara a hard time about anything, he'll deck them."

"Wonderful. Pity he doesn't think more about his wife's feelings when he's off screwing his bimbos," Natalie replied tersely. "And tell him if he even *thinks* about going off on another cameraman again, I'll . . ." She shook her head and went towards her office. "On second thoughts, don't bother. I'll give him a call myself."

"Sure." Danni was only too happy to offload this particular client to someone who knew exactly how to handle him. "But don't forget to call Ken Forde, will you? He was insistent."

Insistent, insistent, Natalie echoed inwardly – they were all bloody insistent, weren't they? Retreating into the sanctuary of her third-floor office with its relaxing views over the Thames, she sat down and slipped off her heels. She used one hand to massage her aching feet and the other to dial the first number on her list – Ken Forde, the increasingly demanding manager of boy band Blast.

"Ken, hi, Natalie here," she began. "Just returning your call. Yes, we've got lots of publicity in the pipeline for the guys this time – nothing confirmed yet though." She spoke quickly in the hope of heading him off at the pass. Ken was the type of manager who wouldn't be pleased even if she'd arranged for the group to make a special appearance on MTV.

"There better be plenty, Natalie – we badly need a number one this time round."

Well, maybe if you lot concentrated less on the partying and more on the music, you just might get one, she thought uncharitably – not at all in the right frame of mind to deal with Ken and his demands. Not when her mind was decidedly focused elsewhere.

"Well, you know we'll do our best to help you achieve that, Ken," she replied instead. "I just have a few things to confirm, and then we'll send over a full publicity schedule. Don't worry, this will be Blast's biggest campaign yet."

"OK, Natalie, I'll leave it in your capable hands," he replied grudgingly. "We'll talk soon."

"Sure, great to catch up," she replied, before ringing off and sighing heavily. She and Danni would have to work double-time to get a decent campaign going for the group, who barely a year ago were UK pop's Next Big Thing, but following some poorly subscribed concert dates, and a lacklustre follow-up to their debut single, were already in danger of becoming old news. Which would make it *very* difficult this time round for Natalie to secure Blast the requisite TV appearances and magazine features and, in effect, the second number one their manager so desired.

And speaking of number ones . . . Natalie moved to the next item on her list, concert tickets for British music's Current Big Thing – a favour to another client.

"Mark? Hi, Natalie Webb here."

"Well, hello there!" the concert promoter, who was one of Natalie's many social contacts, replied. "How's London's sexiest PR queen?"

Natalie grinned. "You sure know how to flatter a girl, Mark Wallis. But listen, any chance you could get me a couple of tickets for The Murderers gig next weekend?"

"Sure, no problem. I didn't know you were a fan."

"I am but they're not for me, unfortunately. Thanks for that, Mark – I owe you one."

"Anytime, Nat. But with all the tight spots you've got me out of over the last few years you know damn well you owe me sod all."

"Cheers, Mark!" Natalie quickly ended the call and made a mental note to get the tickets sent over to Dean Phillips, the MD of a technology company Blue Moon represented. She wouldn't phone Phillips now though, she thought, looking at her watch. It was heading for six o'clock and today she needed to get home early. She glanced guiltily at the rest of her telephone messages. Damn it, they'd have to wait until tomorrow – as would her emails. Normally, she wouldn't dream of leaving a client or contact waiting overnight, but today, she couldn't help it. She just wasn't in the right frame of mind. No, for once, she'd have to give over some of her precious time to her personal life. Hopefully, it would be worth it.

Picking up her Balenciaga bag and D&G trench, Natalie left her office and went back out front to Danni.

Her colleague looked at Natalie and then at the clock,

mock surprise written all over her face. "What's this? The great Natalie Webb leaving for home *before* eight o'clock on a weekday?"

Natalie winked. "I've got a date tonight, remember? A very important date."

"Oh, God, I totally forgot! Yours and Steve's anniversary!"

"Yep. Hence the last few weeks' lipo sessions and yesterday's spray-on tan."

"I see," Danni sat back, a dreamy look on her face. "So where is Mr Wonderful taking you tonight, then?"

Natalie grinned. "As if I'd discuss our bedroom antics with you."

"Oh, you know what I mean!" Her assistant reddened. "What have you got planned? Are you two going somewhere nice?"

"I don't know yet," Natalie told her truthfully. "I think he's planning to surprise me." *And hopefully not just with the location*, she thought to herself.

"You lucky thing," Danni sighed dreamily. "For our last anniversary Lee and I sat in with a takeaway. He wouldn't go out because the Reds were playing, and the only celebrations we had that night were for the ball hitting the back of the net." She sighed deeply.

Natalie said nothing. Danni and Lee had got married early that year and clearly adored one another, and in truth Natalie would have given her right arm to be in Danni's position of cosy coupledom

Well, if all went well tonight, it mightn't be as far away as she'd thought up to now.

"Well, have a great night, and you can tell me how it all went tomorrow," Danni said, shaking her head sadly. "Make me even more jealous that you managed to land a dreamboat like Steve Watson, while I ended up with a yob like Lee."

Chapter 5

Outside the Blue Moon offices, Natalie tried in vain for fifteen minutes to hail a cab. Shit, today of all days she'd hoped she wouldn't have to take the tube. But there was little or no hope of her getting back to the flat any other way, so she'd have to bite the bullet. Tottering along on her heels, she made her way down the street to the nearest underground station, trying to remember the last time she'd travelled this way. Given that she usually left the office sometime after eight p.m., there was never any problem getting a cab, and in any case, she wasn't usually in that much of a rush to get home.

But this evening, the dreaded tube would have to do, despite the fact that the dead air in the tunnels always seemed to tire her out. And Natalie wanted to be fully alert tonight – especially if tonight turned out to be *the* night. It had to be, didn't it? They got on fantastically well, were madly in love and the sex was just amazing!

He'd ask her tonight, Natalie was almost certain of it. He'd been a bit coy and evasive lately, which she thought was a big hint.

No, her boyfriend's confidence and single-mindedness were some of the traits that had made her fall for him in the first place. They'd met at one of the many social events she attended in the course of her work and had been introduced by mutual friends. That night, she couldn't take her eyes off this tall, handsome and self-assured individual who, with his broad chest and closely cropped blonde hair, seemed the embodiment of potent masculinity, and who unfortunately also seemed hell-bent on resisting her charms. It had taken a while (and a few glasses of Veuve Clicquot) for Natalie to break him down and interest him enough to ask her out, but break him down she did, and the two had been together ever since.

Hopefully after tonight they'd be together for good, she thought, feeling the distinctive warm blast of air that signalled the imminent appearance of the next train to the platform. Soon after, she boarded the train and squashed into the carriage with what seemed like half the population of the city, trying her utmost to ignore the sweaty stench emanating from the person brushing up alongside her. It'll be worth it, she told herself. You'll be home soon and will have plenty of time to get ready for tonight.

Natalie's flat was situated not far from Central

London and, luckily for her, only a few stations away. Eventually reaching her destination, she practically raced out of the carriage and away up the stairs towards the exit.

Seven p.m. Steve would be picking her up at eight. Despite their intense relationship, the two hadn't yet moved in together, although this was because of Steve's necessity to be near the airport for all the travelling he tended to do with work. Natalie, on the other hand, had no desire to live outside a five-mile radius of Central London – she preferred the city on her doorstep. Still, she knew this couldn't last forever, particularly if she and Steve were to get married. No doubt he'd want to move somewhere sensible and affordable, whereas Natalie would give anything for a pied-à-terre in Belgravia. Well, a girl could dream.

Reaching her flat, she flung her bag and coat on the sofa and headed directly for the shower. Their housing arrangements were certainly something they'd have to discuss when he popped the question tonight. Well, one thing at a time, she thought, massaging Clarins shower-gel onto her bronzed skin – bronzed courtesy of the good people at Sun FX. If tonight Steve produced the ring, like she was certain he would, they could think about the practicalities some other time.

Half an hour later, Natalie was fully made up and dressed to impress in a strapless raw silk Ben de Lisi, the raspberry colour of the dress setting off her dark eyes and glossy hair, now styled with seductive flicks à la Kelly Brook.

An hour later she was still waiting, the flicks drooping in tandem with Natalie's spirits. Where the hell was Steve? He'd assured her he'd pick her up at eight before heading out to this surprise destination, which Natalie hoped was a suitably romantic spot for a marriage proposal. She'd tried his mobile, which was switched to messages, sent him a text enquiring about his whereabouts and still nothing.

At about nine thirty, when Natalie was just about to give up and change into a pair of comfy pyjamas, ignoring the La Perla ensemble she'd bought especially for the occasion, the love of her life appeared at her door.

"I'm so sorry," he said, when Natalie had thrown the door open, her hands on her hips and the expression on her face leaving him in no doubt that he was in the doghouse. "Something came up at work, and I couldn't get away."

"You couldn't get away for long enough to phone and let me know what the hell was going on?"

"Don't be like that, babe," he said, reaching out and lightly caressing her bare arm. "You know how these things can go."

Almost immediately Natalie's resolve softened. She could hold a conversation with someone as important and charismatic as Bill Clinton any day of the week without batting an eyelid but when it came to this man she was like a piece of limp lettuce. In a way, it was what she loved most about him. He was unpredictable, could be very unreliable yet was totally addictive.

And if he was planning to propose she couldn't go too hard on him either, could she? Heaven forbid then that he might change his mind!

"You could have let me know," she went on, her tone softening.

"I know and I was going to, but I didn't think things would go on this late. If I had known I wouldn't have let myself get caught up in it. Especially when you look so good," he pulled her into his arms, "so good that I don't know if I want to go out at all." He began to gently nuzzle her neck.

"But what about your surprise?" she asked.

He stiffened slightly. "My what?"

"Your surprise," she reminded him. "You told me you were taking me somewhere special for our anniversary, but you wouldn't say where."

"For our what?" Suddenly, Steve released her from his arms and drew back.

"Our anniversary," she said. "Our six-month anniversary?"

Steve gulped. "Em, right, yes."

By his tone, Natalie knew he'd forgotten all about it. He hadn't planned any bloody surprise for them at all, never mind a big proposal! He hadn't even remembered that today *was* their anniversary – that they'd had six whole months of romantic bliss.

"I'm sorry, I erm . . . thought we were just going out for a bite to eat . . . I didn't realise it was that important to you."

Obviously not, Natalie thought, disappointment

flooding through her as Steve went through to the living room. OK, so maybe she'd jumped the gun a little bit with the proposal thing. But she was so sure she'd read the signs right! She and Steve clearly adored one another, and he was always telling her how wonderful she was – particularly in bed, where they tended to spend most of their time.

So why wasn't she wonderful enough to marry? Sod it! Natalie followed him into the room, yet again cursing herself inwardly for wanting it so much – and admittedly so soon. Maybe six months wasn't that long after all – not long enough for Steve anyway. Six bloody weeks had been enough for Natalie to know she wanted to marry him – or indeed to get married at all!

But why *did* she want it so much, she wondered? What was wrong with things the way they were? They got on great and had a great sex life – what more did she want?

But despite her exciting career and lively social life, lately she'd been thinking a lot about settling down and starting a family. At thirty-two she'd been living, working and partying in London for nearly fourteen years and at this stage was beginning to tire of it all. While she adored her work, deep down she felt that there had to be more to life than working eight to eight and schmoozing some of London's most self-important glitterati.

And, she admitted ruefully, her good friend Freya's forthcoming wedding had a lot to do with that.

When Natalie first moved to London almost a lifetime ago, she'd been full of energy and enthusiasm, eager to experience life outside rural Hertfordshire. Hoping for a foot in the door of the London PR scene, she'd applied for a job as a senior publicist's assistant, and it was here that she first came into contact with Freya Parker.

The two girls had hit it off almost immediately and for the next few years they shopped, partied and sampled the best of what the city had to offer, including the men. Naturally confident and incredibly flirtatious, Freya was never short of a man or two, while Natalie's curvy figure and outgoing personality also drew men like flies. Throughout the years, Natalie worked hard at the agency, gained some important clients and even more important media contacts, and it wasn't long before she was headhunted by one of London's most prestigious firms, Blue Moon PR – the improved salary greatly helping to finance her girl-about-town exploits.

In the meantime, Freya met the love of her life, Simon Ford, and soon things began to change. Within a few months, Natalie's best friend had changed from mad, fun-loving, champagne-guzzling Freya to a sensible, more mature, occasional drinker who, instead of partying in some of the city's best bars and clubs, now preferred to host sophisticated dinner parties at the new home she shared in South London with her city broker fiancé.

It was inevitable that their city-girl friendship wouldn't last forever, Natalie thought, but while she was genuinely thrilled for her friend, she still couldn't help thinking that Freya's fabulous new house, her upcoming wedding and her blissful domesticity seemed to garishly highlight her own lack of progress in this regard. Natalie had been ready to settle down and get married for some time, and the fact that Freya had beaten her to it merely made her want it all the more. Not to mention the fact that everyone she knew – Danni (who was only twenty-five!) included – seemed to be getting engaged and married too and Natalie was now in serious danger of being the only one left behind.

Having decided that it was too late to go out to dinner, Steve had since settled himself comfortably in front of the TV. "You don't mind, do you?" he asked.

"No, I don't mind," she said, slumping down on the sofa alongside him, her raw silk Ben de Lisi now decidedly wrinkled from all the sitting around waiting. "I'll be up early tomorrow morning anyway. I've got a lot of work to catch up on."

The comment was intended as a jibe but, sure enough, he didn't seem to notice. Steve was like that sometimes, Natalie thought wryly, the little barbs and remarks that could be so effective at work making no impression whatsoever on her easy-going boyfriend.

Then she sighed inwardly. She hated feeling like this, feeling so out of control, so much so that she'd reduced herself to behaving like some clingy, desperate wannabe. She was thirty-two years old, for goodness sake! Sophisticated thirty-somethings did *not* sit around sulking and pouting like teenagers when things didn't go their way. No, sophisticated thirty-somethings were mature and adult and *dignified* enough to actually do something about those things. So there would be no more pouting and sulking about this, Natalie decided then – instead she'd have to think of a plan of action, something to help put this situation back on track. Feeling better now that she'd reasserted some control, Natalie began to think more clearly. Typically, when she encountered a sticky situation – usually at work – she wasn't the type of person to sit in a corner feeling sorry for herself like she'd done just now; usually she went right ahead and tried to find a solution. But Steve wasn't work, was he? And Natalie couldn't just dream up a fast-fix solution to this particular problem – could she?

Over the last few weeks she'd interpreted the situation very badly by convincing herself that Steve was working up to a proposal. Her usually dependable intuition seemed to have deserted her this time, and she didn't like it. Then again, for some reason her intuition *always* made a run for it when it came to men.

Although she knew Steve loved her (the sex was *amazing* after all and he said himself he couldn't get enough of her), the idea of marriage obviously hadn't yet entered his stupid little head. And this was a problem, because she knew without question that she wanted to marry *him* and had no intention of sitting around waiting for him to realise it.

Natalie's gaze drifted idly towards the TV programme Steve was watching, some holiday programme or other.

Steve yawned. "I could definitely do with something

like that soon," he said, nodding at the screen. "The negotiations for this new deal are taking forever."

And just like that it hit her. A *holiday*! Perfect!

Natalie thoughts began to race a mile a minute. She and Steve hadn't really been spending enough time together lately – a week away at some fabulous sunny destination would surely convince him once and for all that she was the one for him. She sighed blissfully. Imagine a week relaxing in the sun at some fabulous hotel, doing nothing but eating and drinking and . . . well. Natalie grinned to herself as she stared at the TV. By the time she was finished with him, Steve wouldn't be able to remember what life had been like without her!

The following morning, Natalie arrived at the offices of Blue Moon, tired and still deflated that last night hadn't gone exactly as planned.

As she went upstairs in the lift, she glanced critically at her reflection in the elevator mirror. It was no surprise really that Steve wasn't interested in taking their relationship to another level. She looked like absolute shit. Her wardrobe needed serious updating, and she could definitely do with losing a few more pounds. But at least the lipo-dissolve sessions she was getting would sort that out. Still, she made a mental note there and then to book herself a fresh appointment with the image consultant she used now and again. In this business, appearance counted for a hell of a lot and, apart from

Steve, she was lucky that she hadn't frightened off the young footballer and his father yesterday!

Yes, a session with Janet from the Image Agency followed by a good dose of retail therapy at Selfridges would soon set her on the right track. And if she wanted to get to work on Steve properly during their romantic break in the sun, she'd have to ensure her wardrobe was well up to the task!

Finding the time for all this was another story though. What with leaving the office early yesterday evening, and being out of it for much of the afternoon, she'd be lucky if she found the time to have lunch at her desk for the next few days, let alone factor in an image consultancy.

Which made her doubly determined to go and see that time-management consultant Freya had recommended. Her friend had secured someone to help her cope with the time constraints of her forthcoming wedding, and Natalie thought she could certainly do with some of that type of advice too.

"She's fabulous, Nat," Freya had gushed. "She made me break my time down, not into things to do, but into *blocks* of time. And she reckons I'm *way* too generous with people and that I should use my time much more constructively."

Yes, Natalie could certainly do with some of that.

But speaking of consultants, she thought, saying a quick hello to Danni before going into her office and closing the door behind her, she needed advice from someone in the travel business, and quickly.

She had it all arranged within the hour. The travel rep had informed her over the phone that at such short notice there wasn't 'a monkey's chance' of getting availability for her and Steve in her preferred holiday destination, St Tropez, or indeed anywhere in the Cote d'Azur. Instead, for this time of year, she'd helpfully suggested Sharm El Sheikh in Egypt.

"Egypt? Isn't that one of those troublesome places?" Natalie asked, frowning.

"Well, if guaranteed thirty-degree sunshine, warm waters and unadulterated luxury is troublesome?" the travel rep joked. "Honestly, I've been there myself and it's heavenly. Tony Blair goes there all the time – I think he has a holiday home in Sharm actually."

Well, Natalie thought, if it was good enough for the PM, it was definitely good enough for her and Steve. And when the rep mentioned that the place was a treasure trove of beautiful gold jewellery, she nearly burst a blood vessel trying to make the booking.

"So, it's for two adults leaving Saturday?" the other woman clarified as Natalie gave her and Steve's details. "And flying first class from Heathrow to Sharm?"

"That's right." The flight and five-star hotel were going to cost her an arm and a leg but what the hell – Steve was worth it. And if, as Natalie hoped, the romantic trip abroad took their relationship to another level, well, then it would definitely be worth every penny!

He would get *such* a surprise when she told him, she thought, gleefully calling out her gold-card details. And what man wouldn't be chuffed with a girlfriend who arranged last-minute luxury holidays abroad, not to mention Chelsea tickets at the drop of a hat?

That morning before he left her flat to go to work, Steve had casually mentioned that he'd kill to get his hands on tickets for the upcoming Chelsea Champion's League opener in Stamford Bridge. In her line of work, piffling things like football tickets were simple to get, and since the beginning of their relationship she'd been arranging such tickets (*corporate box* tickets) on a regular basis. In fact, she did it so often that anyone would think Steve was seeing her *just* for easy access to the tickets, she thought grinning. But of course they'd be wrong.

"Your holiday tickets will be forwarded to your address within two working . . . actually, because you're leaving at the weekend, it might be best if you collect them," the travel rep told her.

"No problem, I'll send a messenger," Natalie said.

"And of course, you do realise that payment is completely non-refundable at this stage?"

"Of course."

"Great. Well, thank you for booking with us, Ms Webb. I do hope that you and Mr Watson have a wonderful holiday."

Oh, we will, Natalie thought, as she ended the call, *you can count on it.*

Chapter 6

"Mum, can you speak up a little? The line is very bad," Tara urged, pressing her mobile phone more closely to her ear. But no amount of bad lines could obscure her mother's disapproving sniff on the other end.

"It isn't any wonder it's a bad line, Tara," she replied tetchily, "and it all the way out there in the desert!"

Isobel, who had never been abroad in her life, couldn't understand the attraction people had for gadding off on these fancy holidays. And in the desert of all places! "How's Glenn?" she added, almost yelling, and nearly taking the ear off her daughter in the process. Evidently she felt that her voice needed to be raised in order to carry all those thousands of miles so Tara could hear her. "Are the two of you drinking enough water? Or do you have to get it at one of those mirage things?"

Tara bit back a laugh. "Mum, I told you last week – Egypt isn't just desert," she said, her own voice instantly echoing back on the line. "We're staying on the coast in this amazing holiday resort by the sea. Glenn's out snorkelling on the coral reef as we speak."

Yes, they were finally in Egypt and Glenn was in his element. He was a decent swimmer, but as he and Tara hadn't taken too many holidays abroad over the years, he hadn't tried snorkelling until now.

And, she thought, you could get no better introduction to the joys of snorkelling than in the waters of the Red Sea. Even as a non-swimmer, Tara had been able to enjoy the magnificent sea life around the reef of the Egyptian Sinai Peninsula from the jetty by peeking into the incredibly clear turquoise waters and watching a host of colourful tropical fish swim lazily at the edge of the coral reef.

They were staying in a spectacular and sinfully luxurious five-star hotel overlooking the reef, and since their arrival late Wednesday evening, Glenn had thrown himself with gusto into the huge variety of water sports available, leaving Tara relaxing by the hotel's magnificent terraced pool. She didn't mind. It was great to see him enjoying himself and all too soon they would be back home in Ireland to face the wet and cold winter.

Now sitting on her hotel balcony, which overlooked the peninsula's extraordinarily beautiful coastline, Tara once more tried to reassure her mother that she and Glenn weren't at risk of severe dehydration.

"We're having a wonderful time," she told Isobel. "I'll take lots of photographs to show you and Dad. How is he, by the way? And Emma?"

"Your dad's fine and sends his love!" her mother yelled back, but in the next instant her voice lowered and her tone changed as she added mournfully, "As for Emma, well, I suppose it's getting to her that you can afford to go off sunning yourself in Egypt and not a bother on you, while she's going through all this hardship on her own."

Tara gritted her teeth. Bloody hell! What did they expect her to do – cancel her holiday just because Emma was pregnant? And if her little sister would stop chopping and changing jobs every six months or so, then she'd be well be able to "afford" to do it too! But of course it was futile pointing out this to her mother, or indeed pointing out the fact that Tara had been working non-stop for the last three years and might just have earned the chance to "sun herself". Grrr!

"Well, I'll have another chat with her when we get back," she said, trying to keep the frustration out of her voice. "Tell everyone I said hello, and we'll see you all again soon."

"How long will ye be there again?"

Not long enough, Tara stopped herself from saying. "Ten days in all, Mum – we've another full week to go yet."

"OK then, well . . . enjoy yourselves!" Isobel yelled once more, before ringing off.

Dressed in the soft squishy towelling robe and satin slippers the hotel provided, Tara stood up from the patio chair, switched off her mobile and went into the bedroom. Today she would be breakfasting alone.

Although, blast it, she thought, gazing out at the brilliant blue sky, it was such a beautiful morning she might just skip breakfast altogether and head straight for the pool. Tara generally enjoyed a good lie-in on holidays, rather than running around at all hours scrambling to get a place by the pool before anyone else did. She didn't care where she ended up – as long as it was under this glorious sun, little else mattered. But, as the hotel was busy, sun-loungers could be quite difficult to find unless you were up out of bed with the sun.

Still, that morning she was lucky. When she reached the lounge area of the first of the hotel's three cascading pools, there were two recently vacated sun-loungers right alongside the water and, although it was unlikely Glenn would be using one, Tara threw his spare towel on it anyway. He'd have to emerge from the depths of the sea sometime today, and Tara had no intention of sharing her lounger. No, she was quite happy to lie there "sunning herself" all day long, only briefly stirring now and again to cool off in that fabulous pool.

While she'd thought the hotel's luxurious Arabic-style architecture was impressive, the hotel pool area in itself was truly magnificent – a veritable "aqua-oasis" with its three cascading pools, surrounded by waterfalls, whirlpools and tiny grottos, all bordered by a variety of exotic palms and abundant pink and purple bougainvillea.

Yes, Tara thought, as she put on her sunglasses and lay back languidly on her sun-lounger, a relaxing morning here would be just perfect!

She'd been lying there a good hour and was deeply engrossed in the book she was reading when Glenn returned from his snorkelling, his skin still wet and his brown eyes shining happily.

"Guess what?" he said, grinning from ear to ear. "They run scuba-dive courses here."

Tara couldn't help but smile. "And?"

"And I've always wanted to try it – you know that."

She shook her head indulgently. Glenn was an out-and-out water baby, and Tara had known it was only a matter of time before he realised that scuba courses were part of the hotel's facilities. In fact, it was partly the reason she'd chosen this hotel in the first place; it would make the pain of dragging Glenn off to Cairo to see the pyramids some day next week that bit easier. After leaving her alone at the pool while he was off scuba diving and snorkelling, he couldn't really complain about a simple day trip, could he?

"So try it then."

Glenn's eyes lit up. "Are you sure? I've had a look at the course and it seems pretty intensive – it'll take a couple of days at least."

"I know that, don't worry about it."

He looked doubtful. "You're sure you don't mind me leaving you on your own again? As I said, it could be a few days."

"Of course not," Tara assured him. "I'm fine here. You go on and enjoy yourself."

He bent down and gave her a quick kiss – his delight almost palpable. "You're the best, do you know that?"

Tara smiled. "I know."

"OK, well, I'll go and book my first lesson for this afternoon then," he said, getting to his feet. "The sooner I get started, the sooner I can get out on the reef and start diving. I can't wait to tell the lads at work about this – they'll be green."

"Find out first if you're able for it before you start boasting about it," Tara advised, although she knew well that Glenn would take to diving like the proverbial duck to – ahem – water, whereas normally she preferred not getting wet at all! Although in this heat, she didn't have much of a choice but to dip into the pool now and then to cool off.

At times like this, Tara sorely wished she had the confidence to dive straight into the water like everyone else. Wading in bit by bit wasn't half as refreshing, although she supposed it was better than nothing. Once again, she wished that she'd learned how to swim at a younger age, like Glenn had. It was like learning to drive; the older you became, the more fear you seemed to have. And given that Tara wasn't the best driver in the first place, she wasn't about to throw caution to the winds when it came to swimming.

So let Glenn get his scuba lessons; Tara was perfectly fine where she was. She'd stocked up on books at Dublin airport and was looking forward to getting through them. It had been years since she'd had the time to sit and read purely for pleasure, so she was going to make the most of it.

As Glenn once again took off down the stone steps

towards the beach, probably not to be seen for the rest of the day, Tara picked up her book, repositioned her sunglasses on her nose and settled down again to some serious relaxation. But before she could manage to read a single sentence, she was interrupted once more.

"Excuse me – is this bed free?" a female voice asked.

Tara looked up to see a bikini-clad and hugely attractive girl with glossy dark-brown hair smiling hopefully at her.

"Is it free?" the girl repeated. "Or are you holding it for somebody?"

Tara felt guilty. There were no other beds available and it wasn't fair of her to keep one for Glenn when it was unlikely he'd be using it today. And even if he did return to the pool later, Tara was sure he wouldn't mind her giving his sun-lounger away. He certainly wouldn't mind her giving it away to this stunner, she thought wryly, with her huge almond-shaped eyes, full lips and, Tara noted ruefully, even fuller bosom. Tara's chest was as flat as day-old champagne and even Monsoon's industrial strength padded bikinis couldn't do a thing to change that. By comparison, this girl looked like she belonged in a Wonderbra advert.

"Yes, it's free," she said, moving Glenn's things out of the way and giving the girl a friendly smile. "But there's only one so –"

"You're a doll, thank you!" the girl replied in a pronounced English accent. She put her towel on the sun bed and sat down gratefully on it. "One is all I need."

"No problem." Tara smiled and resumed her reading,

but as the other girl settled herself alongside her, she couldn't help notice how remarkably clear and tanned the English girl's skin appeared in comparison to her own.

Not to mention how glamorous and confident she seemed, dressed in a fabulous red bikini that displayed her perfect curves and remarkably smooth, cellulite-free thighs to perfection – she guessed they were both around the same age, and while Tara was riddled with the stuff, this other girl's skin was still baby-smooth. How was that fair? She had to be a model or something, Tara thought enviously, as the girl began applying sunscreen in a sensuous manner that would make even Peter Stringfellow blush. God, now she hoped Glenn did stay away for the afternoon. One look at this girl and he'd be frothing at the mouth!

"I'm so sorry to interrupt you again," the girl said, startling Tara out of her envious reverie, "but would you mind spraying some sunscreen on the back of my shoulders? It's a tricky area to get to and –"

"Of course not." Tara swung her legs off the sun bed and took the bottle from the other girl, doubly glad that Glenn wasn't there!

"Thanks. I normally wouldn't ask, as I'd get my boyfriend to do it, but because I'm on my own for the week –"

"On your own – on holiday?" Tara blurted, before she could stop herself. She couldn't conceive of the fact that this gorgeous creature was on holiday without a man equally as attractive. She knew some people liked to travel alone but . . .

The girl sighed and piled her wonderfully shiny chestnut hair on the top of her head before turning her back to Tara. "Yes, Steve was supposed to come with me but he cancelled at the last minute – while I was on my way to Heathrow, can you believe it? 'I have to work, Natalie,' he says. 'Something important's come up and I just can't get away,'" she mimicked exaggeratedly as Tara sprayed sunscreen onto her shoulders. "Our very first holiday together, and he has to work!"

"That's unfortunate." The job complete, Tara handed her back the bottle and the two resettled themselves on their respective sun-loungers, Natalie lying on her stomach and exposing her newly protected back to the sun.

"Tell me about it," she said, rolling her eyes, before chattily continuing to fill Tara in on the situation. "But I decided to come anyway. I haven't had a break in yonks, and work has been crazy so I figured why waste the opportunity to get away and flop for a while?" She giggled. "Although I suppose there are some compensations. With Steve not here, at least I can just lounge around all day with no make-up on and not have to worry about trying to look effortlessly perfect every minute of the day."

"Now, I don't think you'd have to try too hard to do that," Tara replied with a smile, having already decided that, despite her intimidating beauty, she already liked this girl. And it seemed they had a thing or two in common. Like Tara, this girl evidently had a hectic work life, as it was also her first holiday in ages, and today each had both been more or less abandoned by the men in their lives!

"So thanks very much for the sun bed," the girl went on. "I've only just arrived, and it's so busy down here I really thought I'd have to spend the day in my room – not that that's too much of a problem: have you seen the size of the Jacuzzi bath? Oh, I'm Natalie by the way!" And she offered Tara a perfectly manicured hand.

"I'm Tara – nice to meet you," she replied, trying to hide her own nail-bitten paw. "And yes, the bath is huge, although I haven't tried it yet – despite the fact that we flew in last Wednesday."

"From Ireland?"

Tara smiled and nodded. "The accent is obviously a giveaway."

"Oh, I love the Irish accent," Natalie declared, sitting up. "I worked with a girl from Dublin yonks ago, and we all adored the funny little expressions she always used – 'Jaysus' and 'God Almighty' and all that."

Tara bit back a smile. "Well, I'm from Dublin too."

"Really? How fabulous! I've never been to Dublin, but I've heard it's marvellous fun. Great shopping, apparently. But I expect you probably have much the same stores we have in London."

Tara nodded. "We have some, and yes, Dublin can be good *craic* all right. What about you? You mentioned London – is that where you're from?"

"Yep. Well, I was born in Hertfordshire, which isn't

far, then I moved to London when I was eighteen. I've hardly left the place since. Which, I suppose, is part of the reason I needed this holiday." She sighed.

"And how long are you here for?" Tara asked.

"Just a week unfortunately. But this place is so fabulous, I could easily stay for a year – you?"

"Ten days, and I know what you mean. It's amazing, isn't it?"

"So are you here with your husband then?" the other girl enquired.

Tara shook her head. "Well, I'm not married but –"

"Me neither," Natalie groaned, shaking her pretty head from side to side. "Something I had really hoped to get to work on changing this week," she muttered under her breath.

Tara said nothing, although she was sorely tempted to pry some more into the state of Natalie's relationship, which by the sounds of things didn't appear to be going too well. Naturally curious and, she supposed, because of her profession, Tara was always greatly intrigued by other people's personal lives and what made them tick.

And she was full of admiration for the girl going off on holiday on her own too, especially to such a far-flung destination. But that was London girls for you, wasn't it – so confident and worldly. She chuckled inwardly. Despite herself she couldn't help but compare Natalie's wonderful self-assurance with Emma's annoying listlessness. At times, her sister could be so lethargic that going as far as the corner shop on her own was an ordeal, let alone a country in the Middle East!

The two girls lay side by side in companionable silence for a while, Tara becoming nicely engrossed in her book and Natalie just as engrossed in her sunbathing. Then, before they knew it, it was time for lunch.

Tara, who had anticipated having to do everything alone for the day, decided it might be nice to have some company for lunch, and good company at that.

"Do you fancy getting a bite to eat over there?" she asked, nodding in the direction of the pool snack bar. "They do great sandwiches and pizza."

"I'd love to!" Natalie grinned enthusiastically, before getting up and wrapping herself in a beautifully patterned and indecently short sarong that made the most of those fabulous cellulite-free legs. "In fact, while we're at it," she added with a wink, "we could always try something from the cocktail bar, what do you think?"

They walked together towards the snack bar.

"I'd love a cocktail," Tara agreed, "but it'll be a virgin one for me."

"Oh, you don't drink?"

"Nope," Tara replied and she had to laugh at Natalie's shocked expression. "Not exactly living up to the drunken Irish stereotype, am I?"

The other girl blanched. "Christ no! I mean – that's not what I mean and – oh, I'm frightfully sorry – I really should just quit while I'm ahead." The poor thing looked embarrassed and Tara felt for her. "I'm really sorry. I hope I haven't made you uncomfortable."

"Don't be silly. I'm not an alcoholic or anything," Tara told her easily, as they sat down at a vacant table. She picked up the menu. "I'm just not mad about the taste of alcohol – or the effects, to be honest. I got drunk once in my life and, believe me, once was enough."

"Bad hangover?"

Tara smiled. "Something like that."

"Well, I know where you're coming from! Although, unfortunately, it's never stopped me from going back for more! But I do love a cocktail on holiday – so you don't mind if I . . .?" she trailed off and almost apologetically indicated the menu.

"Of course not!" Tara insisted. "You work away."

It was funny really, she thought, how people reacted to her teetotal ways. Most seemed to automatically assume Tara was an alcoholic and found it hard to come to terms with the fact that she just didn't like drinking alcohol. And for a foreigner like Natalie, who, she supposed, probably associated the Irish with being rip-roaring drunks, no doubt it was doubly confusing!

"I'll have a Mai Tai and a chicken sandwich," Natalie told the Egyptian waiter, who was busily trying to avoid looking at Natalie's magnificent bust, his religion and culture totally at odds with all this Western exhibitionism. But refreshingly, Tara thought, the girl seemed totally unaware of her beauty and the effect she was having on all the surrounding males.

"And I'll have the virgin Poco Loco and a pizza," Tara told him, throwing her usual healthy eating habits out the window. To hell with it, she was on holidays!

"Well," her new friend said, when the waiter had taken both their orders and left, "thanks to you this holiday mightn't turn out to be such a disaster after all!"

Chapter 7

Later that evening, Natalie sat alone in the hotel, still quite unable to believe that she was in this amazing place all alone. It was such a pity that Steve hadn't been able to make it.

Such a pity because he'd sounded so eager when she'd first mentioned her grand plans for a holiday.

"Sounds good," he'd said. "I could do with a break. Like I said, we're in the middle of a huge deal at the moment, and it's been hard going. After all this, I'd jump at the chance to get away."

As a property developer, Steve didn't have to keep nine to five office hours like everyone else and (unlike Natalie) could easily get away at the drop of a hat. This had been the main reason she'd been so confident about booking it at such short notice.

"So, I'll let you know when would be a good time for me, and we'll talk about it then, OK?" he told her.

Natalie gulped. This was obviously not the time to tell him that she'd already arranged the entire thing, first-class flights, five-star hotel, lock stock and barrel and that they were leaving in a few days' time! But she'd been certain that Steve would be fine with it in the end. After all, what man *wouldn't* want to be whisked away on a last-minute holiday by the woman in his life? All men loved an assertive woman, didn't they?

So, later that week, she'd phoned Steve and excitedly left a message on his answering machine, informing him that she'd booked them a fabulous last-minute break in Egypt, and they'd be leaving first thing Saturday morning.

And by the end of that particular week, Natalie sorely needed a holiday herself.

It had easily been the toughest few days at work in living memory. Midweek, Michael Sharpe had been involved in a punch-up with his team-mate, not in a nightclub, but right on the football pitch in full view of the fifty thousand or so spectators at the match. He'd got in a strop because his team-mate, a younger and more inexperienced player, hadn't passed the ball to him at a crucial stage, which Michael believed was an offence deserving of a punch in the eye. But it got worse. When the referee tried to intervene, Michael promptly spat in his face, earning himself an immediate red card and, Natalie reckoned, a three-match suspension for his troubles, if not more. Having just about managed to get the *Sun* story pulled earlier that week, she just couldn't *believe* that Michael had got himself into more trouble so soon. Player altercations she could handle; spitting at referees was a different story altogether. Still, she'd had to do something to try and save face, and that evening she and Danni had stayed till all hours at the office and brainstormed until the two had eventually come up with something that would serve as a decent excuse as to why he'd lost the rag on the pitch.

"We could say that Clara had threatened to leave him unless he stopped his boozing and wandering eye," Danni suggested and Natalie wanted to hug her.

So, with a speed that would put the Schumachers to shame, they'd arranged an exclusive interview with the *Mail on Sunday* for the following afternoon, during which Michael carried off a truly Oscar-winning performance as a ravaged and tormented human being, terrified of losing his family.

"I don't know what I'd do without Clara – she's my rock," he'd sniffed. "I couldn't cope – I try not to bring my problems onto the pitch, but once I got out there, I just cracked. It was all too much for me."

Natalie had to admit that the man was good; for the benefit of the photographer, he had even managed to produce real tears.

"My family mean everything to me!" he wailed. "If I don't have them, all the medals and trophies in the world mean nothing."

Clara had no more threatened to leave him than she had to give up shopping, but painting such a doleful picture of this talented player, haunted by demons and so upset over his family, meant that he at least gained sympathy from fans and, most importantly, from certain sections of the media. Everyone loved a tortured genius.

So, thanks to Danni and Natalie's savvy bit of PR, come Sunday, Michael Sharpe would no doubt be once again restored to his position as England's most adored and even-more-indulged footballer.

But by the weekend, Natalie had been feeling the effects of a full week's troubleshooting and was only too ready for a relaxing week abroad.

However, in the meantime, and with all the hullabaloo with Michael, she hadn't managed to get Steve on the phone, and instead she'd texted him the details of their flight and arranged to meet him at the airport. Obviously, he was trying to get this property deal tied up before they went, so much better to just let him get the job done and then they could both enjoy their time away. Then, on her way to Heathrow in the cab on Saturday morning, she'd sent him another text telling him she'd meet him outside WH Smiths in Terminal 2.

Almost immediately Steve phoned.

"Natalie, I can't go on holiday with you today!" he said, sounding flustered. "What on earth made you think I could?"

"But it's all booked, Steve! We're flying out this morning. You knew that!"

"I did *not* know that! You told me you were thinking of booking a week away for us at some stage. As far as

I was concerned it was just an idea! Then when I got these texts telling me we were flying out this weekend, I didn't know what to make of it. To be honest, I thought you were having me on."

"But –"

"Natalie, are you out of your mind? What made you think I could just drop everything and take off for a week at such short notice? I have a business to run!"

He sounded very upset, considerably more upset than the situation merited, Natalie thought. After all, *he* was the one leaving her stranded, after more or less agreeing to go on the holiday with her!

"Natalie . . ." Steve paused for a moment. "Nat, this is coming across a little bit weird . . . a little bit heavy, to be honest. And the thing is –"

"The thing is what?" Natalie asked, her nerves instantly on alert.

"I don't like being railroaded – into anything."

Sensing that she'd crossed some invisible line, Natalie's heart began to race. "Look, Steve, we obviously got our wires crossed here," she said quickly, her voice unnaturally bright. "I really thought you were fine about this trip, so I went ahead and booked it. Obviously I was wrong."

"Yes, you were."

This was followed by an uncomfortable silence, and Natalie wanted to kick herself. Why oh why had she pushed it – why had she been so impulsive? Of course she should have checked the details with him, of course she should have made sure.

But when Steve eventually spoke again, his voice had softened somewhat. "You're right. Maybe I didn't make things clear enough. But look, why don't you go along without me? You said yourself you badly need a break from work."

The idea of going on holiday alone, quite frankly, sounded a little sad to Natalie, but then again, unlike Steve, she *could* get away. Jordan King had since signed with the agency and her boss, Jack, was so pleased about that, he'd have let Natalie fly to the moon if she'd wanted to.

"Honestly, you should go," Steve insisted. "And I'll pay you back for the money you lost on my ticket."

"Oh, don't be silly. It was my fault for booking it in the first place without consulting you properly." It *had* been rather rash of her. But he'd seemed quite enthusiastic about the idea initially so . . .

"Even so, there is no point in letting a perfectly good holiday like that go to waste," Steve went on, his tone now sounding rather impatient, she thought.

Natalie bit her lip, trying to decide one way or the other. She'd really wanted this time alone with Steve – time to make him see how important she was in his life and how he couldn't possibly live without her. "I suppose."

Eventually, and after considerable encouragement from Steve, Natalie decided that she would go. If anything, it proved to him that she was an exciting, unpredictable woman, who was confident and assertive enough to go on holidays on her own. So, she bid Steve a regretful goodbye over the phone and promised to call him when she got to the hotel in Sharm el Sheikh.

"I'll be very busy over the next few days," he'd told her, his voice sounding tense once again. "So it mightn't be that easy to reach me."

"OK, well, don't work too hard," Natalie said, her eyes welling up a little as she finally began to come to terms with the fact that he really wasn't coming with her. "I'll really miss you."

"Yeah, me too," Steve said, before ringing off and leaving Natalie staring out the window of the cab. From the sound of his voice, the poor thing was obviously very stressed by this deal, she decided, putting her phone back in her bag. Never mind, she'd speak to him when she got back. In the meantime, she'd just have to try and get through this week on her own.

Now, in the hotel, as she got ready to go out for dinner, Natalie sorely wished Steve were there. How the hell had she got things so mixed up? She'd been certain he'd be able to come with her.

Oh, well, there was no point in worrying about it now, she thought, smoothing her dress down over her thighs. She was here – on her own – so she'd better just try and relax and enjoy herself. After all the fretting and worrying she'd been doing lately, she deserved it.

That evening, having spent an enjoyable afternoon sunbathing and chitchatting with Natalie by the pool, Tara got ready to go out to dinner.

Glenn – who'd finally returned to the hotel room a good hour after Tara had finished sunbathing – was still wildly enthusiastic about his scuba-diving lessons, but weary after the initial preparation.

"First, I had to swim a couple of hundred metres, then the instructor got me to tread water for a full ten minutes, which was hard going on the calves I can tell you," he told Tara as they made their way to the Souk, the hotel's popular Bedouin-themed restaurant area. Situated outdoors on the uppermost level of the building and overlooking the bay, the Souk consisted of five different restaurants, some offering traditional Lebanese and Middle Eastern *mezzeh*, curried and spiced meals, hummus and *aish* – a type of Egyptian flatbread. Another specialised in mouth-watering Mediterranean food, reflecting the trad-itional cooking of Spain, Provence, Italy and Greece, while the chefs at the Oriental kitchen prepared seafood, noodles and rice dishes judiciously seasoned with soya sauce, oyster sauce, rice wine, sesame oil and lemongrass. And a typical choice of Indian and Middle Eastern pastries, sweetmeats and Turkish delights from the dessert kitchen nicely finished off a meal.

Guests could, on any given evening, choose from a range of dishes from any of the five kitchens, meaning there was no shortage of variety and little chance of anyone getting bored. The balmy outdoor setting and fragrant mosaic of herbs and spices in the air, set against the background of traditional Bedouin music and rhythmical drumbeat, made for an exotic and enjoyable Arabian experience.

Glenn and Tara both adored exotic food and, upon reaching the Souk, he wasted no time in finding them a vacant table overlooking the tip of Naama Bay, the bright lights of the town twinkling brightly against the darkness. Glenn, however, was less interested in the view and more in getting the attention of one of the waiters, eager to get started on the food.

"I'm starving," he told Tara. "I think I'll try something from all five places tonight."

"Won't all that extra weight affect your buoyancy?" Tara teased, studying the drinks menu.

"I don't know, but all that training sure makes me hungry," he replied, before trying to smother a yawn. "Not to mention exhausted."

"Are you sure you wouldn't rather wait and do this scuba course some other time?" she asked, her voice full of concern. "We're only here for ten days and it sounds like you won't have much time to relax."

According to Glenn, the scuba-diving course was to take place on three consecutive days, and in order to successfully achieve his PADI open-water diving qualification, he would, along with the training, also have to complete two open-water dives – a punishing schedule in Tara's estimation.

"Nah, I'm not bothered about relaxing," he assured her. "I'd much rather be doing something interesting. And I've been dying to do this for years, so I wouldn't dream of giving up now!"

No, Tara thought fondly, you wouldn't, would you? A sports and activities fanatic, back in Ireland (when he wasn't stuck in front of a computer) Glenn was always off rock-climbing, orienteering or taking part in various adventure activities with like-minded friends. So it was no surprise really that he wasn't concerned about missing out on relaxation time. Tara still had to broach the subject of their day-trip to the pyramids, which she hoped to take towards the end of the following week and was something she was sure he wouldn't be too happy about.

Well, there was no point in fretting about it now, she thought, looking around for a waiter who would put the tired and hungry soul out of his misery.

As she did, she caught sight of Natalie being led to a table not far from their own. Tara had thought the girl attractive earlier, but this evening she looked even more beautiful, dressed in a stunning jade satin dress that flattered her curves and accentuated her dusky colouring. By comparison, Tara was struck by how drab she must look in her boring khaki linen trousers and black halter-top.

Tara wasn't usually insecure about her looks, at least not in the way Liz could be sometimes, but she didn't think there was a woman alive who wouldn't be intimidated by Natalie's gorgeousness. But what the hell, it wasn't Natalie's fault she'd been blessed with the beauty gene, and it certainly wasn't any reason not to like her!

Tara had really enjoyed their chat earlier over lunch. There was something very liberating about chatting to someone you hardly knew and who knew absolutely nothing about you. They'd exchanged snippets of each other's lives, Tara telling her all about her and Glenn and hearing about Natalie's glamorous London lifestyle in return. They'd then spent a comfortable afternoon sunbathing and dipping in and out of the pool. Well, Tara had "dipped", Natalie, a confident and elegant swimmer, had *glided*.

Now, in the restaurant, she tried to catch Natalie's attention.

"Who are you waving at?" Glenn asked, turning round in his seat. Predictably, his eyes nearly popped out of his head when he spied the stunning creature walking towards them.

"The girl I told you I met at the pool earlier. She's lovely and she's on her own, so be nice to her."

"Hello there!" said Natalie.

The two women embraced and then Natalie turned to face Tara's companion. "And you must be Glenn," she said, extending a hand to him in greeting. "I've heard all about you. How are the scuba-diving lessons going?"

Glenn couldn't have looked any more shell-shocked than if Pamela Anderson had walked right up and kissed him on the lips. Despite her slight unease, Tara had to laugh at his reaction, which she'd anticipated. He was actually blushing!

"Pleased to meet you," Glenn replied, quickly shaking Natalie's hand.

"You'll join us, won't you?" Tara urged.

"Oh, no, I couldn't – you two are on your own holiday and –"

"Don't be silly," Tara assured her, "we'd love you to have dinner with us, wouldn't we, Glenn?"

He nodded dumbly.

"Well, if you're sure . . ." Natalie smiled at the waiter, who quickly went to fetch another place setting. "I must admit I didn't relish the thought of having dinner on my own. But I feel awful about intruding on your holiday like this, Tara. Please don't feel like you have to take pity on me because I've been abandoned."

"Abandoned?" Glenn enquired.

"Natalie's boyfriend was supposed to come on holiday with her," Tara informed him, stressing the word "boyfriend" just to be on the safe side, although she knew there was hardly anything to worry about. Even if he did happen to fancy her, Natalie was way out of Glenn's league. "But he had to cancel at the last minute."

"Which means you're stuck with me," Natalie finished, her beautiful eyes widening apologetically. She opened a box of cigarettes and went to light up before pausing quickly, her cigarette still mid-air. "Oh God, you don't mind, do you? I know smoking is banned in Ireland so –"

"Only indoors and, no, we don't mind," Tara replied easily. "So, what will I have tonight then? I think I might try the Oriental – I'm in the mood for something noodley."

The three of them chatted easily over dinner, and once again Tara marvelled at how down-to-earth and lovely Natalie was. Then, when the plates were cleared away, Tara suggested the three of them go and have drinks elsewhere in the hotel.

"We could go to the piano bar. It's really relaxing sitting there on the terrace, the music drifting along the air," she told Natalie.

"Sounds great." Natalie looked at Glenn. "Again, if you don't mind –"

"No, you two work away," he replied, stifling a yawn. "I might head off to bed early tonight if that's OK. I'm whacked after all that swimming, and I've an eight o'clock start in the morning."

"You go ahead, love," Tara soothed, and shot a mischievous wink at Natalie. "We'll be fine without you."

"I can't wait to get my PADI cert. Problem is, when I do get it, I'll only get in one or two more open-water dives before we go home."

Tara seized the moment. It was now or never. "Don't forget that next week we need to fit in a trip to Cairo too."

As expected, Glenn wasn't receptive. "Ah, we don't have to do that, do we?" he moaned.

"You know I've always wanted to visit the pyramids, Glenn." Tara was equally petulant. "And it wouldn't kill you to spend even *one* day with me on this holiday."

"But it's such a long trip up there – I'll be shattered after all my training!"

He was right: the day trip to Cairo had a four a.m. start and it would be nearly bedtime by the time they got back. She bit her lip. It was annoying but perhaps it might be too much to ask.

"Well, I'd love to go," Natalie piped up then. "But I

wouldn't dream of going all that way by myself. Anyway, these things are never much fun on your own, so if you don't mind my tagging along, I'd be happy to go with you, Tara. That is, if Glenn doesn't mind staying here by himself."

Glenn didn't mind at all. "That's a great idea – why don't you two go together?" he said, quickly seizing the opportunity to get out of the trip. "As Natalie says, at least then you get to go with someone who'll actually enjoy it. Me, I couldn't give a toss about pyramids and museums and the like. I'd much rather get a few more dives in. What do you think?"

Tara considered it. Granted, it would be much more fun going on the trip with someone who actually wanted to be there, and even though they'd only known each other a few hours, Natalie had already proven to be great company. Still, she felt guilty about leaving Glenn here on his own. They were on holiday together after all. "You wouldn't mind my going up there without you?" she asked.

Glenn laughed. "Believe me, I wouldn't mind at all!"

"Thanks a million," Tara said dryly.

"You know what I mean. It'd be much better for all concerned. I could get another dive in back here, and you can go and visit the pyramids with someone who'd enjoy them."

"And who wouldn't have a face like a wet week on them either," Tara teased.

Glenn was sheepish. "True enough, but it's not my fault that long-dead bodies don't float my boat."

"OK then, great." Tara looked at Natalie. "We could book for Wednesday, let's say? What do you think?"

"Sounds good to me," the other woman replied, smiling warmly back.

True to his word, Glenn headed straight for bed, leaving the two women alone at the table.

"He's gorgeous!" Natalie enthused, when he was out of earshot.

"You think so?" Tara was secretly pleased.

"Absolutely – those amazing brown eyes! And he's quite muscular too, isn't he?"

"Well, no disrespect, but hands off!" Tara joked.

"Oh, my goodness, I didn't mean that! I just meant it, you know, as a compliment."

"I know you did – I was just joking," Tara replied, although the idea that someone as gorgeous as Natalie found Glenn attractive in return was a little unsettling. Still, she knew instinctively that Natalie wouldn't dream of making a play for him. She just wasn't that type of girl. And anyway, she was obviously madly in love with this Steve.

Having decided to skip dessert, the two retired to the hotel bar and settled in for another cosy chat. Over a couple of champagne cocktails, Natalie told Tara some more about her relationship with Steve.

"We have a wonderful relationship and I really feel that he's the one. I just wish he'd get round to popping the question soon. It was our anniversary last week and I'd sort of hoped that it might happen then. And, if not, at least on this holiday."

Tara smiled understandingly. "So how long have you two been together?"

Natalie took a sip from her drink. "Six months."

"Six . . . months?" Tara couldn't keep the surprise out of her tone.

"Yes, I know it doesn't sound like long. But we're in love, and time is moving on – especially for me." She rolled her eyes. "If it doesn't happen soon for me, it never will."

"Why do you say that?"

Natalie shrugged. "The fact that I'm almost forty."

Tara's eyes widened with disbelief. *Forty?* That was it, once she got back home she was going on a *serious* diet!

"Well, thirty-two," Natalie admitted then, much to Tara's relief. "But the point is I'm not getting any younger. This year alone I've watched my assistant and *three* of my best friends get married, and they're all younger than me."

"And do you feel that age alone is a basis for getting married?" Tara said, automatically switching to coaching mode and kicking herself for doing so. "I'm sorry, Natalie – don't mind me," she added quickly, shaking her head. "I'm a life coach, and sometimes I can't help drawing people into personal conversations like this. Sorry."

But Natalie didn't bat an eyelid. "A life coach? How fabulous! My assistant Danni sees a life coach in Bloomsbury that she's always raving about! I keep promising to try one myself some time, but work's been so crazy lately, I just don't have the time."

Tara grinned. Some people were horrified by Tara's job, thinking her some kind of unscrupulous quack, which was the main reason she hadn't mentioned it to Natalie before. But, trust an open-minded Englishwoman to accept her profession without question!

"Well, I do enjoy it, but as I said, sometimes I find it difficult to carry on a normal conversation. The temptation is always there."

Natalie waved her away. "Don't worry, I'm the same. As I said before, I work in PR and at times I can't help but size up every new person I meet as a potentially useful contact. But now I understand why I find you so easy to talk to."

Natalie did seem happy to have someone to confide in and confessed quite candidly to Tara her deep need, almost obsession, with finding a husband.

"I know it's not fashionable to say it, and most of my single girlfriends in London would kill me for even *thinking* it, but it's what I want. I want to be married; I want to be somebody's wife."

"I don't think that's so terrible," Tara commented.

"I'm tired of all the empty socialising and arse-licking," Natalie went on, as if Tara hadn't replied. "London is a big place, and while it's wonderful, it can get lonely sometimes. Now, don't get me wrong, I wouldn't dream of living anywhere else, and most of the time it's great fun, but sometimes I feel like there has to be more to life than parties at Claridges and media launches in Soho."

Tara hid a smile. Parties at Claridges sounded pretty

amazing to her. But no matter who you were and what you did, the grass always seemed greener on the other side, didn't it? She'd seen it time and time again in her line of work.

"I feel like such an idiot for thinking this way," Natalie continued. "As though I'm betraying my womanhood or something. We're all supposed to be independent, women-of-the-world types who don't need men, aren't we? According to the magazines, in a few years' time we'll all be so self-sufficient we'll have no need for them at all! But deep down I really don't feel that way. I want to be a wife. I want to be Steve's wife."

Tara's heart went out to her, this beautiful, successful and self-assured woman who, on the face of it, was the *Cosmo* ideal incarnate.

"Look, don't beat yourself up for feeling that way. My best friend Liz was exactly the same, and since she got married three years ago, I don't think I've ever seen her happier. And there's certainly no shame in wanting to be happy. I never thought any less of her for admitting that she wanted the big white wedding, even though I didn't necessarily feel the same way – and still don't."

"You don't want to get married?"

"Not particularly. I'm perfectly happy the way I am. I adore Glenn and the life we have together. We're very happy – well, most of the time," she added, smiling fondly, "and that's enough for me."

"But don't you think that might change sometime in the future? That you might want something more?"

Natalie persisted, her eyes widening. "Oh, I'm sorry, now I'm being nosy, aren't I? Just tell me to sod off and mind my own business."

"No, it's fine." Tara sat forward, not at all insulted by the question. "But it's funny, you sound just like Liz, the friend I was talking about just now. As I said, she's been married for years, is blissfully happy and for the life of her can't understand why I'm a million miles away from following suit. But in all honesty, I love my life the way it is and I've never had any interest in getting married."

"But why not? Don't you want the fairytale and the big white dress and all the trimmings?" Natalie's face took on a faraway expression. "Personally I can't wait, and I'd give *anything* to walk up the aisle."

"You're certain that's what you want?" Tara asked and Natalie nodded dreamily.

"And what about Steve – what do you think he wants?"

"Hopefully the same thing as I do," Natalie replied. "If not, I'm in a spot of bother, aren't I?"

Chapter 8

Liz strapped Toby into his buggy and took a short walk down the hill from her house, towards the centre of the village. Although the weather was chilly, the sky was a glorious clear blue, and as she crossed the low stone bridge over the river, she thought the large Norman castle after which the village was named had never looked so impressive. The remarkably preserved castle, which, apart from the picture-perfect village itself, served as the main tourist attraction for Castlegate, was positioned on a slightly elevated site at the edge of the town centre. The river wound its way around the castle, serving as a typical Norman moat, so from her side of town, Liz needed to cross the stone bridge above the river in order to get to the centre and to the shops where she was headed this morning.

As she and Toby walked over the bridge, most of the villagers she passed gave her friendly but distant smiles. As well as commuting "Dubs", the inhabitants of Castlegate, a designated heritage village, were of course used to a continual influx of tourists, and so, even with the smiles, she knew she had a long way to go before she was accepted as one of "their own". . . if she ever was.

"Liz, hello!"

She looked up to see Colm, one of Eric and Tara's childhood friends, waving at her from across the road. He was standing outside The Coffee Bean, the popular village café he ran, which was nicely situated directly across from the castle, with magnificent views over the river.

Needless to say, he was running a thriving business, what with the huge amount of footfall the café garnered from the visiting tour buses and the fact that, since its inception by Colm's parents thirty-odd years before, the place had become a Castlegate social institution. He was also one of the few people in the village that Liz had got to know properly since the move from Dublin.

"Hey, Colm!" Liz waved back, before nipping quickly across the road to talk to him.

"Hello there, little lad," said Colm, bending down to talk to Toby and briefly pausing in his task of cleaning the premises' glass frontage. "God, he's gorgeous, Liz! Who would have thought an ugly bastard like Eric would produce a cutie like that?"

"Wash out your mouth, or I'll set my dogs on you!" Liz laughed, and Colm feigned terror.

"Hmm, you didn't threaten to set your husband on

me all the same – he must still be as much of a wimp as ever," he said with a grin. "How is Eric anyway? I haven't seen you two around town in a while."

Liz grimaced. "We haven't been around town in a while, unfortunately. And Eric's fine, working like a maniac lately – he's hardly ever at home." She rolled her eyes. "I'm beginning to think he has a mistress on the go!"

"Well, if he does, he's an idiot," Colm replied, a little more earnestly than the remark necessitated. She was only joking after all.

"So are you coming inside for a cuppa?" he asked then. "I'm trying out a new recipe involving sinful amounts of cream and mascarpone – and I'd love a guinea pig."

Judging by his slim and perfectly toned physique, he obviously didn't try out too many of his creations on himself, or if he did, he was conscientious enough to work the excess off.

Colm managed the café and, knowing what she did about him, Liz had decided that rural attitudes had surely come on in leaps and bounds when the residents of such a close-knit community didn't bat an eyelid at being served tea and coffee by the local homosexual.

"Don't tempt me – not this early in the morning," Liz replied, groaning. "But I might call back later for a coffee. I've got a bit of shopping to do first, and then I'm popping up to Eric's mum for an hour or two. I think she may have forgotten what Toby looks like at this stage!"

Maeve McGrath didn't particularly like animals, so needless to say she wasn't a regular visitor at the cottage. And in truth, she wasn't exactly a huge fan of kids either, a subscriber to the "children should be seen and not heard" camp. So, Liz and Eric usually went to visit her. Liz privately suspected that Eric's mother, with her reserved and standoffish personality, wasn't particularly liked in the village. Colm's response confirmed this.

"How *is* the old bag?" he said, rolling his eyes. "I haven't seen her in donkey's years myself – but of course, she wouldn't *dream* of coming into a place like this. Heavens no!" he mimicked exaggeratedly. "After all, who knows *where* the chef's hands have been!"

Liz smiled. Maeve McGrath was one, and possibly the only, resident of Castlegate who had a problem with the proprietor of The Coffee Bean and, according to Eric, once his mother had eventually discovered Colm's sexual preference, she had never forgiven herself for allowing the two boys to go off camping together when they were growing up. He might have turned her darling, God forbid!

Well, Liz thought now, it was certainly the woman's loss. Colm was one of the nicest and most genuine guys you could meet, and despite being a friend of Eric's rather than one of hers, he was someone in whom Liz instinctively knew she could confide, should the need arise.

According to Eric, Colm had recently begun a serious relationship with a man who was also living locally and, while Liz hadn't yet met the boyfriend, she was pleased for Colm. Living such a lifestyle in a small, close-knit community like this couldn't be easy, but at the same time it was impossible not to love Colm. Outgoing and gregarious, his gossipy mannerisms always made her laugh yet he wasn't over-the-top camp. Liz had really taken to him and decided when she met him first that it was lucky in a way that he was the other way inclined, otherwise she might be tempted to make a play for him herself!

"Tara was telling me she and Glenn met you in the pub last time the two of them were home," Liz said, her thoughts then segueing to her friend, who also knew Colm well.

"Yes, Tara looked stunning as usual," he said. "That girl has such great taste! You know, I still can't figure out how a girl from this dive ended up being so fabulous! She really knows how to make the most of herself, doesn't she?"

"I know what you mean," Liz grimaced, suddenly aware of her own dowdy jeans and boring T-shirt.

"Although, I have to hand it to you, Liz, you've smartened Eric up quite a bit! Honestly, when we were teenagers, we all used to be bewildered as to where that boy got his clothes – especially those reindeer jumpers he loved so much."

Liz giggled. "Reindeer jumpers?"

"You mean you've never seen the pictures?" Colm's eyes widened dramatically. "God, I must hunt them out and show them to you sometime. Eric used to wear this *horrific* knitted brown jumper with patterned reindeer prancing gaily all over the front of it. Can you imagine? Talk about ironic! Honestly, Liz, I'll have a look for the photos. We'd all get a good laugh out of it – especially when it's at Eric's expense." He winked conspiratorially. "Anyway, I'd better get back inside and give the others a hand – I see another horde gathering across the road like lost, and hopefully hungry, sheep."

Liz followed Colm's line of vision and, sure enough, there outside the castle entrance stood a crowd of tourists, the majority by now no doubt having had it up to the gills with hearing about Norman invaders and such like and likely gagging for a coffee break and a slice of creamy cheesecake. Lucky things.

And as well as being endowed with such an amiable personality, Colm had also been blessed with stunning culinary ability. Together with managing the business, he was The Coffee Bean's resident cook, and in conjunction with his delicious savoury breads, tomato chutneys and homemade pesto, the man made the best chocolate and vanilla cheesecake Liz had ever tasted. Evidently, she wasn't the only one who appreciated Colm's talents.

Deciding she'd better not keep him any longer, Liz bade Colm a quick goodbye, having promised to return soon for a cuppa and another chat, and continued on pushing the buggy further along the street to the shops.

Within the next half hour, she'd done most of her shopping and was inelegantly trying to stow her vegetables at the back of Toby's buggy when she looked up and came face to face with another Castlegate resident – one she really wished she hadn't.

"Emma!" Liz blurted in surprise, her face suffused with colour – not just from surprise, but also from her exertions in trying to put away the heavy groceries.

"Oh, hello," said Emma.

Tara's sister was typically off-hand and, maddeningly, looked stunning as usual, dressed in a pretty flower-patterned skirt and stylish white top. Blast it, why hadn't she made more of an effort! Baggy jeans and a sweatshirt that had seen better days were barely suitable for slobbing around at home, let alone going shopping! But Toby had been narky that morning and she'd had a couple of dogs changing over before she left, so really she had been lucky to get out of the house at all. So, trust Eric's ex to look like something from the *Cosmo* fashion pages, all pretty and feminine and glowing with health, while *she* looked like something from *Down-and-Out Weekly*.

Then Liz recalled why it was that Emma looked so glowing.

"Tara tells me you're moving home again," she said, trying to inject some warmth into her tone. Granted, over the years, neither woman had made any bones of their dislike for the other, but Liz saw little reason not to be polite, if not exactly friendly, towards Emma. It was unlikely that the two would ever be bosom buddies but . . .

"Did she?" For a brief moment, Emma looked surprised and, Liz thought, slightly wrong-footed. "I didn't realise my personal life was up for public examination."

Liz gritted her teeth. Right. If the girl wanted to play silly buggers, then to hell with being polite. "Emma, to be honest, I'm not too concerned about your personal life, OK? I was just making small-talk as people tend to do when they bump into one another. But seeing as you're not capable of basic manners, let alone anything else, then good luck to you!" She went to push the buggy away.

"Will Eric be at home this weekend?" Emma enquired pointedly. "I haven't seen him around here in a few weeks. Anyone would think he was staying away on purpose."

Don't let her get to you – it's exactly what she wants, Liz warned herself silently, while inwardly wishing she could smack the cow.

"Of course, where else would he be?" she replied sweetly.

"Oh, I don't know. From what I can make out, he seems to be spending a lot of his time in Dublin. I bumped into him once or twice up there and we had a few drinks. It was good fun actually."

Despite herself, Liz's heart began to pound loudly in her chest. "Did you really?" she asked, trying to sound nonchalant.

"Yes, it was just like old times actually," Emma replied, her voice full of meaning, before walking away in the other direction, her shapely backside moving haughtily from side to side.

Liz's hands gripped the handle of the buggy so

tightly her knuckles almost broke through skin. What the hell was all that about? Granted, Eric had been spending a lot of time in Dublin lately but he was working, wasn't he? She took a deep breath and shook her head, trying to get a grip on herself, trying to contain the jealousy and suspicion that had out of nowhere aroused itself within her.

What on earth was wrong with her? Why did the mere sight of Emma Harrington turn her into some raging, jealous wreck almost every time they met? It had been years since Emma and Eric had been together – way before him and her, she reassured herself as her heartbeat began to slow a little and her stomach stopped spinning. And Eric was married to *her* after all, and as far as she knew had barely even spoken to Emma since God knows when.

As far as she knew . . .

Despite herself, Emma's words planted themselves in Liz's brain. "*I bumped into him a few times – we had a few drinks.*" Had Eric and Emma met up when he stayed over in Dublin? And if they had, wasn't it strange that her husband hadn't mentioned it?

Emma walked further along the road, a mischievous grin plastered across her face. OK, so she shouldn't have said anything to Eric's wife, but she couldn't help it!

For some reason that goody-two-shoes friend of Tara's had always got up her nose, and she couldn't resist telling her that she and Eric had met up in town.

That had certainly wiped the smug smile off her silly little face! The slip of the tongue had been worth it, just to see Liz's stupefied reaction.

Emma smiled and headed for home. Well, she'd lit the fuse: now all she had to do was sit back and watch the fireworks.

Eric returned home from work that evening bustling with energy and all throughout dinner raved enthusiastically about the extra hours he'd secured at work.

"Which means an extra few quid to spend on the house, love," he told his wife, gleefully rubbing his hands together and apparently not noticing Liz's sombre mood.

"Or maybe you might just blow it on your nights out on the town with the boys," Liz replied, the words escaping before she could stop them.

Instantly, the mood changed. "What?" he asked, frowning. "What are you talking about?"

Liz lifted her chin and continued feeding Toby at his high-chair. "From what I hear, you've been having the life of Riley up there, while I'm stuck at home with Toby and the dogs."

Eric set down his fork. "Liz, I don't know what the hell you're going on about but –"

"I'm only telling you what I heard. I bumped into Emma Harrington today who wasted no time in telling me what a wonderful social life you seem to lead in Dublin."

Immediately Eric coloured. "Emma? What would she know about it?"

Why did he look so guilty? Liz thought worriedly. He knew nothing about her true feelings towards Emma and that she'd always felt jealous of her. A wildly jealous woman wasn't attractive, Liz knew that, and so she'd always taken great pains to ensure her insecurities remained hidden.

"Liz, what's going on?"

Unable to stop herself, Liz sniffed defiantly. She knew she was behaving childishly and setting up a conversation that could only end in trouble. Still she couldn't help it. The irrational sense of being hard done by had clouded her judgement.

"You tell me," she snapped. "All I know is that some stranger seems to know much more about your exploits in Dublin than I do."

He frowned. "I still don't understand what you're getting at. OK, so I did bump into Emma up in Dublin. But so what?"

Liz didn't reply; she just sat there looking wounded yet defiant, and with that Eric's temper began to fray.

"Look, Liz, I'm not in the mood for this sulking and childish behaviour," he said shortly, his tone raising a fraction. "If you've got something to say, then just come right out and say it! What's on your mind?"

Just then, Toby let out an anguished cry, evidently unused to his mum and dad speaking to one another like this.

Liz wasn't used to it either and, despite her sense of

grievance, she hated that she was sounding like a nagging wife. But Emma's comments earlier had really unnerved her, and she was determined to demand some kind of explanation.

But it seemed Eric was in no mood to oblige. "Look, it's obvious you're in some kind of a mood, but whatever is wrong with you, don't go taking it out on me." With that, he got up from the table and walked out of the kitchen, Toby still wailing in his wake.

Her mind racing, Liz got up to tend to her son and tried desperately to get a grip on her whirling thoughts and emotions. Why had Eric got so angry when *she* was the one who should be feeling hard done by? When *she* was the one who sat here alone on weeknights while he lived it up in the capital?

It had been mostly his idea to move to Castlegate in the first place after all. "It would be better for the baby and all the space around the cottage would be perfect for setting up your kennels," he'd told her enthusiastically.

And yes, village life had indeed been better for Toby, and setting up the kennels had been a dream come true for Liz, but if living in Castlegate was so wonderful, why did it seem that Eric was lately coming up with more and more reasons to stay away from the village, to stay away from her and Toby?

Her son's cries eventually abating, Liz slumped back down at the kitchen table and put her head in her hands. What was wrong with her? Why did she feel so insecure all of a sudden? Granted this underlying emotion had always been a problem where she was concerned, and she wasn't sure why. She'd lost a few boyfriends over the years as a result, but since then had pretty much managed to keep it in check. And for the most part, she'd never really felt anything other than completely secure and happy when it came to Eric. For the most part.

Except when it came to Emma Harrington.

The idea of Eric and Emma together wouldn't go away – however hard she tried.

It didn't help that she had never been able to communicate her fears to anyone. Tara was her best friend but, of course, she couldn't exactly voice her feelings about Emma to Tara, could she? Irrespective of their relationship, and in all fairness their relationship was pretty good, no girl in their right mind would bitch to her best friend about her sister, would they?

So, Liz stayed silent and never outwardly expressed her doubts and niggling feelings of jealousy. She'd never even properly investigated the reasons for Emma and Eric's break-up. Instead she'd resolved to try and forget about the girl and get on with her own life.

But now something had been sparked off in her that for years she had tried to bury and which, since the news of Emma's surprise pregnancy, had grown and flourished.

She had to get a hold of herself.

Liz took a deep breath and made an effort to think rationally.

There was nothing between Emma and Eric –

nothing. So what if Emma had met him on a night out in Dublin? It wasn't that big a city after all, and there was always a chance they could bump into one another, wasn't there? And just because they'd bumped into one another didn't mean they'd gone off and had a raging affair, did it? Liz felt her heart would shatter at the thought of Eric with somebody else. God, she'd drive herself crazy if she kept thinking like this! How had a simple smart comment from a girl who was known for her deviousness, and whom she didn't like, almost sent her into convulsions of distrust and suspicion?

And why on earth had the news of Emma's mystery pregnancy had such an effect on her? Emma could have a serious boyfriend in Dublin for all she knew. But deep down, Liz knew this wasn't the case. Tara had been puzzled by her sister's pregnancy primarily *because* she hadn't been seeing anyone. And they had both considered the possibility that it might have been the result of a clandestine affair, perhaps with a married man.

But there was no reason, no reason at all, for her to think that this affair could have been with her own husband, was there?

Getting up from the table, Liz reached for a tissue and quickly wiped her eyes and nose. She had to snap out of this. She was being hysterical, over-emotional – completely unreasonable. Emma would be thrilled to see the damage she'd done, and all with a simple little throwaway remark. But it wasn't a throwaway remark either, was it? No, Emma had known full well what she was doing, had known well that she was planting a seed of suspicion in Liz's brain. And of course, any normal, well-adjusted, secure woman wouldn't give it a second thought, would she? But when the woman in question was someone as basically insecure as she was, then . . .

"Honey, what's the matter?" Eric reappeared in the doorway, concern written all over his face. "Why are you crying?"

"I don't know," Liz answered truthfully, her thoughts scattered all over the place as she tried to come to terms with her own feelings. "I don't know why I went off on you like that and I'm sorry. I just . . . I suppose I just find it hard sometimes when you're away from us, and I don't like to think of you off enjoying yourself while you're supposed to be working."

"But I *am* working, love – and working very hard." Eric moved across the room and put a comforting arm around her shoulders. "I thought we'd agreed that I'd put in the extra hours for a little while, so we can afford to get this extension built."

She sniffed. "I know – and I'm sorry, but for some reason I keep having images of you out and about and living it up in the pubs and . . ." She shook her head. "I'm sorry. I'm just being silly."

"Yes, you are," Eric said firmly. "So, are we friends again?"

"Of course we are," she replied, resting her head against his chest and hugging him tightly.

Eric was her husband, the love of her life, the father of her son and the man she really should know better than to doubt. This mistrust, suspicion – there was no basis to any of it – it was all in her own stupid head!

Blast Emma Harrington! As far as Liz was concerned, if she never saw the girl again for as long as she lived, she'd be happy.

But that wasn't very likely, was it? she thought worriedly. Not when Emma was back living in Castlegate and, according to Tara, was very likely back for good.

Chapter 9

Back home in London, Natalie unpacked her luggage and flung various items of clothing into the laundry basket. Despite the fact that she'd arrived at Heathrow a good two hours ago, she hadn't yet heard from Steve. It was strange because she'd had visions of him waiting for her in the arrivals area, all handsome and smiling and ready to whisk her into his arms and off her feet, like something from *An Officer and a Gentleman.* But she'd scanned the crowds a few times upon arrival and there'd been no sign of him.

Despite herself, Natalie was beginning to worry. All throughout the holiday she hadn't heard from Steve once, despite sending him a few texts asking him how he was and if he was missing her, but he hadn't replied to any of them.

And of course she'd checked her answering machine on the way in and there was nothing on that from him either, just a series of messages from the office and a couple from her mum, who'd obviously forgotten she was away. Or had she told her? She couldn't remember. These days she was so caught up in work (or indeed with Steve) that she'd barely had the time to talk to her mother. Oh well, she'd call Imogen later.

She smiled as she held up her favourite Roberto Cavalli dress, the one she'd been wearing the first night she'd met Tara and Glenn. She was so lucky to have met them; the holiday could very well have been a disaster otherwise. Well, lucky to have met Tara anyway – after the first day or two she hadn't really seen that much of Glenn. He seemed just as nice, though, and didn't seem to mind Tara gadding off to Cairo with some English stranger!

They were a good pair who obviously adored one another, though oddly they didn't seem to have that much in common as far as their interests were concerned – she with her pyramids, he with his scuba diving!

But Natalie envied the fact that the other woman would never be lonely with Glenn around – the two of them seemed blissfully happy together, and while Tara had admitted that people were constantly on at her to get married, she wasn't at all bothered. It was a refreshing perspective, but also a little frustrating for someone like Natalie who would give *anything* to settle down with someone nice.

But, unlike Natalie, Tara had someone to come home to every evening. She didn't know what it was like to return to an empty flat after a hard day's work and have nothing but the four walls to complain to. So, she supposed it was easier for Tara to be flippant about her unmarried state.

Having unpacked her suitcase and sorted her clothes, Natalie padded barefoot out to the kitchen and rummaged around in the drawers for a takeaway menu. Although, she thought, there was something nice at the same time about being able to slob around in comfortable jog-suits, something she'd never be able to do if she were living with Steve. As far as she knew, he'd never seen her without make-up. Even when he stayed the night, she always made sure she removed her face only after sex, and as he usually snoozed till noon the following day, she usually had the war paint applied hours before he surfaced.

She picked up her mobile phone to order dinner from the local Chinese but, before she dialled the number, she once again checked her messages. Nothing from Steve.

Not a single reply to the messages she'd sent him while away. Granted, she'd only sent – what – one or two brief texts on arrival in Sharm and . . . oh God, Natalie realised, horrified, as she scrolled through her "Sent" folder, make that eleven or twelve! No, thirteen! How on earth had she managed that? All those late-night drinks with Tara had obviously loosened her fingers, because most of these were very definitely tipsy-texts. Yikes! Steve would think she'd gone mad. She'd better text him now and apologise and –

As if on cue, her phone beeped, and to her delight Steve's name appeared on the screen. Yes! He must have been waiting for her to return home before contacting her. Actually, now that she thought about it, maybe it wasn't possible to contact her through the mobile network in Egypt and that was why she hadn't heard from him.

Excitedly she opened the message. Goody! With any luck she might see him tonight. OK, so she was dog-tired and if he called round the frumpy jog-suit would definitely have to go but . . .

Please stop stalking me.

Puzzled, Natalie stared at the message. *Stalking?* What was he on about? Then she smiled and rolled her eyes. This was obviously one of Steve's little jokes. Still grinning, she hit the "Call" button and waited for his phone to ring. Her boyfriend could be a howl sometimes. But at least now she knew he was in a good mood and –

"Yes?"

Hearing him pick up on the other end, Natalie beamed. "Hi, darling, it's me – I'm just back from –"

"Look, I'm sorry, but I really don't have time for this now," the object of her affection interjected shortly. "Can't you just leave me alone?"

Natalie blinked. "Steve, it's me, Natalie."

"I know bloody well who it is – unfortunately." Steve groaned. "Look, Nat, I thought I made this clear last time."

"Made what clear?"

He sighed. "Look, we had a few dates, and it was great but –"

Her heart began to thump. "But what?"

"But that's it. We're not really suited, you and me. I thought you understood that last week."

"Understood what?"

Steve took a deep breath. "Look, you're great and it's been fun but –"

Her eyes widened in disbelief as she sensed what was coming, "But what?" she repeated timidly.

"Look, I just don't think this is going anywhere."

On his side, Natalie heard another phone ring in the background and guessed he must be at the office.

"Don't be so silly," she said, trying to keep her voice light, "of course it's going somewhere. You have no idea how much I missed you while I was away and –"

"Yes, I do actually – I have all the sodding texts to prove it."

"Right, well, I can explain those." Natalie gave a little laugh. "That night, I'd had one drink too many so –"

"Natalie, I really don't have time to discuss this," he said, his tone now decidedly impatient. "As I said, I just don't think we're suited."

Of course they were suited! She and Steve were great together – perfect together! How could he say that they weren't? Natalie couldn't believe this was happening. Again.

"But – but what about our holiday?" she spluttered. "If we 'weren't suited', as you say, why did you agree to come on holiday with me?"

"What? I didn't agree to anything! It was all your idea and you had it all arranged before you even asked me!" Steve sounded mightily put out. "Talk about railroading somebody!"

"Well, you could have let me know that you didn't want to go instead of letting me down at the last minute like that!" she said, irked that he saw things in such a way. "I paid out a fortune for that holiday!"

Steve seemed to be struggling to hold his temper. "Natalie, I told you at the time that I would let you know if and when I had time to take a holiday and that we would then discuss it! But you didn't listen. You just went right ahead and booked it anyway. Jesus, we barely know one another! In all my life I don't think I've ever met a bird so pushy."

Natalie's heart sank. "We barely know one another? Steve, we've had sex at least a hundred times!"

"Yeah, well . . ." Steve paused for a minute, as if trying to think of the right words. "Look, Nat, as far as I'm concerned it was just that – sex. Maybe you thought it meant something more but . . ."

Natalie couldn't remember ever feeling so low in her entire life. Just sex? What about love and companionship and all the things she thought they'd shared? How could it have been "just sex"?

"We weren't a couple, Nat. I wasn't looking for a relationship. I thought you knew that – especially when I told you I wasn't keen on that holiday, and I'd blown you . . . I mean, hadn't seen you that much beforehand."

"But I thought that was because you were busy with

work! You *told* me you were busy with work! And I was busy too, so I thought the holiday would be a good opportunity for us both and . . ." Natalie couldn't finish the rest of the sentence. She'd thought he'd be thrilled at the idea of the trip, delighted that she'd gone to such effort just for him. But obviously she'd been wrong. "Look, I'm really sorry that I sent you all those text messages when I was away," she babbled quickly. "I was a bit tipsy at the time and I didn't really mean it when I said you were the best thing that's ever happened to me and –"

"Nat, look – it's not going to work, OK?" Steve interjected, his voice softening somewhat. "You're a great girl, but I'm just not ready for a relationship with – with *anyone* at the moment. There's too much going on in my life right now."

"Like what? Maybe I can help," she replied eagerly, heartened by his change in tone. She could help him through whatever was going wrong in his life at the moment. That was what supportive girlfriends did, didn't they? Yes, it would be perfect. They could put their passionate romance aside and she'd just concentrate on being Steve's confidante, his shoulder to cry on, his rock of strength –

"I don't need any help!" he said, becoming irritated once more. "Look, can't you take a bloody hint? I don't know where you got the idea that this was something serious. Yes, we had some good times together but –"

"*Some* good times together! Steve, we were –"

"Ah, Natalie, please just leave me alone, will you?" the object of her affection interjected once again. "Look, if I'd known you'd turn out to be some psycho bunny-boiler, I'd have run a mile! No man in their right minds would want all this crowding and neediness!"

She a bunny-boiler? *Psycho* bunny-boiler? What was he on about?

"But, Steve, how could I possibly crowd you when I hardly ever see you?" she snivelled, sounding even more desperate than she felt.

Steve sighed once more. "I'm sorry, but there's no point in making this any harder for either of us. You're a nice girl, Nat, but it's just not meant to be. See you round."

With that, he rang off, leaving her staring dumbly at the handset for what seemed like an age. What had happened to the grand homecoming she'd anticipated? The big love affair she'd described to Tara in Egypt? Had this really happened? Had Steve – the love of her life, the man she was supposed to marry – had he just dumped her?

She was eventually snapped out of her reverie by the ringing of the intercom. For a brief second, she wondered if it was Steve at the front door, if he had been playing an elaborate (and admittedly cruel) joke on her. But no, it was merely the deliveryman with her take-away.

Wishing that she'd ordered a fattening and much more comforting dish like fried rice and crispy duck in plum sauce instead of a boring and anaemic low-fat chow mein, Natalie went downstairs and dazedly paid the delivery man. Then, her appetite by then having completely deserted her, she went back upstairs and threw the whole lot in the bin, before finally throwing herself on the bed and crying her heart out.

The following morning, as she struggled to gather together enough make-up to cover her tearstained face and the dark circles under her eyes (despite her fabulous tan from the holiday), Natalie thought again about what Steve had said to her on the telephone the night before. His words had kept repeating themselves over and over in her head all night, but she'd been so upset that their relationship was over that she hadn't been able to think clearly about any of it. Now, in the cold light of day, and having let all the hurt and anguish out, she was better able to consider everything somewhat more rationally.

Was she pushy and needy and bunny-boilerish?

Well, she thought huffily, as she applied Clarins Beauty Flash Balm to her face, if trying to show somebody how much you cared about them by booking them on a luxury holiday was being a bunny-boiler, she wished she knew a few more of them herself! Then she shook her head dejectedly. She'd really thought that doing something extravagant like that for Steve would make him happy, especially as he'd been so thrilled when she'd organised prime seats for him and his mates at Stamford Bridge that time. But maybe an exotic holiday abroad had been too much too soon. After all, they had only been together a few months.

And why oh why had she sent him so many texts while she was away? Why had she been so stupid as to think that they had a real future together? She remembered Tara's surprised expression when she'd told her that she was expecting Steve to propose any day now, especially after confessing they'd only been together six months. But she had been so sure Steve was the one for her, the one who'd finally deliver the fairytale she'd longed for since she'd watched her very first Disney video.

Natalie wiped away a stray tear from the corner of her eye. Now she was further away from that than ever, and considering the fact that she was getting older by the minute, she was getting further and further as time went on.

Was it *ever* going to happen? Was she ever going to find someone who wanted her as much as she did them? How many more frogs did she have to kiss before she found her Prince Charming? It was so bloody frustrating.

Natalie began to apply a thick layer of mascara onto her eyelashes, hoping it would obscure her still red-rimmed eyes. With her naturally long and dark lashes, she didn't normally need much, but today she needed to pull out all the stops to ensure that nobody in the office realised she was upset. Appearances were everything in the PR business and it wouldn't do for one of Blue Moon's most trusted publicity managers to come across as anything other than composed and in control. Given that she knew all about the holiday and Natalie's hopes of a romantic week away, no doubt Danni would notice something, but hopefully she would know better than to ask.

Natalie sighed. So much for the romantic week away. How had she got it so badly wrong? From the first minute she'd laid eyes on him at that book launch in Soho, and particularly after they'd seemed to get on so well, she'd decided they were meant to be together. And then after a few dates, things had been so going so well that she couldn't help but start picking out their children's names and . . .

Suddenly, her eyes widened but this had nothing to do with her industrial strength mascara. Was that it? Had she been going about this all wrong? What if all the men she'd met over the last few years were perfectly suitable, yet *she* was the one who'd kept messing things up. Each of them had been all over her at the beginning, some of them admitting that because of her supposed good looks they'd almost been afraid to approach her. But despite their early interest in her, the ensuing relationships never seemed to progress any further than a few months.

And now that she thought about it, the same excuses tended to keep popping up over and over again: "I need some space . . . you're too forward . . . no, I haven't thought about whether I prefer Habitat to Ikea . . ." It was all the same stuff.

Natalie finished applying her lipstick and stared at herself in the mirror. She wasn't that much of a nightmare, was she? Granted, she was so used to being aggressive in orchestrating things at work that perhaps she was unwittingly just as full-on when it came to her personal life.

Before Steve, there had been Gary, and he'd seemed fine at the beginning too until she'd . . . Natalie blushed at the memory . . . until she'd phoned up his mother after they'd been a few weeks together and asked if she could call round and meet her. Gary had gone apoplectic. But he'd been so full-on with her in the early days that Natalie had been certain they had a real future together. He was always staying over at her place and the sex, to the say the least, was pretty intense. So as far as Natalie was concerned this had to mean Gary was crazy about her, didn't it? She grimaced. Once again, she'd got it wrong.

But now that she had the benefit of hindsight, Natalie could admit truthfully to herself that it wasn't so much Gary she'd been interested in back then, but more the possibility of settling down and getting married like Freya and the rest of her friends. And if she was being totally honest with herself, didn't she feel much the same way about Steve? Was she really heartbroken that he'd dumped her yesterday, or was she more upset about the fact that her dreams of domestic bliss had been cut short once again?

She didn't know, she decided, picking up her briefcase and leaving the flat. All Natalie knew was that today she felt doubly eager to get back to work, back to dealing with the kind of problems she understood and therefore knew exactly how to control.

Chapter 10

Despite her determination not to let Emma's comments get to her, over the week that followed Liz discovered that this was way more difficult than she'd thought.

On Friday evening, shortly after he and Liz had finished dinner, Eric announced that he was thinking of going out for an hour or two.

"I thought I might give Colm a ring – see if he fancies a few pints in The Bridge," he said. "You don't mind, do you? I haven't seen him in a while."

"Of course I don't mind," Liz had replied easily.

It was Eric's first night off in a while, and even though she was a little put out that he'd chosen to spend it elsewhere instead of with her and Toby, she didn't blame him. And after their argument about his going out in Dublin a few days earlier, she wasn't about to start behaving like some overprotective shrew. "He was only saying the same thing the other day, actually."

"Yeah, it's been a while since we had a few. And of course, what with the café being so busy, I think he needs to get out and relax a bit."

"I know, the place was packed to the gills the other day when I was in. He really needs to take on more staff."

"Well, he's tried, and apparently they're easy to get but impossible to keep."

Liz nodded. "I can imagine."

"Anyway, I'm sure I won't be too late – Colm won't drink too many pints – you know how these fellas don't like to let themselves go!"

Liz smiled inwardly. Despite his apparent open-mindedness about his best mate, Eric nearly always referred to his friend's sexuality in a joking manner. Typical Irishman, she thought affectionately as Eric went off to get ready to go out.

But her affection turned out to be very short-lived when she discovered who her husband was *really* meeting that night.

Eric was in the shower, his deep baritone singing voice filling the house and causing Toby to look around him in wonder, trying to figure out what the awful noise was. Liz was in the bedroom, putting away some newly laundered clothing, when Eric's mobile phone, which he'd left on a chest of drawers, beeped. She picked up the handset and nonchalantly checked the sender, suspecting that it must be Colm replying to his friend's invitation. But when she saw the name that appeared in her husband's inbox, Liz's blood went cold.

"Emma"

All of a sudden, her knees went weak and, the phone still in her hand, she slumped heavily down on the bed. What was going on? Why was Emma Harrington sending text messages to her husband? And was it Colm he was planning to meet tonight – or was it her? Her hand shaking, Liz dropped the phone on the bedcovers. As much as she wanted to, she couldn't bring herself to read the message. That was crossing a line. But hadn't Eric crossed a line by corresponding with his ex-girlfriend behind his wife's back?

It was obvious they had been in contact before. Emma's name was evidently stored in Eric's phone book, as it had been her name and not her mobile number that had appeared on the screen. So what the hell was going on?

A couple of feet away, Liz heard the water of the en suite shower being turned off and Eric stepping out onto the bathroom floor.

Feeling like some kind of interloper, she quickly dropped the remainder of the laundry on the bed and exited the room.

OK, she thought, trying to get a grip on herself as she went back into the kitchen. It might be nothing – it might *mean* nothing. When Eric came out she'd mention that she'd heard his phone beep. She wouldn't tell him that she knew who the message was from, no – she hoped that Eric would fill in that piece of information without any prompting from her. And if he didn't fill her in, if he didn't tell Liz that the message was from Emma and what it was all about, then . . . then she would have good reason to be worried. So for the moment, she would try to stay calm, try to stay rational and not carry on like a crazed, over-emotional, insecure wreck.

Just then Eric reappeared in the kitchen, clean-shaven and nicely dressed in jeans and a blue button-down shirt. A bit too nicely dressed for a visit to the local? Liz wondered and stopped herself before she really went crazy.

"I think I heard your phone go off while you were in the shower," she said, trying to keep her voice steady. "You must have got a message."

"Did it?" Eric went back into the bedroom and soon after reappeared in the kitchen with the phone in his hand. "It's from Emma Harrington," he said, his tone a little too wary for Liz's liking, although she couldn't help but be heartened by the fact that he'd told her the truth.

"Emma Harrington? Why would she be texting you?"

Eric shrugged. "Oh, that night I met her in Dublin she said something about maybe having a tip for me about a job . . . but she never got back to me about that after . . . "

"So what does this message say?"

"Well, it's a blank message so it's obviously a mistake."

Liz knew he was lying. His face had turned bright puce and he couldn't bring himself to look directly at her. Oh, God!

"Right." Liz's insides burned as she tried to think of a response to this pathetic excuse. A blank message? What planet did he think she was from?

"Anyway, I'd better head away," he said, apparently convinced that he'd come up with a convincing explanation as to why his ex-girlfriend was texting him. "Colm said he'd be there around half seven."

"Right," Liz replied, her brain scrambling desperately to try and explain what was going on. As far as she knew her husband hadn't yet phoned Colm about this unplanned night out, so she wasn't sure how Eric knew what time Colm would be there.

But deep down, Liz knew well that her husband of three years wasn't meeting his best friend. Instead he was meeting the girl who had cast a shadow over Liz and her relationship with Eric right from the very beginning. The girl who was, at this very moment, pregnant with some unnamed man's child.

Later that evening, Eric and Emma sat side-by-side on a wooden bench by the river in the huge but private park at the rear of the castle – as they had done many times before throughout their relationship. The secluded riverside area had always been a favourite for young and amorous Castlegate couples over the years, and although it felt very different to how it was when they were teenagers, for Eric there was still something calming and peaceful about the place.

"I think Liz saw your name come up on my phone

tonight," he told her tentatively. "Emma, I don't think you should do that – it looks bad."

She sighed. "Oh God, I'm sorry, Eric. I just wanted to let you know I'd be late, and to be honest I didn't think for a minute that she'd check your messages like that. Isn't that an invasion of privacy?"

"I didn't say she did, I said I *thought* she might have seen the name," Eric replied testily. "I don't think she did all the same, but I had to admit to her that it was you, just to be on the safe side."

Emma's eyes widened. "And what explanation did you give for that?"

He shrugged. "I said the message had been blank, so it must have been a mistake."

Emma shook her head from side to side. "She's going to suspect something, Eric," she said, running a hand through her long fair hair. "She's not an idiot. And I really think you should tell her."

"How can I?" he cried. "What would she think of me?"

"She's your wife."

"I know but . . . I wouldn't even know where to start and, to be honest, I still don't know how I feel about this myself yet. I'm still trying to come to terms with it . . . I don't want to have to deal with Liz's feelings too. God, I know that sounds awful, as if I don't care how she feels. But right now, I really don't think I could cope with that on top of everything else."

"But what are you going to do in the long run? This needs to be sorted out one way or the other. You can't let it drag on forever."

"I know that," he replied, his voice plaintive. "And I don't know what to do. My head is so fucked up at the moment. This is the last thing I expected, Emma, the last thing I thought I'd ever have to face. And I don't know how to deal with it. I don't want to hurt her . . ."

"People will get hurt whatever you do, Eric, you know that. And the more time we spend just talking about it, and not doing anything, the worse it'll be in the end – especially if Liz suspects something."

"I know, and believe me I'm trying to sort it out but . . ." His voice trailed off and for a long moment the two remained silent, lost in their own thoughts.

Eventually, Eric spoke again. "So what about yourself?" he asked. "How are you feeling now . . . about everything?"

She sighed once more. "It's hard, trying to keep it all a secret when everyone is so anxious to find out who the father might be. It all seems so clandestine and I think Tara thinks I'm doing it on purpose. Still, I swore I wouldn't tell anyone and, Eric, I'm determined to keep to that. Nobody's going to know – well, nobody except you anyway." She raised a tiny smile.

"How did the two of us ever get ourselves into such a mess, Em?" he said, shaking his head, realising only at the last minute that he had addressed her as he used to years ago.

"I don't know – we're some pair all right!" She managed a dry laugh. "Maybe we should have never split up in the first place, then none of this would have happened."

"It wasn't that simple," he said, unwilling to go down that road, about how he had moved away to Dublin and the relationship had eventually fizzled out. Fizzled out because he'd met Liz. He remembered how vibrant and funny his wife had been back then, and he'd fallen head over heels in love with her, completely forgetting all about Emma Harrington. And now, years later, here he was, keeping a huge secret from his wife, keeping a secret with Emma. It was strange how things worked out.

"Tara's trying her utmost to wrangle it out of me," Emma said. "We keep having long chats about how tough it'll be for me on my own, or about how the father should be involved in the baby's life."

"And are you planning on telling her?" he asked.

She shrugged offhandedly. " I can't, can I? Unless . . ." She shook her head. "No, forget it, I know it's not an issue, so I won't even say it."

"It's complicated, Emma, we both know that. And if it ever came out, it would be very tough for everyone involved. Particularly you."

"I know – which is why I swore I wouldn't say anything, remember? It was one night – we were drunk, we were stupid. *I* was stupid and it meant nothing."

"Don't say that – of course it meant something, otherwise it would never have happened, would it?"

"Well, at least the sex was good," she laughed. "I'll remember that for a long time to come!"

He raised a smile, a little taken aback that she could be so candid about the whole thing. Then again, that was Emma – tough as old boots. "Trust you to take something positive out of it." Then he looked at his watch, and his tone grew more serious. "Look, Emma, I'd better be heading away soon. I told Liz I was meeting Colm for a couple of drinks tonight . . ."

"Right," she replied, a trace of annoyance in her tone. Then almost immediately she brightened. "Where are you going? The Bridge?" The Bridge was the busiest place in the village and had always been their pub of choice when they were younger. "I wish I could tag along. Any excuse to get out of that house."

"Your parents are still giving you trouble?"

She nodded. "Well, not exactly – my mother is all over me at the moment and it's really doing my head in." Then she sighed deeply. "It's my own fault for coming home, I suppose. Maybe I should have stayed in Dublin and moved in with Tara or something." Emma giggled. "I'd say she'd love that – little sis moving in and disrupting her perfect life."

Eric could hear the bitterness in her voice and said nothing. In a way he could understand why Emma felt hard done by in comparison. While he and Tara had been close in their younger days, he now saw her more as a friend of his wife's than his own, and lately they no longer seemed to have that much in common. Tara was a go-getter, someone who had made a huge success of her life, with her nice career, nice car and plenty of money. Unlike her little sister, who now had to contemplate an altogether more bleak future as a thirty-something single mother living under her parents' roof.

But no matter how badly Eric felt about that, he couldn't let her come along to the pub with him.

"Emma, if you're thinking of coming with me, I really wouldn't. It's nothing personal, it's just . . . well, it wouldn't be right, particularly not in the circumstances. Not to mention the fact that Colm knows and likes Liz, and the two of them could talk. Anyone could talk."

"Of course I'm not going to tag along! I'm not stupid, you know. If I wanted people to see us together I wouldn't have suggested we meet here, would I?"

Eric stood up, suddenly anxious to get away. "Look, I really should go. Thanks for seeing me tonight – I really appreciate it. I know things aren't easy for either of us, but I suppose we've only got each other to talk to and –"

"Eric, it's OK, I understand. I'd hate for you to have to go through this all on your own. Does Colm know anything?"

"Nah – not the kind of thing you discuss with him, really," he said, shaking his head slowly. "And as I said, he knows Liz so . . ."

Emma looked thoughtful. "I don't think she likes me very much. I met her on the street last week, and she seemed quite annoyed when I mentioned I'd met you in town."

He frowned. "I know – she told me." His tone was disapproving. "And to be honest, Emma, you put me in a bit of a spot. I had to think very fast."

"I can imagine – look, it just came out in conversation," she said quickly. "I didn't mean to cause trouble or anything." She sighed. "Look, are you sure you don't want to tell her? It would make it so much easier for both of –"

"I don't want to tell her, Emma, believe me. She thinks our life and our marriage are perfect and for the most part they are – apart from me being too cowardly to . . . well, look, I just don't have the heart to shatter her illusions about me. Not just yet."

"As long as you're sure," she replied quietly. "But if you are ever ready to have it out with her, let me know. In the meantime, I'm here whenever you need me."

He smiled at her. "Thank you, Emma. I don't know what I'd do without you. You're the only one who understands and, God knows, you've got enough to think about yourself. But you know I'm going to help you with that as much as I can, don't you? It's the very least I can do."

Chapter 11

The following Monday afternoon, Liz approached the coffee shop in trepidation, Toby in tow. She felt pathetic sneaking around behind Eric's back like this, but she had to know. She had to know if her husband had been telling the truth about meeting Colm for a drink the other night. Because if he hadn't . . . well, Liz didn't want to think about that just yet.

She pushed open the door and manoeuvred the buggy inside, smiling gratefully as a man – probably a tourist – jumped up from a nearby table and held the door open for her.

As she headed towards a vacant table, she smiled briefly at one of the staff, who was busy behind the counter serving coffee to customers. But the person Liz had really come to see today was nowhere in sight.

Having psyched herself up to come down here in the first place, Liz felt strangely disappointed that Colm wasn't around. She positioned the buggy against the wall, sat down at the table and picked up a menu, her heart going like a jackhammer. What was she thinking, sneaking around and checking up on her husband? And what had she thought she was going to say to Colm if he had been here? "Hi, Colm, I just wanted to ask if my husband was really meeting you for a drink on Friday night, or if it was just an excuse to go and see his mistress?" He'd think she was some kind of hysterical psycho! Which Liz admitted ashamedly was exactly how she'd been behaving lately.

"Liz, hello!" As if on cue, Colm appeared in the kitchen doorway. "How are things?"

She coloured slightly as if he could somehow read her thoughts. "Great, thanks." Of course, now that he was here, she was totally tongue-tied.

"Can I get you something?" he asked, crossing the room to talk to her. "Coffee, cappuccino – something like that? Or we have these fabulous caramel and hazelnut lattes – how about one of those?"

Liz thought about her thickening waistline and non-existent exercise routine. "A black coffee would be great, thanks."

"And for the gentleman?" Colm bent down and tickled the toddler's chin, Toby smiling happily up at him. "A Coke or a cream bun maybe?"

"Thanks but he's fine – I gave him something before we came out. Anyway, I'd be worried about what he'd do with a cream bun – he can be a nightmare with food and drink!"

Colm laughed. "The apple obviously hasn't fallen far from the tree then because Daddy is a bit of nightmare with drink too! How was he after that last night?" He went to get Liz's coffee. "I swear to God – it's the last time I let him drag me out for 'a quiet drink'. I think it was about two in the morning by the time we left the place!"

Immense relief immediately rushed through Liz. Thank God, thank God. She didn't have to ask Colm anything: Eric hadn't been lying to her at all; he had indeed met his friend for a drink.

But why had she convinced herself otherwise? Really, she'd have to get a hold on herself and stop behaving like a paranoid shrew; otherwise Eric would be perfectly within his rights to look elsewhere!

Significantly comforted, she smiled at Colm. "He *was* back very late that night."

"Late back? You were lucky he went home at all! Himself and Jack Cummins were pleading with poor Paddy to keep serving them. Only for the fact the boys in blue were out and about at the time, I'd say the two of them would still be there propping up the bar." He shook his head. "It was a great night though, and we all had a good laugh – although to be honest, the next morning I was cursing Eric through my hangover. Jesus, Liz, I'm just not able for drinking any more – certainly not the way I was when we were teenagers anyway!"

Liz smiled. She'd heard once or twice from Tara that Colm and Eric had been very fond of a few pints in their younger days. In fact, Tara had confessed once that she worried Eric would turn out like his dad, who had apparently been too fond of the black stuff for his own good and had died of liver failure many years before – well before Eric and Liz met.

"And speaking of teenagers," Colm went on, putting a cup of coffee on the table in front of her, "I found those old photographs I was telling you about – the ones of me, Eric and Tara while we were still at school?"

"Oh, I'd love to see them whenever you get the time," Liz enthused, genuinely interested.

"Well, look, wait here, and I'll pop next door to get them. Nicky can look after things for a minute."

Colm lived in a house adjoining the café – a small, beautifully restored Swiss-cottage-style residence, which, like the café, had wonderful views across the river towards the castle.

While awaiting Colm's return, Liz sat back and exhaled deeply, feeling as though a huge weight had been lifted from her shoulders. She had to snap out of this, this pathetic, unreasonable, unwarranted insecurity. She was Eric's wife and the mother of his child and he loved her. So what if he had a history with Emma Harrington? It was exactly that – history. So she really should cop on to herself and start giving her husband the trust and respect he deserved.

"Here we are!"

She looked up as Colm returned, a small bundle of photographs in his hand. He sat down at the table and slid into the seat alongside her. "I'm glad I went looking for them actually – they're really very funny. I still can't believe how much hair I had back then!"

"Are you sure you have the time to show them to me?" Liz asked, looking towards Nicky who was still busy behind the counter. "I don't want to keep you."

"Not at all, the place is dead at this hour of the day," he said, gesturing around the café, which was indeed somewhat quieter than usual. "Give it another half hour, though, and they'll all be in for lunch."

"Well, as long as you're sure." Liz eagerly picked up the first photo in the pack, a great picture of a teenage Colm and Eric standing on one of the bridges, their arms around each other. Eric hadn't changed much in the ensuing years, but Colm indeed had lots more hair then.

"Obviously he didn't know about me at that stage," Colm provided jokingly, "although, in all honestly, I hardly knew it myself!"

Liz smiled. Eric and Tara had told her before that Colm had been through the usual period of sexual confusion when he was younger, before eventually coming to terms with his true sexuality.

She went on to the next photo, again a picture of Eric, Colm and a couple of other boys around the same age, who according to Colm used to get up to "all sorts of divilment" together.

"That's Dave McNamara, you know – the local councillor?" Colm said, pointing at one of the boys.

"Don't think I've met him yet," Liz said, shaking her head.

"Believe me, you'd remember him if you had! A right ladies' man is our Dave!"

"The Castlegate Casanova?"

"Exactly!" Colm laughed. "But where's Eric in his reindeer jumper? There!" He pointed at another photo. "See?"

Liz's eyes widened in amusement.

"I reckon Mammy McGrath knitted those for him," said Colm.

"Oh dear," Liz laughed, understanding why Colm had been so disparaging about her husband's teenage fashion sense. "I sincerely hope she doesn't start knitting them for Toby!"

"Mmm – as fashion disasters go, they're pretty disastrous all right," Colm laughed, flicking through some more photographs. "Oh, here's a good one of us all – it was taken shortly after we left secondary school – the night of our debs, as you can probably tell. And speaking of fashion disasters, there's Tara."

Liz studied the photograph, unable to believe that this shy, gawky-looking teenager wearing a strapless, shapeless and utterly hideous pink dress could possibly be her stylish, confident good friend. The cerise pink colour clashed massively with her auburn hair, although the blonde highlights Tara sported these days made her hair-colour more strawberry-blonde than auburn. Still, there was no mistaking those lively eyes and that warm smile.

Colm and Eric were there too, smartly dressed in tuxedos and looking stiffly at the cameras. Liz was pretty certain that the bow-ties they were wearing didn't stay on for very long after that photograph was taken.

"See that tall nerdy one with the braces?" Colm pointed to the girl standing alongside him, a tall, shy-looking kid who had evidently been the class geek. Liz hid a smile. "*That's* Natasha Kelleher."

"What?" Liz looked at him, shocked, and then peered closely at the girl in the photograph. "You don't mean the *model* Natasha Kelleher! The gorgeous one who does the shampoo ads?"

"The very one." Colm was delighted with himself. "Hard to believe, isn't it? Little did we know that it would turn out the class nancy brought the class celebrity to the debs! None of us had any idea the ugly duckling would turn out like that, no more than we knew I'd turn out –"

"And who's this?" Liz interjected, pointing to a broad, athletic-looking teenager standing beside Tara.

She missed Colm's surprised look. "He was Tara's date?" she urged when he didn't reply.

"Yes," Colm answered slowly. "He was Tara's date."

"Well, there was certainly nothing ugly about him!" Liz laughed. "Lucky old Tara!"

Colm nodded and forced a smile. "Listen, Liz, sorry about this, but I'd better go back and give Nicky a hand." He stood up quickly. "Do you mind looking through the rest of those on your own?"

"Of course not – go ahead. I'm enjoying myself actually – these are great! And I can't wait to tease Tara about her horrible debs dress!"

Colm visibly paled. "Ah, don't – she'd murder me for showing you these – Tara hated that dress afterwards."

Liz laughed. "Well, I can certainly see why!"

"Liz, really, don't say anything. She can be a bit touchy about it – honestly."

She finally noticed the gravity in his tone and, surprised, found herself nodding. "All right, I won't say a word."

"Thanks, but listen, stay as long as you like, and if you need anything else be sure to ask, won't you?"

"OK, sure," Liz replied, picking up the remainder of the photographs and leaving Colm to get back to work. She was so engrossed in the pictures that she failed to question why he'd felt the need to rush off when the café was the quietest it had been all morning.

Liz's relief about Eric's supposed truthfulness about his night out didn't last long.

A few days later, she was cleaning out one of the kennels when she heard the postman pull up in the driveway. She immediately stopped what she was doing and gave her hands a quick wipe on the towel before going out to meet him. The poor man was terrified of dogs which, given his profession, was understandable.

Approaching the delivery van, she called a greeting. "Morning, Shay! Anything exciting for me today?" Highly unlikely, given that the only post they usually received was circulars, bills and the odd bank statement.

From the driver's seat, the postman flicked through a selection of envelopes. "The usual rubbish, I'm afraid . . . although no, hold on, here's an interesting-looking one here."

"Oh?"

He handed her a pink-coloured envelope and Liz examined it curiously. It was addressed to Eric, marked "*Strictly Private*" and the handwriting was slanting, decorative and Liz decided, her heart skipping a beat, very definitely female. What the hell . . .?

"See you later, Liz!" Shay called as he drove away.

Liz barely heard him. She was too busy trying to figure out what on earth might be in that letter.

Don't be silly, it could be nothing, she remonstrated with herself, and more than likely something to do with work. But why would a security firm send correspondence in a feminine pink envelope? And why would they send it marked "*Strictly Private*"?

Deciding not to jump to conclusions, Liz put the letter away and resolved to ask Eric about it that evening.

"There's post here for you," she said, when he returned from work. She pointed out the girly scrawl and envelope. "Must be from your girlfriend," she added jokingly.

Her heart nearly stopped when Eric blushed almost as pink as the envelope he was holding.

"Don't be silly," he said, quickly tucking the unopened letter into the back pocket of his jeans.

"Aren't you going to open it?"

"I'll open it later, OK?" he snapped, before walking out of the room and leaving Liz in turmoil.

Then, and this was what really sent her insecurities into overdrive, a couple of nights later, while Eric was at work, someone phoned the house.

Someone female.

"Hello, can I speak to Eric, please?" the woman asked in a no-nonsense tone.

"I'm afraid he's at work at the moment. Can I take a message?"

"Is he? That's odd," the woman replied, and as she did Liz was sure she recognised the voice. It was bloody Emma Harrington, obviously trying to stir things up and put doubts in her brain once again! What was she playing at? And why was she doing this?

"I'm sorry – can I take a message?" Liz repeated, willing herself not to come right out and ask what she wanted with her husband.

"No, it's fine. I'll try his mobile," the woman replied easily, as if it were nothing unusual for a married man to have strange women phoning him.

After she'd put the phone down, Liz was almost unable to move.

First the text from Emma, then the confidential strange-looking letter and now this phone call. What the hell was going on?

Chapter 12

It was three weeks after Steve had embarrassingly dumped her but, mercifully, Natalie was now beginning to get over it. What else could she do?

Granted she had sent Steve one or two late-night text messages tentatively suggesting that they talk about things, but she'd given up when he'd eventually replied: *"Leave me alone, you psycho bitch!"*

So that was that. Another love lost, another dream shattered.

In the meantime, she did what any normal broken-hearted girl would do and threw herself into her work even more. Jordan King, her latest recruit, was taking up much of her time, as she and Danni worked strenuously on keeping his profile squeaky clean, and strangely, Michael Sharpe, the regular thorn in Natalie's side, seemed to be behaving himself. Evidently, yet another brush with the FA disciplinary board for kicking a Premiership referee up the arse during a recent match had given him something to think about, and for the moment he was being a good boy. Although God only knew what he was up to in his spare time.

So as usual, work was going smoothly as ever while Natalie's personal life went from bad to worse. And this time, it seemed she no longer had Freya at hand to help her get over it. Her best friend had since moved to an admittedly fabulous stately pile in Richmond – miles away from Central London and way too far for Natalie to pop over and cry on her shoulder like she used to when she lived in town. She'd phoned Freya the night after Steve dumped her – hoping for some much-needed sympathy.

"I always thought he was a prick anyway," Freya told her helpfully. "You deserve much better than that."

"But I really thought he was the one!" Natalie wailed down the line.

"Nat, you think every guy who looks at you half-arsed is 'the one'," Freya sighed. "Remember that time we had to take the tube?" She said the word "tube" as if the word itself was liable to infect her. A London girl all her life, Freya had only once or twice used the London Underground, and only when she was absolutely forced to, so convinced was she that the entire network was one of the Seven Circles of Hell. A while back, when the two needed to get from Oxford Street to Leicester Square in quick time and there wasn't a taxi to be had for love or money, they'd racked their brains for a suitable alternative. Eventually

Natalie tentatively suggested they take the tube.

"Ugh, too icky!" Freya had started scratching herself as if a swarm of ants had suddenly appeared out of nowhere and attached themselves to her Prada coat. But eventually she'd relented, and while on the train Natalie had become convinced that a guy sitting directly opposite and smiling in her direction fancied her, despite the fact that he looked (and smelt) as though he hadn't lived indoors in decades.

"But he *was* kind of cute," Natalie insisted now. "In a rough and ready sort of way."

"Very definitely rough," Freya agreed. "At least Steve was some kind of improvement."

"I don't know what I'll do without him," Natalie said sadly, the mention of Steve's name sending her back into the depths of depression.

"Oh, for goodness sake, Nat – you barely knew him! And you'll find someone else – you always do."

Natalie was taken aback and a little hurt by her friend's irritable reaction. She'd hoped that Freya might suggest coming over for the night, so the two could stay in and spend the night scoffing chocolates and bawling over *Sleepless in Seattle*, the way they used to before she met boring old Simon.

"That's easy for you to say. You're engaged, and happy and –"

"Pregnant," Freya finished dryly.

"What?"

"I'm pregnant. And before you ask, no – it wasn't planned. It very definitely wasn't planned."

"Oh." Natalie didn't know what to think. Freya was not the maternal type. She'd even go as far to say that her best friend hated kids, hated being in same room as them, breathing the same air . . .

So Natalie's first reaction to this news was amazement. And her second was pure and unadulterated jealousy. Freya was getting married with a baby on the way. She was living Natalie's dream.

"I know, I didn't know what to say either when the doctor confirmed it," Freya said when Natalie remained silent. "I've been on the Pill forever and me and Si aren't exactly at it like the newlyweds we're soon supposed to be. But it's happened and he's thrilled, and it's the end of my life as I know it. And of course now we have to postpone the wedding until after it's born, which is obviously a total bore."

She sounded so hard and dismissive about the whole thing that suddenly Natalie wanted to throttle her. How could she be so callous? Did she not realise that she had the perfect house, the perfect man – the perfect life? While Natalie would give anything for a fraction of what Freya had – namely a willing husband-to-be. As it was, she couldn't even find herself a decent prospect, let alone a boyfriend, and had only lately been reduced to making eyes at homeless men on the bloody tube!

"Well, congratulations," she said tentatively, while at the same time bracing herself for an onslaught of abusive outrage from Freya. "What do you mean congratulations?" she could imagine Freya wailing, "This is my worst bloody nightmare!"

But instead her friend replied simply, "Thanks – I suppose. But sorry, Nat, I really can't chat for much longer. Si's parents are coming over for dinner this evening and –"

"That's OK. I'd better go too." *Back to my sad, lonely and pathetic existence,* she added inwardly. "Talk to you soon."

"No problem, darling. And don't worry too much about that idiot Steve. Plenty of fish in the sea and all that."

Natalie smiled tightly. *That idiot Steve was the man I was hoping to marry,* she told her silently. "Of course. See you soon."

Natalie replaced the receiver thinking that she had never felt so lonely in her life. She'd been so sure Freya would understand, had been certain that her friend would be only too happy to help her get over the humiliation of it all – like they'd done for one another all throughout their friendship. And her other close friends, Jodi, Sarah and Rachel, were all either happily married, engaged or long-term attached. No point in phoning them either; no doubt they were just as uninterested as Freya was about the ups and downs of Natalie's pathetic love life.

OK, so she had only been with Steve for a few months at the most. That didn't mean her relationship was any less worthwhile than theirs, did it? Although, evidently, in Happily Married Land, it did. Natalie's repeatedly disastrous love life was now a million miles away from her friends' lives of cosy coupledom and happy domesticity.

At work, Danni had been reasonably sympathetic, although Natalie was loath to go into any detail, other than to let her know that she and Steve had split up. She was Danni's boss, after all, and it wouldn't do to have PR Supremo Natalie Webb letting her guard down in front of the staff.

But now, three weeks on, things were improving, and Natalie was moving on. And as that evening she and Danni grabbed a cab and drove in the direction of Kensington, she found that despite herself she was looking forward to attending the launch of Purple Grapefruit, the newest in a long line of supposedly ultra-trendy London clubs. Although a rival PR firm was handling the account, several invites had been issued to Blue Moon, their rivals evidently hoping that some of the other company's more prolific clients – England international Michael Sharpe, actress Jennifer Cox or the much-photographed glamour model Cassandra – might make an appearance. Cassandra would be there, Natalie knew; the model never lost an opportunity for her and her humongous breasts to be photographed for the tabloids, earning herself a fat fee in return for their usage. The girl was a nightmare to work with, but despite her trashy image was a very shrewd businesswoman, determined to use her . . . erm . . . *assets* to the best of her ability.

Having reached the venue, Natalie got out of the cab, adjusted her brand new blue and green Pucci mini-dress over her thighs and waited for Danni to pay the cab driver.

Natalie had bristled on hearing that they had to pay their own way there. If the events company were any good they would have sent VIP guests a stretch limo, she thought, rather self-satisfied that their rivals evidently didn't have Blue Moon's class. And the red carpet was insane. Didn't they have any imagination?

Now, if the company Natalie used to arrange events for a club this size made such a dismal effort she'd have them strung up! Whoever this lot were, they were clearly amateurs, and if the club's promoters thought they could attract celebrities to Purple Grapefruit on this dismal showing, they really had their work cut out for them.

Apart from Cassandra Natalie wasn't sure whether any other Blue Moon clients would show. Michael had received his invite but was still lying low after the whole kicking-the-referee-up-the-arse fiasco, and she was certain Jennifer was away shooting some movie in Toronto.

But if all else failed, and this launch failed to attract the big stars, the ex-reality TV contestants could always be relied upon to pick up the slack, Natalie thought, spying a well-worn regular standing on the sidelines and gleefully waving at cameras despite the fact that they were pointed the other way. Now, if Natalie had been handling this launch, she wouldn't have let those bottom-feeders near the place. No, the club needed to start as it meant to go on, and if it wanted to attract exclusive high-profile clientele, it needed to invite London's finest. At this rate they'd be lucky to attract extras from *EastEnders.*

But, she thought, as she and Danni entered the club and accepted a glass of champagne – *cheap* champagne, she discovered grimacing (she would have insisted on Laurent Perrier at the very least) – this wasn't her gig, so tonight she could just sit back and relax and if photographs from the event didn't make the papers the next day, some other poor sod could take the rap.

Barely an hour into the event, Natalie was bored senseless. There wasn't a sniff of celebrity, even Cassandra hadn't bothered showing up, and the atmosphere at a chess convention would have been more exciting.

Although Danni seemed to be enjoying herself, she thought wryly, seeing her assistant chatting with a group of men at the bar. Then again, Danni rarely got to attend one of these events outside work and she wouldn't be here at all if Natalie hadn't strong-armed her into accompanying her. She sighed. She was definitely getting too old for this. A few years ago she would have been the life and soul of the party, flitting from here to there and charming everyone – no matter how tedious the company might be.

But these days, she just couldn't be bothered. While she still thrived on the cut and thrust of the day-to-day stuff, dealing with media contacts and managing client accounts, she was beginning to find the social aspect of it all samey and tiring.

Fourteen-odd years working the London scene did that to you, she supposed, and it was inevitable that she'd eventually tire of it all. And once again she sorely wished that, like most of her thirty-something friends, she had a warm house and welcoming partner to come home to.

Realising that lately she seemed worryingly prone to gloominess, Natalie took a large gulp from her glass of cheaper-than-cheap fizz and strode resolutely across the room to Danni and her new friends. She'd better snap out of this and start working the room – otherwise, word would get round that Natalie Webb had lost her edge and she'd be on the scrapheap in more ways than one!

"Natalie, there you are!" Danni beamed at her, a smile that would have looked warm and welcoming to anyone else, but which Natalie knew meant "please save me!". "Everyone, this is my boss, Natalie Webb."

As Danni didn't offer any further introductions, Natalie just smiled and said hello to the three men, who all looked to be in their mid-to-late thirties and were dressed in a mixture of Hugo Boss and Paul Smith. The bald one, despite his thick gold wedding ring, seemed to be flirting unashamedly with Danni, while the others alongside him looked on, mildly amused. City types, Natalie decided instantly, thinking that she recognised at least one of them from some other event she'd attended recently. The kind of people who often got invited to these events to make up the numbers.

"You work in PR too?" One of the men, also sporting a wedding ring, asked Natalie as the bald man renewed his onslaught on Danni.

"Yes."

"Sounds like an exciting job."

"It can be."

"Bet you get invited to parties like this all the time."

"Yes, but to be honest, most of them are a little more exciting than this," she couldn't resist saying. So she shouldn't bitch, but she was in a foul mood, and she'd wasted her first outing in her new Pucci dress on this poor showing!

"Really?" the third man interjected. "You're not having a good time?"

"Not exactly." Natalie wrinkled her nose. "Are you?"

"Well, we've got excellent food, champagne and a great atmosphere – what more do you want?"

Deciding instantly that she didn't like this guy with his haughty eyes, aquiline nose and slightly weird accent, Natalie squared up to him.

"A little bit of imagination might be nice," she said, having met his type many times before. "Champagne and foie gras are old news."

"I know what you mean," he agreed to Natalie's surprise, while one of his companions gave him an odd look. "I suppose they could have tried something different."

"Something different – they could have made an effort to start with! This is supposed be a fun, trendy London club, not a reception for the Queen! Now if I were organising a party like this, I'd give it a theme," she went on, warming to her subject. "A launch for a club like this is crying out for a theme."

"Such as?"

"Purple, of course!" she said grinning. "I'd instruct the organisers to use a purple entrance carpet to start with. What were they *thinking* using the tried and trusted red? Purple is the obvious choice and something to really get the cameras clicking. And while we've got a theme going, why not serve Kir Royale instead of cheap sparkling Cava?"

"Purple drinks for Purple Grapefruit," he said, nodding solemnly.

"I know – and there's this fab Lebanese lemonade you can get that would be perfect too." She shrugged. "Of course it's unbelievably tacky, but tacky's in these days, and celebs love it."

"I see. So tacky's the way forward, is it?"

"For a place like this – definitely."

"Right, next time we arrange an event of this size I must call on you for advice, Ms . . . what was it again?"

She stared at him warily, for the first time wondering if she'd drunk and said too much. "Webb, Natalie Webb from Blue Moon PR. And you are?"

"Jay Murray," he replied, shaking her hand. "Labyrinth Event Management."

Natalie closed her eyes. Oh shit.

Right at that moment Natalie understood well why Tara, the girl she'd met on holiday, had taken the decision not to drink. If she'd put her foot in it the same way that Natalie just had, then who could blame her!

She gulped and swallowed hard as she realised she had just insulted the work of one of London's most prolific event-management companies – a company that

Blue Moon had used on numerous occasions, but one with which Natalie had never dealt directly. How could she have been so stupid as to openly criticise the party in front of the very people who'd organised it? Or automatically presume that Jay Murray, with his Hugo Boss suit and stuffy, buttoned-up appearance, was simply a hanger-on?

Usually these guys looked like a cross between Jean Paul Gaultier and David Beckham with their ultra-trendy clothes and frequently effeminate exterior. Still, given that he wasn't racing around the venue like a headless chicken, it was unlikely Murray was one of the planners. Which meant he had to be Labyrinth management.

Even worse.

"So I take it you're not a big fan of canapés and champagne, Ms Webb?" he asked, his dark eyes mocking her.

Natalie instinctively straightened her dress and tried to regain some composure. She glanced across at Danni, who was still trying to fend off the advances of the bald man and, mercifully, seemed totally oblivious to her boss's faux pas.

"It's Natalie," she said, with a nervous laugh. "And of course I am, but I thought that a place like this could . . . could do better, that's all . . ." she trailed off, too embarrassed to elaborate. Thanks to the aforementioned Cava, she'd already said way too much. "Look, I'm very sorry if I insulted you – I had no idea –"

"No idea that we'd spent weeks on end organising

this . . . wait a second . . . what was it you called it again? Ah yes . . . 'a reception for the Queen', wasn't it?"

Natalie bit her lip, mortified.

"But it's OK," he went on. "As it happens, I agree with you, and it's good to get the feedback. I like to get a feel for what people really think of our events, which is why I try to blend in at these things."

"Blend in or go in disguise? When we were introduced, I had you pegged as a City trader."

He glanced down at his none-too-casual attire. "Really? I thought all the party people dressed like this," he joked, before adding, "But as I remember it, Ms Webb, or should I say Natalie, we weren't actually introduced before you so eloquently voiced your opinion of my company's work."

Yikes! She'd walked into that one. Saying nothing more, Natalie took another gulp of champagne, wishing that she were anywhere else but here. She hadn't really wanted to come to this sodding party in the first place – fitting that, like everything else in her life these days, it should end up in disaster!

"Anyway, as I said, I think you're right in what you said," Murray conceded. "We had some great ideas for this launch, but the club management wouldn't go for any of it. Although, to be honest, nobody had come up with your purple carpet suggestion, and now that I think of it, you're right – it is the obvious choice. You could have a future in this kind of thing, Natalie – your talents are obviously wasted in PR."

By his tone, Natalie knew he was teasing her. Thank goodness. At least he hadn't taken serious umbrage at her remarks. Some of these events and promotions types could be very touchy indeed, and Jack Moon would kill her if he found out she'd managed to alienate one of the city's top promotions people.

"Yes, well, it was just a suggestion," she said, cringing as she realised how stupid her tacky ideas must have sounded to someone of his expertise. "I see a lot of this kind of thing and, well, it would be good for once to experience something different."

"You work with Blue Moon, you said?"

"Yes, I'm an account manager there."

"Great company – Jack Moon's a good man."

"Yes, he is."

"Tell him I said hello, will you?"

"Sure." Shit, Jay Murray and her boss obviously knew each other. *For God's sake, please, please, don't tell him I made a fool of myself tonight!* Natalie pleaded silently. The last thing she needed was her work life going to pot too. Work was the only thing in her life that was going smoothly. If only she hadn't opened her big fat mouth!

Murray was now leaning casually against the bar, and Natalie realised that the two of them had gradually moved away from the others and were now having a private conversation.

"So, Natalie, do you think the place has any chance of being the next Ivy? And this time, give me your honest opinion – I wouldn't want you to hold back or anything." His mouth curled up into a not altogether unattractive smile and yet again Natalie tried to place that accent. It was British but with a faint tinge of something else . . . Scottish maybe?

She smiled back, thankful that the tension had finally been relieved. "Well – no offence – but with a damp squib like this for a launch, I doubt it." She shook her head from side to side. "Never mind celebrities, it's not even the kind of place *I'd* hang out."

"I see, and where would that kind of place be?" he asked, looking her squarely in the eye, and with a jolt Natalie realised he was flirting with her.

In fact, he probably had been all along, but she'd been too caught up in her embarrassment to notice.

She took a second or two to study him properly. He was tall, so tall he towered above her five-foot-five frame by a good six or seven inches. And he seemed well built, although it was difficult to tell what lay underneath that banker's suit. But while he had a nice face, he wasn't conventionally attractive, save for his dark, almost black, eyes and, now that she thought about it, rather arresting presence.

Natalie only wished she'd taken notice of that powerful presence long before she'd started shooting her mouth off about the crappiness of the party. Yes, she decided as Jay Murray's dark eyes stared back at her own, he wasn't bad at all.

Almost instinctively she straightened up, subtly thrust forward her boobs and flashed him her most alluring smile. In that same split second, she forgot all about Steve and her shattered, never-to-be-repaired heart.

"A million miles away from where supposed City-types like you hang out," she replied, her smile widening.

Freya had been right, Natalie thought happily, there *were* plenty more fish in the sea, and she'd just decided she might like to try and land this one.

Chapter 13

"So how's everything?" Tara asked her mother. It was her first visit to Castlegate since her return from Egypt, having been up to her eyes in work after the ten-day break.

"Everything is the same as it always is, Tara," Isobel replied with a put-upon sigh.

"And Emma? How is she now? Has she said anything at all about the father yet?"

Her sister was fast asleep in bed right then, apparently "worn out from the stress of her pregnancy".

Isobel shrugged. "If she doesn't want to say anything, then none of us can force her."

"Still, Mum – don't you think all this secrecy about it is a little bit foolish, not to mention over the top? Fair enough if she doesn't want to tell him, but why not tell us?"

"Well, it's her own business, isn't it? And anyway,

who's to say that telling the father will make things better? He could be an awful layabout for all we know."

That was true, Tara thought, guilty of the fact she hadn't before considered that Emma was being secretive about the father simply because she wanted nothing to do with him. But for some reason she didn't think that was the case. Emma had given little sign of being troubled in this way, and Tara truly believed that all the secrecy was just her sister being her usual melodramatic self.

"Well, yes, of course it's her own business, but by refusing to ask him for help, isn't she making things hard on you and Dad too? It's hardly fair that at thirty-one years of age she should be moving back home and expecting you to look after her."

Isobel smiled. "Emma was always a home-bird," she replied fondly.

Tara said nothing. Having got over the initial shock of Emma's pregnancy, Isobel had now resumed normal service and was back to feeling sorry for – and needlessly indulging – her youngest daughter. Of course, Tara couldn't blame Isobel for wanting to help Emma out in her hour of need, but still she felt annoyed at the girl for blatantly exploiting her mother's generosity. Oh, well, she thought with a sigh, those two had always had a close relationship, and she knew Isobel would go to the ends of the earth just to keep Emma happy.

"I'm sure she has her reasons for keeping it a secret," Isobel went on, "but, to be truthful, I'm wondering lately if she might have been in contact with him. She's going out in the evenings a lot these days and doesn't say where."

"Oh?"

"Yes, she goes out for a couple of hours at a time, and then when she comes back she's usually in much better form."

"I wonder is it anyone from around here then?" Tara wondered out loud. They'd all assumed the father of Emma's baby was some guy she'd been seeing in Dublin during her short stint living there. But perhaps not. Still, who could she possibly be seeing from around here?

"I don't know," Isobel replied, "but whoever he is, there's no fear of her telling us anyway."

With that, Emma appeared at the doorway, and Tara and Isobel looked at her guiltily, both wondering if she'd overheard them talking about her.

"Emma, pet!" Isobel cried, getting up. "Did you manage to get any sleep?"

Her daughter gave a deep sigh in reply. "Actually, I was just about to drop off when I heard Tara come in."

This sounded innocent, but Tara knew her sister well enough to understand that there was a deliberate dig in there.

"Did you have a nice holiday?" Emma asked then, and again there was an edge to her tone.

Tara smiled, unwilling to let Emma's theatrics get to her. "It was great, thanks. Sorry I haven't been to see you before now. Work has been manic."

"Oh, that's OK – I'm sure you've got much more

important things to be doing than worrying about me," her sister replied mournfully.

"Sit down there and take the weight off your feet, pet," Isobel urged, going over to the sink and filling the kettle. "Would you like a cup of tea?"

Tara marvelled at the way she fussed over Emma. Fair enough, she'd been sickly as a child, and this had always given Isobel reason to worry, but by the way her mother carried on, you'd swear Emma was still a helpless baby, not a fully grown adult!

It hurt too that her mother had never fallen over herself to do the same for Tara, but the Harrington family dynamic had always been the same, and at this stage in their lives it was hardly going to change. Especially not now, when Emma was in real "trouble".

"I was just telling Tara all about Dave McNamara getting engaged," Isobel said and, confused, Tara's head snapped up. When Isobel flashed her a pointed stare she realised that their mother was trying to give Emma the impression that she and Tara had been partaking in a bit of local gossip rather than discussing her.

"Yes," she replied after a beat, deciding to play along, despite the fact that this was the first she'd heard of the aforesaid Dave's engagement. But perhaps this time her mother was right; Emma seemed in bad enough form as it was without thinking she was being talked about. "That's a bit of a surprise, isn't it?"

"I suppose so," Emma replied sourly, evidently unimpressed by the news of the local councillor.

"He's about the same age as you, isn't he, Tara?"

Isobel persisted as she stood waiting for the kettle to boil.

"Yes – we were in the same class at school." Tara grinned. "It's funny – he used to have a bit of a crush on me, actually."

"He had a crush on *everyone*, Tara," Emma said testily, angry spots of colour appearing on both cheeks.

"Right – I take it he tried it on with you too?" Tara replied laughingly, but inside she was a little miffed by Emma's reaction to what had only been a jokey comment. Not unlike Isobel, her little sister seemed to really enjoy cutting Tara down to size. "Well, he hasn't changed much over the years apparently."

"Dave's a nice lad, though," their mother said. "He's done great things for the village over the last while, so whoever she is – a Dublin girl, I've heard – I hope she makes him very happy."

Again Emma rolled her eyes – Dave McNamara and his happiness were evidently the last things on her mind.

"So how have you been?" Tara asked cheerfully, changing the subject. "Morning sickness any better now?"

Emma looked at her as if she'd grown two heads. "Morning sickness?" she grumbled. "It lasts all bloody day!"

"There's been no let-up at all, sure there hasn't?" Isobel added, putting a mug of tea in front of her youngest daughter. "She's been terribly misfortunate altogether with it. I never really suffered with that kind of thing at all when I was carrying ye, thank God."

Hearing this, Tara quickly admonished herself for being so unfeeling about her sister's plight; Emma was pregnant after all and must be finding it all hard going. Still, try as she might, she just couldn't help but feel that Emma was keeping them all in the dark about the father of her baby for a very good reason. And if her sister had been messing around with someone she shouldn't have been – namely a married or already attached man – then it was very difficult indeed to feel sorry for her.

Emma had always been the same at school – only interested in the boys who weren't openly interested in her. Was it the challenge, the thrill of the chase? Tara couldn't understand it. She knew that women like that existed, women whose only way of validating themselves was by proving their power over men – especially other women's men – but she'd never been able to truly understand the psychology behind it and she hated to think that her sister might be one of them. What was the point?

Then again, she'd never been able to truly understand Emma anyway, the way her sister was so determined to feel continually hard done by and so quick to play up to people in order to get out of anything she couldn't be bothered doing. Like getting a job and earning enough money to put a roof over her own head instead of going back to her parents looking for handouts. Like taking responsibility for her own actions.

Then again, Tara thought, as she watched her mother

fuss around her youngest daughter, why should Emma trouble herself about such things when the people around her were fully prepared to do all of them on her behalf?

Later that evening, having just about had enough of Emma and her "misfortune", Tara went to visit Liz.

"You would have loved Natalie – she was an absolute scream," Tara told her friend, as the two of them sat in Liz's kitchen having coffee while Tara told her all about the holiday. "We had a such a laugh the day we went visiting the pyramids. And do you know, I've never known anyone to be so frank and open about what they really wanted in life. The girl is beautiful, successful, has this amazing, glamorous life and," she told Liz enviously, "from what I've seen, a better wardrobe than Kate Moss, so she's obviously loaded too. Yet all Natalie wants is to get married. Strange, isn't it?"

Liz said nothing.

"To be honest, she reminded me a little bit of you in a way," Tara went on. "You know, the way you were so excited about the prospect of marrying Eric and having a family of your own. It was all you wanted back then, wasn't it?"

"Maybe the girl should be careful what she wishes for," Liz said, her tone uncharacteristically sullen.

Tara looked at her, an amused expression on her face. "What? This coming from the happiest married woman I know?"

But her friend stayed silent, and just as quickly Tara's amusement changed to a frown.

"Liz? What's the matter?" she asked, setting down her coffee mug. "Has something happened?"

"I don't know," her friend replied.

For the first time, Tara noticed how drawn and anxious Liz looked today. She hadn't really noticed anything untoward up to now but, come to think of it, *she* had been doing most of the talking for the last half hour or so, whereas Liz had just sat there quietly listening and saying little more than a brief "really?" and "that sounds nice".

Tara sat forward in her chair. "What do you mean you don't know?"

"I . . . I'm not sure. I could be just imagining it, but I think Eric might be . . . well, as I said, I'm not sure."

"You think he might be what, Liz?"

Then Liz quietly told her about Eric's seemingly strange behaviour and the longer and more unusual hours he lately seemed to be working.

"But what makes you automatically think he's having an affair?" Tara asked, shocked by the admission. Liz never behaved like this before; she had always been one of the most rational people Tara had ever come across, and to see her worrying like this now was very disconcerting. *Was* there a chance that Eric was cheating on her?

"Tara, I don't know how to explain it, and maybe it sounds silly to you, but I just know. Call it what you want, female intuition, whatever. He's my husband, and lately he's been acting very strangely, staying in Dublin for long periods of time – things like that. And then, when he is home, instead of spending time with us he goes out with Colm . . . and sometimes he even goes out in the evenings and doesn't tell me where he's going."

At this something niggled in the back of Tara's mind, but she was so surprised by Liz's revelations that she couldn't think of what. "But wasn't that the plan? That he'd do all these extra hours so you could get the house finished?"

Liz shook her head. "Maybe it all sounds totally irrational to you, but you don't know what's been going on."

"So tell me! Tell me what makes you think your husband, who I know adores you, is now cheating on you. Liz, it doesn't make any sense."

Liz's expression closed over. "Fine – I'm sorry I said anything."

"Oh, don't be like that! I'm merely trying to get to the bottom of this, maybe try and give you a different perspective –"

"Tara, don't use your pyschobabble on me," Liz cried suddenly. "I'm not one of your clients!"

"No, but you are my friend, and I'm trying to help you." This was *very* worrying. Liz and Eric were as solid as any couple Tara had ever known. "Look, maybe the move down here has taken its toll on Eric a bit more than it has on you. After all, he thought he'd find work of some sort here, didn't he? It must be hard on him having to go back and forth to Dublin and leaving you and Toby so often, mustn't it?"

"He doesn't seem to have problems leaving us to go out with Colm," Liz said petulantly.

"But he and Colm are friends, and you said before that it's been difficult for you and Eric to get out together or find someone to look after Toby." Then she had a thought. "Look, why don't I ask my mum to pop over some night and keep an eye on Toby? Or, even better – I could ask Emma. She isn't doing much these days, and it would do her good to get in some practice before –"

"No, thanks," Liz said sharply, and Tara looked up, surprised by the vehemence in her tone. "Seriously," she added, her voice softening a little, "I'm sure we'll be fine. And you're right – I probably am just imagining things."

For a few minutes, the two of them sat quietly at the table, neither of them sure what to say. Shortly afterwards, the sound of the phone ringing broke through the silence and Liz stood up to answer it.

"Hi, Eric." The cordless handset still held to her ear, she returned to the table and sat back down across from Tara. "Oh," she replied then.

Tara looked up at the tone of her friend's voice.

"I'm sorry to hear that, love."

Well, Tara thought, whatever problems the two of them might be having, at least they were still on decent speaking terms. But by Liz's concerned expression, it seemed that Eric was passing on some bad news. She stood up from the kitchen table and wandered into the living room, wanting to give her friend some privacy.

"I know that," she heard Liz saying in the background, "but you and your mum will just have to go yourselves. Well, we can't very well drag Toby along with us. It's a long drive up to Belfast, and anyway, what about the dogs?" There was a brief pause. "Yes, I know that, but there's not a whole lot I can do about that. I have Bruno coming again on Thursday, and there are another two booked in so . . . look, we'll talk about it when you get home, OK? All right, love – I'll have a dinner ready for you. See you then."

"Trouble?" Tara enquired, coming back into the kitchen.

"Eric's uncle just died," Liz said sighing. "He was Maeve's only brother, and he's being buried on Saturday in Belfast, where the family's from. Thing is, much as I want to go with Eric, I can't just drop everything and go all the way up there for the removal on Friday evening – not with Toby and the dogs and –"

"I'll do it," Tara offered quickly.

"What? How can you?"

"Honestly, Liz, I'll do it. Go with Eric on Friday – and stay for the full weekend if you like. It would give me an excuse to spend some time with my godson – I don't see enough of him as it is, and every time I do he seems to have grown another foot or aged another year." She smiled at Liz. "Honestly, it would be no trouble. I have a couple of appointments Friday morning, but I can arrange to do those and the ones I have in the afternoon over the phone from here – if that's OK with you. And I don't work weekends so –"

"You can do that? People won't mind?"

"Not at all." Well, no doubt some of them *would* mind having their sessions over the phone, Tara thought, but the prospect of a reduced fee would soon quieten them. And if her offering to baby-sit made things that bit easier for poor Liz, who seemed to be having a tough time at the moment, then it would be worth it.

"You're sure? But what about the animals?"

"You let me worry about that. Looking after my favourite godson should be no bother, and walking and feeding a few dogs couldn't be that difficult either." OK, so she wasn't the world's greatest dog lover, but it couldn't be *that* bad, could it?

"Tara, I really couldn't ask you to do that," Liz said.

"You're not asking – I'm offering, actually I'm *insisting*. Go to Belfast with your husband for the funeral. I'm sure he'll need you."

"Well, I don't know if he and his uncle were *that* close, but Maeve would obviously like us to go so . . ." Liz was finally coming round to the idea. "Now, are you sure you'll be OK with Toby? He can be a bit of a handful, you know."

"Me and Toby will be fine," Tara insisted. "We'll have a ball. And I'm well able to look after a few mangy dogs."

Liz grimaced. "Please, don't say that in front of their owners, or I won't have a business when I get back!" she said, raising a smile for the first time that day. Then she shrugged. "But, if you're sure."

Satisfied that Tara really wanted to do this, Liz flicked through her kennels diary. "Like I thought, there are only three dogs and one cat booked in over the weekend, which isn't too bad. One dog is already here, and the others are due in on Thursday evening. Obviously, I won't take any more bookings in the meantime, and I'll make sure I'm back early on Sunday evening, so you won't have to deal with any of the owners."

"Grand," Tara replied briskly. "I'll be down Friday morning and you can show me what needs to be done."

"What about Glenn?" Liz enquired. "Won't he mind?"

"Are you mad? Glenn will think he's died and gone to heaven having the house to himself for a weekend. He'll be able to watch Sky Sports morning noon and night! Although, now that I think of it, he's working Saturday morning anyway, so I'm sure he won't miss me."

"I suppose," Liz looked thoughtful. "Do you know, it will be really strange – I don't think me and Eric have had a single night to ourselves since Toby was born. I know Maeve will be there of course, but still."

"Well, maybe the time away from here will do you two a bit of good. Help you get to the bottom of whatever it is that's bothering you."

Liz coloured a little. "I know – maybe I am just imagining things. You're right, we might get the chance to have a proper chat in Belfast over the weekend. Maeve will want to stay at the family home, which means me and Eric will probably have to get a hotel somewhere. The circumstances aren't ideal, but at least I might get the chance to find out why he's been acting so strange lately."

"Exactly," Tara said, pleased that her friend's spirits had lifted a little. "And I guarantee things will seem much better after that, Liz, and you'll come home feeling silly for even thinking those things about Eric."

The following Friday afternoon, Tara was sorely regretting her generous offer.

That was *it*! she told herself, panting. No way. No *way* was she ever giving in to Glenn's pleas and getting one of these things. No bloody way!

They were rough, smelly, thick as a ditch – totally at the other end of the *spectrum* compared to soft, cuddly, intelligent and *clean* cats. She didn't know *how* Liz did this for a living!

"Are you sure you don't mind looking after the place for us?" Liz had asked for the umpteenth time, before she and Eric left for Belfast earlier that morning.

"We'll be fine," she'd told her, shooing her out to the car. "And if I get into any trouble – which I won't," she added quickly, when Liz looked worried, "I can always call on Dad."

"Right, well, you have the number of the hotel we're staying at, and of course you have my mobile too."

"Yes, I have. Now go!"

Understandably, Eric had been very quiet when she arrived at the house. Probably eager to get going, Tara mused.

As predicted, Glenn hadn't been too upset that she'd be out of the house for a night or two, although he offered to come down after work on Saturday afternoon to help with the dogs.

But Tara wasn't convinced she'd need his help at all. In fact, she was looking forward to spending some time in the little village; it might help her decide whether or not she wanted to move back there for good.

But right then, Tara was sorely regretting her enthusiastic offer. As per Liz's instructions, she was taking the dogs for their afternoon walk, and one of them, a huge brute of a thing called Bruno (and the most hyper and unruly animal Tara had ever come across), was practically dragging her across the fields behind Liz's house. And these two little rat-like terriers who hadn't a hope of keeping up with the bigger dog, but insisted on trying, kept getting their leads entwined around Tara's feet and tripping her up. It was bloody annoying and quite dangerous given that she was carrying little Toby in his harness – as Liz usually did. But judging from his excited giggles, the little boy was thoroughly enjoying his outing, and Tara couldn't help but wonder if his mother knew some kind of calming command that she didn't, something that could slow the bastards down.

Then, out of nowhere, Bruno took off at a hare's pace, dragging Tara and the others along behind him. She groaned.

"Bruno! Come back!" she called breathlessly, as the little rats started yapping in annoying unison.

Just then Toby squealed excitedly, and as Tara spotted a small rabbit hopping some way in front of them, she understood why Bruno had taken off like one the hounds of hell. Bloody rabbits!

By the time she and her motley crew returned home an hour later – the dogs still hyper and excited and not in the least bit tired after her strenuous efforts, Tara never wanted to see another animal again. At least Liz's two, Ben and Jerry, were able to run around the place of their own accord, and she didn't have to walk them too. Thank goodness for small mercies and big back-yards!

But it seemed there was no let-up with the boarders. Liz had instructed that Tara should take each dog out of their holding-pen to do their business an hour or so after feeding.

And while the rats seemed perfectly happy to do her bidding, the huge mutt seemed to treat the whole thing as some big game, and instead of obediently doing his thing in Liz's prescribed "area" in the yard, began to merrily lead Tara in circles around the back garden. Tara swore the dog knew she hadn't a clue what she was doing and was acting up on purpose just to annoy her.

Honest to God, Toby was a saint to look after compared to this fella, she thought, trying in vain to steer him towards the yard. Then, the savage somehow got it into his head that he'd rather drop his load in the garden of the next house! At that stage, Tara was sick to the back teeth of his antics, it was beginning to get dark and she didn't have the inclination or the energy to stop him from going outside the boundaries. Not that there were actually any boundaries between Liz's garden and the adjoining grounds. The old cottage had been vacant for years and the "garden" was overrun with weeds, so as far as she was concerned Bruno could do what he liked.

In fact, she might suggest to Liz upon her return that she use the overgrown garden for this purpose, rather than have to shovel up the stink from her own back-yard. Tara's stomach turned as she thought about cleaning up after the dogs – especially this one! No, it was just as well that Bruno had taken a fancy to this particular spot – at least that would be one less load to deal with.

Holding Bruno by the lead, she turned her head away, as the dog squatted bang-slap in the middle of the garden.

"Hey, what the hell do you think you're doing?" an angry voice cried, and Tara nearly jumped ten foot in the air with fright.

She looked around to see a tall, well-built and very annoyed-looking man coming out of the supposedly abandoned house. Yikes! Liz hadn't mentioned that the house had been sold – or that the Incredible Hulk had bought it!

"Oh, my goodness – I'm so sorry," Tara began breathlessly, her cheeks reddening, as she quickly yanked Bruno towards her, the dog still in mid-effort. "I didn't realise anyone lived –"

"Oh, so it's OK for your bloody dog to mess up the place, just because there's nobody here?" the man retorted in disbelief.

"No . . . I mean . . . well, he's not actually mine," Tara spluttered, mortified that she'd been caught out in such a manner. She'd *strangle* that dog when she got him home! "And no, I don't think it's OK, but he was determined to do it here, and I'm really sorry."

"Well, I suppose I'll let you away with it this time."

Tara watched in surprise as the man bent down and rubbed Bruno behind the ears. She didn't think she had ever seen a man so huge. With his broad shoulders and thick muscled arms, the guy looked like a pro-wrestler.

"He's gorgeous, aren't you, lad?" he said. "Despite the fact that your mammy is happy to let you make a mess of my lovely garden!"

Despite herself, Tara was annoyed. "Well, he's such a pain in the backside that I didn't have much choice in the matter!" she said, putting a hand on her hip. "And as I told you before, I'm not his bloody mammy!"

"He's not yours?"

"Certainly not," Tara replied, thinking that she wouldn't wish Bruno on anyone, yet slightly miffed that a perfect stranger could so easily calm the errant mutt. "I'm looking after him for a friend, who usually looks after him for . . ." she sighed. "Look, it's a long story and I'm sure you don't want to hear it. Let me just say that I'm really very sorry about your – um, garden," she gave the weeds a sideways glance. "I'm sure you worked very hard to get it that way."

"I quite like the natural look, actually," the man replied in an amused tone. "And isn't she very bold, calling you a pain in the backside?" He said this to Bruno, who was now the picture of well-behaved innocence.

"If only you knew," Tara said, rolling her eyes. "But look, I'd better get back – my friend's son is having a nap, and I don't want to leave him too long on his own."

"Oh, you're a friend of Liz's then?"

Tara looked at him. So he did know Liz – which meant that her friend must have known that the house had been recently sold but hadn't mentioned it. Pity that she hadn't – then Tara wouldn't have dreamed of allowing Bruno near the place!

"I bought this place a few weeks back," he told Tara, "and I met her a couple of times since. She was a little worried about the kennels being so close to the house and hoped the barking wouldn't disturb me." He grinned widely. "But I grew up on a farm, so noisy animals are par for the course for me."

"Well, rather you than me. Bruno here has got a bark that would break the sound barrier. But look, I am really sorry about your garden."

"Don't worry about it – if I'd known you were a friend of Liz's I wouldn't have shouted at you like that. I just thought you were some passer-by taking advantage. The fields behind seem to be used quite a bit by ramblers and dog-walkers, and because I haven't yet got round to putting up a fence, they tend to wander in."

Well, Tara thought, deciding that Liz McGrath was

a very dark horse indeed. With all her worries about Eric, she had neglected to mention that she had a new and (if you liked the meat-head look) quite good-looking neighbour.

"You don't need to apologise," she replied, feeling slightly flustered in his company. He was just so . . . big! "It was my own fault for letting him get the better of me. But I really should get back to Toby. It was nice meeting you."

"You too," he replied easily, "and say hello to Liz for me, won't you?"

"I will," Tara answered, but it was only after Bruno had dragged her back to Liz's house that she realised she didn't know his name.

Chapter 14

"Oh, that was Luke!" Liz told her on the phone the following morning, when Tara mentioned the encounter. "He's gorgeous, isn't he?"

Well, Tara wouldn't say that exactly. Yes, she supposed there was something attractive about those muscled, hardy-looking, outdoorsy types, but brawn had never been her thing. No, Tara had always been attracted to dark, brooding, creative types and wouldn't normally look twice at someone like that.

"I was too embarrassed to take any notice," she told Liz breezily. "I really wish you'd told me there was somebody living there, though. The place looks just as abandoned as it was when I was growing up, so I'd no idea –"

"To be honest, *I'd* no idea he'd be moving in so soon," her friend replied. "He's abroad a lot – I think he works in different countries out on oil rigs or that type of thing.

Last time I bumped into him, he said he had a long stint coming up and wouldn't be back until after Christmas. That was just after he bought the house."

"Well, he's definitely here now," Tara said with a sigh, "and Bruno gave him a lovely welcome."

"Didn't I tell you to be firm with that fella? Otherwise he'd walk all over you."

"Tell me about it," Tara groaned.

"Listen, I'd better go – Eric and I are just heading over to the house now. Will you give Toby my love and tell him Mummy and Daddy were asking for him?"

"Of course, I will." Tara rolled her eyes good-naturedly. This was the *third* time Liz had asked her to pass on such a message to Toby.

"And thanks again for looking after him – I really appreciate it."

"No problem. How's it all going there anyway? Did you two get any time on your own?" Then she added, "Or can't you say anything at the moment?"

"Not really," her friend replied quietly, and Tara understood that Eric must be in the room with her. She really hoped that, despite the circumstances, some good might come out of their time away.

"Well then, say hi to Eric and Maeve for me, and I'll talk to you tomorrow afternoon."

"You too. And tell Toby I –"

"Yes, Liz – I'll tell Toby you and his daddy were asking for him. Take care."

Smiling, Tara replaced the cordless phone in the receiver and went back into the living room where

Toby was playing happily on the floor with his toys.

She checked the clock on the mantelpiece and groaned. It was almost eleven – time to bring those mental-cases for another trek in the fields. Tara almost felt as though she were preparing herself for battle as she fetched their leads and went to let them out of their kennels, the dogs leaping about excitedly upon her approach.

An hour or so later, she, Toby and the dogs returned to the house. The animals had been much better behaved this morning, or perhaps she was getting better at handling them, she wasn't sure. Then, as soon as they were all safely inside their kennels, she went inside and began preparing Toby's lunch.

"This is quite good fun, isn't it, Toby?" she said, as she rummaged through the fridge for something to make, Toby sitting quietly in his highchair as he watched her move around. He was a dream to look after, really, she thought, deciding that while he was the image of his father, he had definitely been blessed with Liz's temperament. Her friend was so calm, so docile and unassuming, which were mostly lovely traits but could often work to her own detriment. She had urged Liz to use this weekend to find out what exactly was going wrong in her marriage, but she doubted very much that her friend would confront Eric. Liz hated confrontation and –

Hearing a loud roar from outside, Tara stopped short. Blast it – was one of the dogs due to leave today? No, that couldn't be it, and even if that was the case, it was highly unlikely the dog's owner would be shouting his head off outside the door, wasn't it?

Then, she thought of something. Oh, God, had one of the animals escaped from its pen – maybe got out and bit someone?

Tara rushed to the back door. "Stay right there," she told Toby, although there was little chance of the baby going anywhere strapped like that into his high chair. "Aunty Tara has to go outside and check on the doggies, OK?"

Toby giggled and clapped his hands excitedly at the mention of the word "doggies", no doubt thinking he was due another outing in the fields. Fat chance of that, she thought wryly.

Going outside, Tara headed straight for the kennels, Ben and Jerry circling around her feet. As she drew closer, she saw that littles and large were still in their individual holding pens and, amazingly, all three were fast asleep. Thank God for that!

She turned away and was just about to go back inside the house when she heard someone curse loudly.

"Stupid friggin' things!" a man's voice hissed.

Following the direction from which the voice had come, Tara went towards the adjoining house. As she did, she spotted muscleman Luke standing outside his own back door, his face red and his fists clenched tightly.

"Is everything OK?" Tara called across to him. "I heard someone shout."

"Everything's fine," he replied, through gritted teeth. "I just have a couple of unwelcome visitors."

"Oh." Someone must have dropped by unannounced, she decided. Her own mother hated that too, hated people calling to visit when the house was in a state, so in a way she understood how he felt. Still, the cottage hadn't been lived in for years and was bound to be less than perfect, and it seemed a bit rude of Luke to go running out of the house screaming about it.

"Do you think you could get rid of them?" Tara heard him ask then, his tone softer and a little hesitant.

"Excuse me?"

"I mean, do they bother you? Are you afraid of them?"

"Well," Tara wasn't sure how to answer that. Why the hell would people visiting *his* house bother her? "I'm not sure if . . ."

"I hate the little fuckers, always have. It's embarrassing but . . ."

Oh, now Tara got it. Whoever his guests were, they must have brought children with them, and evidently Luke wasn't a fan – to say the least. Glenn could be a bit like that too and would often run a mile whenever Liz or any of her other friends brought their offspring to their house. Though if Glenn were to express himself in such a horribly violent way, she would have something to say about it. In such an *unbalanced* way . . . Tara began to feel a bit nervous. Was he quite sane?

And how he expected Tara to deal with these people on his behalf when she didn't even know *him* was beyond her . . .

"I think they're under the sink," he added then,

confirming for Tara that he really wasn't the full shilling.

Under the sink?

"I opened the door, and two of them ran straight out," he informed her, grimacing. "One of them ran right over my hand! Jesus, I can still see his bloody tail!"

Tail? But right then it hit her and she understood exactly who, or rather *what,* had paid Luke a visit. She tried to smother a laugh.

"Mice?" she clarified, her eyes widening in mirth. "You're afraid of tiny, harmless, little mice?"

Luke's expression paled at the mention of the word. "Rub it in, why don't you? I know the place is old, but I thought it was so old that the little fuckers wouldn't be bothered with it." He shook his head. "There could be hundreds in there for all I know."

"Oh, for goodness sake!" Tara was still struggling to keep a straight face. "Imagine someone your size being afraid of a tiny, harmless little animal like that!"

"Yeah, yeah, I know. But I can't help it, OK? It's just something that's in me and I can't help it. Some people are afraid of heights, others of spiders. Me, I'm afraid of mice."

He said this in such a way that Tara knew it was killing him to have to admit it, especially in front of a woman.

"So do you think you could . . . you know . . . go in and take a look around? See where they went?"

Tara was laughing openly now, but felt almost guilty when she saw his petrified expression. This really was killing him. "OK, then. But let me get Toby first – I left him inside on his own when I came outside to investigate all the noise you were making."

Luke looked sheepish and, still smiling, Tara quickly went back inside to Toby, who was chattering happily away to himself and totally out of harm's way.

"Sorry about this, pet," Tara told him as she lifted him out of the chair and strapped him into his buggy, "but the scaredy cat next door needs our help."

"Ca!" Toby pointed out happily, as the two of them passed the cattery on their way through the garden to Luke's house.

Leaving Luke to keep an eye on Toby (or indeed the other way round) Tara was in and out of the place within a few minutes, having opened and closed all the old cupboards and checked in various nooks and crannies, but there were no "visitors" to be seen.

"I know you think this is hilarious, and I don't blame you," Luke said, when Tara eventually reappeared outside, "but I can't help it. My mother used to freak whenever one appeared in our house when I was younger, so I suppose I've carried the fear since then." He shrugged. "Stupid I know but . . ."

Tara was sorely tempted to keep teasing, but a look at his mortified expression told her it was unfair to embarrass him any further. "Like you said, it's a genuine fear and most of us have them."

"It's stupid," he insisted and Tara suspected he was trying to convince himself more than anyone else. "I know they're only tiny, but . . ." he winced again, "those bloody tails!"

"Well, they seem to have gone into hiding now. But I doubt that's the last you'll see of them so you really should think about setting down traps."

"Ugh!" Luke shuddered.

"Well, if you're not up to it, you'll have to get somebody else in to do it. The place has been vacant for so long now, I'm surprised it isn't ten times worse than it is," she added thoughtfully.

"You know the place?"

"Yep. I grew up here in the village – and me and my friends used to come up here when we were teenagers to drink and chat and . . . you know."

Luke smiled. "Right."

"That's why I got such a fright the other day. Nobody's lived there for so long that I just assumed –"

"I know. And I still feel bad for shouting at you. But to be honest, the renovation work is not going as well as I'd thought." He rolled his eyes. "Those bloody TV programmes make it all look so easy."

"True," Tara laughed. "In twenty-four hours, *you* can make your rundown cottage into a show-house mansion! It's not quite the same when you get down and dirty with it, is it? Although in fairness, I'd love to have a house of my own to decorate. The one we're in now is rented. But it'll be a long time before I can afford to get any house in Dublin, let alone one I can restore to its former glory."

"Oh, you don't live in the village any more?"

"No, I'm just looking after the place for Liz. Oh, and speaking of looking after the place, I'd better go – this little fella will be needing his lunch soon."

"Well, look, thanks a million . . . um . . . I'm sorry, I don't know your –"

"It's Tara."

"Tara. I owe you a cuppa, only I don't even have a kettle in there yet. Speaking of which, can you recommend anywhere in the village for food? I was in that coffee shop yesterday, but they do all this organic muck, and I'm not really into –"

"Why don't you come back next door with me?" The words were out before she realised it. "I was just having lunch anyway. I could do you a fry-up or an omelette or something."

"Are you sure? I'd love that, but I really don't want to impose."

"Don't be silly. After the shock you've had, you need a strong cup of tea," she added mischievously.

"I won't argue with that," Luke said, his form greatly improved as he closed the back door of his cottage behind him. "And I'd kill for a decent cuppa. Those choco-mocco things they serve in that café taste like shaggin' dishwater!"

Chapter 15

So far, the weekend was not going well.

On Friday morning, Liz and Eric had left for Belfast (picking up Maeve on the way) and Eric had been largely uncommunicative throughout the drive north.

Understandably, he hadn't exactly been in high spirits since learning about his uncle's death, but at the same time he barely knew the man. Liz had never met him; in fact, Pierce hadn't even been in attendance at their wedding three years ago, so she knew he and Eric weren't close.

No, Liz knew her husband well enough to know that there was something else bothering him – something other than the death of an estranged relation. And, over the course of the weekend, she hoped she'd get the opportunity to find out exactly what that was.

"It'll be nice to get some time on our own, just the two of us, won't it?" she'd said while packing a weekend bag for them to take to the hotel. "It's ages since we've been anywhere without Toby."

"It's my uncle's bloody funeral, Liz," he'd replied shortly. "It's hardly a romantic weekend away."

"Oh, I know that, love – that's not what I meant." Liz could have kicked herself for sounding so unfeeling. But she'd been thinking out loud more than anything else. "I was just saying that it will be strange the two of us being away from Toby for the first time, that's all."

In Belfast, after the removal Friday evening, they'd spent much of the night at the family home, before eventually getting back to their hotel around midnight. So there had been very little opportunity for Liz to get her husband on his own and have the chat she so badly wanted.

It was only late Saturday evening after the funeral, once they'd again left Maeve with her family, that she and Eric got any time on their own.

Liz suggested going for somewhere local for dinner.

"I don't know if I fancy it, Liz – I'm fairly whacked after today."

"I know but we haven't eaten anything other than salad sandwiches all weekend," she argued. "All right then, forget about going out – let's just have something here in the hotel."

Eventually Eric relented, and now, possibly for the first time since the birth of their eighteen-month-old son, Liz and her husband, the man she loved with all her heart, were alone. But now that they *were* finally alone – sitting across from one another in the hotel dining room, Liz had no idea what to say to him.

Eric seemed miles away, his thoughts clearly still elsewhere. Should she risk it, she wondered, her heart rate accelerating. Should she just get it over and done with and come straight out and ask him if he was seeing Emma? If he had fathered her unborn child? Tears prickled at her eyes as she realised how unhappy they both seemed. This was no way for a married couple to behave. Tara had been wrong; far from bringing them closer, the time on their own seemed to only highlight just how far apart they were.

Still, she had to try. Something was wrong and she needed to fix it.

"I spoke to Tara on the phone earlier," she said, trying to sound light-hearted. "She and Toby are having a great time, and he doesn't seem to be missing us at all! It was good of her to baby-sit him, wasn't it?"

"Good old reliable Tara," Eric replied, and Liz thought she noticed an edge to his tone.

"The dogs are fine too, which is great," Liz babbled on, deciding to talk about things that made her feel comfortable, normal everyday things. "I must admit, I did wonder how Toby would get on without us. He's not used to being left with other people and I thought he'd be a bit teary."

"Well, if Tara says he's fine, then I'm sure he is," Eric replied in a rather bored voice.

"Still, he's been a bit troublesome lately," she said. "I hope he hasn't been getting up to mischief." When

Eric didn't reply, she continued, "Yes, it was really great of Tara to offer to baby-sit this weekend, and she also said that if ever you and I want to go away for a weekend in a hotel somewhere, she'd love to do it again."

"Did she offer to pay for the bloody hotel too?"

This time there was no mistaking his tone and Liz frowned. "What do you mean by that?"

"Well, Tara seems to enjoy throwing her money around, doesn't she? The fancy clothes and fancy car. Next she'll be buying a mansion in Dalkey."

Liz was taken aback. She'd never heard Eric criticise his old friend like that. "Tara works very hard for her money, Eric. Same as you, me and everyone else. And I don't think anyone can begrudge her anything, considering." She looked away. "Look, Tara was just being kind, and all she did was offer to baby-sit in order to give us the opportunity to get away now and again. We've barely had a second to ourselves since we moved to Castlegate. I'm always busy with Toby and the kennels, and if you're not working, you're out with . . ." She let her voice trail off, afraid that if she mentioned his nights out with his work friends or with Colm that it would sound like she was nagging. And Liz didn't want that, not when she was trying to get their relationship back on track. "But if you don't think we should accept her generosity again, then we won't. But you know as well as I do that we have nobody else to ask."

It was a barely disguised jibe at the fact that Maeve

McGrath had never offered to baby-sit her grandson; in fact, she had never gone out of her way to spend any time with him at all. It hurt Liz that Toby's one and only grandmother wasn't really interested in him. Granted she wasn't interested in Eric's sister's kids either but they lived much further away in Kerry. With Toby she didn't really have an excuse.

"I know what you're getting at," Eric said. "And yes, maybe Mum should help out some more. But she's getting on now, Liz. She wouldn't be able to handle Toby."

"I suppose."

In truth, when push came to shove, Liz knew she wouldn't be altogether happy with Maeve looking after her baby. The woman was guarded and standoffish and didn't seem to have a friendly bone in her body. Liz only put up with her because she was Toby's only grandmother, but the woman's continued refusal to visit their home (supposedly because of the dogs) was becoming annoying.

But she didn't want this to spark off a disagreement between herself and Eric, so she decided to change the subject.

"How's your lamb?"

Eric had so far spent much of the meal simply picking at his food. "It's OK, nothing special."

"Here, have some of my sea bass," she offered, pushing the plate towards him. It was pathetic the way she kept trying to ingratiate herself with him, but she didn't know what else to do. Tara wouldn't behave like this; no, if she were in this situation, she would just come right out and ask Eric what the problem was, instead of just sitting there, timid as a mouse, pretending that all was well. Liz cursed her own cowardice, cursed her inability to confront the situation head-on and ask her husband what the hell was wrong with him.

The problem was that, deep down, Liz really didn't want to hear the answer. She didn't want to hear Eric admit out loud that something was indeed wrong. At least this way, she still had a hope that their marriage was OK, albeit a slim one, and could convince herself that they might get through it.

But then again, how could they, when she didn't really know what there was to get through? And what kind of marriage could they have in the future if they couldn't talk to one another now? Liz sighed inwardly, at a loss as to what to do next and sick to the back teeth of worrying about it.

"I'm all right, thanks," Eric said, refusing her offer of the sea bass. "I'm not very hungry, to be honest."

"Eric, are you OK?" Liz blurted, deciding to just bite the bullet and ask him straight out what was wrong with him – like any self-respecting wife would. "You seem very down in yourself lately."

"I'm fine," he replied and her heart plunged to her stomach when she realised that he wouldn't look her in the eye. "Just a little tired."

"Well, do you want to head back to the room after this? I'm quite tired myself, actually." She pushed her plate away. "Now that I think of it, maybe we shouldn't go anywhere on our own – without Toby, we're both so tired we can hardly talk."

She got a brief smile in return.

"I suppose it was nice of Tara to offer to take him again all the same," he said. "But don't you feel that sometimes she can overdo things?"

"What do you mean?"

"This whole 'look at me – I'm so successful' carry-on?"

"Well, she *is* successful, but as far as I'm concerned she's no different to how she was when we first met. And you know as well as I do that Tara deserves every bit of success she has now."

"I suppose you're right," Eric conceded. "But it must be tough on Emma though when –" He stopped short, as if he'd spoken out of turn, and Liz's heart skipped a beat. "Why do you say that?"

Eric sat back in his chair. "Well, there's Tara with this great career, nice car and what have you, and on the other hand there's Emma, pregnant and having to give up her job and move home."

"*Having* to give up her job" was a bit of an overstatement. According to Tara, Emma (after her first bout of morning sickness) had simply packed in the job and gone running home to Mammy and Daddy. But she didn't share her thoughts with Eric.

"Yes, but it's not as though she won't get plenty of support – much of it from Tara, I'd imagine," she added quietly. Then, she took a deep breath before adding, "Seeing as the baby's father doesn't seem to want anything to do with it."

"And what makes you think that?" Eric replied, his tone measured.

"I'm only going on what Tara told me. I don't really know Emma, after all."

"Well, I do, and from what I can make out, things are hard enough on her as it is, without Tara gossiping to all and sundry about it."

"All and sundry? I'm one of Tara's best friends!" Hurt that he had so easily come to Emma's defence, Liz couldn't help her voice from rising. "And she's not *gossiping* about Emma, she's worried about her! Anyway, how do *you* know so much about how hard things are for Emma?" she added petulantly, and immediately wished she hadn't. Now, she sounded like a jealous nag.

"Oh for God's sake, Liz, don't start! Emma's an old friend, you know that. OK, so we went out with one another before I met you – big deal! I didn't marry her, did I?"

No, Liz replied silently, *but perhaps now you wish you had.*

Instead she replied, "I know that, but to be honest, Eric, since we moved to Castlegate, sometimes I can't help feeling a bit left out."

There, she'd said it, she'd finally admitted that she felt an outsider in the village, that the idyllic life they'd envisaged in the country hadn't quite materialised. "You know so many people, which is of course understandable seeing that you're from there, but I . . . I don't know . . . people in Castlegate are friendly, but I can't help feeling like an outsider."

Eric sat back. "But that's only natural, Liz. We've only been there less than a year. These things take time."

"I know, but I just get the sense that it'll always be like that. I mean none of the locals have used the kennels yet –"

"That doesn't mean anything. Part of the problem is that everyone knows their neighbours so well that they don't need to put their dogs in kennels. They can just leave them with one another. Don't read too much into that, Liz. Anyway, what about Colm? Don't you get on with him?"

"I do, but I suppose he's still really your friend. I don't really have any friends of my own." She hated the way this all sounded so whiny. With the way she was carrying on, why *wouldn't* Eric cheat on her?

"Well, then you have to get out and about more. Bring Toby to one of those mother and toddler groups or something."

Liz had thought of that, but it was difficult to arrange it around the kennels. She had to be available in the mornings to take in and discharge the animals. Maybe when she was fully booked she needn't worry about it, but for the moment she needed to look after her customers' every whim, so she couldn't go gadding off to playgroups.

She sighed. "Maybe you're right. I suppose I just need to give it time."

"Of course you do," Eric soothed, but Liz suspected he wasn't really taking her concerns seriously. "Now, will we get the bill? I think I'm ready for bed."

"Sure."

But much later, as she lay beside a heavily sleeping Eric, who had meant he was ready for sleep, and not for the lovemaking his wife had sorely hoped would bring them closer together, Liz wondered if giving it time would be enough.

Chapter 16

Sunday lunchtime, Eric and Liz returned home from Belfast.

While both were obviously excited to see Toby after the few days, Liz in particular seemed over the moon to be back, and upon arrival she practically swooped on the baby and covered him in kisses. Toby, in return, seemed just as pleased to see his mum and giggled with delight at Liz's exuberance.

Eric kissed Toby too, but Tara suspected that he was somewhat annoyed by his wife's overly demonstrative behaviour.

"Liz, leave him alone – you'd swear we'd been away for weeks," he admonished, but not in the usual playful manner Tara would have expected from him. In fact, now that she'd observed him up close, Eric didn't seem himself at all. She was certain he'd lost weight, and the sunny and good-natured manner she'd associated with him for as long as they'd known one another now seemed curiously absent. Instead he looked drawn and solemn and, Tara thought worriedly, a little uncomfortable and out of place with the cosy family reunion. Tara now understood why Liz had been so worried. Eric looked like a man who had the weight of the world on his shoulders.

"Thanks for looking after him," Liz said, coming over and giving Tara a hug, Toby still in her arms. "I hope he was OK."

"Liz, it was a pleasure – he wasn't a bit of bother."

"He wasn't?" Liz replied, looking oddly at her son. Then she coloured slightly and gave a sideways glance at Eric, as if ashamed. "Well, you're obviously much better at this than I am – I'm finding him very hard going lately."

"Liz thought the place would be in chaos without her," Eric drawled, and Tara could have kicked herself. The last thing Liz needed was to feel insecure about her mothering skills, especially when she was feeling so anxious about everything else these days.

"Not at all. To be honest, I think he was so amused by me trying to handle the dogs that he didn't have the heart to make things any harder," she joked. "And of course, it's always a novelty to have someone else looking after you, isn't it?" she added, tickling the little boy, who began to giggle. "But I'd say he can be a little terror when he sets his mind to it, can't you, Toby?"

"Or maybe you're simply much more of a natural at this than I am," Liz insisted tiredly.

Tara decided not to push it any further and her mind strained to think of something that would change the subject.

"Oh, I hope you don't mind," she said then, "but I had your new neighbour over for lunch yesterday."

"What new neighbour?" Eric asked, frowning.

"The one who bought the place next door," Liz told him.

"That old rundown shack? I didn't know anyone had bought that."

"Well, I told you," Liz said with a jaded sigh.

Tara couldn't believe how sullen and distant she and Eric seemed around one another. For a couple that had always been so fun-filled and relaxed together, it was especially difficult to comprehend. Tara didn't have to wonder too much how their weekend had gone – she could see it all reflected in their faces. Liz was understandably delighted to get back to Toby, but the strain between Eric and her was evident.

"I'd better head back home," she said, feeling again as though she should change the subject. "After a few nights surviving on takeaways, no doubt Glenn will be expecting a decent dinner." She shook her head in feigned exasperation.

"Oh, he didn't come down on Saturday night, then?" Liz asked.

"No, he got stuck at work till all hours. Apparently he and the boys were right on the verge of cracking some incredibly important line of code – don't ask me!" She rolled her eyes. "I wouldn't be surprised if he's still at Pixels in front of the PC surrounded by empty pizza boxes." Glenn was like a dog with a bone when it came to computers so Tara wasn't at all surprised when he'd phoned to say he wouldn't be joining her. And she had to admit she didn't mind either. She liked having a weekend to herself – well, she admitted guiltily, not quite to herself, as she'd shared most of the previous day with Liz's friendly new neighbour.

She'd really enjoyed their lunch yesterday. Contrary to first impressions, Luke Cunningham was intelligent, talkative and very good company. Tara was surprised by how clued-in and sharp he seemed about everything, considering he spent months on end away from civilisation and surrounded by what he laughingly called "serious alpha-males". Tara didn't want to admit that she'd immediately dismissed Luke as one himself after their first meeting – although the incident with the mice had quickly dispelled that.

And (beefy biceps aside), he was also very attractive and, from what she'd gathered, single, seeing as he'd mentioned he was doing up the house himself. Not that she cared, of course, Tara reminded herself quickly, as she collected her belongings and went outside to put them in the car.

"Nice machine," Eric commented, joining Liz and Toby out front to say goodbye. "That must have cost a few quid."

"It was all Glenn's idea," Tara said, shaking her head in exasperation as she struggled to cram everything into the convertible's tiny boot. "Never again will I take the advice of someone who reads *Max Power* magazine."

In truth, she was actually quite fond of the car now, but something in Eric's tone stopped her admitting it. For some reason, she got the impression that he begrudged her the little luxury. Had his return to Castlegate had that much of an effect on him – that he, like so many others, hated to see one of their own doing well? Well, if he did feel that way, he had an absolute cheek. Eric of all people should understand how difficult it had been for her to get to where she was now.

And in fairness, what with all the whispering that used to go on when they were younger about Eric going the way of his misfortunate father and turning into a no-hoper, she'd have expected better of him. And no one was happier than her when Eric grew out of his wild youth and moved to Dublin to get a proper job instead of staying at home and becoming a troublemaker, like everyone in the town expected him to.

So what the hell was wrong with him now? Or more importantly, Tara wondered as she drove away from Castlegate, what was wrong with *them*?

Was Liz right – instead of making their lives easier, had the move away from Dublin driven them apart? Or was there another reason for Eric's odd behaviour lately?

Realising that his comment about the car sounded suspiciously like something Emma would say, Tara bit her lip, her unease about the situation growing by the second.

Over the course of the weekend, when reflecting upon Liz's remarks about Eric going "off somewhere in the evenings", her heart thudded as she'd remembered her mother mentioning Emma doing the same.

Now, Tara wondered if Liz's suspicions might not have been that far off the mark at all, and she wondered if her friend had made – like she'd just had – a connection between Eric's strange behaviour and the announcement of Emma's secret pregnancy.

Liz had told Tara that she felt Eric might be having an affair. Her friend hadn't mentioned anyone by name, of course, she was far too respectful for that, but now that Tara thought it about it, it was very possible that Liz just might have put two and two together and come up with Emma.

And of course, Emma had made it all too clear that the father of her unborn baby was off-limits, leading everyone to suspect that she'd got involved with someone she shouldn't have. Tara's heart raced in her chest. Could it have been Eric? she thought panicking. *Could* he be Emma's mystery man? Surely not. Then again, given their history . . .

With all her heart, Tara hoped this wasn't the case because she loved Liz like a sister and wouldn't be able to come to terms with the fact that her own flesh and blood could do her friend such damage.

Why couldn't Emma find a man of her own anyway? Why did she get such a kick out of wanting something she couldn't have?

But, unfortunately, Emma had always been like that.

If she put as much effort into building a life for herself as she did trying to wreck other people's, she'd be running the country by now. It was such a shame. Then again, Tara thought, who was she to pass judgement?

Maybe Emma thought *her* life was weird. Maybe *she* thought that Tara was mad for not getting married and settling for a simple, but admittedly boring, life with Glenn. Liz certainly did. But then again, as Liz had discovered herself only recently, married life didn't necessarily guarantee infinite happiness, did it?

When she reached home, the house was strangely silent. On any typical Sunday afternoon, Glenn would be flaked in front of the TV watching the football and surrounded by a mountain of junk food. So Tara was surprised to see that the living room was not only unoccupied but, amazingly, free of clutter.

"Glenn?" she called out as she walked through the house looking for signs of life. Surely he wasn't still at Pixels trying to crack that bloody code? Although nothing would surprise her when it came to Glenn and his beloved computers.

Going through to the kitchen, Tara became even more puzzled. There were no dirty dishes piled in the sink, no sloshes of spilled coffee staining the worktop . . . again it looked as though the kitchen hadn't been used all weekend.

Curiouser and curiouser . . .

Trying not to read too much into it, Tara went back

out to the car to unload her stuff, before going upstairs and dumping her bags in the bedroom.

"You're back early!" Glenn's voice floated up from the hallway, and in the distance, she heard the front door bang behind him. Ah, he must have been out at the shops or something.

"Yes," Tara replied, going back downstairs to meet him, "Liz and Eric were back at lunchtime, so I . . . what are *you* doing here?" Her eyes widened at the sight of her sister standing in the hallway behind Glenn. Speak of the devil . . .

"That's a nice way to greet your baby sister," Emma replied, but her tone was light. "I was in town for a scan on Friday afternoon, and it was late by the time I got out of the hospital. So, I thought I'd pop over and say hello – maybe stay the night."

Right. That was pure Emma to just decide to drop in unannounced whenever she pleased and expect everyone to run around after her. God forbid that Tara might have something else to do. And since her pregnancy, this kind of behaviour had only got worse.

"It's a pity you didn't phone first – then you would have known I wouldn't be here."

"Oh, it didn't matter," Emma replied nonchalantly. "When I arrived, Glenn told me you'd gone baby-sitting for the weekend."

"But didn't Mum tell you?"

Emma shrugged and walked into the kitchen. "She must have forgotten. Anyway, I was so tired that I couldn't face the long bus journey home, so Glenn very kindly offered to let me stay anyway, didn't you?" She flashed a beaming smile at Glenn, who nodded.

"I thought it made sense," he said. "I had to go into work on Saturday morning anyway, so as long as Emma didn't mind being here on her own . . ."

Emma nodded beatifically. "Of course I didn't!" she said cheerily. "Anyway, you kept me company on Saturday night, didn't you?"

"Strange you never said anything about Emma being here when I spoke to you on the phone," Tara said, addressing Glenn.

"I know but to be honest I was up to my eyes at work, and at the time the fact went completely went out of my head."

"I suppose." That was understandable. When Glenn was in cyberspace Tara was lucky to get a word out of him, never mind anything else!

Just then, Emma was helping herself to something from Tara's fridge. "I'm starving! Glenn," she said, resting her hand lightly on his arm, "is there any chance you could make me another one of those yummy toasted sandwiches you do?"

Like every other man on the planet, Glenn seemed powerless to resist Emma's blonde, blue-eyed charms. "Sure." He looked at Tara. "I'll make one for you too, if you'd like. Or did you have lunch at Liz and Eric's?"

"No, a sandwich would be nice," she said, eyeing her little sister, who as usual was only too happy to have someone else dancing attendance on her.

Despite herself, she didn't like the idea of Emma

being here at the weekend when she herself wasn't. OK, so she was her sister, but it just didn't seem right having her lazing around the place when no one was home. And of course, with everything that was going on with Eric and Liz, and her suspicions about Emma's possible involvement, she now wasn't in the best frame of mind to have to indulge the little madam.

"So, how did the scan go?" she asked Emma, as the two of them went into the living room, leaving Glenn to make lunch. This was another surprise, given that Tara was still trying to get over the fact that he'd kept the house clean and tidy while she was away. It had to have been Glenn; in Emma's "condition" Tara certainly couldn't see her sister tackling any housework!

"Fine – everything seems fine." Then she sighed loudly. "I feel so tired all the time, though. I hope you didn't mind Glenn staying here to look after me instead of going down home to you."

Tara's eyes widened. She wouldn't have put it quite like that. According to Glenn it had been work that had stopped him from coming down on Saturday evening, and he hadn't even remembered Emma was there! Not to mention the fact that she couldn't see Glenn signing up for a weekend running around her pregnant sister.

"It's no problem – I quite enjoyed having the weekend to myself actually." Well, not quite, she added inwardly, again remembering that Luke had been there for a lot of it.

"I had to get out of the house for a while," Emma went on, as she put her feet on the coffee table and waited patiently for lunch to be served up to her. "Mum is driving me demented with all her running around after me, asking if I'm OK. She can be a bit of pain sometimes, can't she?"

Tara held her tongue. It really wasn't her place to point out to Emma that their sixty-year-old mother shouldn't have to be running around after her in the first place, let alone be criticised for doing it. But that was bloody Emma – selfish to the last!

"Well, I'm sure Mum just wants to make this as easy as possible for you," she said evenly. There was no point in having a row with Emma over it – especially not here. From experience she knew that Emma was more than likely to go home to Castlegate in a huff and, no doubt, crying to their mother that Tara had been inconsiderate to her. So Tara couldn't win, no matter what she did.

"Oh, I know, but there are times when I really wish she'd just leave me alone. Glenn's been great, though," she added smiling. "And he's so good with the housework and everything, isn't he? You're so lucky to have him."

Tara tried not to roll her eyes. "So, are you planning to head back home this evening? It's just, after taking last Friday afternoon off, I have a busy schedule in the morning. So I won't really be able to sit and chat or anything . . ." She was hoping Emma would get the hint.

"Oh – I'd thought we might go shopping or something," Emma said petulantly. "I've hardly seen you since you came back from the holiday."

"Emma, I have appointments tomorrow. I can't just take off and go shopping. People are depending on me."

"Right," Emma replied in a disapproving tone that was remarkably reminiscent of Isobel's and suggested that Tara was putting other people over her own family. Especially in Emma's hour of need!

"But we'll do something else soon," Tara said, trying to appease her. Although she'd enjoyed spending time with Toby, she was tired after her exertions at the weekend and didn't have the energy for one of Emma's moods. "And maybe you could stay tonight anyway."

"I think I might," Emma replied, smiling gratefully at Glenn, who'd just come in carrying a tray laden with tea, coffee and a plate of toasted sandwiches. Tara looked at him in shock, suspecting he must have been hit over the head with something recently.

"So," Emma asked then, as she took a hearty bite of her sandwich, "how *are* Eric and Liz these days? Still love's young dream?"

Tara looked at her, and if she didn't know better she could have sworn that there was something very smug in her sister's tone as she said this.

Her heart sank, and she looked away, almost afraid to reply. Maybe there was a lot more to Liz's suspicions that she'd thought.

Chapter 17

Jay was definitely the one – Natalie was sure of it!

They'd been inseparable for the rest of the night at the Purple Grapefruit launch, and when Danni had eventually made moves to leave around midnight, Natalie had ensured her assistant was safely ensconced in a taxi home before she herself went back inside the club to continue chatting (and flirting) with Jay.

Though, unfortunately, and much to Natalie's disappointment, he hadn't been able to accompany her home that night, as he was still officially on duty with Labyrinth and needed to stay behind for a party post mortem with the club's management.

But that didn't matter. When Natalie eventually left the club sometime after two, he'd escorted to her cab and given her a highly satisfying kiss goodbye, having already asked for (and received!) her number. And first thing the following morning he'd called and invited her to dinner this coming weekend.

Natalie couldn't believe how quickly she had fallen for him – well, she did tend to fall for most men pretty quickly, but this was different. Jay was mature, thoughtful, *very* attractive and absolutely perfect for her!

Thinking of it now, Steve had been in totally a different league and Natalie didn't know why she'd been so upset that an unsophisticated and totally immature footie fan was out of her life. If anything, it was a blessing in disguise, because if she'd still been with Steve, then she wouldn't have gone to the launch of Purple Grapefruit and so she wouldn't have met the wonderful Jay, who really was everything her ex-boyfriend wasn't. Successful, sophisticated and senior management in a dynamic and well-respected company, Jay Murray was most normal women's idea of a perfect catch. Also – and this was a first – he was Irish! Well, apparently he'd been living in London for yonks but had grown up somewhere near Dublin, which is why at first Natalie hadn't been able to place his odd accent.

But of course, once Jay had confessed his Irish heritage, it made perfect sense as to why she'd warmed to him so quickly. He was funny, charming and had that lovely down-to-earth quality that most Irish-born men seemed to possess.

Still, however much she liked him, this time Natalie wasn't going to mess it up. She wasn't going to rush into things like she had before and make a complete shambles of the relationship before it had even begun. This time, she was going to play it to perfection, and seeing as her past record in this regard had proved so hopelessly inept, this time she was going to call in the experts.

Natalie sank back onto her comfy office chair and hummed softly as she dialled the number.

"Hello?" A groggy-sounding male voice answered after the fifth or sixth ring.

At the sound of his voice, Natalie instinctively looked at her watch. She hadn't called too early, had she? It was after eleven o'clock on Monday morning, and she was pretty certain that Dublin operated on Greenwich Meantime too, didn't they?

A little perplexed, Natalie spoke into the receiver. "Hello, is that Glenn?"

"Yeah, who's this?" he replied testily, and Natalie gulped. She'd obviously rung at a bad time, or else Glenn was in what Tara had called in Egypt – much to Natalie's amusement – one of his "quare moods".

"Glenn, hi – you might not remember me, but we met on holidays a few weeks back. In Egypt? I went to Cairo with –"

Almost instantly, Glenn seemed to perk up. "Oh right, Natalie, is it? How are you?"

"I'm good! How are you?" she replied cheerily. "I hope I didn't wake you – you sounded a bit sleepy when you answered."

Glenn yawned again. "Well, I was on a late shift last night, but not to –"

"Oh, silly me, I'm very sorry," Natalie blustered. "I had no idea."

"Not to worry." Then, when she didn't say anything else, he said, "Erm, did you want to speak to Tara?"

"Oh goodness, yes, sorry – that's why I was ringing in the first place. Is she free?"

"I'm not sure – she might be with a client. No – hold on – she's just come into the room. Hey," he said then, and Natalie knew he was talking to Tara, "it's for you – that good-looking English girl we met on holidays."

Natalie raised an eyebrow at this description of her, but quickly lowered it again when she heard Tara on the other end of the line.

"Natalie? Hi, how are you?" The other woman seemed pleased, but also a little perplexed, to hear from her. People exchanged phone numbers all the time on holiday with no real intention of keeping in touch, Natalie knew, and most of the time they were never to be heard from again.

But this was different, and just then Natalie realised that meeting Tara in Egypt like that might not have been accidental. Their paths had almost certainly crossed for a very good reason. It was a heartening thought and one that convinced Natalie beyond doubt that she was doing the right thing.

"I'm good – and you?" she replied. "How was your flight home? Great holiday, wasn't it?"

"Brilliant – I'm still telling people about our Cairo trip," Tara said warmly. "And the flight was fine – *long*, but fine. How are things with you? It's good to hear from you."

"Well, it's great to talk to you too, although I must admit that I have an ulterior motive for calling."

"Oh?"

"Tara, I wanted to ask for your help."

"My help with what?"

"With my love life!" Natalie blurted, dying to tell her everything. She hadn't bothered telling Freya about Jay – no doubt her friend would be too wrapped up in her own life to care. "I've just met the most *amazing* man, who I think could really be the one and I don't want to –"

"Whoah, hold on a minute," Tara interjected. "What about Steve – the guy you told me was the love of your life, the one who was just about to propose?" Then she paused for a moment. "Or did you decide to dump him after he'd bowed out of the holiday?"

"Well, no, not exactly." Natalie wasn't about to go into the shameful details of her multiple text messages or indeed Steve's "psycho bunny-boiler" comments – not when she'd already convinced Tara that he'd been the man of her dreams. "I think we both realised that it just wasn't meant to be, in the end," she said with a deep sigh. "So I told him it would be better to move on."

"That's a shame."

"But it doesn't matter because I'm over it now, and the other night I met the most amazing man and he's taking me out to dinner on Friday night!"

"Well, that's wonderful, Natalie. I'm delighted you and Steve sorted things out so amicably. If you don't mind my saying so, I had a feeling from what you were telling me that he might not have been the right man for you."

"Did you?" Natalie wrinkled her forehead. She didn't know where Tara had got that idea. Maybe she wasn't all that good at this relationship lark after all, she realised, her heart sinking.

No, that was being stupid. Tara was a life coach for goodness sake and from what Natalie could tell, a very good one at that. She remembered how she'd so admired the other woman for the calm, controlled and serene way she seemed to live her life. And in the end Tara had been right, hadn't she? Steve obviously *wasn't* the man for her and Tara had seen that way before Natalie had. So, yes, of course she had made the right decision in getting Tara on board to help with Jay. Although she wasn't actually on board yet because she had yet to ask her . . .

"Well, I didn't want to say anything but it did seem as though you and Steve wanted different things," Tara went on. "Anyway, I'm pleased you found someone else. I never doubted for a second that you would."

"Thanks, Tara. Oh . . . can you hold on for a second? I've a call coming through on the other line."

Hoping it might be Jay, Natalie decided to take the call, but was sorry she did when it turned out to be one of the brats from Blast whining about the lack of press interest in their latest release. The cheek of the child, ringing her directly! Natalie would certainly have a word with his manager about that! After listening to his rants for a minute or two, she eventually fobbed him off and returned to Tara.

"Hi – sorry about that – that was just some spotty boy-band member I handle, who thinks he should be treated like a rock god just because he's got his nose pierced. Ozzie Osborne, he isn't," she added wryly. "Anyway . . . oh, God, are you still there?"

There was a smile in Tara's voice. "Yes, I'm here."

"Good. Now, where was I? Oh yes, as I was saying, I've met this new guy now – an Irish guy! Well, he grew up somewhere in Ireland, so *obviously* I immediately thought of you and decided you'd be the *ideal* person to help me!"

"Help you with what?"

"Well, with making this relationship work," Natalie replied, as if it were the most obvious thing in the world."

"But how can I help with –"

"Because you're Irish, of course! You know how Irishmen's minds work."

"Natalie, I really don't think –"

"Please, Tara," Natalie interjected before the other girl could say any more, "I *really* want the relationship to work – I *need* this relationship to work. I can't mess it up." Then suspecting that she might as well come clean, Natalie sighed. "Look, Tara, I haven't exactly been honest with you. I didn't ditch Steve – he ditched me."

"Oh, I'm very sorry about that, Natalie."

"He told me I was needy and stifling! God only knows where he got that idea," she said huffily. "And, Tara, he called me a sodding bunny-boiler!" There it was out, and surprisingly, Natalie felt liberated.

If this was going to work Tara needed to know the truth, the whole truth and nothing but. She needed to know *exactly* what kind of raw material she had to work with if she was to help Natalie get this dating lark right. So she might have been full-on and stifling when it came to Steve, but she was trying to change, wasn't she?

"Gobshite," Tara replied in that lovely Irish brogue of hers. "No wonder he didn't reply to your text messages."

Then, for a split second Natalie wondered whether Tara meant that she and not Steve was the "gobshite" in question.

"Well, maybe I overdid it on the text messages," she said quickly.

"How? You sent him what – two or three in an entire week?"

"Um, thirteen actually," Natalie clarified meekly.

"Oh."

"It was a bit much, I suppose."

Tara seemed at a loss what to say. "I suppose it must have been."

"So, Tara, this is why I'm phoning you now. I don't want to make the same mistakes with Jay as I did with Steve or any of my old boyfriends. I don't want to frighten him away, nor do I want to act too cool and distant either. It's like in that Goldilocks story, I want to get this one just right. And I want you to coach me how to do it."

"You want *me* to coach you? But Natalie, there are hundreds of relationship coaches in London that you could use and –"

"I want you, Tara. As I said, Jay's Irish, as you are, so you'll know better than most how Irish guys' minds work. You're perfect for this. And," she added quickly, "I suppose I don't want everyone in London knowing that I'm taking dating advice. I know it's silly, but –"

"Well, of course – I can understand that, but still –"

"Please, Tara," Natalie interjected plaintively, "I really need you to help me do this. My love life has been a disaster for so long, and no matter what I do, I always seem to get it wrong. Now I'm thirty-two years old and evidently I haven't learnt *anything*. I need help."

"I know but, the thing is, I'm not convinced that what I do exactly suits your needs. I usually help people work through emotional problems and –"

"But this *is* an emotional problem!" Natalie interjected, now decidedly harried. "To be honest, I'm getting quite emotional as we speak. I want this to work!"

There was a brief silence at the other end, and Natalie worried that she'd said too much.

"Look," she said, softening her tone considerably, "there's no point in my muddling along forever and messing things up even further, is there? That would be foolish. I need to get this problem sorted."

"Yes, but it's not that simple."

"Tara, if I'm carrying a few pounds, I get them lipo'ed, if I spot a few wrinkles, I get them botoxed, so why should this be any different? At our age, I'm sure you know as well as I do that holding onto our looks is as much a battle as holding on to a relationship. And as one mostly depends on the other, I have to do something!"

Tara laughed. "I've never heard it put quite like that, but you sound very sure."

"I'm sure, Tara. I've never been more sure of anything in my life."

Tara seemed to be thinking about it. "It's not usually the way I operate, Natalie. Coaching has a very defined mode of operation and just because he's Irish doesn't mean I can –"

"Tara, I just need some help!" Natalie cried. "I just need some guidelines as to how the hell I should handle this! And if you don't help me, I don't know who can!"

"Well, what about your girlfriends?"

"They don't care," Natalie groaned. "They're all too busy with their own lives and their own relationships. None of them have been on the scene for years, and they're bored with me and my relationship problems." Natalie was silent for the moment. "Will you help me, Tara?" she then asked, her voice plaintive. "Because I really can't afford to fuck this up."

"But you said you barely know this fella Jay – how do you know he's worth all this?"

"Well, I suppose I *don't* know that yet, but for once,

I'd like to give it a fighting chance. I've been trying to get it right for so long and failing that I don't know what right *is* any more. I'm either too full-on or too indifferent or –"

"I should tell you that I'm no expert either, and I can only go on what you tell me –"

"You'd be fantastic – I know it. And obviously I'd pay whatever rates you charge like any normal customer –"

"Well, we can work all that out some other time," Tara interjected, "but –

"So you *will* help me then?" Natalie cried gleefully. "You'll help me with this, coach me on how to properly handle Jay?"

"Well, if you're sure you really want this, then I'll certainly try," Tara finished, with the resigned tone of someone who was seriously wondering what on earth she'd let herself in for.

Chapter 18

Tara settled herself comfortably on the couch and tucked her legs beneath her. It was the following afternoon, and she and Natalie were having their first telephone coaching session.

In all her years in coaching, she had never come across someone like Natalie, someone who seemed to know *exactly* what she wanted. Usually, her clients' main problems were that they *didn't* know what they wanted, and this could only be discovered by gently discussing the workings of their lives and eventually coaxing out their ultimate ambitions. Then, having come to this realisation, the coaching process could begin, and once they'd achieved their aims, her clients generally went off and did their own thing. Tara had never yet been approached by someone who already knew exactly what he or she wanted and simply wanted her help in achieving it. Which meant that her usual more rigid coaching methods had to go straight out the window.

Tara had begun by asking Natalie some background information about her relationship history so far and was quite frankly shocked at what she'd heard.

It was pretty obvious from the outset that Natalie had been incredibly (almost scarily) full-on with her previous boyfriends. In fact, it was horrifying how quickly she pushed on, trying to bring the relationship further in order to achieve her ultimate aim – a ring on her finger.

"So you've already decided that this Jay person might be the one," Tara said, keeping her voice neutral. "Do you feel you already know enough about him to make a judgement like that?"

"Probably not," Natalie replied sheepishly. "I'm just going on how he makes me feel."

"OK, so he makes you feel good – why do you think that is?"

"I don't know. I suppose it's because even though I know I like him and he likes me, I still don't know where it will all go from here."

"And that excites you?"

"Yes."

"More than Jay himself?"

"Well . . . well, yes and no."

"Yes and no?"

"I mean, yes, of course Jay excites me, but the idea that this could really be the right man for me excites me just as much."

"Just as much – or more?"

"Oh, Tara, I bloody well wish you'd just come right out and say what you think!" Natalie said irritably. "All these questions are getting us nowhere."

"That's how coaching works, Natalie. You're the one with the answers – not me."

But she decided to change tack and, rather than talk about Jay, proceeded to talk some more about Natalie's previous relationships. "Tell me, why do *you* think your other relationships haven't lasted the course?" she asked casually. "That they haven't resulted in the proposal you wanted?"

"Well, I've been thinking about that," Natalie replied solemnly.

Tara couldn't help but smile at her earnestness. When faced with a question like that women often blamed themselves – their weight, their clothes, their attractiveness. But, she suspected, not this woman.

"I suppose some men might be quite frightened of me. Now, not wanting to blow my own trumpet here, but, as you know, I'm very successful in what I do. I have my own place here in London, a fantastic social life, lots of good friends and a bloody great lifestyle. So when it comes to men, perhaps I'm not really giving off the right vibes – you know, the 'nicey-wifey' type vibes. I think I might be too self-sufficient, too independent for them to think seriously about marrying me. And that's what I've been trying to change."

Tara thought for a moment before speaking. "OK, so you treat the entire process like a piece of PR then?"

"What?"

"Well, you just admitted that you think that you, the real you, isn't doing the job. You think men are threatened by you. So you consciously try to change that."

"I suppose I do, yes."

"So if you try to control the way the man you're with thinks about you, you don't really behave like yourself around men then, do you?"

"What? Of course I do!"

"No, you don't. Maybe you think you do, but, Natalie, from what you're telling me, you don't. Don't you think that's a strange irony? That you're so focused on directing the relationship where you want it to go that you don't seem to focus on whether or not *you* actually want it – or if you're really enjoying it? You said that you went to a cricket game with some guy, even though you hate cricket?"

"Well, yes. But relationships are all about give and take, aren't they?"

"Of course they are, but didn't this imply that you were prepared to sacrifice your own enjoyment simply to take the relationship to the next level?"

"I suppose that could be true. But it didn't matter – I had nothing else on so . . ." The rest of her sentence trailed off.

"Still, by doing this, you effectively compromised your own enjoyment in the hope of moving the relationship forward. How did you know that you even liked this man enough to want to settle down with him?"

"I suppose I didn't," Natalie said simply.

"OK, then," Tara clarified, "from what you've told me, you meet a man, start going out with him and then do your utmost to push the relationship to where you want to get it. You don't seem to believe in letting things just run their course and go where they will. Instead, you're determined to direct proceedings – yes?"

"But I can't afford to just wait around for things to happen!" Natalie argued. "That's not in my nature."

"I know, but think about what you're really doing. Aren't you trying to control and manipulate your relationships in the same way you try to control and manipulate your clients? Don't get me wrong, I can completely understand why you do it, but the important thing is that it's not yielding the results you want."

On the other end of the line, Natalie was silent.

Tara went on softly. "Natalie, don't you think that you're so obsessed with your long-term goal – that is, the ring on your finger – that you haven't given any thought to what will happen after that? Tell you what, let's imagine that one day you do achieve that goal – how will you feel then?"

"I'll be the happiest woman alive!" Natalie joked, but Tara sensed there was truth behind her words.

"Happy that you've found a man you really love and that you can happily spend the rest of your life with? Or happy because you've finally got the ring on your finger? Have you ever really thought about what might happen after that, Natalie?"

"Not really," she admitted shamefully.

"Look, I'm sorry if this sounds harsh to you, but the

point I'm trying to get across is that you need to think seriously about what happens after the ring and the big white wedding. You need to think long-term. My advice for when you meet this guy Jay on Friday night would be to try your utmost to put the long-term aim out of your mind. Try and decide if you actually like him or enjoy spending time in his company. If all you focus on is whether or not he might be the one, you've lost the battle."

"All right then," Natalie replied gamely. "I promise I'll do just that." She paused for a second. "Thing is, he really *could* be the –"

"Natalie."

"OK, OK, I'll try and control myself."

"And, speaking of control," Tara said, a smile in her voice, "I don't want you sleeping with him on the first date either."

In preparation for what lay ahead, Tara had earlier got some indication of how Natalie usually behaved on a first date so she knew this piece of advice would *not* go down well.

"What?" Natalie's reaction was as she'd anticipated. "But, Tara, you should *see* him – he's so sexy!"

"Maybe, but if you do that you're clouding the issue."

"But why not? It's going to happen anyway, so why delay the inevitable?"

"Haven't you ever heard of playing hard to get?"

Natalie was petulant. "I tried that once, and the guy told me I was a prick-tease and never called me again."

"Well, did you ever stop to think that he might just not have been the right guy for you?" Tara felt the need to speak frankly. Unlike most of her clients, she already knew enough about Natalie to know that she didn't respond to subtlety. "Natalie, I hate to say it but don't you think that by sleeping with these guys too easily you're killing off the chase? Taking away all the mystery?"

"Mystery? What mystery? If a guy asks me out on a date in the first place he obviously fancies me – if I go, I fancy him too. Where's the mystery?"

"But what about romance, seduction, delayed gratification?"

"That's just a female thing – men don't like that."

"And who told you that?"

"Another ex-boyfriend. He reckons that women's magazines have fried our brains. Men don't care about the mental stuff: they're led by their anatomy."

"Well, if that was the case, how do people stay married, stay with the one woman for the rest of their lives? There has to be more to it, doesn't there?"

"Look, Tara, maybe things are different where you come from, but here, women are more sexually liberated. We don't beat around the bush, as it were."

Tara's eyes widened, then she smiled despite herself. "Natalie, I really don't think this has anything to do with where you come from. The fact is that by going straight to sex you're killing off the prospect of romance. What about fun? Look, if this is going to work, you really will have to try and change your approach. The first piece of advice I'm going to give you – and please try to stick to it – is: you are *not* to sleep with Jay on Saturday night."

"But he'll think I'm a prude or a prick-tease or –"

"Get those stupid expressions out of your head. The guys who told you that have nothing to do with anything. You need to change your approach, that's what you told me, isn't it?" Tara had long since dispelled with the usual life-coaching principles. Rather than the softly softly approach, some serious straight-talking was in order when it came to Natalie.

"Yes."

"Right then," Tara said determinedly. "We're changing your approach. Now, where's he taking you on Friday?"

"Some posh French place in Covent Garden."

"Nice."

"Not really – I'm not really into truffles and foie gras and all that. We do so much of that kind of entertaining during work that it gets rather boring after a while. To be honest, I'd much rather a nice Tex-Mex or something."

"Well, did he ask if the restaurant was OK with you?"

"Yes."

"And did you tell him you'd rather not go for fine dining?"

"No – if he wants to do that, it's fine by me."

"OK, we'll let it pass for a first date, but remember what I said before about you not being yourself. You must stop that, OK?"

"OK."

"So, when Jay arranges something for your next date – if there is one and, by God, I'm determined there will be – and you don't like where you're going, you'll have to speak up."

It amazed Tara how full of contradictions Natalie was. She'd happily swap bodily fluids with the man, yet was afraid to be upfront in the simplest of ways. Unconvinced that Natalie truly understood the message she was trying to put across, Tara decided to put it across in another way.

"May I be blunt?" she asked her.

"Please do."

"Well, don't you think that if a guy wanted a wishy-washy, do-anything-to-please him girlfriend that he'd be much better off just buying himself a blow-up doll?"

When there was no reply from Natalie for some time, Tara briefly wondered if she'd gone too far. Then, on the other end of the line there came a burst of laughter.

"Bloody hell!" Natalie chuckled. "You don't pull any punches, do you?"

Chapter 19

One evening, about a week after their return from Belfast, Eric announced yet again over dinner that he was going out for a while.

"Where to?" Liz asked, her heart dropping like a stone.

"I'm just popping down to Mum's," he replied, as he got up from the kitchen table. "I haven't seen her in a few days."

"But it's your first night off in weeks," she said, disappointment coursing through her. Couldn't he go at least a few days without seeing *her*, whoever she might be?

You know damn well it's Emma Harrington and the sooner you admit that the better, Liz admonished herself, her heart twisting as unbidden images of Emma and her husband together filled her brain.

But she couldn't do that, not just yet, she thought,

trying to get a grip on things. Because as soon as Liz admitted to herself that Eric really was having an affair, then her life as she knew it was over. She couldn't carry on like this – *they* couldn't carry on like this, pretending that everything was OK on the outside, when inwardly they were both falling apart. Well, Liz was anyway. Maybe Eric was finding this all very straightforward and *she* was the one feeling the strain.

"I know, but I promised Mum I'd call and see her this week," Eric told her. "She's probably still feeling a bit down after the funeral."

"OK then, why don't we all go?" Liz suggested, trying to keep her voice casual. "We'll leave the washing-up till later. I'm sure she'd like to see Toby too."

At this, she could clearly see his facial muscles twitch. "Well, yeah, good idea, but won't one of us have to stay behind and look after the dogs?"

"Oh right, I'd almost forgotten." Liz *had* forgotten all about the dogs and the fact that one of them was being collected tonight. "I suppose I'd better stay."

"You don't mind me taking Toby, then?" Eric seemed thoughtful. "You're right, I'm sure Mum *would* like to see him."

Liz sat back, her mind racing. He wouldn't dream of involving their son in one of his trysts, would he? No, she was being over-sensitive now. If Eric was taking Toby with him, then he evidently *was* planning to visit his mother and her mind was simply running away with her. There was no question but that he wouldn't stoop so low as to bring his son, *their* son, to a meeting with Emma. Because if there was, then Eric really was no longer the man she'd fallen in love with and a million miles away from the man she'd married.

When Eric had settled Toby in his pushchair, and the two were ready to leave, Liz bent down and lightly kissed the top of Toby's head.

"OK, then," she told the two people she loved most in the world. "Have fun."

"He looks like you," Emma said, laughing gaily.

"Do you think so? Everyone else says he looks like Liz."

"Naw, he's too good-looking," she joked.

"That's not very nice."

"Oh, you know I'm only joking, Eric. Don't take it all so seriously." She sat back down on the park bench, the two having once again convened at their preferred meeting place, the park behind the castle.

Eric shifted uncomfortably in his seat. He hadn't liked the idea of taking Toby with him, but Liz was right, it had been a while since his mother had seen her grandson and it would have looked odd if he hadn't wanted to bring him. So, in order to avoid suspicion about his whereabouts, he had indeed gone to visit his mother. But only briefly.

And he'd got even more of a fright when, within about five minutes of their arrival at the park, they'd spotted someone walking along the pathway towards the river.

"Shit, who the hell is that?" Eric asked, his face paling at the thought of someone seeing them together – and with Toby here too!

Emma too looked concerned, but as the person drew closer, they realised it was no one they knew. Eventually, having bid them a friendly hello as he passed, the man, who was carrying a fishing rod, continued further down the river.

"Relax – it's nobody from around here – probably just some tourist doing a spot of fishing."

Thank God, Eric thought silently. Now he turned to Emma, who this evening was looking very pretty, dressed in a pair of tailored trousers and a pattered top, her bump now becoming visible beneath it.

"So how are you feeling?" he asked.

She made a face. "Like death. Although at least the morning sickness seems to have calmed down a bit. But I've put on lots of weight and it's driving me mad. My face looks like somebody stuffed cotton wool in my cheeks and my breasts are getting bigger by the day! Although maybe that's not such a bad thing, eh?" she added jokingly.

Despite himself, Eric reddened. "It's good that you're over the morning sickness anyway," he said, gulping slightly. "But how do you feel about, you know, everything else?"

She rolled her eyes. "Tara and my mum are still driving me mad – trying to find out who the father is and why I'm hiding it. But they can keep trying." She looked at him. "How's everything with you?"

Eric sighed. "Things are getting worse. You know Liz and I were away last weekend?"

"Sure, how did it go?" Emma tried to sound off-hand.

"The usual. She spent the entire time talking about Toby and the house and the dogs – it's all she cares about now. It's as though I no longer have a part to play in her little world." He sat forward. "At one stage, I was almost tempted to come right out and tell her."

"You can't," Emma warned. "Not yet – not until it's all sorted."

"I know, but I feel so guilty keeping secrets from her. After all, this affects her future too."

Emma put a hand on his arm. "Promise me you'll give it just a little more time before you tell her. Now is not the right time. And if she finds out that *I'm* involved, all hell will break loose. She'll want to throttle me!"

"Liz wouldn't dream of doing something like that." Despite his guilt or perhaps because of it, Eric felt obliged to defend his wife.

"Right," Emma snorted, "I'm sure she's a *very* understanding person."

"She is actually."

"OK then, how understanding would she be if she found out that you've brought your son to one of our meetings?"

He bowed his head. "It wasn't like that. I didn't bring him here on purpose, and we went to see Mum first."

"Liz might not see it that way."

"I know.

Emma reached across and kissed him on the cheek. "Look, try not to worry about it too much for the moment. We'll think of something. In the meantime, we'll both keep our mouths shut – about everything, OK?"

"OK."

"It'll all work out for the best, I promise you."

"Will it?" Eric asked, thinking that things certainly couldn't get much worse than they'd been recently.

Chapter 20

Natalie's first date went spectacularly well. That Friday night, she took Tara's advice and admitted from the outset to Jay that the restaurant was wonderful, but truthfully she'd prefer something a little less formal.

"I get so much of this kind of thing with work," she told him, her tone apologetic, but not too much. No simpering, Tara had warned her.

Jay laid down his leather-bound menu. "You know, you're right. I'm the very same. We entertain clients in places like this all the time, and while the food is great, it's nice to be able to go somewhere where you get by with using just one bloody fork instead of four."

"Or maybe even eat with your fingers," Natalie added.

Jay picked up the wine menu and gave it a cursory glance. "Or have a cold beer instead of a fifty-pound bottle of wine."

"Mmm, now you're talkin'," she said, before cocking her head towards the corner of the dining room. "Or listen to rock music, instead of frightful screaming accordions."

Jay laughed and followed her gaze to where the restaurant's resident musician was happily providing what had to be described as very much *foreground* music. While it stamped an air of French authenticity on the place, it was invasive and largely not conducive to cosy chat. Although the restaurant was expensive and upmarket, it was also very much in demand, and private tables were at a premium here, so much so that Natalie and Jay were practically bumping elbows with the party seated at the table next to them. That particular evening, the place was full of self-important business types, all of whom were too busy trying their best to look sophisticated to enjoy themselves.

"I'm sorry," Jay said, evidently reading her thoughts. "I've made a mess of this already, haven't I? Here was I thinking you'd be impressed by all this grandeur when all the time you're hankering for TGI Friday's."

Natalie grinned. "Well, perhaps not quite there, but somewhere a little more fun, maybe?" Then she realised something. With all her talk about purple carpets and purple cocktails and now TGIF's Jay would think she was a right chav!

When she said this to him, he laughed out loud.

"No, I just think you're someone who knows how to have fun," he replied cheerily.

"I suppose that's what it's all about, though, isn't it?"

she said, echoing Tara's earlier words. "Having fun."

And to Natalie's surprise, she believed them. For once, she wasn't concentrating on whether or not she looked good in the dress, or if her make-up had run, or when she'd get to meet Jay's mother – instead she was concentrating on just enjoying being with him. And she admitted to herself, she didn't have to try too hard to do that.

Also, knowing that the decision of whether or not to sleep with him had already been made – "Most certainly *not*!" Tara had ordered – there was a certain freedom in just kicking back and relaxing.

All throughout dinner, she and Jay entertained themselves by trying to apply silly chain-restaurant names to the fine-food dishes they'd ordered (Jay's truffles were 'Viagra Mushrooms' and Natalie's rare-cooked duck was 'Quacking Daffy'). They'd laughed so much that at one stage the resident musician had come over to their table in an attempt to drown out the noise.

"This is terrible," Jay joked. "We really should be giving these lovely truffles the respect they deserve."

Natalie looked down at her meal. If she was going to be honest, she might as well be honest about everything.

"Do you know something? I really don't know what all the fuss is about."

Jay raised an eyebrow. "About truffles?"

"Yes. At eight hundred quid a pound, I suppose there has to be something to it, and I know the way they can only be found by a certain breed of animal is believed to be very romantic and so on. But tell me, how on earth is the idea of pigs snuffling round dirty ground looking for wild bloody mushrooms romantic?"

Jay's lips were pursed, so she wasn't sure how he'd react to this. She knew how Freya would react – her friend would think that Natalie had taken leave of her senses. "But truffles are simply fabulous, darling!" she'd purr, irrespective of whether or not she really enjoyed them. No, the fact that truffles were considered a delicacy and so expensive only a certain type of person could afford them – Freya's type – would be enough for her. Personally Natalie had never understood what all the frenzy was about and, by admitting this to Jay, she was, without knowing it – and possibly for the first time in her dating life – using a subconscious test on him.

Jay looked at her. "Is it a case of Emperor's New Clothes, do you think?"

"Would it be so awful if I told you that's *exactly* what I think?" she replied, setting down her knife and fork.

Then, to her surprise, Jay nodded vigorously. "Well, I do enjoy the taste, but I know what you mean about the hysteria. Everyone else raves so much about the bloody things, you'd wonder if they had magical properties."

"*Phew!* So I'm not the only one then!"

"I doubt it very much," Jay told her, smiling. "You know as well as I do how the glitterati fall over themselves to appear exclusive, when all they're doing is following the horde." Then he smiled wickedly. "So if we're going to take the piss out of expensive delicacies, what are your thoughts on caviar? Horrible bloody stuff, isn't it?"

By the end of the evening, Natalie's sides ached from laughing, and for once she didn't worry about whether or not she'd impressed him enough to want to see her again. In fact, it was no longer an issue – during dinner Jay had already promised to take her to the Hard Rock Café the following weekend.

"Then we can do the reverse – their curly fries will be 'delicately sautéed potatoes' and their burgers 'ground-up fillet de boeuf with tomato jus'," he joked, as they went out to the street afterwards, Jay casually linking her arm in his as if it was the most natural thing in the world.

"I'll have to have a proper think about what to call buffalo wings then," she replied, enjoying the unforced intimacy. He wanted to see her again and they'd had a great night tonight!

Tara was an absolute genius.

The second date was even better. They did go to TGI Friday's for Saturday lunch (apparently there was a waiting list for the Hard Rock Café, something Jay found hilarious) and again spent the entire time taking the piss out of the menu, while trying to speak over *The Best of Bon Jovi* blasting out over the speakers.

"Lunch is good," Tara had declared approvingly, during their last coaching session. "It means he wants to spend time getting to know you, instead of simply wanting to jump your bones."

"I don't know if that's a good or a bad thing," Natalie murmured. "He's gorgeous, successful, good fun – why hasn't anybody snapped him up yet?"

"You're gorgeous, successful and good fun too – why hasn't anyone snapped *you* up yet?" Tara retorted before launching into another diatribe on how Natalie really should think of herself as the prize catch, instead of the other way round.

She was unbelievably bossy when she wanted to be.

Now, sitting in TGIF's staring at the remains of her "boeuf" burger and listening to Jay recite funny anecdotes from Labyrinth's most recent event, she wondered why she had ever bothered with a loser like Steve, whose idea of interesting conversation was how Chelsea's latest signing had turned out to be the greatest load of bollocks.

When they'd finished, Jay once again insisting on paying the bill, Natalie wondered what on earth they were going to do next. It was the middle of the afternoon, for goodness sake – it wasn't like they could spend the rest of the time wandering around the shops.

Still, she supposed they could go for one or two quiet drinks somewhere. No, on second thoughts, she'd better not suggest that. Tara would *not* be impressed if Natalie ended up getting sloshed in some pub and then launched herself on Jay, which is exactly what would happen if they went for "a quiet drink".

She looked across the table at Jay, who was busily signing his credit card slip.

"So, are you heading away somewhere now – back

to the office, perhaps?" she asked, when they got up to leave.

He frowned. "Why on earth would I do that?"

Recalling how Steve often used to abandon her for the office at weekends, Natalie was just about to say something about him being very busy and all that, when she remembered Tara's words about being too simpering. She shouldn't let him think that she believed his work was more important than their time together – that was laying the groundwork for bad habits in the future, she reminded herself.

Instead she smiled. "Well, I'm glad to hear it. I'd no intention of being brought out to lunch, and then dropped like a hot potato in the middle of the afternoon."

"Believe me, there will be no hot-potato-dropping today – with luck there won't be anything dropping," he said, raising a cryptic eyebrow at her.

"What?"

He smiled but ignored her question.

Outside, on the street, she watched, confused but intrigued, as he hailed a black cab.

When they got in, she heard him ask for Jubilee Gardens on the South Bank.

"What's going on, Jay?" she asked, not too thrilled at the idea of having to duck and dive through one of London's busiest tourist spots. "Why are we going there?"

"I want to do something different," he said, his dark eyes twinkling. "Have you ever been on the London Eye?"

Natalie groaned inwardly, her initial anticipation rapidly deflating. This wasn't her ideal way of spending a Saturday afternoon. With the capacity to handle hundreds of visitors every hour, a trip on the London Eye wouldn't exactly be relaxing. For one thing, they'd be queuing for up to an hour just to get a ticket for the wheel, and then another queuing to get onto the bloody thing! Not to mention eventually being packed inside a tiny capsule with fifty-odd other sardines of various nationalities!

"Well, no – I know it's strange, the thing has been there for six years, but I've just never got round to it. Probably because there are so many bloody queues. Are you sure you want to do this? We'll be there for a while."

Jay nodded. "So what – it'll be a laugh, won't it?"

Wonderful! Natalie thought, as she slunk back down on the backseat of the cab. Now, if Tara were here, she'd probably advise her to put her foot down and inform Jay that she had no intention of standing in the freezing cold for up to three hours in Prada heels waiting to get onto a bloody tourist attraction!

But she just couldn't bring herself to do it. Jay was almost childlike in his enthusiasm for this and seemed to think it would be a great way to spend the afternoon. And because he had at least made the effort to do something fun and different, Natalie thought she shouldn't really complain. Well, wait until he realised just how bad the queues really were. Then he might change his mind pretty fast!

"Here you go, mate – seven quid please."

As she got out of the taxi and stood on the bridge waiting for Jay, Natalie looked down at the crowds gathered along the bank of the river and tried to establish how busy it was. Again, she groaned inwardly.

People were swarming around in their hundreds, all of them no doubt heading towards the London Eye. Almost instinctively, the soles of her feet began to throb, probably in protest at the notion of having to stand in impossibly high heels for a couple of hours. This was crazy – she'd have to say something. Effort or no effort . . .

"Jay, are you sure you want to do this today? It looks frightfully busy."

"It does, doesn't it?" he said, lightly holding her elbow as she tentatively negotiated the stone steps down to the pier. "But we're not in any rush, are we?"

"Well, no, not really, but . . ." Natalie grimaced as he wandered on ahead of her towards the attraction's entrance, seemingly oblivious to the crowds and the fact that he'd bypassed the ticket office and instead was heading directly to the boarding area. She shook her head. Evidently, he didn't realise the extent of the wait, and she hoped fervently that he'd change his mind pretty smart when one of the security guys told him where to go.

"Natalie – over here!"

But strangely enough, she noticed, as Jay beckoned her to follow him, the staff surrounding the metal detector hadn't told him off. Instead they were holding back the crowds in order to let them through.

"What's going on?" she asked, pink-cheeked with embarrassment, as a couple of tourists who'd been just about to go through the gate muttered profanities at them.

"Why are we skipping the queue?"

"If you could just wait until the capsule comes round, Mr Murray," a security guy was saying, and Jay nodded his head politely, a self-satisfied look on his face.

"Jay?" she asked again.

"I knew you probably wouldn't want to wait around . . . especially in those shoes," he said with a grin. "So I made some alternative arrangements."

"Alternative . . . what?"

"Here we are, mate!"

Natalie stared as an empty capsule stopped at the boarding gate and the security people ushered them inside.

No, she corrected herself as she stepped into the capsule, it wasn't quite empty. To one side stood a small table and perched upon it was a bottle of Cristal cooling alongside a pair of tall champagne flutes. She'd only just about managed to take in this surprising sight when she realised that the doors had closed behind them, leaving Jay and her on their own inside.

Natalie looked at him, open-mouthed. "How did you . . . where did you?"

Jay looked sheepish. "I wanted to do something different. I know the guys here – we've booked private capsules for a number of different events over the last few years – so it wasn't too difficult. I thought it might be nicer with just the two of us, rather than being crammed into another one full of tourists."

"*Nicer* – it's fantastic!" she cried.

As she looked around the empty capsule, at the champagne and everything else, Natalie didn't know what to say. And just then, she felt tears prick at the corner of her eyes. No one had *ever* done anything like this before – something so special and thoughtful and . . . romantic.

It felt . . . strange.

"Oh shit, have I seriously fucked up?" Jay asked, looking concerned. He reached across and cautiously laid a hand on her arm. "You're not afraid of heights, are you? Because if you are, I can try and get them to let us out before we move up any further and –"

"No," Natalie sniffed and shook her head from side to side, unable to speak for a couple of seconds. Then she straightened up, telling herself that she must not make an idiot of herself over this. She looked at Jay. "It's such a lovely surprise. I . . . never expected anything –"

"Well, thank goodness for that," Jay interjected, his shoulders visibly relaxing. Then walking over to the other side of the capsule, he took the uncorked champagne out of its cooler and went to fill a glass. He glanced hesitantly at the bottle and then again at Natalie. "I wasn't sure what you'd like, so I went for –"

"Are you mad?" she cried, practically snatching the glass of bubbly from him. "Who *doesn't* like Cristal?"

"Well, seeing as you seem to have such strong opinions on things like this," Jay laughed, as he filled his own glass, "I'd hate to get it wrong."

"No chance of that today," Natalie replied with a smile.

He joined her at the front of the capsule as the wheel moved slowly upwards.

Then, as they lightly clinked glasses and continued to stare at the panoramic view of the city of London beneath them, Natalie suspected that Jay Murray was a man who very rarely got things wrong.

Chapter 21

"He's just too easy-going sometimes," Tara grumbled to Liz.

The two were in The Coffee Bean in the village, and Tara was grumbling about the way Glenn had run around looking after Emma when she'd stayed the previous weekend.

"I mean – it's not that I mind Emma coming to stay, of course I don't, but I hate the way she just drops in unannounced and expects to be entertained! And I wouldn't mind, but Glenn was nice as pie to her all weekend, and then as soon as she's gone, he goes back to leaving dirty dishes all over the place for me to clean up! I mean, honestly!"

Liz said nothing, and too late Tara realised that the last person she should be complaining to about Emma was Liz. But unfortunately, old habits died hard. Liz had spent years listening to Tara moaning about her sister and knew well what she was like. But that was no excuse and just then Tara felt like an insensitive idiot. But of course she couldn't let on to Liz that she had her suspicions about Eric and Emma too, could she?

She took a sip of her coffee. "So, you and Eric didn't get much of a chance to talk while in Belfast?" she queried. It was obvious by Liz's demeanour that nothing had changed.

"No, we didn't get much of a chance to talk about anything, other than Toby or the house or the dogs. He was just so distant, Tara." Tears prickled at Liz's eyes. "And I just wish I had the courage to ask him straight out if he was seeing someone. That's what any normal self-respecting woman would do, isn't it?"

"It's not always that straightforward," Tara replied, thanking her lucky stars once again that she'd stuck with Glenn. Between Liz and Natalie (although admittedly things were starting to look positive there), she wondered if men were really worth all the hassle.

Liz was still talking. "I'm praying that it's just my imagination going into overdrive, that I'm seeing things that aren't really there. But yet, deep down I know that something isn't right. Why else would he be spending so much time away from me and Toby? Why else does he go out in the evenings for no particular reason?" Then she looked at Tara and blurted quickly. "I think it might be someone from Castlegate."

Tara held her breath. "Do you?"

Reading between the lines, she knew that Liz was trying to broach the subject of Emma, but she just couldn't bring herself to do it. And Tara couldn't do it either, because she knew that once it was out in the open, their friendship would be fractured forever. Even though Tara had no control over Emma's (or indeed Eric's) behaviour, whatever way you looked at it there was a clear clash of loyalties. The problem was that Tara wasn't exactly sure where her loyalties lay. Yes, Emma was her sister but, if she was carrying on with Tara's best friend's husband, that would be very difficult to forgive.

"Tara," Liz said then, glancing sadly at Toby, who was sitting in his buggy alongside the table, "would you have any idea, any idea at all, who it might be? Who Eric might be seeing?"

Tara could see that Liz was steeling herself for the worst, steeling herself for the fact that she could very well be the last to know what the rest of the village already did, and her heart bled for her friend.

"Do you honestly think, if I knew for definite that Eric was fooling around with someone here, that I wouldn't tell you? Of course I would! After I'd given him a punch in the nose!" she added vehemently, meaning it.

Liz gave a half-hearted smile.

"Who's punching who?" Colm magically appeared at the table, bearing a tray of freshly prepared cheesecake.

"No one," Tara said abruptly.

"Well, I hope it's not you punching poor Glenn!" he joked as he unloaded the cheesecake, but by the look on Tara's face he quickly wished he hadn't. "Jeez, aren't you two a couple of rays of sunshine?" he said, rolling his eyes at them both before sidling off in the other direction.

Liz raised a smile. "I think you might have been a bit hard on him there."

"Serves him right for listening to other people's conversations," Tara muttered, and a brief silence fell upon the table as the two women made inroads into their respective plates of cheesecake.

"I hate this," Liz said eventually.

Tara looked up. "What?"

"This. The two of us sitting here depressed and miserable, and me moaning again about bloody Eric! I feel bad you coming all the way down here to visit me and all I do is whinge, whinge, whinge."

Tara didn't mind at all, but the whinging (as she called it) certainly wasn't doing Liz any good. She took a deep breath. Maybe it was time for drastic action.

She set down her fork. "All right then. Let's do something fun – something that'll cheer us both up."

"What – now?" Liz said, taken aback.

"I don't mean now – I mean tonight or tomorrow night – soon. Can you even remember the last time the two of us went out somewhere?"

Liz looked guilty. "I know, and I'd love to but –"

"But nothing. Eric is off nights this week, yes?"

Liz nodded.

"Well, you've put up with enough of his disappearances over the last few weeks – let him put up with one of yours. Come out with me tonight, and let Eric look after Toby and the dogs for a change."

Liz looked at her son doubtfully. "I don't know . . ."

"Why not? Surely you deserve a night out too? Let Eric take the responsibility for once. I'm sure he'd jump at the chance to have a boys' night in with his son. You said yourself he doesn't get enough time with him. And I'm sure Glenn won't mind – it just means he'll be free to get lost in cyberspace without feeling as though he has to sit downstairs watching telly with me." Tara squeezed her friend's hand. "Come on, Liz, we'll have a ball!"

Later that evening, Liz was getting ready to go out and hit the hotspots of Castlegate village.

To her surprise, Eric had readily agreed to look after Toby and hadn't batted an eyelid when she'd informed him that she and Tara were thinking of going out for drinks.

Liz, who'd been expecting some kind of argument, or at least a barrage of questions about her plans, was relieved, but also a little uneasy. Eric didn't seem to give a damn about her life lately. It was almost as though they were beginning to live separate lives, with Toby as their one remaining connection. She wondered how much longer this could go on.

But she wasn't going to think about it now, she told herself, as she stood in her bedroom and tried to decide what to wear. Tara was right: there was no point in trying to second-guess what was going on in her husband's head; she'd drive herself crazy. No, tonight was about having some long overdue fun with her best friend, and knowing Tara, it was bound to be a good night – never mind that Castlegate wasn't exactly hot and happening and the bars were more *The Quiet Man* than *Sex and The City*.

She searched through her wardrobe, trying to find something decent to wear, something that at least wouldn't make her look such an overweight frump alongside Tara. To her dismay, she realised that all her clothes were dark, dowdy and downright depressing and mostly consisted of shapeless tops and too-big jeans, a throwback to her post-pregnancy days.

Before she became pregnant with Toby she wouldn't have been seen dead in block colours, and had a selection of vibrant, multicoloured tops and dresses that showed off a pair of legs that back then would have made Liz Hurley jealous.

And of course in those days she'd had the figure to wear them, whereas now she was still carrying the extra stone and a half she'd gained while pregnant. Which was also the main reason she hadn't gone clothes shopping in ages – all those gorgeous flimsy tops and clingy dresses she loved, but now hadn't a hope of fitting into, mocking her into hiding. Hence the uninspiring wardrobe better suited to a convent than even Castlegate's finest.

Liz sighed. How had she so easily let herself go? Since she'd had the baby, moved to Castlegate and started working with the dogs (who, in fairness, couldn't care less what Liz wore as long as they were fed and watered), she hadn't given her appearance much thought. Despite her energetic walks with the dogs, she'd made no real effort to shift the weight, and of course with Eric away most evenings it was all too easy to sit in front of the telly with a four-stone bag of Minstrels and a gallon of Coke. No wonder Eric had gone off her, she thought as she examined herself in the mirror. She was turning into Jabba the Hutt!

"Liz, Tara's here!" Eric called down the hallway, and Liz jumped. Shit! Tara – here – now? She was nowhere *near* ready!

"OK, I'll just be a second!" she called back, hoping that her friend wouldn't mind waiting a few more minutes.

She riffled through her wardrobe once more and eventually chose an ancient pair of black straight-leg trousers and a black chiffon top. A nice, safe but utterly boring option.

Having got dressed, Liz caught sight of herself in the mirror, not exactly thrilled by what she saw. Was it a fun night out or a funeral she was dressing for? She hoped against hope that Tara wasn't dressed in one of those up-to-the-minute outfits she wore for nights out in the city and had toned down the style a little for rural Castlegate. But no, if anything, Tara would no doubt make double the effort at looking glam here – primarily with the express intention of getting up some of the more disapproving villagers' noses!

Just then there was a soft knock at the bedroom door. "Liz?" she heard Tara call from outside. "Can I come in?"

"Sure." Deciding that she'd just have to make do, Liz went to the dressing-table and quickly began to apply some make-up.

Liz had been right about Tara's chosen outfit. She entered the room wearing a flamboyant emerald and purple patterned top over skinny indigo jeans and stiletto boots. A shimmering purple headscarf held back her golden locks and, with her chunky beaded necklace and bohemian gold hoop earrings, she looked dazzling – an exotic butterfly to Liz's garden-variety housefly.

All of this must have been written on Liz's face because the very first words out of Tara's mouth were: "What's wrong?" She quickly raised a hand to her face. "Did I overshoot my lipstick?" she said jokingly. "Is my mascara running . . . what?"

Liz had to laugh. "No, no, you look perfect, stunning in fact. And I look like such a bloody frump beside you." She sighed and stared again at her reflection in the mirror. "Tara, when did I turn into a middle-aged woman? No, I take that back – most middle-aged women look a million times better than I do these days."

"Don't be silly, you look great! Although, you could probably do with a little more colour. Here!" She quickly removed her sparkling headscarf and tied it jauntily around Liz's neck.

Instantly the outfit came to life and Tara's cheery optimism (and her nifty accessorising) had the effect of erasing all of Liz's insecurities and buoying her mood.

"Oh, I couldn't . . ." she began, wishing that instead

of whinging about her lack of colourful clothes, she'd thought about accessorising what she had. But that was Tara, full of great ideas.

"Of course you can – it's gorgeous on you," Tara replied, waving away her protests. "Now, do you have a thick bangle, or some dangly earrings perhaps? Something like that and a pair of silver strappy heels, and we're away!"

"Will these do?" Liz held up a pair of drop diamante earrings and Tara nodded her approval. Then, quickly finishing her make-up, Liz checked her appearance once more before they headed back out to the living room and said goodbye to Eric and Toby.

"Have a good night," Eric said with a smile, and Toby, who didn't seem in the least bit bothered that his mum was leaving him, waved half-heartedly as she went out the door.

So much for being indispensable, she thought wryly, as she and Tara went on their way. She'd thought that there'd be mighty histrionics when she went to leave. But, she supposed, this was even better – now she didn't have to feel guilty.

Feeling happier and more confident than she'd been in ages, Liz followed her best friend down the driveway and prepared for a rip-roaring night out on the town.

As she and Liz made their way across the bridge to the centre of Castlegate village, Tara breathed an inward sigh of relief. This girly night out had been a brainwave.

During the short walk from her house, Liz had been chatty, animated and was behaving much more like her old self.

Tara knew her friend seriously needed the opportunity to have fun and take her mind off things – especially her worries about Eric.

As well as worrying about her marriage, Liz was in all likelihood also feeling a little lonely and out of place while trying to settle into motherhood and life away from Dublin – which was understandable, really. It was plain to see that the move to the sticks hadn't had yet yielded the lifestyle improvements she and Eric had anticipated – if anything it had been the opposite. And while it wasn't as though the villagers here were clannish, Tara knew better than most that they were set in their ways and it could well be very difficult for a "stranger" to easily become part of this community.

At the moment, Liz was simply finding it difficult to adjust, but with a bit of time, she'd be fine.

Tara's heart had gone out to her when she'd seen her standing in front of the mirror, her insecurities about her appearance written all over her face. Though she managed to conceal the fact, she knew at once that Liz had been worrying about what to wear, particularly as she and Eric had been trying to save money in order to do up the cottage, and Liz hadn't gone clothes shopping properly since having Toby. And of course, she was still carrying the few extra pounds she'd put on while pregnant, which Tara understood didn't particularly make you feel like a million dollars. For this reason, she'd insisted that Liz borrow her sparkly head-scarf and wear a pair of glam heels. When it came to boosting self-confidence, Tara was a firm believer in the power of fabulous shoes. Although perhaps some of the male clients she coached might not agree, she thought with a grin.

Now, if Liz were a client of hers, Tara would spend time helping her realise that she was feeling insecure and worried because she was finding it hard to settle and could very well be expressing these feelings as anxieties about her marriage. But Liz *wasn't* a client, so it was doubly important for Tara to refrain from using her coaching techniques in this regard.

Instead, she'd try to do what any decent friend would, and just be there to cheer Liz up and make her feel better about her troubles, rather than try to solve them for her. Liz wouldn't appreciate being "coached" by her best friend and it would be wholly unethical for Tara do so, although it was frustrating watching her wrestling with her insecurities like that. And she had enough on her plate at the moment coaching Natalie – although she wasn't really a friend. She was more of a close acquaintance, really, which is why Tara had eventually acquiesced to helping her out, albeit in a less formal coaching scenario. Still, tonight would be good for Liz, and despite her earlier concerns about her wardrobe, she now seemed raring to go.

Tara looked at her watch. "I booked The Steakhouse for seven thirty, so we've still time to get in a quick drink in The Bridge beforehand."

"Great, I'm absolutely starving, but I wouldn't mind a drink to kick things off."

"Now, now, take it easy, you," Tara scolded good-naturedly. "It's been a while since you've done this, remember?"

"I know and I think that's half the problem," Liz grinned. "It's been so long since I've been out, I can barely remember what the inside of a bar looks like." She pushed open the entrance of the pub and Tara followed her inside. "No, hang on – I think it's coming back to me!" she added with a delighted wink and sounding much more like the old Liz.

The two took a seat at the bar and Tara promptly ordered a glass of champagne for Liz and asked the barman to fill another glass with sparkling lemonade for herself. Liz had been thrilled at this little luxury but the champagne flutes caused much consternation amongst some of the locals present, who thought it outrageous altogether that these two glamour-pusses should be drinking champagne like celebrities (despite the fact that Tara was having mere lemonade). And one of them supposedly married and with a baby! Who did they think they were?

Keenly aware of the stir they were creating, the two girls grinned at one another as they clinked glasses and drank to a good night out, Tara remembering too late that her showy antics had probably scuppered any chance Liz had of fitting in here now! But these begrudgers weren't the kind of people her friend would want to get to know anyway. Quick to criticise and even quicker to judge, that was most of the older inhabitants of Castlegate, and Tara had spent much of her adult life trying to rise above it.

"Hello, Tara – isn't it well you're looking these days?" said a male voice from behind them.

Tara looked around to see Dave McNamara, yet another old school-mate of hers, approach the bar.

"You, too, Dave," she replied warmly. "How have you been? I haven't seen you in ages."

"Not too bad." Dave nodded a greeting at Liz, whom evidently he didn't know.

"This is Liz McGrath," Tara said, remembering her manners. "Liz, meet Dave – he was in the same class as me and Eric. Dave – this is Eric McGrath's wife, Liz. She runs the boarding kennels across town." She was extra careful to give Liz's business a bit of a mention, seeing as Dave was not only the local councillor but also head of the Castlegate Heritage Committee. As a result he was hugely influential in the village and could possibly put some business Liz's way.

"Pleased to meet you, Liz. How *is* Eric these days? Keeping well, I hope."

As Dave flashed Liz his best politician's smile, Tara hid a grin. A notorious womaniser when they were younger, it was no real surprise that Dave McNamara had ended up employing his legendary charm in politics.

"So can I get you two ladies a drink?" he asked, nodding at the barman.

"Thanks, but no, you work away," said Tara. "We're moving on soon."

Dave stood alongside them at the bar as he waited for his pint. "So, I hear that Emma's moved back from Dublin and returned to the Castlegate fold," he said conversationally to Tara. "Any sign of yourself doing the same?"

"No fear of that. Anyway, after all this time I don't think Castlegate would be able for me. Oh, by the way, congratulations!" she said, remembering. "I hear you got engaged recently?"

Dave nodded proudly. "I did indeed. I'll bet you're sorry now you missed the boat! I tried my best with this one a long time ago," he said to Liz, who looked perplexed, "but she didn't want to know, so eventually I had to look elsewhere."

"And look elsewhere you did – everywhere else!" Tara joked, while Dave looked bashful.

"Better not let my other half hear that – she's from out of town and knows nothing about my sordid history."

"Well, she's probably better off." Tara was enjoying teasing him. "But I hear she's lovely, and rumour has it she's also the right one to keep you on your toes! Have you set a date for the wedding?"

"Sometime next year – after the next election anyway."

Tara smiled. "Of *course*."

Dave picked up his newly poured pint. "Well, I better head away now and let the two of you get back to your night out. It was nice seeing you, Tara – and you too, Liz."

"Good seeing you too."

When Dave was out of sight, Liz raised an amused

eyebrow. "He's right," she said, eyes widening, "I think you did miss the boat where he's concerned. He's *very* cute."

"Not my type," Tara said, "but unfortunately it took him a very long time to get the message. Even up to a couple of years ago he was still trying it on, and as a result Glenn can't stand him."

"I can imagine."

Tara grinned. "I suppose I could view it as some form of weird victory that I'm about the only girl in the town he hasn't 'conquered' over the years! I think he even fancied his chances with Emma at one stage," she added, recalling her sister's recent disparaging remarks about Dave. "Anyway he's engaged now, so the women of Castlegate are finally safe – or sorry, depending on who you ask," she added wryly.

Soon after, they decamped to The Steakhouse where for close to two hours they enjoyed a thoroughly satisfying girly chat over steaks the size of Texas.

"This was a brilliant idea, Tara," Liz said, taking another sip from her wineglass. "I didn't realise how much I missed this kind of thing. I suppose I took it all for granted before I had Toby. Not that I'd change things for the world," she added quickly, "but sometimes it's nice to just be me again, not just somebody's mum."

"I know. You and Eric should try and do it more often too. I know it's hard, what with him working all hours and that, but you two spending time together as a couple is important too."

Liz's looked wistful. "You know, I can barely

remember what it was like before we had Toby. How easy it was just to go out to dinner or the pub on the spur of the moment. Now, it's such a military operation that you think it's hardly worth it."

"It's always worth it."

"You're right. Eric and I should do more things like this. But he's been so wrapped up in work, and I've been so wrapped up in the dogs and Toby, that we can't raise the energy at weekends. Not to mention raise any baby-sitters – other than yourself, of course," she added with a smile. "Maeve is no help and . . ." Letting the rest of her sentence trail off, Liz suddenly set down her wineglass. "Do you know something?" she said, and Tara could hear her voice slur a little from the effects of the wine, which she had of course been drinking on her own.

"What?"

"I've been acting like such an idiot lately whinging about Eric and thinking that he would cheat on me! If I really thought about it properly, instead of just jumping to conclusions, then I'd realise that he would *never* do something like that to me. For God's sake, it's not all that long since we had Toby."

Tara wished with all her heart that her friend was right.

"I have to stop feeling sorry for myself like this," Liz went on, after taking another sip from her wineglass. "I have to stop worrying about things and try and be more confident about things – like you. I think I might just talk to Eric about it when we get home and –"

"Liz, I don't know if that's such a good idea – not tonight anyway. Why not wait until both of you are sober, and you have your wits about you?" Tara was mindful of the fact that Eric could very well come right out and admit that he had been having an affair. And that would be a complete disaster.

"I suppose, but I really want to clear the air and find out what's *really* bothering him, instead of making up all these stupid scenarios in my head."

"Seriously, I would wait until tomorrow, at least," Tara persisted. "For when you're fully sober."

"Maybe you're right. But Tara, I have to get it out of my head. It's been driving me mad lately. I'm so miserable and emotional and . . ." Tears sprang to her eyes. "I thought this move would be a good thing for us. I thought that getting out of Dublin and having a quiet life down the country would be brilliant. But it's not. And I don't know whether the problem lies with me or with Eric or with both of us."

"Well, I'm sure you two will get to the bottom of it but there's definitely no point in trying to solve anything tonight. And speaking of getting to the bottom, look at all the wine you've drunk!" Tara said jokingly.

"You're right – who knows what kind of rubbish I'd start spouting!" Liz replied, picking up the bottle and looking surprised at the amount of wine she'd taken.

"Here, have some of this," Tara said, pouring a glass of water for her. "We've still got a few hours of this night left, and I don't want you wimping out on me before time!"

"Thanks, Tara, you're a pal," Liz grinned and took a huge gulp of the water. "But if anything, I'm glad I got that off my chest. Now that I did I can't believe how pathetic it sounds. Eric having an affair – imagine!" Liz gave an amused roll of her eyes and tucked into the remainder of her dessert.

Chapter 22

After dinner, the girls moved on to the pub for one more drink before returning home.

Liz felt on top of the world. It was as though a huge weight had been lifted from her shoulders when she'd finally realised how stupid and paranoid she was being.

But Tara was right. There was no point in talking to Eric about it, especially not tonight and maybe not at all. Instead, she'd just try and get back to her normal self and try not to read something into his every move or utterance.

What had made her distrust him so much in the first place? A few nights out and a text? Big deal – that could happen to anyone. No, she'd talk to Eric about maybe downscaling their plans for the renovations, which would hopefully allow him to work less and stay home more.

And she might bite the bullet and go to some group

or club in order to meet some more people from the community – or network, as Tara might say. And if she ended up getting some more business from the locals, then the kennels might bring in the extra cash they needed.

Fully determined to put her worries behind her and her marriage back on track, Liz followed Tara into The Wishing Well, a lively but comfortable pub situated right in the centre of the village. It had already been a highly enjoyable night, and she was delighted Tara had made her agree to it.

"A white wine spritzer and a Coke, please," Tara told the barman.

While they were waiting for their drinks to be served, Liz looked up and spied a familiar face sitting alone at the opposite end of the bar.

"There's Luke," she cried excitedly to Tara. "And look, he must be here on his own. Let's go over and say hello."

"Ah no, Liz, let's leave it."

"Why?" Liz gave her a strange look. It wasn't like Tara to be unsociable.

"It's . . . well, maybe he wants to be on his own." Tara paid the barman and picked up their drinks.

"I doubt it. He's only new in town, so he probably doesn't know anyone. I'm going over to say hi, anyway. He's my next-door neighbour, and I don't want to be rude."

"Oh, all right then." Tara picked up her drink and grudgingly followed her over.

As the girls approached, Luke looked up and spotted them.

"Well, hello there," he said, his rugged, friendly face lighting up at the sight of them.

"Mind if we join you?" Liz asked and, strangely, she sensed Tara stiffen alongside her. What was the matter with her? It wasn't as though Luke was a stranger – in fact she probably knew him better than Liz did!

"I'd be delighted," he said, nodding a greeting at Tara who did the same back. "Pull up a stool."

"So how come you're back in Castlegate?" Liz asked, settling herself alongside him. He was a lovely guy and, seeing as he would be her next-door neighbour, she was determined to help him settle in. "I thought you wouldn't be starting the move until after Christmas."

"Well, our last stint on the rig went better than we thought, and we hit our quota, so I thought I might as well make a start. There was no point in paying the mortgage on the cottage and rent on my old flat."

"I wish you'd have told me. I could have turned the heat on, or opened the windows, or at least bought in some groceries – something to take the bare feel out of the place."

As Tara had so far said nothing but a brief hello, Liz attempted to try and draw her into the conversation. "Although, I hear Tara gave you a bite to eat last time – you two got to know each other, didn't you?"

"We did," Luke replied, smiling at Tara. "She makes great a fry-up. And she's pretty handy when it comes to pest control too."

"Pest control?" Liz was lost.

"I thought I'd better bring the subject up first, just in case you decided to out me in public," he said, eyeing Tara who smiled mischievously.

"Pity, I was thinking of saving it for ammunition," Tara replied. "Just in case you decided to sue me and Bruno for pooping in your *lovely* garden."

"I told you – it took me ages to get it just like that."

"What?" Liz looked at Tara. What the hell were they talking about? "What did Bruno do?"

"She might be good with mice, but she's not so good with dogs," Luke told Liz. "Or am I allowed to say that?" he added, winking at Tara.

"I mightn't be so good at handling big strong animals, but at least I don't start screaming like a baby at the sight of one the size of my thumb."

"I didn't scream: I shouted – once."

Tara grinned. "No, you screamed – a big girlie, Ned Flanders-type scream."

"I did not –"

"Um, sorry to interrupt but could one of you please tell me what the hell you're talking about?" Liz asked, wide-eyed. "And who is Ned Flanders?"

"Liz doesn't watch *The Simpsons*," Tara informed Luke.

"You don't watch *The Simpsons*?" he repeated in mock horror. "What planet are you on?"

"Well, I don't have time to watch cartoons!" Liz said, getting frustrated. "Anyway, what's all this got to do with pooping in gardens and screaming like a girl?"

Tara and Luke's eyes met.

"You tell her," Tara challenged. "I swore I wouldn't say a thing."

"Pity you didn't keep your word, then," Luke countered, before turning to Liz. "I suppose I'd better come clean. I'm afraid of – no, strike that – I don't particularly like mice."

"Nope, he's terrified of them," Tara interjected, laughing.

Luke silenced her with a look. "I don't *like* mice, but unfortunately they like me, or at least, they like the inside of my house."

"Ah," Liz said, understanding. They had that problem in their house too – especially around this time of the year. But she used one of those electronic plug-in things, the ones with the high-pitched sound that scared the mice out of the house. She wouldn't dream of using one of those horrible mousetraps or anything inhumane like that.

"So, anyway, the last weekend I was here, I was going about my business and cleaning out the cupboards when two of the little feckers leap out at me. Naturally, I got a bit of a fright –"

"And ran screaming from the house like a girl," Tara finished, trying not to laugh.

Luke feigned a glare. "Excuse me, I thought *I* was telling the story."

"Sorry." Tara winked at Liz, while trying to stifle a chuckle.

"And your friend here, suspecting that I might have been in a bit of bother, came running to my rescue."

"What can I say? For a big strong man, he's a bit of a wimp really."

Luke and Tara were now smiling at one another like there was nobody else in the room, and just then, Liz understood why Tara had been initially so hesitant to join him. The sparks were flying in all directions between these two!

She studied her friend, who was still in mid-banter with Luke. Tara was radiant. Her eyes were sparkling with amusement, and her face glowed as she and Luke continued to try and better one another.

God, these two were perfect for one another, and if Tara couldn't see that, she was a fool! As Liz had long since tired of telling her, her friend had spent way too long in the comfort zone, afraid of not being in control, terrified of letting herself get hurt. And while this had worked out well so far for her and Glenn, it was surely inevitable that Tara would need something more, someone who could complete her life in a way that Glenn never could.

Now, looking at the two of them together, it was perfectly clear that they only had eyes for one another, and if Liz decided to slip away without saying anything, they'd hardly notice. She knew Luke was single; he'd told her a while back that his last relationship had finished some time ago, so there was no barrier on his side. Tara, on the other hand . . . well, if she was going to pursue this – and in Liz's opinion she really should – Tara would have to start thinking about herself and what she really wanted. Although, if Glenn were to get wind of the obvious attraction between these two, given what Tara had said about that guy Dave earlier, Liz didn't even want to think about how he'd react.

Still, judging by the banter going on just now between Tara and Luke, she thought wryly, Tara – unlike herself – didn't seem to be at all worried about what Glenn might think!

"I don't know how you sleep at night," Tara was saying now, and Liz tried to tune into their conversation once more.

"Are the mice that bad?" she asked Luke. "You really should invest in one of those plug-in things – then they wouldn't keep you awake at night."

Tara and Luke looked at one another and grinned – *again*. OK, Liz thought, it was starting to get a bit annoying now!

"We stopped talking about the mice ages ago, Liz," Tara said. "I was just asking Luke how he can justify what he does for a living."

"Why should I have to justify it?" Luke gave a nonchalant shrug. "It's what I do."

"Are you joking? Drilling for all that oil? You're raping the earth's resources."

Liz groaned and reached for her drink. "Oh dear God, *please* don't get her started on the environment!"

"Ah, so Tara's a Green, is she?"

"Of course I'm a Green. Why wouldn't I be? Why wouldn't *anyone* be?"

"So, you reuse and recycle and you've got your own compost heap, and all that stuff?"

"Of course." Tara nodded proudly. "We all have to take responsibility for the environment, an environment that the likes of you and your oil companies are destroying."

"I see. So you regularly use recycling centres then?"

"Yep. I take my bottles and cans there every week."

"Every week?" Luke raised an eyebrow. "Well done, you."

"It's not that much of an effort. It's only a few minutes away in the car."

As soon as Tara had said the words, Liz realised that she was blindly falling into the trap Luke was so obviously setting for her. But she said nothing.

"Oh. So you *drive* to the recycling centre, do you?"

Tara hesitated slightly. "Well, I have to – it's a mile away from our house."

"I see. So, it's OK to drive your car and send all that carbon monoxide into the atmosphere because you're going to the recycling centre, is it?"

"Well, no, but . . ."

"Take any holidays recently?" Luke asked then.

Liz smiled. An almighty battle was about to commence, and by the sounds of things, she'd be much better off staying out of it. Tara had finally met her match.

"Yes," Tara replied hesitantly.

"Oh, where did you go?"

Her mouth set in a hard line. "Egypt."

"I see. And did you happen to get on your bike and cycle all the way to Egypt, and then sleep under the stars with the Bedouins, before cycling all the way back home again?"

Tara was silent.

"Well?" he prompted.

She rolled her eyes. "No, I flew."

"What? You flew?" Luke pretended to be aghast. "A conscientious environmentalist like you got into one of those nasty machines that uses jet fuel and pumps out gallons of pollution into the atmosphere? That same atmosphere you're so obsessed with saving?"

Liz wanted to laugh, but one look at Tara's expression made her think better of it.

Luke shook his head. "And you have the nerve to criticise me!"

"Look, I never said anything about going overboard!" Tara cried, totally wrong-footed now. "I just think that all of us should do our bit to help the environment. I mean, what about global warming and the melting icecaps and all that?"

"A myth," Luke said, reaching for his pint. "The atmosphere's been heating up and recooling for centuries. It's nothing new."

"But it is!" Tara retorted. "The icecaps are melting, there are floods and weird weather and droughts and it's all because of –"

"So, you think you can solve all that by bringing a few bottles to the bottle bin? Get real, Tara. The earth's been around for millions – billions of years. Why is it that the likes of us – who have only been around for half a second in the scheme of things – are so bloody egotistical as to think that *we* get to control the environment? The earth survived without human intervention for billions of years, and I'm sure it will do just fine without us."

Liz looked at Tara for a reaction to this, but none was forthcoming. For the first time as long as she'd known her, Liz saw her best friend rendered utterly speechless.

Yep, she thought, shaking her head at the realisation, they really were perfect for one another!

Chapter 23

"He sounds so sweet," Tara sighed on the other end of the telephone line when Natalie told her all about Jay's London Eye surprise.

"He is," she agreed. "It's weird, Tara – I've never had anyone do something like that for me – ever."

"Neither have most of us – but this guy certainly seems to know how to push all the right buttons. You're certain he's not married?"

Natalie could understand why she'd asked the question. She'd wondered the same thing herself, feeling that a man with money, good looks and a personality had to be too good to be true. But no, she and Jay had discussed their respective love lives at length that Saturday when, after their highly enjoyable trip on the Eye, they'd gone for a drink in Momo, a cosy Moroccan-themed wine bar in Mayfair.

She'd discovered that Jay was thirty-six, lived near

Finchley and had worked in events and promotions for twelve years.

"I'm at Labyrinth for almost six years now," he told her. "I love it and we've got an amazing team, but I think I'd like to go out on my own someday."

"I sometimes feel like that," Natalie admitted and with a start realised that she'd never verbalised this largely latent ambition. "But I just don't know if a one-man or *woman* outfit would attract the calibre of client that Blue Moon does."

"You've got an amazing reputation, though – I'm sure that would count for something."

"Do I really?" Natalie teased. "I see someone's been checking up on me."

Jay gave her a sheepish look. "Well, I mentioned your name to a couple of people – all of whom had nothing but good things to say." He smiled. "They were especially complimentary about your bum."

"Sexist bastards!" But Natalie smiled too. She'd never had an issue about using her sexuality in this line of work (within limits of course) and she was pleased to learn that the lipo-removal sessions were paying off. Although, if she continued scoffing burgers at TGI Friday's, that wouldn't be the case for too much longer!

But it was telling that Jay had asked around about her. It meant that he was interested enough to do so – although after what he'd arranged for their date that day, Natalie was no longer concerned about that. Even Tara would have to admit that any man who went to the trouble of arranging a private trip on the London Eye was interested!

"So, you're heading close to the big four-oh then," Natalie stated, taking a sip from her wineglass.

"Yes, and with very little to show for it, unfortunately."

Her eyes widened. "A house in Finchley, a career in the legendary Labyrinth – how's that nothing?"

"It's just material stuff, though, isn't it? And money, success and all that doesn't count for a whole lot when you get down to it."

"So you never married, then?" Natalie asked, seeing as he'd steered the conversation towards the personal stuff.

He gave a faraway smile. "Never really found the right woman, to be honest. Don't get me wrong, I've had my fair share of long-term relationships and 'nearly' women."

"Nearly women?"

"Ones that might have made the cut, but didn't."

"'Made the cut'?" Natalie repeated, raising an eyebrow.

"Jesus, that sounds really pompous," Jay jumped in quickly. "What I meant was that I could have married certain women back then – simply for the sake of getting married. But somehow, I knew deep down it wouldn't last and so I thought what's the bloody point?"

That's the difference between you and me then, Natalie thought suddenly. Because she'd been with lots of men she knew weren't quite right, but wanted to marry them anyway because she just wanted to be married. Jay was right. It was crazy to mess around with something like that, simply for the sake of it.

Tara had of course told her the same thing, but it hadn't really hit her how stupid she'd been about it all until now. At this stage, she could barely remember the faces, let alone the names, of some of the men she'd seriously considered as husband material. She'd been so desperate to settle down, she'd felt that any man at all would do. She'd been that pathetic.

Still, now that she'd come to that realisation, it made her all the more determined not to get it wrong this time. So, she wasn't going to get carried away into thinking that Jay might just be the one, but at the same time, she didn't want to let him slip through her fingers either.

"What do I do next?" she asked Tara now. "Do I phone his office and thank him for a lovely day, or do I text in the hope of organising another one."

"Don't you even think about texting him!" Tara warned her. "I know what you're like with a mobile phone!"

"OK." Recalling her behaviour with Steve, Natalie was duly convinced.

"He didn't say anything about going out again when he dropped you home?" Tara asked her.

"He didn't drop me home as such – he just came as far as my place with me in the cab and then went home to his own. Tara, I was dying to ask him in! Especially after the cocktails at Momo."

"Didn't I tell you not to drink too much?" Tara scolded although her tone was light. "Still, I'm proud that you resisted the temptation all the same."

"Well, I knew I wouldn't hear the end of it from you if I didn't," Natalie grunted. "Still, it leaves me in a bit of a pickle as to what to do next. Maybe he didn't say anything because he was miffed that I didn't ask him in."

"From what you've told me about him already, that doesn't seem his style."

"Yes, but he organised this amazing thing with the London Eye with champagne and all that and got nothing at the end of it?"

"Natalie, I've told you before – it's not about rewarding someone. Just because a man does something nice for you doesn't mean that you have to automatically sleep with him. You have to get out of that mindset."

"Yes, yes, I know. But that still leaves me at a loss as to what to do now."

"You do nothing, my dear," Tara assured her confidently. "You just continue to play it cool, sit tight and let him come to you."

And yet again, Tara called it right. To Natalie's delight, Jay phoned her midweek at work to arrange another date for the following weekend. Natalie was amazed at how much the other girl knew about handling the opposite sex.

"I've got Glenn, haven't I?" Tara laughed, when Natalie told her this. "And through him, I've learned all there is to know about handling men."

"But you're so good at this anyway! And I honestly don't think that the fact Jay is Irish has much to do it. You're just a natural, Tara! I can't understand why you don't become a *dating* coach, instead of just a life coach!"

"Maybe I will after this," Tara quipped, "and while I'm at it, I might become a marriage counsellor, a pregnancy counsellor and, if all else fails, I suppose I could always fall back on a career in pest control."

"Sorry?"

"Oh, never mind," Tara said with a little laugh. "It's just this guy I met recently that lives next door to Liz. He's afraid of mice and, as they don't bother me, he asked me to help chase them out of his house."

Natalie grinned. "Does anything *at all* bother you?"

"What do you mean?"

"Well, you just seem so calm and in control of everything. I thought the same when I met you in Egypt. Nothing seems to faze you."

"Things faze me," Tara replied simply, "but I've learnt over the years not to let anything *really* get to me. What's the point?"

Natalie shook her head. "I really admire you, Tara. You've really got it all under control – you and Glenn, your career, family, friends."

"Under control? I wish!" Tara laughed easily. "Natalie, my youngest sister is pregnant by a mystery man, which of course means the whole family is up in arms, my best friend is going through a marriage crisis and these days Glenn and I are so busy with work that we barely see one another. It's not *half* as calm and controlled as you make it sound!"

"And then you've got me whining on about my relationship problems too," Natalie said, feeling guilty. "God, I'm frightfully sorry, Tara – I really didn't mean to take up so much of your time."

"Oh Natalie, no, don't be silly, that's not at all what I meant! To be honest, I'm enjoying this – and I think we're making very good progress."

"We certainly are!" Natalie laughed, relieved that at least Tara seemed to be getting some enjoyment out of all of this. "But are you sure you've got time to deal with me and my stupid problems too? It sounds as though you've got a lot going on at the moment."

"Natalie, honestly – if I didn't have you to boss around at the end of the day, I don't know what I'd do! So, stop going on about it – I'm really having fun with this, honestly."

"Well, as long as you're sure."

"Believe me – I'm sure."

"Your sister is still keeping mum about the father of her baby?" she asked, recalling how Tara had confided this while they were on holidays.

"Yep – there isn't a peep out of her and if I didn't know better I'd swear she was enjoying all the attention she's getting by keeping us in the dark. So, of course, the rest of us are driven mad trying to figure out who it might be – my friend Liz in particular," she added, almost as an afterthought.

"The one who's having the marriage crisis?" Natalie

clarified, and the penny dropped. "Oh. Does your friend think it might be –"

"Honestly, Natalie, I'm not really sure," Tara interjected quickly. "I don't think it's a possibility but . . . well, you just never know. Anyway, we shouldn't really be talking about me and my situation – what about Jay? What did he sound like when he phoned earlier?"

Natalie knew when she was getting the brush-off. Tara was probably uncomfortable discussing her best friend's private business with a complete stranger, although Natalie was hardly that now. The two of them had spent ages over the last few weeks discussing what was the best way forward with Jay, and Natalie had already admitted all her past embarrassing mistakes. In fact, she thought, Tara Harrington now knew more about her than possibly all of her friends put together! She and Freya phoned one another now and again, but there was little to say.

Freya was dreadfully irritable because of the pregnancy and clearly wasn't the slightest bit interested in hearing about Natalie's life, and while of course Natalie wanted to be there for her friend, she knew deep down that Freya didn't need her. Why would she when she had Simon and all the other yummy mummies in Richmond to confide in? And at the end of the day, they could give her a lot more advice than Natalie ever could about what she was going through.

Maybe things would get better when the baby was born, or maybe not. Perhaps Natalie just had to come to terms with the fact that the friendship she and Freya now had was based on mental nights out in London many years ago, and while they'd had lots of fun in their twenties, there just wasn't enough in the friendship to sustain it into their latter years. Latter years? Goodness, now she was thinking like a pensioner!

"Well," she told Tara, in response to her earlier question about Jay, "apparently, this time, he's cooking dinner for us at his place."

"I'm beginning to get a teeny bit concerned about this guy," Tara said, although her tone was humorous. "He's gorgeous, successful, single – and he can cook too? Are you absolutely sure he's an Irishman?"

Natalie laughed. "I know – besides being Irish, I'm beginning to wonder if he's really a man at all! But, Tara, you know this will be a serious test, don't you? Me being with him on my own – in private?"

"Let me have a think about this for a second. It's been, what, three or four weeks since you two first met, and this will be the third date?"

"Yes." Natalie was beginning to get excited. Would Tara give her permission to sleep with Jay this time? If so, she was going straight to Selfridges after work to pick up some decent Agent Provocateur underwear and –

"No, it's still not time. I think you should definitely hold off for one more date."

"What?" Natalie wailed. "But I'll be at his place, near his *bedroom* and –"

"I'm serious, Natalie, don't give in just yet. Anyway, speaking of giving in, he hasn't been pushy about that, has he?"

"Well, no."

That was a good point, Natalie decided. Jay hadn't tried anything – at all. They'd kissed, of course, nice but brief goodbye kisses in cabs at the end of the evening, but nothing major or spine-tingly. Goodness, he'd better not be gay, she thought, horrified. Maybe that's why he seemed so bloody perfect!

Tara was right. Forget the new underwear. She'd go to his place on Saturday night for dinner and just wait and see what happened. And if Jay *didn't* make any sort of move on her, well, there was no bloody point in her jumping on him, was there? If he were the other way inclined, which she now thought was a bloody good possibility, then no amount of push-up basques and silk stockings would do it for him, would they?

"So," Tara asked the all-important question, "on a scale of one to ten, ten being totally committed, how committed are you to not sleeping with him on your next date?"

"Ten, definitely ten," Natalie replied with feeling.

"Good woman. It'll be worth it in the end, you know that, don't you? And this upcoming date will be a very good test."

Yes, Friday night would certainly be a bit of a test, Natalie agreed.

And she hoped to goodness that Jay Murray would pass it with flying colours.

Chapter 24

Dinner at Jay's place for their next date had sounded straightforward enough, but as Natalie discovered while the train they were on zipped forward to its destination, there was nothing at all straightforward about Jay Murray.

She supposed she should have realised something was up when they spoke on the phone earlier in the week to arrange it, and Jay had insisted on sending a cab to collect her at her flat, instead of just giving her his address.

Then, when the cab did collect her, the driver had eventually dropped her off at Waterloo station, where a smiling Jay greeted her at the entrance.

"What's going on?" Natalie asked, bewildered, as they walked inside the train station. "Why are we here?"

"I told you – we're having dinner at my place."

"Yes, but I thought you lived in –"

"I do, but I have another place elsewhere, so I thought I'd cook for you there if that's OK."

"Another place? Where?" Natalie was in no mood nor in the right state of dress to go trekking down to Dorset or wherever it was that well-off London executives had second homes these days.

She'd chosen a deliberately provocative yet understated outfit this evening: a red low-cut V-neck cashmere sweater worn over a slim-fitting black satin pencil skirt and the obligatory five-inch heels. She didn't want to look too dressed up for a quiet night in, yet she wanted to be sure she looked good enough for Jay to at least *want* to tear her clothes off!

Now that the idea he might be gay had inveigled itself into her thoughts, Natalie couldn't think of anything else. It had to be the reason he hadn't yet been snapped up by some woman, didn't it?

"Why don't you go and get a coffee while you wait?"

Wait for what? Natalie wanted to scream with frustration at him, but just as quickly he answered her unspoken question.

"I'll just go and get our tickets."

Natalie ordered a latte for herself and another for Jay before sinking gratefully into one of the coffee bar's oversized armchairs, her mind racing as she tried to figure out what on earth was going on. Why was he being so mysterious? And what idiot thought that taking a girl on a train on a busy Friday evening was a nice idea for a date?

A few minutes later, Jay appeared alongside her

table. "Ready to go? Sorry to rush you, but our train is just about to leave."

"Where are we going, Jay?"

"Oh, didn't I tell you?" he said, his tone cool as a cucumber. "On the Eurostar."

Natalie's mouth dropped open as the penny dropped. "To Paris? You have a house in *Paris*?"

Jay smiled insouciantly at her. "Well, it's an apartment actually. Is that OK with you?"

"But – but what about a quiet night in sampling your cooking?" Natalie was so overwhelmed she could hardly take it in. Paris! Thank *God* she hadn't decided to dress down in a pair of jeans or something like that. At least the Audrey Hepburn-style outfit she was wearing would look fine alongside Parisian haute couture. But Paris – oh wow! Natalie grinned delightedly.

"Well, that's still the plan," Jay told her. "I thought it might be a nice idea to go and cook up something nice there instead of Finchley."

"But . . . don't I need a passport or . . . oh God, it's at the office. Danni needed it to arrange some visa or other for a trip I'm taking to the States soon."

Jay smiled knowingly. "That's what she told you."

Natalie looked at him, shocked, as all at once she realised that he had arranged all this behind her back with her assistant as a willing accomplice. She'd kill Danni on Monday morning for making her give up her passport under false pretences! Well, no, she wouldn't really, because this was just wonderful – a truly wonderful surprise.

Here she was expecting a straightforward night in at some townhouse in North London and instead the man was whisking her off to Paris! Funny, she thought absently as she and Jay took their (first-class) seats on the Eurostar, how people always used that word "whisk" when speaking about being brought to Paris.

But in this case it was certainly true, Natalie thought now, as the train zoomed towards the most romantic city in the world – a city she'd always wanted to see, but would never dream of visiting on her own.

Paris wasn't the kind of place a girl visited other than with someone special, and none of the men in Natalie's life would have ever dreamed of taking her there. But it was becoming all too clear that Jay Murray was different to any man Natalie had ever been involved with before. She found the idea thrilling but also a little bit terrifying, the idea that there must be something wrong with him becoming all too sharply ingrained in her mind.

Yet, something Tara had mentioned before now came to the forefront of her mind. Why *shouldn't* she be treated like this? Why shouldn't a man like Jay want to impress or do something special for someone like her, Natalie Webb, who (according to Tara anyway) was just as attractive and as good a "catch" as he was?

And there was nothing wrong with *her*, was there? Well, she thought grimacing, apart from the fact that she had a tendency to come over a little on the "strong" side whenever a man paid her some attention. But she was over all that now.

And, speaking of Tara, she would be totally *gobsmacked* when she heard about this!

"You're very quiet," Jay remarked from alongside her. "Is all this OK with you? I hope I didn't overwhelm you too much or make you uncomfortable – it's just I wanted to do something special."

"Are you mad? This is amazing! No, I'm just thinking about how jealous everyone will be when I tell them all about this."

"Phew!" he said in mock-relief. "I was thinking I might have made a serious cock-up. It's just . . . Natalie, I know you're used to being wined and dined in the best places in London, and you admitted yourself that you're bored with all of that. I suppose I'm deliberately trying to up the ante by trying to be a little bit imaginative."

He sounded so sincere that Natalie wanted to hug him. Imagine doing all this just for her!

"Jay, please don't think that because I've overdosed a bit on foie gras you have to do all this. I'm just happy spending time with you, and it doesn't matter if it's afternoon tea at the Ritz or greasy burgers at TGI Friday's. Now, don't get me wrong – I'm loving all this, and visiting this city has been a dream of mine for as long as I can remember – but you really shouldn't feel you have to do something extravagant all the time." She grinned broadly. "Paris, I can't wait!"

"You're going to love it," Jay assured her, taking her hand in his.

* * *

His "place" was an amazing Haussmann-style apartment not far from the 4th Arrondissement, which, considering property prices in Paris were some of the highest in Europe, must have cost him an absolute fortune.

"It's a leaseback actually," Jay told her, when Natalie remarked how expensive it must have been. "I get to use it for only a couple of weeks a year, and I have to book them well in advance, no matter whether I use it or not. So this wasn't as spontaneous as it might look," he added wryly, pouring her a glass of wine, while she sat at the counter and watched him prepare dinner. "I knew I'd booked it free this week, and again for a couple of weeks at the end of the year, so I thought why not make the most of it? And of course," he said with a wink, "it gave me the perfect opportunity to impress you."

"It certainly did. So how does the leaseback thing work, then? The rent pays your mortgage?"

Jay nodded. "It's part of a scheme operated by the French government. I paid upfront for the property, and they gave me twenty per cent of the asking price back. So in effect, you're only paying eighty per cent of what it's worth. Then the leaseback company take charge of renting it out and all that, and as you say the rent pays some, but not all, of the mortgage. I need to contribute something too. But hopefully by the time the leaseback period is finished, it will be worth something so . . ." He shrugged as if being the owner of an amazing city centre Parisian apartment was no big deal.

"Great investment," Natalie agreed. "I wish I'd

thought of doing something like this ages ago, but I suppose I'm still hanging onto my dream of affording something in Belgravia." She sighed dreamily.

Jay laughed. "You publicists are obviously earning much more than I thought!"

"I *did* say it was a dream," she replied, making a face at him. "But honestly, I really adore this place – your own little piece of Paris, it's heavenly."

"I'm glad you like it and, to be truthful, it's nice to have someone to enjoy it with."

Natalie raised an eyebrow. "You didn't bring any of your previous girlfriends here?" *Or boyfriends*, a wicked voice piped up inside her, and she gulped.

"I've only had it a year, and seeing as I broke up with my last girlfriend over a year ago . . ." The rest of his sentence trailed off, as he went to check the food in the oven. Behind his back, Natalie smiled, pleased that he'd taken the bait, and even more, that his reply had put to rest the idea that he might be gay.

From what she could make out, he was preparing some kind of casserole, which in a way was a little bit of a letdown. There was a side of her that was sorry they weren't going out to some cosy Parisian restaurant on the Left Bank – despite her protestations that she'd tired of fine food – but no doubt whatever Jay had in mind would be gorgeous.

It was. When they eventually sat down to eat, not two hours after their arrival in the French capital, Natalie realised that, along with all his other attributes, Jay was a seriously good cook.

"What's the catch?" she asked him, as she tucked into the most fantastic beef bourguignon she had ever tasted. "What am I missing here?"

"Catch – what do you mean?" Jay said, looking a little worried.

"Well, this is clearly the nicest beef thingamajig I've ever tasted, and most men I know can barely boil a kettle, so what gives?"

"The best you've ever tasted? Wow, that's a hell of compliment. I'll be sure to pass it on to the boys."

"What boys? Oh, let me guess, you've got an army of bloody servants dancing attendance on you too, have you? Bloody hell, Jay, who *are* you?" she said, dropping her fork. "I'm sorry that I haven't had time to Google you before now. When I do, I'll probably find that you're a descendant of the Queen!"

"Do people really do that?" Jay said, laughing. "Look people up on the Internet?"

"Of course. Don't you?"

"Um – no," he said as if the thought had never, ever crossed his mind.

"Well, you should – you never know who you're dealing with these days."

Jay chuckled. "Now I know why you're so successful in your work. You know everyone's deepest, darkest secrets."

"Don't change the subject," Natalie said, taking another forkful of food. "*Do* you have an army of servants dancing attendance on you, and making delicious beef thingamajigs for your lady friends?"

"I told you – I don't know who all these lady friends are that you're talking about," he insisted, before adding casually, "and the boys I referred to are Marks and Spencer – this is from their Finest range – six ninety-nine a piece."

For a long moment, Natalie just stared at her plate. "Bloody hell! I *definitely* eat out too much!" she laughed, before launching straight back into her food.

They chatted for ages over dinner, finding out more about one another's likes and dislikes, where they'd travelled, where they'd like to travel in the future, and the more they talked the more Natalie found herself liking him. This – date or relationship or whatever it was – was so different to anything that had gone before. They had so much in common and seemed to share so many similar values that it was quite frightening really. Was this what Tara had been talking about? About Natalie finding out these things about the men she dated instead of just zooming onto the possibility of marriage like a radar missile? If so, she had to admit it was pretty good advice. Totally obvious, of course, but sometimes these things needed to be pointed out; in her case they'd *certainly* needed pointing out!

So, by the time they'd finished their second bottle of wine, Natalie decided she couldn't hold out if Jay made a move tonight, which he surely would, given that he'd brought her all the way to the most romantic city in the world – and to his own *place* in the most romantic city in the world – he was hardly going to have her sleep on the couch, was he?

As if reading her thoughts, Jay began to speak. "Look, Natalie, we've had a great time this evening, but . . . well, I didn't want to be presumptuous or anything, so I booked you a room at a small boutique hotel not far from here – just in case you thought I was pressurising you to spend the night," he added quickly, "with me."

Her heart sank to her stomach. What kind of man would book a girl into a hotel in Paris when he had his own apartment? He was *definitely* gay after all, she decided regretfully, or else he found the thought of sleeping with her so repulsive that –

"Of course," he added, twisting a strand of her hair around one of his fingers, his breath warm and tingly on her skin, "if you decide that you'd *like* to stay over, well, I won't argue with that either."

Then before she could think any more about it, Natalie threw her arms around Jay's neck and pulled him roughly towards her. Sod Tara and her rules, she thought as he returned her kisses with a fervour that banished all Natalie's doubts about his sexuality and pushed her back on the couch, his hands roaming freely over her body.

When it came to being committed to *not* sleeping with Jay just then, on a scale of one to ten, Natalie was minus one million!

Chapter 25

One afternoon, Luke was out digging his garden when he spotted his next-door neighbour return from walking the dogs in the fields.

He liked Liz and since he'd moved into the house properly had been seeing her every day heading off over the fields with the dogs. She was a lovely woman, always so friendly and chatty. A good-looking woman too, he noticed, but what was most appealing about Liz was that she seemed to have a slight frailty about her. In fact, with her dark hair and ladylike ways, she reminded him of his youngest sister, although Ingrid wouldn't go near a dog to save her life.

"How's it all going?" she called, giving him a friendly wave while trying to herd the dogs back into their individual kennels. "Doing some work on the garden, I see?"

"I'm nearly sorry I started, to be honest," he called

back, standing up and leaning on his shovel. "It's bloody hard work! But I thought I'd better do something with it. Actually," he added, sticking the shovel into the dirt and coming across to chat to her, "your friend Tara shamed me into it with all her talk about it being a wilderness."

"Really?" Liz smiled. "Yes, Tara can be a bit persuasive all right."

"Did you two enjoy your night out on the town that time? Apart from having to make conversation with me."

"Don't be silly – it was a great night, and once Tara got started there was no fear of us running out of things to say. But I'm sorry she went on at you like that about your job and everything."

"Yes, she speaks her mind all the same, doesn't she?" he laughed and Liz laughed too.

"Bit of an understatement, I think!" she said. "Yes, Tara doesn't hold back."

"I think she told me she grew up in the village?" Luke queried. "I take it you did too?

"Oh God, no! Can't you tell from the accent? I'm a true-blue Dub."

"Oh, I just assumed you two were childhood friends and your accent isn't particularly noticeable."

"No, we used to work together in Dublin. But my husband Eric is from here. That's how we met actually – he's a school-friend of Tara's and she introduced us."

"I see."

Luke hadn't met the husband yet, but he remembered Liz saying something about him working in Dublin. Lucky bastard, having a lovely wife and kid like that. At thirty-six, and having done the run of night-clubs and speed-dating and what have you, Luke had just about given up on finding himself a decent prospect, let alone a half-decent woman. Well, at least until now.

"So," he began, trying to sound offhand, "does she get down to visit you all that much or . . .?" He let the rest of the sentence trail off, as at this Liz smiled knowingly, a bit too knowingly, he thought, reddening a little. Shit, had he made it that obvious?

"She comes down to visit her parents a lot," said Liz, "so, yes, we do see her quite a bit."

"Still, I suppose she's busy in Dublin with her job and everything – she told me all about it when you were away," he said casually, afraid that he was revealing too much interest in Tara's life.

"Well, she is busy, but as I said we do get to see her a lot." Liz met his eyes, her look conveying to Luke that she was very much aware of his reasons for asking. "Why? Are you worried that you might bump into her again? And that she'll castigate you about your job?"

"Well, if she does, I'll have an answer for her," Luke replied, feeling cheered by the fact that Liz hadn't mentioned anything about Tara having a boyfriend. With her good looks and seemingly fun-loving personality, he'd thought there might have been someone on the scene. But Liz, who clearly knew he was fishing for information about her, hadn't said a word about Tara being attached. This was good news.

"Yes, you two seemed well able for one another that night!" Liz laughed.

"Hello there!"

Luke and Liz were so busy laughing about Tara that they hadn't noticed the man come out of Liz's house. The guy had such a look of suspicion on his face that Luke immediately twigged it was the husband, evidently wondering who it was that was making his wife laugh like that. And so he might.

"Oh, Eric, hi – you're home!" Liz cried. "Come and meet Luke, our new next-door neighbour." She turned and looked questioningly at Luke. "You two haven't met yet, have you?"

Eric stepped forward. "Nice to meet you – I hear you moved in recently. Sorry I haven't bumped into you before now," he said amiably, holding out his hand.

But as Luke went to shake the other man's hand and got a proper look at his face, he realised that Eric was correct in saying that they hadn't met but was wrong in his assumption that they hadn't bumped into one another.

They had, Luke thought, as he studied his new neighbour's husband, but at the time Eric had been sitting on a park bench, deep in conversation with a woman who was definitely *not* his lovely wife.

"I just don't know how to thank you!" Natalie gushed down the telephone line to Tara. It had been over three weeks since her trip to Paris with Jay, and the two had been inseparable since.

"Well, I'm still not happy that you broke your promise not to sleep with him," Tara reminded her briskly, "but I'll admit that had I been in your situation, I would probably have had problems keeping it too."

"Ubercalm and controlled you? I don't believe it for a second!" Natalie joked.

"So things are still going well then?" said Tara, although any fool could tell from Natalie's elated tone that things were going very well indeed.

"He's wonderful, Tara, and we get on so well. We have the most amazing chats that last for hours, and at the end of it all, we can barely remember what we've talked about. I've never felt so . . ." she seemed to be struggling for the right word, "so on a par with a man before. I'm not always worried about how I'm putting myself across or what'll happen next – I'm just being myself. And, yes, I know it sounds corny, but it's true!"

"I'm thrilled for you, Natalie – I really am. Jay sounds terrific – almost too good to be true." He did sound wonderful – sensitive, thoughtful, romantic – and seemed to treat Natalie the way every girl would like to be treated. Tara sorely hoped that the man was everything he seemed to be. Having genuinely fallen for someone this time, it would just be Natalie's luck for him to turn out to be married or something.

"He is! Oh, Tara, you'd love him – you really would."

"I'm sure I would. So tell me, do you want to continue our sessions for a little while longer? Or are you happy enough to keep going on your own now? To be honest, I don't think there's a whole lot else I can help you with. You seem to be doing just fine on your own."

"Well, there is one more thing," Natalie said. "I'd really love for you to . . . I don't know . . . observe us together."

"Observe you?"

"Yes, I'd love to hear your opinion – not only on Jay, but also on how the two of us interact. You know, just to be sure that it is as good as I'm making it all sound!"

Tara smiled. "Don't be silly. You certainly don't need my blessing – not at this stage anyway."

"But I'd really love for you to meet him, Tara – I mean, it's all because of you that we're together in the first place."

"Um, I think your good looks and sparkling personality might have had something to do with it," Tara laughed.

"Nope, I was a disaster before you went to work on me, you know that. And if I didn't have you coaching me through our dates, I would have messed up this relationship just as easily as I'd messed up all the others. It was you, Tara – you made this happen."

"Maybe I *helped* make it happen, Natalie, but all I did was give you a little push in the right direction. I certainly don't deserve all this praise."

"But you do! Will you come to London and see us? And let me thank you properly for the wonderful help you've given me. Don't worry – I'll take care of the flights and the hotel and all that kind of thing."

"Don't be silly – I wouldn't dream of letting you do anything like that."

"It's not a problem – it'll be my way of saying thank you, seeing as you refused point blank to take any payment from me," she chided. "But will you come, though? Besides meeting Jay, I'd love to see you again too. We could all go out for dinner somewhere, the four of us. I'm sure Jay would get on great with Glenn."

Tara shook her head. Whatever about her taking off to London to see Natalie, there wasn't a hope in hell of convincing Glenn to tag along. He was just way too busy with work at the moment and, in truth, she couldn't see Glenn being the slightest bit interested in coupley dinners with Natalie and her new man. When she said this to Natalie, the other girl sighed.

"I understand. But couldn't you come on your own then? I know it mightn't be as much fun, but you could stay with me and we could go shopping or . . . no, wait – why don't you bring that friend you're always talking about?"

"Liz?" Tara sat back in her seat. *That* wasn't a bad idea. Although she seemed to have cheered up a little in recent weeks, Liz had been going through such a hard time with all this business with Eric that it would be nice for her to get away and enjoy herself. Considering she'd got such enjoyment from their night out a while back.

Liz would adore London. The two of them could go over on a cheapie weekend with one of the low-cost airlines and stay in a nice hotel in town. They could go and meet Natalie (who Liz would love) and the famous Jay, and then they could use the rest of the weekend for shopping and maybe some beauty treatments. It sounded glorious now that she thought about it. She and Liz never did anything like that.

And it would be nice to see Natalie again. She'd enjoyed her company so much in Egypt that when they'd exchanged phone numbers and addresses at the end of the holiday, Tara had every intention of keeping in touch. So it was great that Natalie had made the contact first.

"Well, what do you think?" Natalie asked again. "Will you come for a visit?"

"I think it might be fun," Tara replied, and instantly a high-pitched squeal was to be heard from the other end.

"It'll be brilliant!" Natalie cried. "And hopefully it'll prove to you once and for all that Jay really is as wonderful as he sounds!"

Later that evening, Liz went out to the hallway to answer the ringing telephone, leaving Eric in the living room watching TV.

To her relief, things had improved somewhat in the McGrath household lately. Eric's frequent disappearances had lessened and he seemed to be spending much more time at home. And although he still tended to be moody and pensive at times, he seemed to be taking more of an interest in Toby.

However, the majority of the changes were of Liz's own doing.

After her night out with Tara, she'd decided not to mention her suspicions to Eric about his having an affair and had come to the conclusion that she'd been imagining the whole thing.

After all, had there been any concrete evidence to suggest that he was cheating on her? The woman phoning the house looking for Eric that time could simply have been someone from the office who only sounded like Emma because Liz was paranoid about her. And Emma's apparently "blank" text message appearing on his mobile phone could have very well been as Eric had described it – an accident.

And of course that time she'd suspected that he wasn't (as he'd told her) going out for a drink with Colm had turned out to be exactly that. As had his visits to his mother. And the weird hours and late nights he'd been working in Dublin were for a very good reason – extra cash to renovate the house. And in fairness, she couldn't really have expected him to be chatting and laughing like a maniac in Belfast when they'd been there for a family funeral, could she?

So Liz had finally come to the conclusion that she'd imagined the whole lot of it, had spent the last month or two working herself into a frenzy about nothing.

And it was all because of some stupid comment Emma Harrington had made that day in the village, a stupid comment that meant absolutely nothing. So what if Emma had bumped into Eric? How, from that simple remark, had Liz made the giant leap to think that Eric was the mystery father of her baby? Eric was her husband and he loved her.

It was mostly her own fault, though, she knew that. Insecurity was something Liz had lived with for most of her life and she couldn't help it. It was only natural that when she'd finally got the life she wanted, the life she'd dreamt about, a home and family to call her own, she'd be terrified of it being taken away from her. She'd been that way all her life. When she was younger, it seemed that every time she'd begun to settle in with one of her brothers and his family, circumstances would change and she'd be uprooted and brought to live with another. Since she lost her parents twenty years before, nothing, least of all family, life had ever been stable in Liz's life and she supposed it was understandable that she'd worry about the stability of her own. Subconsciously, she'd often worried that the wonderful life she had with Eric and then Toby seemed too good to be true and was probably only looking for something to go wrong.

But, she realised now, through her own stupid and pathetic insecurity, she could very well have ruined everything she had all by herself. So, in the last few weeks, she'd tried her utmost not to let things get to her, not to fret over Eric's distant moods and working hours, tried not to turn every molehill into a mountain.

And wasn't she so glad now that she hadn't confided her fears to Tara? Imagine accusing her sister of having an affair with her husband when there was absolutely no basis for those allegations whatsoever. She surely would have lost Tara as a friend – no matter how close she and her friend were, blood was thicker than water, and even if Tara had understood that the accusation stemmed from Liz's own insecurities, there would surely always be a faint tension between them. Even though Tara and Emma's relationship was at times unsteady, there was no question but that Tara would be upset at the idea. Liz would be upset if any member of her family was accused of being a home-wrecker, despite the fact that these days she only saw them once or twice a year.

So Liz was incredibly grateful now that she'd held her tongue and hadn't confided her fears to anyone. If she had, who knew what kind of a situation she'd be in now?

As it was, she still had Eric as a husband, Tara as a friend and the life she'd always dreamed of. And she wasn't going to do anything to jeopardise that.

She picked up the ringing phone to find Tara on the other end.

"Do you fancy coming to London with me next weekend?" her friend asked without preamble.

"London? What for?"

"Well, Natalie – you know, the girl I met in Egypt, and the one I've been coaching recently?"

"What about her?"

"Well, she persuaded me to come over for a visit, to meet the man of her dreams and the reason she asked for my help in the first place. Apparently she needs my blessing!" Tara added good-humouredly. "Anyway, you'd love her, Liz – she's a gas woman. And I'm sure she'd know how to show us a good time. She just phoned to tell me she's organised a gorgeous hotel in Kensington for us, and no doubt she'll take us somewhere swanky for dinner on Friday night so –"

"For *us* – she wouldn't mind me coming too?"

"Of course not, she suggested it in the first place! So does that mean you will come?"

Liz bit her lip. It sounded wonderful. She hadn't been out of the country since her honeymoon in Portugal three years ago. And wouldn't it be great to get the chance to go shopping in London – especially with Tara. Her friend would know all the right places to go and would ensure she had her wardrobe updated in no time!

"Oh, I'd love to," she said, "but I suppose I'd better ask Eric if he's OK to look after Toby first. Can you hold on?"

Laying down the receiver on the hall table, Liz went back into the living room.

"Didn't you say earlier that you're not working next weekend?" she asked her husband, unable to keep the excitement out of her tone.

Eric didn't look up from the TV. "Yeah – why do you ask?"

"How would you feel about looking after Toby and the kennels while I go to London with Tara?" Liz held her breath, waiting for him to make up some excuse not to do it. "We're hoping to go Friday and it'd just be for the weekend and –"

"No problem – go for it. I'll be coming off nights early Friday morning, and I'm not back in until the following Monday night. So it should be fine."

"But won't you be tired, having just finished your shift and everything?"

"Not at all! I'll get a few hours sleep in before you leave, and I'll be grand."

"Are you sure?" Liz couldn't believe he'd agreed so readily.

"Honestly, Liz – go. You'll enjoy it."

"I can go!" Liz laughed down the phone to Tara afterwards, feeling happier and more optimistic than she'd felt in ages.

"Fantastic! I'm about to book the flights online as we speak. How about a lunchtime flight on Friday and a late one back on Sunday evening?"

"Sounds fine to me – just let me know how much I owe you."

"Don't worry about it," her friend insisted. "Natalie's insisted she'll look after it."

"Really? That's so generous of her! Oh, Tara, thanks for asking me! I really can't wait," Liz cried. "This will be great fun!"

"It certainly will," her friend laughed, "and I really think it'll do us both the world of good!"

Chapter 26

The following Thursday afternoon at five p.m., Tara sighed with pleasure as she closed the office door behind her and raced upstairs to get changed. That was it, she thought, as she cast off her work clothes and changed into a pair of denims and a T-shirt – no more clients until the following Monday. And in the meantime she and Liz were going to have a wonderful time visiting Natalie in London. She couldn't wait.

She went downstairs and opened the fridge, wondering what she could make for dinner. Glenn's shift ended at seven this evening, so for once he'd be home for dinner.

Tara debated whether to go to the trouble of cooking something or just order in. Blast it, she'd order in, she decided, closing the fridge door and rummaging in the drawer for a takeaway menu.

Glenn wouldn't mind – in fairness, most of the time

he preferred takeaways to what he described as her "bland" cooking. Understandable, she supposed, given that she preferred using lots of fresh vegetables and lean meat, instead of the fat- and additive-laden stuff from the fast-food places.

But tonight Tara didn't care. The odd takeaway now and again wouldn't kill either of them. Still, Glenn would probably be living on them while she was away in London, wouldn't he? She bit her lip. Maybe before leaving tomorrow she should prepare a few things in advance for him to reheat while she was gone – a few simple pasta dishes or something.

But blast it, she'd probably only be wasting her time. If Glenn had his way, he'd live on pizza and Chinese, and it was highly unlikely he'd go to the trouble of reheating something of hers. Oh well, she decided eventually, he was a big boy and she'd have to leave him to his own devices.

She was really looking forward to this trip and couldn't wait to meet up with Natalie again. The girl was so vivacious and fun-loving, Tara just knew she'd go all out to ensure she and Liz enjoyed their stay. And after all this time, it would be nice to put a face to loverboy Jay and suss out whether he really was as good as he seemed. She hoped so. Natalie was a pet who, after so much disappointment, really deserved a good man in her life.

And apparently she was pulling out all the stops for Liz and Tara's visit – despite Tara's protestations that she didn't owe her anything. Instead of just meeting her and Jay for a quiet dinner, Natalie had used all her (and Jay's) connections and had actually arranged a table for them in the celebrity restaurant the Ivy for tomorrow night! Liz had nearly fainted with excitement when she'd heard this, before immediately becoming hysterical over what to wear.

"Oh my God! What if David Beckham is there?" she'd cried. "I'd keel over if I walked in and saw him and Posh sitting at the table next to us or something!"

"Well, seeing as he's living in Madrid these days, and will probably have a game on Saturday, I doubt very much that he'll be there," Tara told her calmly.

Liz sighed. "Pity."

"But we're bound to spot *somebody* interesting," Tara added. "So be sure to let Eric know his wife will be mixing with the rich and famous. Get him worried that you might arrive home with some male model on your arm or something!"

They were getting a lunchtime flight the following day, so the plan was for Eric to drive Liz to Tara's house, and she would drive them both to the airport from there.

So they should get into Heathrow around early afternoon and then . . . Tara frowned and set down the takeaway menu.

What would they do from there? She hadn't been in London in donkey's years. Was there a train they could get into Central London, or would it be quicker to just get a taxi? Tara wasn't sure, but she supposed she'd better find out. Natalie had the restaurant booked for early evening so, by the time they got to the hotel and changed, there really wouldn't be a whole lot of time, and she couldn't take the chance of being late. Especially when Natalie had gone to so much trouble.

Deciding she'd better ask Natalie what was the best thing to do, Tara picked up the phone and dialled her work number, but it went straight to voicemail. Tara was tempted to leave a message asking her friend what they should do upon arrival at the airport but then she realised how silly that sounded. Talk about Irish country bumpkins! There was no point in bothering Natalie – she could easily find out herself on the Internet.

Tara went into the living room and sat down in front of Glenn's laptop. Her office computer had the previous week been infected by some Internet virus and despite Glenn's best efforts was still off-limits as far as Internet access was concerned. So in the meantime, she'd been using Glenn's for her online coaching sessions and for researching her trip to London.

She'd try the site she'd used a few days before when looking up the exact location of the hotel that Natalie had arranged for them – that had loads of tourist information about London.

But when she went online, she found she couldn't for the life of her remember the website address . . . was it *londonhotelbookings* . . . *londonhotels* . . . *hotelslondon*? Nope, obviously none of those, Tara thought frowning as the *"address not found"* page kept coming up on the screen.

Then she thought of something. As she'd accessed it only recently, the site would still be saved on the Internet history file, wouldn't it?

Tara clicked on the *"history"* button, feeling rather pleased with herself that she'd remembered to do it. Ha! Glenn wasn't the only dab hand at computers in this house!

A list of recently viewed pages appeared on the screen, and Tara scanned through them, hoping to spot the one she was looking for. But something else caught her eye instead, a web page she knew she'd find the answer on in any case: the *celticfemmes.com* forum.

The forum was a mine of information – its hundreds of members continuously exchanging information on everything from fake tan to failed relationships. Tara had posted a request for information on Sharm El Sheikh on the site before eventually choosing it as a holiday destination, and she'd been inundated with lots of very helpful information and useful advice. So, why shouldn't she do the same for London? *Someone* would know about how difficult it was to get a taxi from the airport into the centre of the city and how much it would cost.

She clicked onto the travel section and posted a new topic, labelling it, *"Weekend in London"*.

"Hi everyone," Tara typed, *"am off to London tomorrow for the weekend and wondered about the best way to get from Heathrow to Kensington in Central London. Is there a train I can get from the airport to this area, or should I get a cab to go directly? Would prefer not to use the tube if*

possible. Any info would be greatly appreciated. Thanks, Pixie."

"Pixie" was Tara's username for the forum, as like many other Internet users she generally preferred not to use her real name. She then hit "send", and waited for the page to reload and her query to appear at the top of the travel section. And within seconds, there it was.

Grand, she thought, standing up from the laptop. She'd disconnect from the Net and then come back after dinner to see what the femmes had to say and hopefully . . . Tara's eyes widened as she realised she already had a reply and another member's nickname, *"Obi-wan"* had appeared beside her topic. That was quick.

"Good woman," Tara muttered as she clicked into the topic once more to see what advice Obi-wan had given her.

But when the page reloaded, Tara frowned. There was nothing there but her own query – no reply from anyone in the last few seconds.

Perplexed, she refreshed the page again, thinking that the reply might not yet have properly registered, but then something caught her eye.

The topic she'd posted *was* there, but instead of registering as being posted by her own user name, "Pixie", it was showing as being posted by someone called Obi-wan.

Flummoxed by this, Tara sat back in her seat and stared at the screen.

How had that happened? Her user name was definitely Pixie: it was the nickname she used for the various websites and forums she belonged to.

So how had her query ended up as being posted by Obi-wan?

Then, she looked at the login details displayed at the top of the screen.

It read: *"You are logged on to celticfemmes.com as Obi-wan."*

Of course! Tara grinned as the penny dropped. She was using Glenn's computer now, wasn't she? So, obviously, Glenn had visited this particular site before her and had logged on with his own user name, Obi-wan – a name that made sense, really, if she thought about it for half a second: Glenn was such a *Star Wars* fan that she should have guessed at once!

So, obviously what had happened was that Glenn had stayed logged into the forum after his last visit, and Tara's new query was automatically recognised as being from Obi-wan when she posted it.

Then she thought of something. Why would *Glenn* be a member of a mostly female-friendly site? And what had he been enquiring about?

Tara smiled. She shouldn't do it really but, at the same time, this could be interesting.

Still grinning to herself, Tara clicked onto the *"View Member Profile"* section. This revealed that Obi-wan had joined the forum a couple of weeks back and had posted on only three occasions.

Without thinking too much more about it, Tara

clicked into the *"View all Member Posts"* heading. She knew she shouldn't be so nosy, but she couldn't help it. She was *dying* to see what information Glenn might have wanted from *celticfemmes*! Knowing him, it was probably computer-related – though, considering his level of expertise, why he would go to the celticfemmes was beyond her – or, in fact, and this was probably exactly what it was, she thought now, it could be something to do with scuba diving. Since the trip to Egypt, Glenn had been trying to arrange to go on some more dives here in Ireland. He could very well have come across the celticfemmes website through a search for Irish scuba-diving information on one of the search engines. It seemed the most likely explanation anyway, Tara mused.

But the topic he'd apparently been interested in was labelled: *"Serious shit – advice needed."*

As she began to read through the topic, Tara began to wish she hadn't been so inquisitive. But once she'd started she just couldn't stop – she couldn't tear her eyes away and her heart raced as she read the words.

The topic had been started by a member called Mattie who was asking for advice on some "serious shit" all right.

"I need some advice from a female perspective as this is something I'm finding hard to deal with and I can't exactly talk to my mates about it," Mattie wrote. *"My girlfriend's seven weeks pregnant and is thinking of having an abortion. I don't want her to do it – I'm totally against that kind of stuff – but I also know that she is determined to go*

through with it, and the longer we fight about it, the more the baby will grow and the worse it'll be if she does do it in the end."

The topic had lots of responses from regular posters on the site, some passing judgement, others giving him genuine advice. Heart pounding, Tara scrolled down through most of it until she found what she was looking for, which was Obi-wan's reply. Evidently this topic interested Glenn enough for him to sign up for membership to the site in order to reply, as non-members were not allowed to post or reply to topics. But what would Glenn know about things like abortion?

Knowing full well she shouldn't be doing it, and sensing that she wouldn't like what she found, Tara couldn't help but continue down the page until she found Glenn's reply. Now she knew why Liz had felt so awful about checking up on Eric. It was like being drawn to something like a magnet.

Finally, Tara reached Obi-wan's – Glenn's – reply.

"I hear you, man, and I understand what you're going through. I'm in the same fucked-up boat. I got involved with someone I really shouldn't have, and now she's pregnant too. Because of our situation, we can't tell anyone about it, and we've talked about the possibility of her having an abortion too. I think she wants to, but I don't want her to do it. It's just not right. We looked it up, and I think it's OK up until twelve weeks but after that . . ."

Stunned by what she was seeing, Tara couldn't read any more. What the hell was he talking about – or playing at? Was this some kind of joke?

Tara's heart pounded in her chest as she thought about it over and over again. Glenn, *her* Glenn, getting some girl pregnant? How was it possible? Her mind struggled to take in the enormity of it all while she stared at the screen as if in a trance.

Then she read back through the words again. He'd said, *"I got involved with someone I really shouldn't have"*. Who the hell was that?

Then, almost instantly, Tara sat up in her seat as she remembered something – something that hadn't bothered her too much at the time, but perhaps it should have. Emma arriving unannounced at her house the weekend she was baby-sitting Toby while Liz and Eric went to the funeral.

Glenn suddenly deciding not to join her in Castlegate . . . the two of them looking very cosy coming in the door when she returned home on the Sunday. Glenn running around after Emma and making her sandwiches and . . .

No, it couldn't possibly be . . . it would be crazy to even *think* . . .

But Tara couldn't come up with any other possible explanation. She thought about everything that had happened recently, Emma's refusal to talk about the father of her baby, her insistence that she wouldn't or perhaps *couldn't* say a word. Then Liz's concerns about Eric, her unspoken belief that he might be the father of Emma's – her sister's – baby.

As the realisation hit her hard, Tara put her head in her hands.

Liz had been worrying for nothing. The mystery of the father of Emma's baby had finally been solved, and it almost certainly wasn't Eric.

It was Glenn.

Chapter 27

One look at his expression told Tara everything she needed to know.

She'd sat stunned in front of the computer for what seemed like hours, but was actually only a few minutes, and was only woken from her trance when she heard Glenn's key in the front door.

"Tara? Are you here?" He'd moved around the kitchen for a minute or two before eventually finding her in the living room, sitting dazedly in front of the laptop.

"What are you doing? I thought you were finishing work early this evening, and . . . hey, what's wrong?"

When she didn't answer, wouldn't look at him, he asked again. "Tara?" Then he looked past her face to the computer screen, and his face paled. It was then that Tara knew for sure that her worst fears had been realised.

"What the hell is going on, Glenn?" she whispered, barely able to find her voice. "Is this . . ." she turned to the computer screen, "this person really you? Or is this all some kind of joke?"

But Tara knew deep down that it was no joke; Glenn's face had drained of colour and he wouldn't meet her eyes.

"What are you talking about?" he said, but his words held no conviction.

"I'm talking about *you* giving advice on some Internet site about pregnancy and abortion! What the hell would you know about things like that, Glenn?"

"So you're checking up on me now – is that it?" he countered, but Tara knew it was only for show.

"I wasn't checking up on you! You know I've had to use this computer while mine is out of action! I was looking for something totally different and I just happened to . . . Anyway, that's not the point," she went on, eyes flashing with anger. "What the hell is this all about? Tell me, Glenn!"

He ran a hand through his hair and began to pace the room. "Look, I was going to tell you –"

Right then, Tara thought she actually felt her heart split in two. Oh no . . . please no. "When?" she cried. "When were you going to tell me, Glenn? When she had the baby? Or were the two of you planning on keeping that a secret from us too – hoping none of us would know any better?"

"I just didn't . . ." Glenn was lost for words.

Tara felt the room swim out of focus. She couldn't

believe this. How could he? How could *she*? How on earth could this nightmare have happened?

"Tell me, Glenn!"

"It wasn't going to be a secret much longer. I was going to tell you soon. Her parents already know."

"I see, so it's OK to tell her parents but not me –" Then, she shook her head wildly as his words penetrated her brain properly. "Hold on a second, what do you mean her *parents* know? You mean it's not Emma?"

Glenn looked like she'd punched him in the face. "Emma . . . what the fuck? Are you crazy? Emma's your *sister*, for fuck's sake! What kind of a sicko do you think I am?"

Tara didn't know whether to be relieved or upset or even more angry. In all honesty, she just didn't know how to feel. "But if it's not Emma then . . . who?"

Glenn was still shaking his head. "I can't believe you thought that I'd do something like that with Emma. That's sick!"

"Well, if it's not Emma, then who the hell is it, Glenn?" Tara repeated vehemently.

"I was going to tell you," he repeated, "but I just couldn't bring myself to. Look, you've been in such good form since we came back from the holiday – I didn't want to ruin things for you. And I know you're worried about this thing with Emma too and you've been up and down to Castlegate a lot –"

"Oh, so while the cat's away, the mice will play, is it?" Tara challenged.

He shook his head from side to side. "No, it wasn't that. Look, I just couldn't find the right time."

"Now is a good time," she said, her tone hardening. "Or should I just scroll down through the rest of the forum?"

"I still can't believe you spied on me like that."

"It wasn't like that. I was looking for something else and I came across the webpage. I had no idea you were a member of this website. What were you doing giving people advice like that? Were you not afraid of being found out? Jesus, Glenn, of all people you should know enough about computers to realise that you shouldn't have let yourself stay logged in like that. Or didn't you care whether or not you were found out? Is that it?"

"Believe me, I didn't know that would happen. I was sure I'd logged out last time I was in, but the cookies must have saved it and –"

"Spare me the technical stuff, Glenn, and please tell me what the hell is going on! Who is this girl you've got pregnant?"

Glenn sighed. "It's difficult to know where to start,"

"The beginning will be fine," she said, trying to keep her voice even.

He sighed deeply and took a seat on the armchair across from her.

"Her name is . . . Abby," he began, his eyes studying the carpet. "We met a couple of months back . . . in Egypt."

Tara couldn't believe what she was hearing. "In

Egypt . . . while you were supposed to be on holiday with me?" she croaked.

He nodded, ashamed. "She was taking the scuba-diving course too, and she's Irish – from Donnybrook – and over the few days going out on the boat, we sort of . . . hit it off."

Now Tara understood why he'd been so unconcerned about her going off to the pyramids with Natalie. In fact, he'd practically insisted she go! And why not – when it would free him up to go off and chase some girl! How could he? How could he deceive her like that? Glenn had never been the secretive type: they had always been straight up with one another.

Or so she'd thought.

"So, let me get this straight. All those times I stayed around the pool and you were supposed to be going off on the boat, you were actually off with some girl?"

"No, I *was* going off on the boat. I did take the course. She was taking it too."

"I see – very convenient, wasn't it?"

Glenn wouldn't look at her. "I'm sorry – it just happened."

"And now she's pregnant," Tara stated acidly. "When did this happen? On some plastic sun-lounger in Egypt, or did you continue seeing her after we got home?"

Still, he wouldn't look at her. "We met up a couple of times afterwards, yes," he said shamefully. "And then . . . it happened. Look, we didn't mean for it to –"

"Oh, spare me that bullshit! You know as well as I do that these things don't 'just happen'!"

"I said I was sorry," he replied, his tone hardening somewhat. "This is hard enough for me as it is, without feeling guilty about you too!"

"You selfish . . . why shouldn't you feel guilty, going around behind my back like that? And what else did you think I'd feel?"

"I'm sorry . . . I just . . . I'm sorry," Glenn repeated as Tara stared into space, unable to believe what was happening.

Eventually, Tara got up and walked out, unable to stay in the same room as him any longer. She went into the kitchen and put her head in her hands. In a few months' time, Glenn – her Glenn – would be the father of some strange girl's baby.

What on earth was she going to do?

The following morning, a bubbly and energetic Liz arrived at the house, Eric having driven her all the way from Castlegate. Tara and Glenn had sat up for hours the previous night discussing everything that had happened, Glenn apologising over and over, Tara trying in vain to come to terms with it all. She'd lain awake for hours in bed afterwards, wondering what on earth would happen to them now. Glenn had insisted he was going to stick by this . . . this Abby (Tara could barely bring herself to utter the girl's name).

"She's carrying my child, and she needs my support," he told Tara, when she'd calmed down somewhat from the shock of her initial discovery. "You must understand that I have to stand by her."

"Do you love her?" Tara asked him.

Glenn was hesitant, and again he wouldn't give her a straight answer.

"I . . . I don't know. I think so," he said, while inside Tara's heart shattered.

So it seemed he had it all worked out. He was standing by this girl – this soon-to-be mother of his child. Good for him, she'd thought, as she lay wide awake well into the night. He'd had weeks to come to terms with this, to think about what it meant for his future. But what about her? What about what *she* thought? Didn't that matter to him at all? Did he think that she'd just stand by, say nothing and accept things as they were? That saying sorry would be enough?

Tara didn't know; and that morning she could barely see straight from lack of sleep, let alone get excited about the upcoming trip.

Earlier that morning, Glenn had gone out to work as usual and had given her a warm hug, before urging her apologetically to "try and enjoy it" and that they'd talk some more on her return.

Tara hadn't returned the hug and almost wanted to laugh out loud at the idea of enjoying herself. A jaunt to London was the last thing she wanted or needed after the bombshell he'd landed on her, but at the same time she didn't want to let Natalie, or indeed Liz, down.

"I'm so looking forward to this!" her friend squealed, as she excitedly dropped her bags in the hallway and followed Tara through to the kitchen. "And Eric was *fine* about my going – he actually told me I deserved the break – which was a turn-up for the books, I can tell you, and . . ." Her words trailed off as, in the bright light of the kitchen, she properly caught sight of Tara's drawn and anxious face. "What's the matter?" she gasped. "Tara, what's wrong?"

"Oh, Liz – everything's such a mess!" Unable to hide her distress any longer, Tara sank into a kitchen chair and put her head in her hands.

"What is it? What's happened?"

"It's Glenn!" she cried. "He's made such a mess of everything!"

And through her tears, Tara spilled out the whole sorry tale to Liz, including the part where she'd suspected that Glenn might have been the father of Emma's baby.

"I suppose that's the only positive thing to come out of this," she said afterwards, grimacing through her tears. "If it *had* been Emma he'd been seeing, I don't think I could have ever got over that – none of us would."

Liz said nothing, and Tara knew the mention of her sister's name raised the question of her pregnancy and the elusive father once more. In fact, if Glenn *had* been revealed as the father, then Eric would have been off the hook, wouldn't he? And all of Liz's worries would have been at an end. But Tara couldn't think about that now.

Eventually Liz shook her head. "I can only imagine what you're going through," she said, her voice gentle, "but at least he admitted everything and was willing to talk about it with you. And no matter what he might have done, Glenn is still a good and decent guy. You'll work it out between you, I know you will."

Tara sniffed. She wasn't so sure whether or not she wanted to work it out. It might be easier to just throw Glenn out on his ear and let him and his girlfriend go it alone. But deep down, she knew she wouldn't do that. She and Glenn had been through too much over the years, and despite what had happened, she loved him like crazy.

"I just don't know how to deal with it," she told Liz sadly. "He's going to be a father soon, he and some slapper he barely knows! He's said he wants to stand by her, that he has to stand by her. And if he's so determined to do that, so determined to become involved in this girl and her baby's life, then, Liz, where on earth does that leave me?"

Chapter 28

They arrived at Heathrow that same afternoon, and Tara resolved to try and take her mind off things for a while, at least until they'd met up with Natalie and her boyfriend. Then, as Liz said, the two of them could spend the rest of the weekend "locked in the hotel with chocolate and ice-cream" if Tara preferred. She certainly knew she wouldn't be up to going shopping in Oxford Street on Saturday afternoon or anything like that. She'd be lucky if she got through the day as it was.

"I'm so sorry for ruining your weekend," Tara said, as they travelled towards their hotel in the taxi (which, she thought sadly, had "cost" her a lot more than she'd anticipated – and not financially), "I know how much you were looking forward to this."

"Don't be stupid," Liz replied, looking horrified that she should think – let alone say – such a thing. "In fact, I think you're amazing for going through with this at all. If it were me, I know for a fact I'd be buried under the duvet with one of my four-stone bags of Minstrels!"

Tara raised a smile. "Well, everything's arranged and, to be honest, I don't think Natalie would hear of it if I told her we weren't coming. Let's just say she's a pretty determined girl."

Liz sat back and stared out at the London streets, which were today covered with mist and rain. "I'm looking forward to meeting her and this lovely boyfriend of hers."

"Yes," Tara replied, hoping she'd be able to get through tonight without letting Natalie know she was off form. She knew how much Natalie was looking forward to their visit and showing off Jay. She really didn't want to ruin it for her. "It should be an interesting night all right."

That evening, Liz checked her appearance in the mirror for what must have been the thousandth time in the last hour. Not that it mattered an iota what she looked like in the scheme of things, she thought guiltily. Here she was, idiotically concerned about her clothes, when poor old Tara, who was getting ready in the hotel room's en suite bathroom, was going through a terrible time with Glenn.

Liz still couldn't believe that he'd got some girl pregnant. Who'd have thought he had it in him? Especially when he'd never really seemed that interested in anything other than computers and bloody football! But, as that old saying went, she thought sadly, it's the quiet ones you have to watch.

And now poor Tara was devastated over it.

Liz sighed. She hated herself for it, but for one brief second when Tara was explaining how she'd suspected that Glenn might have been Emma's mystery man, she'd almost hoped it were true.

Not that she'd ever wish something like that on Tara – no way – but from a purely selfish point of view, it would have meant that she could finally rule out it being Eric. And Liz wanted that more than anything else: she wanted to know for certain that her husband hadn't been unfaithful to her, that his association with Tara's sister was based purely on an old friendship and nothing more.

And discovering that someone else was the baby's father would certainly give her that. Although it was awful to think that Glenn and Emma could have been . . . Liz shivered at the notion of it. Still, there was that horrible tiny part of her that had grasped at the explanation, and now she despised herself for it.

Why would she want to visit such a thing on Tara – her best friend of many years, the friend who'd been there for her through thick and thin, and in fairness probably suspected too that Liz was worried about Eric's part in this, but was too much of a friend to vocalise it?

Instead she'd chosen to support Liz as much as she could, by offering to baby-sit Toby so Liz could spend some time alone with Eric, and getting her out of the house nights – and then at the first opportunity Liz goes and wishes that.

It was pathetic, *she* was pathetic, and the more she thought about it, the more she decided that when she got home she was going to face up to the problems in her marriage once and for all. If it meant she had to face up to the fact that Eric had done the unthinkable, then she'd just have to do it. After all, Tara had had to face worse than this, much more, and she'd come through it all, hadn't she?

Even now, at her lowest ebb, Tara was still putting a brave face on things – trying to overcome and put aside her hurt and disappointment with Glenn, at least for the moment. And although her friend looked wonderful in the black trousers and Karen Millen jade-green velvet and lace cami-top she was wearing tonight, there was no mistaking the pain behind her eyes.

"Will we go?" Tara said, as Liz couldn't help checking her reflection once more.

God, thought Liz, could she not stop obsessing about stupid trivial things? With all that was going on, she should have more bloody sense! But at this stage, her self-esteem was almost at rock bottom and her insecurity now second nature. Another reason, she thought, to confront the situation when she got home.

"Are you sure you're OK to do this?" Liz asked again, deciding that it was about time she started acting like a proper friend. "We could always call Natalie and cancel, say you've got a headache or something."

Tara managed a rueful laugh. "Believe me, Natalie

would be over here with the cavalry and armed with a multi-pack of Paracetamol! No, it's fine, Liz, honestly, and in all fairness it might be the best thing for me – help me to take my mind off Glenn for a while."

"Well, as long as you're sure."

"I'm sure," Tara replied and the two closed the hotel room door behind them and headed off to the West End to meet Natalie and man-of-the-moment, Jay.

At first, Liz didn't actually notice anything out of the ordinary. Anything, that was, other than the restaurant's wonderful décor and its remarkably welcoming and friendly maitre d' as he took their coats. And of course she was too busy trying to spot well-known faces amongst the tables to concentrate too much on who they were meeting.

But as they approached their table, at which sat a woman so incredibly stunning she would make Jennifer Lopez feel like Quasimodo, she noticed Tara suddenly stiffen and then stop dead in her tracks.

"Are you OK?" she queried, as the gorgeous woman – evidently Natalie – smiled and waved in their direction. Liz put a hand on Tara's arm. "Because you know we don't have to do this if you don't want –"

"Sweet Jesus, don't do this to me," Tara whispered, and when Liz glanced quickly at her friend, she realised that Tara was speaking, not to her, but almost to herself. "Please, don't do this to me – not now!"

Confused, Liz followed Tara's gaze to the table where

Natalie and her companion, a tall and, fittingly, equally attractive man, watched their approach.

Then, properly catching sight of the man, she blinked and looked again, wondering if her eyes were deceiving her. Could it be? But how . . .?

Then, as she and Tara drew nearer, her friend moving alongside her as if in a daze, Liz took a better look.

No, it wasn't who she'd thought it was at first, but by God there was one hell of a resemblance! Obviously Tara had noticed it too, which was why she was acting so strangely.

But when he finally turned his face to the light, Liz realised she *did* recognise this man, but when she'd seen him he'd been much younger and much less distinguished, standing alongside her best friend who was dressed in a cerise-pink taffeta dress.

"Tara," she said in hushed tones, almost stopping too as the image from the photograph Colm had shown her flashed into her memory, "isn't that – ?"

"Yes," her friend replied shakily, before Liz had a chance to finish the question.

"Yes, it is."

Chapter 29

Tara didn't think she could endure this for much longer.

Natalie, God love her, was trying her best, and Tara's heart went out to the girl who she knew couldn't understand why the mood at dinner was so subdued.

But, mistakenly thinking it was Liz who was the source of discomfort, Natalie spent much of the meal trying to entice her into conversation.

Liz, of course, had figured things out immediately. How could she not, seeing Jason up close like this?

Tara still didn't know how she'd found the strength to shake his hand when Natalie introduced them.

"Tara, this is Jay. Jay – Tara."

The shock and surprise in his eyes mirrored her own. As recognition dawned, she saw his expression turn from amiable to downright disbelieving.

"It's . . . nice to meet you," he stuttered, briefly shaking her hand, while she wished she could just race out the door and never come back.

Out of the corner of her eye, she could see Liz watching her carefully as they shook hands, but luckily Natalie noticed nothing.

"And this is Liz."

"Hello, very pleased to meet you." To her credit, and possibly so as not to arouse Natalie's suspicion, Liz tried to make up for Tara's lack of enthusiasm as she in turn shook Jason's hand.

"And, Liz, as you can probably guess –" Natalie went on, giving Tara a look of feigned disapproval for neglecting to introduce her friend, "I'm Natalie, and I'm so delighted to meet you. Is this your first time in London?"

"Great to meet you too, and, no, this isn't my first time, but I haven't been here in years. Thanks for inviting me."

When they went to sit down, Natalie insisted Liz take a seat alongside her at the table, leaving Tara no choice but to sit beside Jason. Natalie continued to chat to Liz about their flight over, if the hotel was OK and what she thought of the restaurant, while Tara, still reeling from the shock of seeing him again, just stared dumbstruck at the menu.

In truth, Tara was also shocked by how little he'd changed and how handsome he still looked after all these years. In a way, seeing him face-to-face, and sitting in close proximity to him like this, almost reduced her to the naïve, love-struck teenager she'd been back then. Almost, but not quite. The ensuing years had made sure of that, had guaranteed that Tara's carefree teenage years were long gone.

And so Tara sat there, within a couple of inches of the only man she'd ever truly loved, a man who'd broken her heart and trampled on her dreams, her silly pathetic teenage dreams of a great romance and a future together. And the reason she'd never ever allowed herself afterwards to get involved with someone who could hurt her like he had. Despite Liz's and everyone else's insistence that she should seek out real love and passion in her life, Tara knew that if passion led to such heartbreak and pain, she never wanted to experience it again. And as for love, well, she'd thought Glenn would give her enough of that. But as she'd only recently discovered, maybe she had been wrong in thinking that her life was under control, that by not allowing herself to fall in love again she would be immune from sorrow and pain.

'Calm, controlled and serene,' Tara remembered Natalie describing her one time, but what she didn't know was that Tara was that way for a very good reason.

And now, almost the instant she'd set eyes upon Jason (or Jay, as Natalie called him – why had she never considered there might be a connection, as he was from Dublin?) that old Bryan Adams song, "Heaven", began to play in her head. Their song – and the song that Tara had never since allowed herself to listen to in its entirety: whenever it appeared on the radio she had always steadfastly changed the channel. It was something that amused Glenn no end.

"Why do you hate that song so much?" he'd laughingly ask her, and Tara would nonchalantly declare that it was "cheesy and pathetic" while inside she'd try desperately to banish the memories the song and its lyrics always triggered. Memories of a time that Tara wanted to forget, but never, ever could. Jason had made sure of that.

"Whew! I'm stuffed after that!" Natalie declared, pushing away the half-eaten plate of roast duck in front of her. "How was yours, Tara? Was it any good? Tara?"

"What?" Tara suddenly realised that someone was speaking to her.

"How was your food? You've hardly eaten anything."

"Oh, it's great," she said, trying desperately to raise a smile, as she felt Jason's gaze on her.

"Are you sure? You haven't eaten much at all – we can send it back if it –"

"Honestly, Natalie, it's great, thanks a million. I just don't have much of an appetite this evening. Sorry."

"With all the travelling and everything," Liz inserted by way of explanation, even though their plane had been in the air barely forty-five minutes.

But Natalie didn't seem to notice anything out of the ordinary. "I know, air travel can be so tiring!" she agreed, turning once again to Liz. "I suffer from terrible jet-lag at times, do you?" she asked chattily. "Jay, you like flying though, don't you?"

"Yes."

He was being as uncommunicative as she was, Tara

noticed, resolving to try and buck herself up before Natalie noticed that something was seriously wrong. It wouldn't be fair of her to ruin this dinner, not when Natalie was making such an effort – especially with Liz.

At that moment, Natalie's eyes widened and she elbowed Liz's arm. "Do you know, I think I just saw Jodi Marsh go into the Ladies'!" she declared, and despite herself, Liz's eyes went wide as saucers.

"Are you serious?" she asked, undoubtedly unable to help herself, and Tara smiled sadly. In normal circumstances this night would have been great fun.

"Come on!" Natalie said, putting her napkin on the table and standing up. "Let's do a little celeb-stalking!"

Liz looked unsure. "Aren't you coming too, Tara?" she asked, remembering herself.

"No – you two go ahead."

"You're sure . . .?" Liz gave her a questioning look, as she followed Natalie away from the table, and Tara nodded briefly.

When they'd left, Tara truly understood the expression "you could cut the atmosphere with a knife" and she wondered how and why the gods had engineered this nightmare.

"Tara," Jason began softly, in that familiar velvety voice of his, "this is very . . . very unfortunate. I really had no idea."

Tara's voice was brittle, and as she spoke she really wasn't sure how she was getting the words out. "Unfortunate is a bit of an understatement, Jason – or should I call you Jay?"

There was a slight pause. "It's a nickname that started in uni, and it stuck. Everyone calls me that now."

"Really? So you went to university then, did you? How wonderful for you – I never got that chance."

"Tara . . . believe me, I thought about contacting you many times after –"

"And why didn't you? What stopped you? Too worried that I might tie you down, cramp your style – all those stupid expressions that people use when talking about people like me. But you wouldn't know anything about that, would you, Jason? No, you got out quick, long before the name-calling started."

"It wasn't like that – I . . ." The rest of his sentence trailed off, and he shook his head.

For the next few minutes, there was a deathly silence and right then Tara realised how crazy this was, the two of them meeting here, in a place like this, a place of wealth and opulence and celebrity, while their romance had taken place in an innocent, old-fashioned country hotel in Ireland – a million miles away from somewhere like this. Yet it was here they'd ended up.

"Tara, you must believe me when I tell you how sorry I am," he said again. "But I didn't think, I couldn't think . . . we were so young, and I just didn't know how or what . . . I was so scared –"

"Jason, you were two years older than I was! I was seventeen, barely seventeen, and I was bloody scared too! But then that didn't last long, because after that being scared was the least of my worries."

"I'm sorry," he repeated.

Yet again the two were silent, Tara twisting her cotton napkin so tightly in her hands she thought it might shred.

Eventually Jason turned to face her – the first time he'd looked at her properly all evening. "So how is . . ." he began, before pausing to take a deep breath. When he spoke again, his voice was shaking. "How is –"

"How is *Glenn*?" Tara interjected breezily. "Well, I'm delighted to say that he's grown up to be a mature, responsible and utterly wonderful young man."

Finally, she looked Jason directly in the eye. "Nothing like his father."

Chapter 30

In that instant, Tara was back on the dance-floor of the Castlegate Arms Hotel, barely seventeen years old, and in the arms of the man she'd adored for so long. The dress was, in her opinion, the most beautiful ball-gown ever created. It had taken absolutely *ages* to find but it was worth it, and as soon as Tara had tried it on in the shop, she'd known it was the perfect dress for her. The colour was her favourite – deep cerise pink – and the bodice and overskirt were made of lovely shiny satin that shone under the lights when she moved, and the lovely flowing skirts shushed along when she walked.

Jason had loved it too, and when he'd called to collect her from home earlier, he'd told her she looked "amazing". Tara was pretty certain that if she'd been going to the debs ball with any of the lads from Castlegate they wouldn't have even noticed her dress, and certainly wouldn't have called her "amazing".

Instead they'd have called to the door, fidgeted impatiently for the photographs and talked about hurrying up so they could go and meet "the boys".

But Jason Murray wasn't like any of the lads in Castlegate (thank God!) and instead of trying to avoid the photographs like Deborah Murphy's boyfriend Conor had, he'd even offered to take one of the family, Tara standing in the middle between her mam and dad and a narky-looking Emma kneeling in front and whinging about "being swallowed up in a pink meringue". And he hadn't batted an eyelid when they'd reached the hotel and Colm had insisted on getting a group photo, even though Tara knew that he was slightly uncomfortable around her friends, whom he didn't know all that well.

Now, as Jason and Tara danced slowly to Bryan Adam's "Heaven", Tara's favourite song, his arms wrapped around her waist and his cheek resting lightly against hers, she thought the lyrics had never seemed more appropriate. She truly *was* in heaven, and he was all that she wanted, that she'd ever wanted.

She still couldn't believe he'd agreed to go to the debs ball with her, this mature, sophisticated boy from Dublin who'd holidayed with his family in Castlegate every summer for as long as Tara could remember.

He and Tara had struck up a close friendship over the years, and every time he came on holiday they'd spend ages just chatting about nothing in particular and enjoying each other's company. Tara fancied him for ages, in fact all the girls in the village had fancied him for ages, but it had been Tara he'd eventually agreed to go to the debs with. And she knew all of her fellow sixth years in Our Lady's Secondary School were pea-green with envy that the fine thing from Dublin had chosen Tara Harrington to go to the debs with. Even Emma, who was only a kid, and didn't know much about fellas yet, was wide-eyed with awe when Tara told her who she was taking to the ball.

Her mam and dad hadn't been too happy about it, though.

"He's a bit old for you, love," her mother had said. "Why couldn't you have gone to the debs with one of the local lads, like that nice fella Colm Joyce or maybe Eric McGrath?" Tara had groaned inwardly at the notion. Colm was totally hyper and you wouldn't get a word in while he was around, and all Eric wanted to do was smoke fags and talk about boring stuff like football. Anyway, none of them were in the *least* bit good-looking, although this never seemed to stop them from getting girls – Colm in particular was meant to be a "demon with the women", whatever that implied.

But what Tara's parents especially didn't realise was that age didn't matter when you had something special like she and Jason did. He didn't talk about Man United and boring things like hurling; he talked about travel and was into astrology, same as she was. Jason Murray was her soul mate, she was sure of it.

And tonight, as Bryan Adam's throaty voice and romantic lyrics filled the room, Tara closed her eyes and felt more certain than ever. The only thing was, she thought, opening them just as quickly, the room was beginning to spin a bit now, and it wasn't from dancing. She'd better slow down a bit on the drink. Tara wasn't a big fan of drink, and she'd never been interested in going off down the park behind the castle, drinking flagons of cider with the boys, like some of her classmates did.

In all fairness, even Emma was able to hold her drink better than Tara, and she was only fourteen! Of course, Tara had tried to have a word with her about it, but she might as well be talking to the wall. Emma wanted to do her own thing, and nobody, least of all Tara, could stop her. She knew Emma thought she was a bit of a goody-two-shoes really. Well, she supposed she was. But she couldn't help it that she didn't like the horrible taste of cider or the way it made people act the eejit and fall all over the place, like Eric McGrath. She adored Eric, but there was no need for him to carry on like that, and when he was drinking he turned into a different person altogether. Tara thought he'd better control himself soon enough or he'd end up a drunkard just like his poor father.

No, drink just wasn't Tara's thing, but the problem was, she couldn't very well refuse the drinks that Jason had been good enough to buy her tonight, could she?

And they were expensive drinks too – Southern Comforts, he'd told her – as if she should be impressed by this. Maybe this was some sophisticated drink that they all drank up in Dublin or something, so it might be rude to say no – especially when he'd agreed to come to her debs. So, feck it, for tonight only she'd have a couple of drinks, but she'd sip them slowly, and then, hopefully, she'd be grand.

"Did I tell you, you look beautiful in that dress, Tara?" Jason murmured in her ear, and as she pictured how they must look together, Tara immediately felt like Baby in the film *Dirty Dancing*, when Patrick Swayze did that slow dance with her. That had been a great film and really romantic. And of course Baby and Johnny were different people from different backgrounds, just like her and Jason, yet they'd fallen in love and to hell with anyone who tried to stop them!

"Thank you – you look funny in a suit, but it's nice," she giggled and then kicked herself when she realised how unsophisticated that sounded. Here he was complimenting her like a proper grown-up, and she giggled back at him like a schoolgirl! Well, as of three months ago, Tara was no longer a schoolgirl – she was now a seventeen-year-old woman with the world at her feet. Not that she had much of a clue what to do with that world, she thought ruefully. At least not until she got the Leaving results anyway.

She might like to go to college – she wasn't really sure. Some of the other girls in her class, like Deborah, couldn't wait to go to college and "finally get out of this kip", whereas Tara didn't think she ever wanted to leave Castlegate. She loved her hometown and the yearly influx of tourists (like Jason) every summer, all anxious to visit the pretty village and famous Norman castle that she was lucky enough to have been born near.

Tara loved the castle and often spent hours thinking about and trying to recreate the lives of the kings and queens who had lived there and she also loved the fact that her little village had such a wealth of history behind it. So, at the moment, she didn't want to leave Castlegate.

No, what would be perfect would be if Jason and his family moved here from Dublin or something, and then she could see him all the time, and their great romance would last forever. Yes, that would be perfect.

Then, as if reading her thoughts, Jason turned his head and kissed her gently on the lips. As she kissed him back, Tara's head swam with the romance of it all, the softness of his lips, the taste of him on her tongue, as Bryan Adams was just about to finish the song with that amazing guitar solo. This truly *was* heaven and it was most definitely love, she was sure of it.

"I want to be with you, Tara," Jason whispered then. "You're beautiful."

Tara's heart soared as they kissed again, this one deeper and much more passionate. She knew it! Jason felt the same way she did, and he wanted to be with her here in Castlegate too! This was turning out to be the best night of her life. Never mind all the others throwing envious looks at her – from the looks of things there was no point in them being jealous. Jason loved her, and that was that.

Then, the wonderful slow song ended, and all too soon some noisy Madonna number broke the spell. Tara loved Madonna as much as the next girl, but at that moment she really wished that the DJ would play some more romantic numbers, so she could stay wrapped in Jason's arms forever. Although, she thought, as Jason smiled and led her away from the dance floor and back to their table, now she wouldn't ever forget that song. "Heaven" would be *their* song from now on, hers and Jason's, and whenever she heard that song on the radio in the future it would remind her of tonight – the happiest night of her life.

"Let's go outside for a while, will we?" Jason said, interrupting her musings. "It's baking hot in here."

Tara smiled. She loved his Dublin accent and the funny expressions he came out with sometimes. Castlegate people would *never* say "baking". Instead they might say "it's "boiling" or "roasting", but she didn't think they would ever say something like *baking*. It made Jason seem all the more special.

"Out to the garden?" she said, as Jason picked up her drink – another yucky Southern Comfort, she noted.

"We could go for a walk down by the river, maybe?" he suggested with a smile that made Tara's heart turn over in her chest. "It's always nice down there. And if it gets cold, you can always take my jacket."

Tara's heart soared. "I might as well bring my cloak too," she said, referring to the silk shawl-type thing that went over her dress. Although she probably wouldn't need it – the fine summer weather was lasting well into September and the evening was mild, so she'd be plenty warm as she was. Either way, she certainly wasn't going to refuse. The riverside park behind the castle had always been a popular spot for couples in love – couples like her and Jason. She couldn't wait to spend time alone with him in one of the most romantic places she could think of – especially tonight, with a full moon out.

This truly was turning out to be the best night of her life.

Chapter 31

It was, she supposed, every teenage girl's nightmare, discovering they were pregnant after having sex for the very first time. And she'd been stupid, she and Jason had been stupid that night after the debs ball, when drunk on romance (and Southern Comfort) they'd gone down to the romantic, moonlit park behind the castle and made love for the first time by the riverbank, having found a comfortable and private spot for them to be alone.

And it wasn't all horrible and fumbling like Deborah Murphy had said it was for her – for Tara it was the perfect expression of their love for one another. OK, so it was a bit uncomfortable at first, lying on the ground with only his coat and her shawl beneath them, but eventually she gave herself up to the pleasure of just being with him and enjoying what they were doing.

Afterwards, as they lay sleepily in one another's

arms, Tara thought about how wonderful it had been and how this had to be true love. She knew they had some problems to surmount, certainly – what with Jason living in Dublin and she in Castlegate – and she knew her parents already disapproved of the fact that he was that bit older than her. But this was meant to be, and they'd get through those problems, wouldn't they? They were soul mates.

Tara's euphoria was short-lived, however, when Jason – who'd dozed off for a short while immediately afterwards – woke up properly and began fretting over the realisation that they hadn't used contraception.

Tara's heart sank to her stomach, as the dreamlike state she'd been in all evening began to wear off, and Jason's anxious behaviour brought her right back to reality. He wasn't having second thoughts about their night together, was he? No, she told herself, he was merely worried that she might get pregnant or something.

But Tara was certain it should all be fine. She'd only had her period the week before, and judging from what she'd learnt in biology at school, she was probably safe enough. Still, she should have thought about it, of course she should, and right then as Jason continued to worry over their carelessness, Tara admonished herself for being so stupid and causing all this worry.

"I don't make a habit of this kind of thing," Jason told her, obviously horrified that she might think he slept with girls without protection on a regular basis.

Tara had quickly assured him that there was nothing

to worry about and that they should be fine, all the while trying to conceal her hurt and disappointment at his distant demeanour and her humiliation at his eventual admission that their night together had all been "a big mistake".

Shortly after that, they gathered their things and left the park, Tara still distressed and humiliated over what he'd said. But just before they parted, Jason kissed Tara goodbye and gently told her he'd see her soon.

Buoyed by this, Tara again reassured herself on her way home that his slightly standoffish behaviour earlier had more to do with their not using contraception than his having regrets about what had happened. After all, Jason was her soul mate, and he loved her, didn't he? No, all would be well and she was worrying for nothing.

But she'd been wrong.

Six weeks later, long after Jason had returned to Dublin, Tara's worst fears were realised in more ways than one.

Upon discovering that her period was late, she realised she had a much greater problem than a broken heart to contend with. She was barely seventeen years old and almost definitely pregnant with Jason's child, and although she'd convinced herself it was a child conceived out of love, Tara wasn't naïve enough to think that this fact alone would make it any easier for her parents to accept.

She was right. Her mother was apoplectic, and although her father tried at first to remain calm and non-judgemental, he too was obviously very upset.

"The little shit!" her mother raved. "Isn't it well for him taking off back to the city and leaving us to deal with his mess!"

"It's not a mess, Mam," Tara insisted through her tears. "We love one another. Yes, we made a big mistake, but it'll be OK. Jason loves me – he'll come back and look after us. It'll be OK."

But it wasn't OK. When Tara finally plucked up the courage to phone Jason and tell him the news, his reaction wasn't quite what she'd expected.

"I . . . I don't know what you want me to do," he'd said, after what seemed like an interminably long silence. "I'm starting college next week and –"

Immediately, Tara dropped the phone. Naïvely, she'd hoped against hope that Jason would immediately rush to her side and proclaim that he was going to take care of her and the baby, that there was no need for her parents to worry, that he would face up to his responsibilities because he loved Tara and wanted to be with her forever. Stupidly, she'd even allowed herself to pretend that the pregnancy might force his hand and get him to move here for good. But instead, he'd acted cold and uncaring, a million miles from the Jason she knew before their night in the park.

"What did I tell you?" her mother ranted. "Of *course* he's going to tell you it's your own tough luck. That's what happens in these situations. You're the one – or should I say *we're* the ones – who'll be left to shoulder the burden – so you might as well get used to it."

Looking back, the words seemed unnecessarily cruel, but a teenage pregnancy in the family – a respectable family in a small, quiet village – was every parent's nightmare.

But the words remained with Tara and, right then, she knew that if she stayed and tried to bring up the baby under her parents' roof, when they were so obviously disappointed in her and resented her situation, she'd regret it for the rest of her life.

So, when she'd eventually got over the disappointment and devastation of Jason's rejection of her, Tara resolved to take the "burden" and shame away from her family and deal with it all herself. And when, a few months later, an adorable bundle of dark hair and laughing brown eyes was born to her, Tara resolved to go it alone.

She knew what to do; she'd thought about nothing else for the last while and had set the plans in motion during the final months of her pregnancy, had spoken to the relevant authorities and knew exactly where to go and what to do next.

She'd prove to everyone that she could do this on her own, and she never wanted the baby – Glenn, she'd called him – to feel that he was an outsider or resented by anyone in her family or the community.

So, at barely eighteen years of age, Tara got out of Castlegate and went to Dublin, bringing her three-month-old baby son with her. For the first few months of his life, she'd ensured she learnt how to cope properly with him, how to feed him, how to respond to his cries, and while she had no illusions about how difficult it would be, she felt confident she could go it alone.

Much to her mother's protests. "What do you think you're playing at?" Isobel had sniggered when Tara told her she didn't want to burden her any longer. "How are you going to feed him and yourself?"

"I'll get by," she said defiantly. "Other people have to do it."

Her mother shook her head. "Nonsense! You'll be back here within a week!"

But Tara would not allow her son to be a burden on her parents, and she knew that if she stayed she would become resentful and bitter and that her mother would remind her every single day that she was beholden to them.

Granted, it wasn't exactly a bed of roses being beholden to the state services either, as Tara was in the early days. She knew that the benefits given to single mothers were a constant source of ire to the working population, but at barely eighteen years of age, she hadn't much of choice but to rely upon them. She couldn't go out to work just yet, as there was nobody to look after Glenn, so she'd had no other option but to take the "handouts" she was, apparently, legally entitled to.

They'd also put her on the housing waiting list, and in the meantime set her up in a tiny, airless bedsit on Dublin's northside, in what could only be described as a "troubled" area. But within the community Tara eventually made some good friends – especially amongst the other single mothers – and although life was very tough for the first few weeks, as far as she was concerned it was only temporary. As soon as Glenn was old enough to go to playschool, she'd come off the benefits, get a job and begin to make some kind of a life for them.

Still, in the first few weeks they'd barely coped, and many times Tara seriously considered going back home to her parents but her pride wouldn't let her. Then, almost two months after she first left Castlegate, her mother – grudgingly impressed by the strength and determination shown by her eldest daughter and ashamed at her immediate response to her plight – had insisted she come home and raise the baby there.

"We can look after the baby for a couple of mornings a week if you want to go out to work," she'd offered. "Anything to make it easier on the two of you."

Initially, Isobel had been so consumed with anger and upset (not to mention embarrassment) at Tara's stupidity that she'd been quite prepared to let her go it alone and get it out of her system. It wouldn't be too long before she'd come crawling back to Castlegate begging for help. But when the weeks passed and that hadn't happened, Isobel had to admit that her daughter's tenacity surprised her. Then again, with the kind of handouts the young ones got these days, maybe it was no surprise after all. Still, the state of the places they expected them to live in! Isobel had been horrified at the sight of roaming horses and burnt-out cars on her first time visiting the flat where Tara and the baby were living, and after that, she vowed that she'd look after them both properly.

But Tara didn't want to be "looked after"; at that stage she didn't want anything from her mother that could be construed as charity. She didn't want to go back living under her parents' roof and have it held against her for the rest of her life, as her mother surely would. She knew she'd never be allowed forget it. And by then, Tara had gone through enough without her mother's help. She'd got over the worst of it.

So, she'd faced her mother down and told her that she didn't want to go home to Castlegate, to be "looked after", and that she was perfectly fine staying in Dublin, but if Isobel and her dad wanted to contribute to their grandchild's upbringing by giving her a hand to look after him now and again, they were most welcome.

That was a proud day for Tara. She hadn't asked, she hadn't begged, yet her mother was offering to help with the baby, not because she had to, but because she *wanted* to.

And Tara accepted the offer with a pure sense of relief, relief that she no longer had to do it all alone, that her parents would be involved in Glenn's life too, but by their own choice. This way, she and her mother were closer to an equal footing – they were both adults, sharing the burden (and the joys) of looking after the baby, rather than Glenn and Tara living at home and always having to feel grateful because her mother had no choice but to help her out.

Her dad had been wonderful too and, as a young

toddler, Glenn loved going down to the house in Castlegate now and again to work out in the garden with him, while all the time his mother strove to build a decent life for them in Dublin.

Eventually, when Glenn was old enough, Tara enrolled him in the local playschool and herself in a state-sponsored "back to work" programme, working mornings in a nearby centre for troubled kids.

The scheme was designed so that she could contribute to the community, learn some new skills and at the same time hold on to her benefits. It was a godsend for Tara, who had been terrified she'd become like some of the other unmarried mothers she knew, perpetually dependent on the state, with no desire or no incentive to do anything else. Whereas nothing mattered more to Tara than to have the chance to get out of the poverty cycle and try to make a better life for herself and Glenn.

So, by the time Glenn was eight years old, and with his grandmother on board to look after him (on *Tara's* terms, she'd been clear about that), Tara had gone on to complete a variety of similar schemes and had built up a decent portfolio of different skills, so much so that she'd decided that community and social care was what she wanted to do. But, jobs were limited and she discovered, when finally coming off benefits, wages were very low, and the centres where her skills were most needed were chronically under-funded.

Still, this was where Tara's interests lay, and while Glenn was in school during the day, she kept them going by working in a telesales company and then took a correspondence course in social studies by night. And by the time she was twenty-five years old, Tara had a decent job, her own rented flat (not much bigger than the one the state provided but, most importantly, paid for out of her own wages) and had completed a university diploma, all with an eight-year-old son in tow.

But – and every day Tara thanked her lucky stars for this – Glenn was a wonderfully mild-mannered child who loved nothing better than sitting quietly in front of his computer, playing games. Initially, Tara had been concerned at his apparent contentment with his own company, but according to his teachers, he had lots of friends and was very outgoing at school so this wasn't an issue.

"Tara, look, see what I can do!" he'd say, calling her into his bedroom, hoping to impress her by displaying his skills on some confusing computer game that would leave his mother dizzy trying to keep up with him.

"Why doesn't he call you 'Mammy'?" her mother asked one day. By then, the two had long put aside their differences, and Isobel was very much involved in her grandson's life. "It seems strange that he calls you by your name."

Tara shrugged. "Do you know, I don't really notice it any more," she said truthfully. "It was funny in the early days when he started doing it as a toddler – probably because he never heard me being called anything other than Tara by the other mothers and kids in the estate. But I never really corrected him, so I suppose it stuck. I don't mind, though."

Isobel said nothing, feeling that it wasn't really her place to criticise her daughter's child-rearing skills at this stage, not when she'd done such an amazing job, particularly in the early days when she'd gone it alone. But it was a bit strange all the same.

Eventually, and especially once Glenn hit his teenage years, Tara began to carve out more of a life for herself, and so she went about setting up her life-coaching consultancy. It was ironic, really, that this work could be carried out in her own home now that Glenn was old enough to do his own thing; whereas when he was a baby there been no option for her to do anything other than go out to work.

And the last few years had been great for them – they had an incredibly close relationship, Glenn very aware and evidently respectful of the sacrifices his mother had made for him, and he'd never given her a bit of trouble or a night of worry.

Of course, she was occasionally concerned about him falling in with the wrong crowd, but seeing as most of his mates were computer geeks just like him, she'd little need to worry!

And when earlier that year she'd learnt that Glenn had passed his Leaving Certificate exams and had gained enough points for computer studies (what else?) in university, she'd never felt so proud. It had been worth it, all the pain, all the heartache and poverty, and years missed going out and enjoying life like other girls her age. Glenn was her life, and everything she'd worked for had come good.

She hadn't lied when she'd told Jason that he'd grown up to be a decent, respectable young lad. He had, and sometimes his level-headedness worried her. Immediately after finishing school and his exams, instead of taking it easy for the summer as most other seventeen-year-olds would do, he'd taken the junior analyst's job at Pixels, which he hoped would give him lots of experience in his chosen field. But the truth was that Glenn's first love was and always had been computers. It was only surprising he hadn't been born with a keyboard in his hands, she thought smiling, such was his love for all things cyber.

Now, lying awake in bed for the second night running, Liz sleeping soundly in the bed next to her, tonight's nightmare dinner with Jason and Natalie finally over, Tara worried once more about Glenn and the situation he was facing. She'd no right to criticise; after all, the same thing had happened to her and everything had turned out OK, but didn't he have any idea how hard it was going to be?

She wanted more for him, of that there was no doubt. But she couldn't help but be impressed by his determination to stand by this girl Abby and shoulder his responsibilities. Whether or not this optimism would still be around by the time the child was born was another thing, but at least he was giving the girl the support she needed.

The kind of support that Tara had sorely craved from Jason.

The Murrays had never again returned to Castlegate

for the holidays, and after that initial phone call to tell him she was pregnant, Tara had never again heard from Jason.

In fact, she hadn't thought about him for a very long time, and certainly hadn't expected to bump into him again at this stage, and especially not in London. Back then, Tara had tried to convince herself that her reasons for moving to Dublin were purely for Glenn's good, but thinking about it, maybe there was a tiny part of her that subconsciously hoped she might bump into Jason again in his home city, although apparently he lived in a big house south of the capital along the coast, a million miles from the run-down part of the city she'd had to settle for.

But he must have moved to England in the meantime – Natalie had mentioned he'd gone to university in London – so in reality there had been little chance of her seeing him during Glenn's early days.

Anyway, over the years it was very likely he had forgotten all about Tara and the baby he'd fathered but had never seen. She smiled through her tears. It was strange, until tonight he would never have even known if it was a boy or a girl.

How sad for him, she thought now, her anger at Jason and his treatment of her having long since dissipated, how sad that he had missed, and never could share, the wonderful experience of being Glenn's parent.

There was a lot of Jason in Glenn, of course, especially in appearance, so much so that even Liz had spotted the resemblance when she'd first seen him at the restaurant. They had the same dark colouring, strong jaw-line and proud Roman nose, the same chocolate-coloured eyes. And they also had that same quiet, gentle way and restful personality that had made Tara fall for Jason in the first place.

And when tonight she saw how handsome he still looked, and how over the ensuing seventeen years life had evidently treated him very well, she couldn't help but feel bereft once more at what she had lost. She'd loved him deeply – so deeply it hurt – and she didn't think she'd ever really got over that.

Of course, there hadn't been too many opportunities to see other men, not in her situation and, in all honesty, she didn't care.

All throughout her late teens and twenties, her priority had been Glenn, and despite Liz's insistence now and again that she should try and find someone special, someone for herself, she just didn't have the urge.

There had been a couple of dates now and again once Glenn was old enough, but it was just for the sake of it and very much a case of going through the motions. Tara's heart just wasn't in it. Her son gave her all the love and companionship she needed, and although she knew deep down that the time would come when Glenn would grow into adulthood and likely leave her to her own devices, she just hadn't imagined it would happen so soon.

But, this time next year, Glenn would have his own responsibilities and a child of his own to look after. Who knows, maybe he and this Abby girl would make a go of it together and he'd have a family of his own too? And Tara would no longer be the most important thing in his life – she'd be just his mother, there in the background, loved certainly, but no longer needed in quite the same way. She'd have to face up to that now. Face up to the fact that, for the first time in her thirty-four years, Tara would be facing life alone.

Chapter 32

"I really hope you didn't mind my telling her," Liz said to Tara, the following morning over breakfast at the hotel. "I just thought it would make things easier for you, and easier for us to leave."

Liz still couldn't believe that the dream man Tara had been helping Natalie with had turned out to be Glenn's father.

She'd seen the resemblance straight away in the restaurant of course; it was very difficult *not* to, when they looked so alike, and she'd even gone as far as to think that it had been *Glenn* sitting at the table with Natalie. But then when she realised how tense and upset Tara was, the penny soon dropped. And of course, now she understood why Colm had thought it strange at the time that she'd asked who the guy in the debs photo with Tara was. With the benefit of hindsight, it should have been obvious *exactly* who he was. But while she had, of course, known that Tara had given birth to Glenn at a very young age, she had no idea he'd been conceived on Tara's debs night.

No wonder then that Tara didn't want to be reminded of that night, and no wonder Colm had been insistent that Liz shouldn't mention the photograph to her.

Of course, it was different now, and these days it was more of an excuse for a party than anything else, but back when she and Tara were teenagers, a girl's debs night was supposed to be a very special night – often one of the most special nights of a girl's life, and the man she chose to bring was so important.

"Of course I don't mind you telling her," Tara said, replying to Liz's question as to whether or not she was right in confiding to Natalie in the Ladies' that Tara wasn't in great form because of some problems she was having with Glenn.

Natalie had been inconsolable. "Bloody hell, now I feel awful that she came all the way over to visit me. If I'd known, I'd never have expected her to come! Oh, Liz, I feel so guilty now!"

"Don't feel guilty, you weren't to know," Liz had said, wondering how poor Tara was getting on alone out there with Jay. But she'd thought it better to accompany Natalie to the toilets and give them some time alone and Tara seemed OK with her doing that. Evidently, Natalie didn't know anything about Jason being a father, and certainly not being Glenn's! "But I'm sure you can appreciate that she's worried about him, so she's not her usual self."

"I know, I know, and I did wonder why she was being so quiet. Oh, God, Liz, we'd better get back – I'd hate for Tara to feel that she has to make stupid small talk with someone she doesn't know. Come on!" And with that, the two of them returned to the table – to a quiet and uncomfortable-looking Tara and an upset-looking Jay.

Later, Natalie had taken Tara aside and told her that she so appreciated her coming and that she felt so awful that she'd come at all, and she certainly didn't expect her to have to put on a brave face just for her sake.

"We'll go home soon, Jay and I – and you go back to the hotel with Liz and get a good night's sleep. And I'll arrange for early flights home for the two of you tomorrow if you like. Please don't feel as though you have to stay in London any longer on my account. I'd much rather you went home and sorted it all out with Glenn. Liz didn't give me too much detail other than . . . well, you know," she looked embarrassed, "but if you *do* need to talk sometime, let me know. I owe you one. It's all because of me that you had to come here in the first place, so it's the very least I can do." And with that, she hugged Tara tightly and after dinner she and Jay bade Liz and her goodnight.

Liz knew that the idea of going home early was a godsend to Tara, who had got so many shocks in the last day or two it was a miracle she was still standing. What with learning about Glenn's impending fatherhood, and then meeting her first love, the father of her teenage son . . . well, it was enough to make Liz thank her lucky stars for her relatively trouble-free life.

At least for the moment anyway. And it was also enough for her to want to confront Eric about his strange behaviour. Tara was an incredible woman who had been through so much and yet still managed to keep all the balls in the air, whereas Liz was a wimp who should be ashamed to call herself a woman. If Tara could get by without a man for all these years, then so could Liz. If Eric had betrayed her, then he wasn't good enough for her, or indeed for Toby.

"And how do you feel this morning? About everything?" she asked Tara now.

"I'm not sure. I suppose seeing Jason reminded me that Glenn's girlfriend, if I can call her that, is about the same age as I was when I had him. So I'm not really in a position to judge. I wanted more for him than this, but . . ." she shrugged, "I have to admire the way he's dealing with it – well, the way he's *proposing* to deal with it. Who knows how he'll cope when the baby is born and he has to support them. But honestly, Liz, the thing that bothers me the most is that he's all grown up now." There were tears in her eyes as she spoke, and her voice was full of regret. "He no longer needs me. And when someone has depended on you for half your lifetime, that takes some getting used to. Although now I think I understand why my mother and Emma have always had a much better relationship than she and I did. With her childhood illnesses, and now her pregnancy, Emma has always needed her, and my mother likes to be needed. Whereas I made it clear very early that I didn't need her, that I could stand on my own two feet, irrespective of what I was going through. I grew up too fast, and to this day I have never let her see anything other than the strong Tara, the Tara that can take on the world and whom nothing fazes. I think my mother doesn't know how to deal with that; she doesn't know what her role in my life has been for a very long time." She shook her head sadly. "Whereas Emma has always needed her – she was always in trouble with jobs, men . . . and now this. And don't get me wrong, I don't resent the fact that this will all be so much easier for Emma to deal with than it was for me; after all, she's much older and times have changed, and there will be none of the shame and disgrace that I experienced." She exhaled deeply. "And I suppose I have to be careful now not to do the same thing with Glenn. I have to let him know that I'll be there for him and Abby whatever they decide to do. And I'll do my best to help them out with my . . ." she laughed as if unable to believe she was actually saying the words, "my grandchild. Imagine, Liz, a grandmother at thirty-four years of age!" Then her face changed slightly. "Although make that an over-the-hill grandmother with no life of her own. Do you know, you were right all along. I should have thought some more about finding someone to share my life with, someone just for me."

"It's not too late to do that, you know," Liz told her gently. "You might be a granny soon, but you're still only in your thirties."

Tara shook her head. "I couldn't do it, Liz. I wouldn't even know where to start. I know nothing about men.

The last time I had any sort of relationship was when I was barely seventeen years old, and look where that led."

"You know as much as any of us do. Look at all the help and advice you gave Natalie . . ." She winced, realising what she'd just said.

But Tara laughed. "Good God, isn't it mad when you think about it? Here I was, coaching Natalie on how to nab this so-called man of her dreams, when all along he was the man of my dreams too!"

"And how do you feel about him now?"

Tara looked her straight in the eye. "To be honest, Liz, I feel sorry for him. Look at what he missed out on. Glenn is a wonderful gift, and I treasure every second I've spent with him. Yes, it was unbearably tough sometimes, but my love for him and wanting to do the best for him kept me going. But Jason experienced none of that. He decided he didn't want to experience it a long time ago. But I did fine. And to be honest, I could look him in the eye last night and honestly tell him that I did a good job. And I did. At least," she said, eyes dropping to the tablecloth, "at least I thought I did until the day before yesterday."

"You did do a fantastic job," Liz assured her. "And you know better than most that a teenage pregnancy doesn't have to be the end of the world."

Natalie and Jay were having breakfast in her flat.

"God, Jay, I felt so awful! I had no idea she was

having problems of her own. Typical me, too obsessed with myself to notice anyone else."

"Don't be silly, you weren't to know," Jay said, his voice soft and, Natalie thought, sounding tired and weary.

"Did you sleep OK last night?" she asked him. "I know my bed isn't as comfy as yours but –"

"No, it was fine – I just have a couple of things on my mind at the moment, that's all."

"I still can't believe she came all the way over just to see me – and you, of course," Natalie went on, regardless, "when all the time she was worrying about Glenn!"

She spread some strawberry jam on her bagel. "I have to say, I'm surprised at him; he seemed like such a level-headed guy."

Jay's head snapped up. "You met Tara's son?"

"Yes, on holidays in Egypt. Remember, I told you that's where I met Tara in the first place?"

"What . . . what was he like?" Jay asked gently.

"Like? I'm not too sure really – I didn't get to talk to him much. A typical seventeen-year-old, I suppose. Mad into sports – he did a scuba-diving course when we were over there. Although I will say I thought he was very good-looking. I told Tara that too and . . . what . . . what's wrong, Jay?" It was weird, but if she didn't know better, she'd swear that Jay's eyes were glittering with tears. He mustn't have got a wink of sleep in her bed. Well, that was his own fault for refusing to let her help tire him out, she thought, still a little miffed that last night, after their return from the restaurant, Jay hadn't been in an amorous mood. "Jay? Are you all right?"

"Nothing, sorry, I was just thinking about something – what were you saying?"

"I was just saying Tara's son was very good-looking and mad into sports. But I really am surprised at him. He seemed like such a gentle sort, the type who wouldn't look twice at a girl – let alone get one pregnant. And apparently he met her in Egypt too –"

"I'm sorry, what did you say?" Jason interjected shortly.

"Jay, I really wish you'd wake up. I said he met this girl in Egypt."

Jay looked pale. "So, Tara was upset because Glenn – I mean, her son – got a young girl pregnant?"

"Yes, she only found out the day before yesterday. I thought I told you this. It was why she seemed so preoccupied last night."

"You told me she was having problems of some kind but you didn't tell me what."

Natalie shrugged and took a bite of her bagel. "Well, I suppose as a single mother of a guy that age, it's to be expected that she'll have all sorts of problems to deal with. I must say I really admire her, though. Given what she's had to deal with, she's incredibly cool and in control. Of course, I suppose she had to be, considering the fact that Glenn's father, cowardly bastard, ran out on her when she was just seventeen. Can you imagine it?" She shook her head at Jay. "I'm so relieved that kind of thing never happened to me at that age – it must have been a nightmare. And in all seriousness, what kind of man must he have been to turn tail and run when the going got tough like that? Honestly, Jay," Natalie asked, shaking her head in disgust, "what kind of horrible, selfish coward would do something like that?"

As promised, Natalie had organised and paid for flights to get Liz and Tara home late on the Saturday afternoon instead of Sunday evening as had been arranged. It was a relief really, Liz thought, as she didn't think poor Tara could cope with having to try and keep up a brave face for her sake. Liz knew that if she was in Tara's position, she'd just want to lock herself away from everyone and have a good cry, but true to form Tara was trying to keep up a steady stream of chat on the way home in the plane.

And when they reached Dublin airport close to six p.m., Tara insisted on driving Liz to Castlegate.

"No, you head home," Liz said, dismissing the offer. "I'll give Eric a call. The traffic will be light this time on a Saturday evening, and he'll be here in no time."

But Tara wouldn't hear of it and so, earlier than expected, Liz arrived back from her weekend away, tired but thankful she didn't have Tara's worries to deal with.

Waving her friend goodbye from the gate and thanking her profusely for the lift home, Liz walked round the back to take a quick check on the dogs before letting herself in the back door.

There was no sign of life in the kitchen, so she threw her bags on the kitchen table and went to look for Toby and Eric in the living room.

Expecting to see a cosy tableau of her husband and young son sitting in front of the TV, perhaps with the dogs at their feet, Liz couldn't believe what she was seeing instead.

"What the hell is *she* doing here?" she shouted from the living-room doorway, as a shocked Eric, a delighted Toby and a brazen Emma turned around to face her.

There the cow was, sitting cosily in Liz's living room with her husband and son and behaving as if she belonged there all her life!

"Liz – what are you doing here?" Eric asked, all the colour draining from his face.

"What am I doing here? I *live* here!" Liz raged. "And I asked you a question! What is *she* doing here? Jesus Christ, Eric, do what you like behind my back, but how dare you, how *dare* you bring this floozy into my house and flaunt her in front of my son! How dare you!"

Emma raised an eyebrow. "Wow, and here I was thinking you were the mousey type! Shows how much I know."

"You keep your fucking mouth shut, you little tramp!" Liz said. She couldn't help it, something inside her had snapped seeing that girl there, knowing that she had the power to break up her life, mess up her family, in fact had probably done so already. So what was the point in hiding from it any more? She had no respect for Eric, and certainly none for that rap Emma, but she owed it to her son at least to show some backbone, in the same way that Tara had for hers.

"Liz! What the hell is wrong with you?" Eric cried. "Don't use language like that, especially not in front of Toby."

As if on cue, the baby started to cry and Liz immediately marched into the room, brushed past a shocked Eric and took Toby in her arms. "It's all right, honey, Mummy's here, now." She kissed her son gently on the head, swearing blindly that Eric could do what he liked but he would never, ever hurt this child. She turned to Emma and Eric. "Get the hell out of my sight, the two of you, and carry on with whatever you were doing somewhere else."

"Liz –"

"I don't want to hear your pathetic excuses, Eric. Be man enough for once in your life to tell the truth."

"Wow, I *definitely* had you pegged wrong," Emma said, and Eric silenced her with a look.

"Emma, I think you'd better go," he said softly to her.

For Liz, the gentle way he spoke to the other girl was like a red rag to a bull.

"Didn't you hear what I said?" she cried. "I want both of you *out of my sight*! This instant! I don't care where you go or what you're doing – to be honest, I really couldn't give a f—" she caught herself just in time, "a damn about what's going on between you. So you," she pointed at Eric, "can take that pregnant tramp and get away from me."

"Liz! What are you – ?"

"I don't want to hear it, Eric!" she raged. "Just leave me alone, both of you!" And with that she turned on her heel and marched into the kitchen.

Then, hands still shaking with anger, she put Toby on her lap and her head in her hands and cried.

In the living room, Eric and Emma stared at one another, unsure what to say.

"I think you'd better leave," Eric said finally, as Emma got to her feet.

"Well, it seems you're most definitely in the dog-house now," she told him resignedly.

"Emma, please, just go – I need to sort this out."

"Are you going to tell her?"

"I think I have to," Eric replied levelly, as he met her worried gaze. "I have to tell her something – especially now that it's all come to a head. But I really had no idea she'd come back early today and –"

"Look, do what you have to do," she said, sighing deeply. She picked up her bag and headed for the door. "I think everything has to come out now anyway. It was bad luck my being here, wasn't it?"

"Yes," Eric replied firmly. "Yes, it was."

Chapter 33

"Liz, listen to me."

"I don't want to hear it, Eric, I really don't. How dare you bring that tramp into our home!"

When Emma had left and Eric had followed Liz into the kitchen, evidently wanting to talk, she had put on a Disney video for Toby, who was now watching it happily in the living room and, Liz thought, hopefully oblivious to his parents' "discussion".

"Why are you behaving like this, Liz? And as for calling Emma a tramp, what's all that about?"

"Oh, believe me, I could think of plenty other names to call her," Liz said, lifting her chin, "but I'm not going to – not with our son in the next room."

"Liz, I don't understand, what's brought all of this on?"

"What?" She whirled around to face him, amazed at his brazenness. "What's brought all of this on? I come home early from a weekend away, away from worrying about our marriage, to find you, your pregnant girlfriend and my son happily ensconced in my front room – *that's* what's brought all of this on! How did you expect me to react, Eric? Did you think that I would come in, pull up a table for Emma to put her feet on and offer her a cup of coffee or something? How can you be so callous, bringing her here, flaunting her in front of everyone and, worse, in front of Toby? What the hell is wrong with you?"

"Liz –"

"I said I don't want to hear it, Eric! I've seen and heard enough already. All I want now is for you to just get out of my sight – just pack your stuff and leave. Get out of the house. I'd go myself only I don't feel as though I should have to. This is my home, after all, my dream house, our dream house. Except it didn't turn out exactly like that, did it?" She bit her lip, willing the tears to stay away.

"Liz, you have things totally wrong!" Eric cried, white-faced. "I don't know why you think there's something going on between me and Emma – she just called over this afternoon to say hi! I didn't know she was coming, and I certainly didn't think it would be –"

"Oh for goodness sake, why can't you just come right out and admit it! All those secret meetings with her that you think I didn't know about, the texts and phone conversations, all the sneaking around behind my back. How long did you think it would be before I found out? This is a small town, Eric – as you should well know."

Eric blanched. "You seriously think I was having an affair with Emma?"

"Why not? She's the famous ex-girlfriend, isn't she? The one who supposedly broke your heart for some unexplained reason all those years ago. The one I've had to try and live up to ever since we moved to this godforsaken place."

"Liz –"

"So, you go and do what you like now – go ahead, you're free. Free of me and Toby and the drudgery of married life. Although, seeing as she'll be ready to give birth in a few months, it won't be long before you're back in the same mindless, boring existence you're in now."

"Mindless, boring existence . . . what the hell are you talking about? I love you and Toby, but you're too wrapped up in him to notice or care!"

"Don't make this about me, Eric, don't you dare make it about me or blame me! You and Toby were all I ever wanted, a happy family is all I ever wanted, you know that."

"I do know that, which is why I've always done everything in my power to make that happen! I do know how much it means to you, and it means everything to me too. But I did something stupid, Liz, I did something that could destroy all that and I couldn't tell you."

"Getting another girl pregnant was a funny way of keeping our family together, Eric," she said bitterly.

"Liz, for Christ's sake, will you listen to me! I did

not get Emma pregnant. I am not having an affair with her!"

Something deep inside Liz began to flutter awake, but she didn't dare believe him, not just yet. "What about all those secret meetings? The texts . . . the sneaking around?"

Eric sat down alongside her at the kitchen table. "It wasn't like that. As you know, Emma and I used to be friends and –"

"I think that's a bit of an understatement, don't you?"

"Liz, you have to understand that Emma, and also Tara to a certain extent, understood what I was going through growing up here in this town. My family weren't liked, because of my dad's drinking – I wasn't liked . . ." He shook his head. "But she and Tara were good friends to me back then. And when I moved back to Castlegate –"

"You remembered how good you were together and decided to take up where you left off all those years ago?"

"That's not it. When we first moved here, things were going great. You said you'd never been so happy as in this house, with Toby and being able to run the kennels. I knew it was up to me to keep that going. I wanted you to be happy – for us to be happy. But recently it's seemed that Toby and the dogs are what's keeping you happy, not me."

"Oh, for goodness sake, Eric, spare me the 'my wife doesn't understand me so I was forced into another woman's arms' bit. It's a bit clichéd, don't you think?"

"It wasn't that. I felt a bit . . . isolated from it all. And it was weird, because it had been my idea to move here and make a new life for ourselves in Castlegate, so I could hardly turn around and tell you that I wasn't enjoying it as much as you were."

"But you were commuting to the city! You weren't here often enough to enjoy it! You were too busy enjoying yourself in pubs in Dublin!"

Eric looked right at her. "I wasn't enjoying myself in Dublin pubs. Liz, I was working in them."

"What? What are you talking about?"

"Liz, I got laid off from Securitex a couple of months ago, not long before Tara went on holiday. I couldn't tell you because you were so excited about living here and about getting the house sorted properly, and I didn't want you to feel as though you had to succeed with the kennels right away to keep us going. I didn't want to put you under any pressure."

"But how could you not tell me you got laid off?" Liz gasped, stunned.

"I thought I'd find something soon enough, and again, I tried a couple of places in Castlegate. But Liz, as you know, nobody needs security guards in a tiny place like this. I couldn't find anything different, and it wasn't easy getting in somewhere in Dublin either. So I went back to bar work. I was doing days in a hotel in Leeson Street and some nights – the nights I told you I was working overtime at Securitex – in a place in Temple Bar. That's why it worked out so well this weekend and I 'supposedly' had the time off while you went away. Anyway, one night, Emma happened to walk into the place I was working, and I was rumbled. So I had to tell her what had happened."

"You told *her* – but you couldn't tell me!"

"I couldn't tell you, Liz. I knew you'd be devastated."

"And you didn't think I'd be devastated even more to think that you were the father of Emma Harrington's child?"

"Liz, never in a million years did I imagine you'd think something like that! Why would you?"

"Because of all those secret meetings and texts, which I'm still not convinced were innocent, by the way! What was going on? What else were you hiding from me? Because there had to be something else, Eric – losing your job is no big deal in the scheme of things. You'll easily get something else – and I'm sure if you sat it out long enough you'd get something here."

"You see, this is why I didn't want to tell you! I knew you'd try to convince me to get a job here! And when I didn't find anything – when I was sitting at home twiddling my thumbs while my wife had to look after other people's dogs to keep things going, then everyone would say that they'd been right all along, that I was Pat McGrath's son after all – a waster and a drunk."

Liz was amazed at the pain in his voice. She'd never really understood why Eric felt he had to prove something to the people in the village. Tara had mentioned that his father had been troublesome and that she'd been afraid Eric would turn out the same, but because his father had been dead for years, Liz hadn't really known what she meant by this.

But she couldn't let talk of all this distract her from what she really wanted to know, the real reason Emma and Eric had been in contact.

When she said this to Eric, he sighed loudly.

"Well, when I said Emma agreed to keep my secret, about working at the bar, it turned out to be quid pro quo. I eventually discovered that she had a secret too. When she came in that first night, she was with a few others, and we started chatting. She seemed in really good form, and she eventually told me all about this great guy she'd been with, although she wouldn't mention any names. Emma is a bit like that, a bit secretive."

"I'll say," Liz replied shortly. "So how did you find out about her pregnancy?"

"By accident really. She started to come in to the pub a bit more after finding out I was working there. To be honest, I think she was a bit lonely in Dublin, despite this new man she'd found – at least that's what I thought at the time. And of course, when she came in, we used to chat a lot, chat about harmless things and people we both knew and all that. And then one time, I made a casual, offhand comment about a particular person we both knew, and her face crumpled. It *crumpled*, Liz – I've never seen Emma let her guard down like that. So, after a lot of persuading, she broke down and eventually told me what had been going on – that the person I'd so casually mentioned in conversation, the *man* I'd mentioned, meant something to her. Meant a lot to her. And she was heartbroken."

"Heartbroken over the guy she was being secretive about – the mysterious father of her baby?"

Eric nodded. "But at this stage she hadn't admitted she was pregnant. I only knew about that when you mentioned it here in this kitchen. But of course I put two and two together, and when I asked her about it, she'd no choice but to admit that, yes – she was pregnant by the same person we'd spoken about before."

"So, you knew who the baby's father was," Liz stated. "And Emma knew about you losing your job and working in the pub –"

"Yes, but things got worse for me shortly after that. Just when I thought I was getting back on track and earning a decent wage, the pub in town began to cut my hours back. So I panicked, thinking that I was further away from getting things sorted – and in effect, further away from telling you – than ever. I was desperate. And seeing as Emma was the only one who understood –"

"Well, of course she was the only one who understood!" Liz retorted, stung. "She was the only one you told!"

"I know . . . I know and that's not what I meant. I'm sorry . . ." Eric shook his head. "Look, because Emma and I both knew what the other was . . . going through, we began meeting up now and again, just to let off steam."

"While you kept secrets from everyone else – secrets from me."

"I know, and, Liz, you really don't know how hard it was to –"

"So who is it?" Liz interjected, cutting him off. "Who's this mysterious person Emma's been seeing? Is it someone from the village?"

Eric shook his head, his expression guarded. "Liz – she swore me to secrecy about it."

"Why – is it because it is someone from the village, someone I know?" Liz asked, her curiosity now getting the better of her. She was *dying* to find out who this man might be, the mysterious man that had managed to break the heart of ice-queen Emma Harrington. "Who *is* he?" she urged.

Eric sighed deeply. "Look, I promised Emma I wouldn't tell anyone, but I'm going to tell you because you're my wife, and I don't want any more secrets between us. But you can't breathe of word of it, Liz – too many people will get hurt by it. Emma made a silly mistake, and she got caught out. This is a difficult situation for everyone involved, and it'll do no one any good if it gets out."

"Who is it, Eric?"

"You have to understand that Emma has always got what she wanted, all the way through life. She's been indulged, spoiled – she managed to get every man she ever set her sights on. Except one. And I'm sure you know from Tara that she's the kind of girl who doesn't like it when she doesn't get what she wants, that it merely makes her want it all the more. And there's always been one person Emma wanted that she could never have, and it's something that's plagued the poor girl for a very long time."

"Eric, who the hell is it?" Liz insisted impatiently. "Who is the father of Emma Harrington's baby? Tell me!"

Eric took another deep breath. And then, when he finally did tell her, Liz's jaw dropped to the floor.

Chapter 34

Having left Liz and Eric's house, Emma hurried across the bridge towards the centre of the village, her heart racing in panic and her cheeks burning with humiliation in anticipation of what she now had to do.

Damn, damn, damn! Eric would have told Liz by now – he had to have told her by now. He'd need to in order to explain Emma's presence in the house, particularly when Liz was so sure Eric was the father of her baby. And of course that was her own fault for messing with Liz's head this last while, wasn't it? God knows she was sorry for doing that now – if she hadn't sent the text and made that stupid phone call, then Liz wouldn't be so paranoid and Eric wouldn't have to pacify her.

And when Liz did find out who the father of Emma's baby was, then of course she would be only too delighted to tell everyone else – after all that had happened lately, Eric's wife certainly didn't owe her anything.

Damn Liz anyway for coming home so early! Emma had been looking forward to a quiet evening chatting with Eric at his house, although in truth he had seemed rather uncomfortable earlier when she'd arrived at his doorstep unannounced.

She'd known, of course, that Liz had gone away for a weekend with Tara, so the coast was clear, so to speak. But never mind trying to make Liz jealous, which, Emma admitted to herself, had been good fun initially but had begun to wear thin – she found she really did enjoy talking to Eric about everything. She enjoyed getting her worries off her chest. And while Eric had always been sympathetic, Emma lately got the feeling that he was sorry all the secrecy had ever started.

He was clearly very much in love with Liz and worried for his family, and as time went on Emma did feel truly sorry for him that he couldn't find a proper job. At first, it had been a bit funny, happening upon Eric working behind the bar in Dublin like that, and the poor guy obviously so embarrassed about it and desperate to keep it a secret. But when his hours were cut and his worries multiplied, Emma realised that it was no joke at all.

And, yes, maybe her own worries were just as valid, but lately she got the impression that Eric was tired of listening to her moan about her woes and wanted her to think seriously about getting everything out in the open.

"It can't stay hidden forever, Emma," Eric had insisted at his house earlier. "When he sees how big you're getting and realises that you *are* pregnant, surely he'll put two and two together? Maybe he already has."

Emma shook her head. "You know I've been avoiding him ever since – as far as I can tell he doesn't know anything at all. Too wrapped up in his own little life," she added bitterly. "And I'm not really showing enough yet for the gossip to start."

"Yet," Eric repeated meaningfully. "OK, so he might not suspect anything now, but he certainly will in a few months' time when the baby is born. The man isn't stupid, Emma – he'll work things out for himself!"

"Being with me in the first place was stupid of him, Eric!" Emma retorted quickly, the beginnings of tears in her eyes, "And what he did afterwards was even worse! Why mess around with my head like that? Why sleep with me at all if he knew it wasn't going anywhere, if his heart was somewhere else?"

"I know. I know." Eric was soothing. "I wish I knew. But things have always been complicated where he's concerned – you know that better than I do."

Emma nodded but couldn't reply as she tried to stop the tears from coming. She certainly did know that, but still it hadn't stopped her from thinking that their night together had meant something more. Having sworn for most of her adult life that she'd never, ever make a fool of herself over some man like her sister had, she'd then gone and stupidly done the very same thing. She'd been an idiot.

"He's bad news where women are concerned, Emma – always has been."

"Maybe, but that doesn't change the fact that I really cared about him," Emma said sadly. "And he used me. And just because he was unsure about what he really wanted, I'm left in this position."

Now, as she made her way across the bridge, Emma came to the conclusion that there was no point in keeping her pregnancy a secret from him any longer. Eric was right. He had to know, and soon.

Very soon, before Liz McGrath had a chance to tell the whole world about it.

A few minutes later, Emma stood outside his front door.

Steeling herself for the confrontation to come, she tried to keep calm as she rang the doorbell. She stood back from the doorstep and fastened her coat up to the neck in a conscious attempt to keep her condition concealed. OK, so she might have come here with the express intention of telling him, but she didn't want to make it all so obvious from the outset. And she certainly didn't want him to panic at the sight of her bump and maybe quickly close the door in her face. Who knows how he'd react to something like this?

Suddenly, the door swung open and there he stood in the doorway, looking as handsome and wonderful as ever, and as she caught sight of him once again, Emma's breath caught in her throat. God, how she wished she didn't feel like this! But it was pointless wishing – for some reason, he had always had a profound effect on her, and despite her attempts to deny it, she just couldn't help how she truly felt.

"Emma, hi! This is a surprise . . . how are you?" By the slight wariness in his tone, she knew immediately that there was someone else in the house with him – and she could guess exactly who. Well, she wasn't going to keep him very long.

"Well, I'd like to say I'm fine, but that would be a lie," Emma said shortly, lapsing into defensive mode.

"Oh?" He looked confused. "What's up? And how can I help?"

"That night . . ." she began, staring straight at him, her eyes cold and her chin upturned. "The night we –"

He visibly winced. "Emma, I'm sorry . . . but can we talk some other time?" he said quickly. "It's been a busy day and now is not really a good time for me . . ." Then he gave a surreptitious glance behind him, as if afraid that his companion might come out to investigate.

The casual, almost indifferent reaction and the disinterested way he'd tried to brush her aside set off something inside Emma, and right then, all thoughts of breaking the news softly to him went right out the window.

"It was a good time for you a few months ago, though, wasn't it, you two-faced bastard!" she blurted, her tone rising. "Back then, you had plenty of time for me!"

He looked stunned for a moment. "Emma, please . . .

calm down!" He looked worriedly up and down the street.

"Why should I? Are you afraid that everyone will find out about you? Afraid they'll all find out that the person they think is the salt-of-the-earth is nothing but a heartless, using bastard?"

"Heartless, using bastard . . . what's all that about?" he said, looking genuinely puzzled. "How did I use you? As far as I was concerned that night was just a bit of fun – for both of us. Something stupid after a few drinks too many."

Emma couldn't believe it. He had no idea – no idea at all that she had real feelings for him. He'd really thought their night together was no big deal. *Just a bit of fun?* Having known all about this man, having always known deep down that she couldn't – *shouldn't* – put any faith in him, still she'd thought it meant something. But she'd been silly to think about trusting him, because most of the time the same man couldn't even trust himself.

"Look, Emma, I'm sorry if you thought that . . . well, I didn't mean to . . . as I said, we'd had a few drinks, and it was just a bit of a laugh, wasn't it?" He was talking as if it was all perfectly reasonable. "I didn't think for a second that you might think something would come of it. I mean, you know as well as anyone the story with me."

"Well, something did come of it, actually," Emma replied, her heart racing as she said the words. "I'm pregnant."

She watched his face drain of colour, as his gaze quickly moved to her abdomen.

"I don't believe you!"

"Well, you'd better believe me, because it's no bloody joke."

The two of them stood there for a while, both silent as he tried to take in the news. "Emma, I don't know what to say," he said eventually. "This is . . . well, to be honest, I'm completely shocked."

The fact that he hadn't immediately closed the door in her face, the fact that he looked almost . . . fascinated by this news, buoyed her a little. Maybe things wouldn't be so bad after all. Maybe the two of them might just be able to muddle through. But just as quickly, Emma remembered what Eric had told her, remembered the reasons she'd kept this a secret in the first place. There was no future for her with this man – nor would there ever be.

"But why didn't you tell me before now?" he asked then.

Emma looked quickly down at her feet. "I was going to, but then I heard from Eric that you'd . . . well, that you'd found someone else – someone serious."

He coloured slightly. "That's true. But Emma, you and me, that night . . . well, to be honest, after that I did feel a bit strange . . . a bit confused, I suppose – and I felt I was back to square one again, back to not knowing what I wanted. But then, shortly afterwards, I met Nicky, and right away I knew I didn't have to make a choice. It just felt right . . ."

His words trailed off, as the aforementioned Nicky appeared behind him in the doorway.

"Is everything OK, Colm?" he asked, glancing at Emma warily.

Emma looked from one man to the other and all of a sudden felt very foolish indeed.

Eric had been right; she'd been stupid to think that she had a chance just because the long-time object of her affection hadn't been living an openly gay life. Colm had struggled for years with his sexuality (when they were younger, in this village an admission would have been impossible) and she'd been stupid to think that he would – or even could – change his mind.

But you couldn't help who you fell in love with, and unfortunately for her, Emma had been in love with Colm for a very long time. Despite what Eric had told her, despite what she knew herself to be true, for as long as Colm struggled, she'd always thought she was in with a chance.

And when, a few months ago, just before taking the new job in Dublin, she'd worked her final shift alongside him in The Coffee Bean and Colm had brought her out for a farewell dinner and then back to his house to share a bottle of wine, Emma tried to take that chance.

Colm was right, it had all been a laugh at first and, in fairness, she had more or less thrown herself at him, but at the time, he hadn't refused. And over the days that followed, Emma had been certain that their night together had made things clearer for him, that it meant that for him all those years of experimentation and uncertainty were finally over.

And she'd been right, albeit not in the way she'd anticipated. It appeared that their night together, along with Nicky's subsequent appearance in the village – ironically to act as Emma's replacement in the café – had made Colm decide on his path once and for all.

Emma still recalled the devastation she'd felt when Eric had one day mentioned in passing that Colm had finally started a proper gay relationship. It had only been a few weeks since their night together, and she'd been too busy settling into her new job and new place in Dublin after the initial move to come home since.

"So it seems Colm has finally bitten the bullet and decided to swing one way once and for all," Eric had said with a grin.

And thinking that Colm had told Eric about their night together, Emma smiled coquettishly.

"Really? How so?" she'd asked, expecting Eric to start teasing her about it. But she'd nearly fallen off the chair when he told her Colm had begun openly seeing Nicky, some guy who'd recently moved to Castlegate and started working at the café.

And then, to complete her upset and utter embarrassment about the situation, soon after that, she discovered she was pregnant. She immediately resolved not to tell Colm or indeed anyone else who the father was. Pregnant by the town gay? How mortifying!

But now, it finally was all out in the open, and Colm knew everything.

And strangely, Emma thought, as she stood on the doorstep outside his house, he didn't seem all that upset by her news – certainly not as upset as she'd expected him to be at any rate. Yes, there would be plenty to sort out, but for some reason, Emma suspected that things mightn't be that bad after all.

Still slightly dazed, Colm looked from Emma to Nicky and back again. Then, he shook his head from side to side. "Emma, please come inside for a cup of coffee," he said, smiling faintly at the absurdity of it all. "I think the three of us have a lot to talk about."

•

Back at the McGrath house, Liz was still trying to pick her jaw up off the floor.

"Colm from the café?" she spluttered. "*Gay* Colm?"

"I know," Eric said shrugging. "Believe me, I was as surprised as you are. Although, probably not as shocked," he added wryly. "Colm is a very confused man – has been for a very long time."

"I'll say!"

"Remember I told you before that he was a bit of a catch with the girls in the village when we were younger?" Eric shook his head in exasperation. "To be honest, over the years I think he's had some sort of fling with most of the girls from around here."

Liz was still shaking her head. "Well, fair enough if he's confused – I've known guys like that myself – but what on earth was *Emma* thinking? Colm's in a relationship – with a man! Surely she didn't expect him to forget all about that for her? I mean, I know she's good-looking but she's not *that* –"

"He wasn't with this guy when he and Emma . . . got together," Eric explained. "And afterwards, she really thought she was in with a chance. Turned out it was the complete opposite. I felt a bit sorry for her, to be honest. She really was mad about him."

"I can't believe this!" Liz gasped. "What kind of weird people live in this village?"

Despite himself, Eric raised a smile. "Look, I know it sounds a bit weird to you now, but you don't know what Colm is like. Ask Tara – everyone here has always known that Colm wasn't quite sure himself about his own sexuality, and all this excessive womanising was simply part of that. And, as you can probably imagine, it certainly wouldn't have been easy for him to come out properly – not in Castlegate anyway. But then, when Nicky came along . . ." Eric shrugged, "he told me he'd eventually decided to hell with the begrudgers after all – he was happy with this person and he wasn't going to give that up simply because of what people thought. I suppose the fact that he's more mature and now much better able to handle it all helped."

"And times have changed – even in Castlegate."

"Yes. Look, Liz, Colm still doesn't know Emma's pregnant, by the way – undoubtedly as far as he's concerned it was just another of his idiotic attempts at figuring out what the hell he wanted. Look, I know what you're thinking, but believe me Emma's realised just how stupid she's been, and she's terrified that it'll get out that they've slept together. She hasn't been keeping the father a secret because she's afraid he'll find out about it, Liz; she's keeping it a secret because she's embarrassed about the entire situation. Seducing the town gay? Think about it."

Liz didn't know whether to laugh or cry. She believed her husband when he said he hadn't been cheating on her and that he'd been meeting Emma because they knew one another's secrets. But she was still hurt that he hadn't felt able to tell her about losing his job. She could imagine just how delighted the vindictive little cow would have been about finding out Eric's situation and helping him keep it hidden from his wife.

And she was convinced that Emma had in the meantime been purposely trying to plant seeds of doubt in her mind about Eric. Why else would she be blatantly sending him texts and making supposedly innocent phone calls? The bitch had known exactly what she was doing in trying to make her suspicious and it had worked! Though convincing Eric of this might be difficult, given that he seemed to see Emma as some kind of confidante.

And although it still galled her to think that Eric and this horrible person had for the last while been meeting in secret to talk through their individual problems, she knew that she couldn't say too much about it. They were old friends at the end of the day and there was nothing Liz could do to change that. Granted, she'd make sure Eric stayed well away from the little witch for the next while, and Liz would ensure she stayed well away from Emma herself – otherwise there was no knowing what she'd do!

"So, now you know," Eric said then. "Now you know that I wasn't cheating on you. Although I can't believe for one second that you would think something like that, and if I had known you'd even suspected it . . ." The rest of the sentence trailed off. "Liz, I love you so much. All I've ever wanted was to make you and Toby happy, to look after the two of you like my dad never did for me and my mum. That's why I didn't want to tell you I'd lost my job – at least not until I'd had a chance to try and find another one, a decent one. I just didn't want to disappoint you." He shook his head and took Liz's hands in his. "You two are my life, and I don't know what I would do if I lost you. I would never sacrifice that – you've got to believe me."

Liz looked into her husband's face and knew instinctively that he was telling the truth. OK, so she still didn't fully understand his need to keep the news about his job a secret from her; after all it wasn't as though he was sitting on his backside refusing to do anything else. He still was working – even if it was just in a bar. But Liz knew only too well that it was very difficult to try and live up to other people's expectations, and sometimes even more difficult not to. She had to give him the benefit of the doubt.

"I do know that, love," she replied, squeezing his hand. "But I think you and I have a lot to sort out. I'm hurt that you didn't tell me, and doubly hurt that you felt able to confide in someone else. And it's not a question of you having to take care of me and Toby. We're a partnership and we look after one *another*."

"I know, but can you at least understand how all this happened? As far as I was concerned, it was all innocent between Emma and me. I had no idea you suspected anything about the two of us. As far as I was concerned, we were just two old friends discussing our individual troubles. Of course, Emma turned to me a lot because she didn't have anybody else, and also because I know Colm well, so I could understand better than most why it had happened. She's so embarrassed by it, Liz."

"And well she should be."

"But look, now that I've told you everything, including Emma's private business, will you promise not to breathe a word to anyone about it? Not even Tara?"

Liz sighed deeply as she thought about it. "Well, I don't like the girl, you probably know that by now, but at the same time it's none of my business what she does – thank God," she added, eyeing Eric who smiled ruefully. "So I won't say a word." And despite all that had gone on these last few months, she felt a stab of pity for Emma and her pathetic existence.

So what if Colm had been the love of her life but ultimately rejected her for a different lifestyle? All it meant was that for once Emma Harrington didn't get what she wanted. But by pursuing such a foolhardy and destructive course of action, the girl had eventually ensured that she'd got a hell of a lot more than she'd bargained for.

But thank God, thank God, it wasn't Eric.

Chapter 35

"Tara, it's Natalie."

It was the day after their return from London, and by the other girl's tone Tara knew instinctively that she knew – that Jason had told her the whole sorry story. It was a relief in a way; it meant that she wouldn't have to pretend anything if Natalie excitedly asked her what she thought of him.

"Hi, how are you?" she replied guardedly.

Natalie's tone was solemn. "I know, Tara. I know about you and Jay. He told me everything. I can't tell you how sorry I am to have put you through all this. I had no idea. I knew there was something familiar about him when I met him – maybe it was because he reminded me a little bit of Glenn – although obviously I didn't know that at the time."

"How could you know? How could either of us have known that we had that much in common?" Tara attempted a short laugh. "But Natalie, please don't let this affect your relationship with Jay. It was a long time ago – a lifetime ago – and it shouldn't affect how you feel about him."

"It doesn't," Natalie said simply, and for reasons she couldn't quite fathom, Tara felt a little wounded. "But look, that's not the real reason I'm phoning. Jay is here, and he wants to talk to you."

Tara stopped breathing. "Natalie, no, I can't –"

"Please. He really wants to talk to you – to explain."

"Natalie, there's nothing to explain – it was seventeen years ago. You and Jay should just get on with your lives and leave me and Glenn to get on with ours. I realise that you and I have been close this last while, but surely you realise now that our friendship can't really continue?"

"I understand that, but if our friendship ever meant anything to you, then can I ask you to just talk to him, just hear him out? After that, I promise I'll leave you alone." Then she sniffed. "But I'll miss you, Tara – you've been a rock to me."

Tara's heart went out to her. It wasn't fair of Jason to involve her in this, to use her as a go-between in an attempt to salve his conscience. "I'll miss you too, pet. But it's better for both of us."

"Will you talk to him? For me?"

Tara sighed. She might as well get this over with. "All right."

Then Natalie was gone, and before Tara had any real chance to prepare herself, Jay's all too familiar voice appeared on the other end of the line.

"Tara? It's me," he said, and immediately she tensed.

"Pretty cowardly of you to get Natalie to do your dirty work, isn't it?" she replied.

"It wasn't like that," he said. "I knew it was the only way to get you on the phone."

"We have nothing to say to one another, Jason. You said it all seventeen years ago."

"I didn't say anything," he countered softly. "You wouldn't let me. You'd hung up the phone before I even had a chance to think. Tara, the same day you rang me, I'd been out earlier shopping for stuff for college. It was a total shock, and I couldn't think straight."

"How nice for you," she said bitterly.

"Look, what I mean to say is . . . that I wasn't in the proper frame of mind to tell you what you needed to hear – which was that I'd try to support you every way I could. But I couldn't say those words back then, Tara, because in all honesty I couldn't *be* sure that I could support you at all. I had no job, no prospects – we didn't even live in the same town for goodness sake!" When Tara said nothing, he continued. "I told my parents, who as you know were horrified and more than a little embarrassed. They'd visited and had friends in Castlegate for many years, and then their son goes and gets a local girl into trouble. They wouldn't speak to me for weeks. I was confused, upset; I hadn't a clue what was going on."

"And how do you think I felt?"

"I know. Look, I'll admit I tried at first to put it out

of my head for a while, tried to convince myself – as my parents tried to – that there was nothing I could do. I was too young to provide for you properly, they told me, better to let your family rally round and help you out. And I thought that was what would happen – you were seventeen after all, barely out of school . . . so I thought I was doing the right thing – they'd convinced me I was doing the right thing. Looking back now, I know they were just trying to make sure I went to college and got my education. They didn't want me wasting my life on some young girl I'd met on holiday. But they didn't realise how close we were and how much I cared about you."

At this Tara's heart twisted, and she closed her eyes.

"And I did care deeply about you, Tara. I never lied about that. The closeness we shared over all those summers was real and it should have . . . I should have stood up for that. But I didn't, and by the time I realised that I couldn't leave you to your own devices, it was too late. I phoned your house one day and your sister told me that you'd moved away somewhere with the baby, moved away on your own. And when I asked her for your contact details she said she didn't know them – said that it was somewhere in Dublin but she didn't know where. And when I asked to speak to your parents, she told me that there was no point because they wouldn't want to speak to me."

Upon hearing this, Tara's eyes narrowed. Emma had spoken to Jason, he'd phoned the house looking for her and she'd never said a word! How could she? How could her little sister have so much hate and badness in her that at fourteen years of age she'd conspire to keep them apart? But then again, Emma was only young so perhaps she'd forgotten the conversation almost as soon as it had finished. And she wouldn't have known Tara's exact address at that stage either. So, she supposed she had to give Emma the benefit of the doubt. If she didn't, Tara didn't know what she'd do, and in truth, she'd had enough to deal with over the last few days never mind discovering that her little sister had a part in it all.

"I didn't know that."

"Tara, I'll admit that I was stupid at the beginning, that my reaction was wrong and very hurtful. But you have to believe me when I tell you that I never meant for this to happen. I truly, honestly cared about you, and I don't know if we could have made it work, but now I really wish that I had tried. That I had tried to help you raise our . . . raise Glenn. You don't know how much I regret everything that happened back then. I know it affected your life in an immense way, and I know you probably don't want to hear it, but it affected me too. I've never forgotten you or the baby. I always wondered about you and every time I went back to Ireland I used to imagine I'd bump into the two of you on the street some day. Yet at the same time, I was afraid that I *would* come face to face with you again because I knew you'd probably hate me for what I'd done. But you were my first love, Tara, and I've never forgotten you."

Tara felt an immense lump in her throat. He sounded the very same as he had all those years before, all those summers when they were falling in love. She wanted so much to believe that he was being sincere, that he was telling the truth when he said he'd never forgotten them, that he'd regretted not trying harder to find them, that he'd wished he'd had the courage to try and make it better. But no matter how convincing he might sound, Tara knew deep down that if Jason had really wanted to find her and Glenn, he could very easily have done so. So, she really couldn't let him persuade her otherwise. OK, so at the time he was only a teenager, and it was a relief to know after all these years that he had really cared about her and wasn't the heartless cad everyone had believed him to be, but still, this didn't change what had happened.

"At the beginning of our relationship," he went on, "Natalie asked me why I'd never married and I told her it was because I'd never found the right woman. But the truth was I'd never really got over what had happened with you, and how I'd made a mess of it all. You know how close the two of us were back then, how close we'd become during all those summers I came to Castlegate. And then I ruined it all – I ruined our relationship and, by abandoning you like that, I ruined your future too. And as I got older, I began to realise even more the damage I'd done and how much I'd hurt you. And I really did care for you back then, Tara. I know that probably sounds crazy to you now, but it's true. But we were young, and I was stupid and I didn't know what to . . ." His voice trailed off then and he took a deep breath. "Remember when we used to talk about being soul mates, and how the universe had conspired to bring us together?"

Tara nodded, but then remembering he couldn't see her, she croaked, "Yes."

"Well, if you believed in that then, don't you think that maybe the universe just might have conspired to bring us together once again?"

Tara swallowed as Jason continued, his tone gentle.

"That there was a reason that you and Natalie met in Egypt, perhaps so she could eventually put us in contact again, and we could have this conversation. So that I could tell you how sorry I am about everything and how I wished things could have been different."

"Is Natalie there with you now?" Tara asked, wondering what the other girl was making of all this. She didn't want Natalie hurt – she didn't deserve that.

"No, she went out for a while to give us some privacy." There was a brief silence. "I know I said I never found anyone to live up to the closeness I had with you, Tara, but with Natalie, I think I have."

Tara closed her eyes, unsure how she was feeling about the whole thing. She didn't want Jason back, of course she didn't, but the emotions she was feeling just then were all-consuming and she hadn't felt like that in a very long time.

"I'm pleased for you both," she said eventually. "Natalie is a wonderful person, and I know you'll be very happy."

"Thank you – it means a lot to hear you say that."

"Jason, I appreciate you telling me that you at least tried to contact me. And maybe you do have your regrets. But it doesn't change the last seventeen years of my life, and it doesn't change the fact that Glenn has no idea who you are, nor does he want to."

"I understand that."

"And I'm not going to tell him I met or have spoken to you recently. He's got too much going on in his life right now."

"I understand that," Jason said politely. "And I don't blame you. I would hate to stir things up for either of you."

"But . . ." Tara said then, and she could almost hear Jason hold his breath, "one of these days I will tell him about you. To be honest, up until now, strangely, he's never been too bothered or terribly inquisitive about you. But that might change once he has a child of his own. And when I do tell him who you are and where you live, it'll be entirely up to Glenn what he wants to do. I won't hold sway over him either way. If he wants to see you, well and good; if he doesn't, I won't force him."

"Thank you, Tara," Jason breathed, relieved. "I know I don't deserve that much."

"No, you don't," she said seriously, but then she smiled. "But I think I'd like you to meet him one day all the same. He's an honest, decent and very special person."

"Then he most definitely takes after his mother,"

Jason replied quietly, and for a long time after that, the two of them just stayed on the line saying nothing because – Tara realised, tears streaming down her cheeks – after that there was nothing more to say.

Chapter 36

A few weeks later, Glenn arrived home for dinner with a visitor in tow.

"Tara, this is Abby," he said, his cheeks colouring slightly as he introduced a petite and timid-looking dark-haired girl.

"Pleased to meet you, em, Mrs Harrington," the girl said, limply shaking Tara's hand.

"Call me Tara," Tara said with a friendly smile, although inwardly she wondered how on earth a girl this young and harmless-looking was going to deal with a pregnancy. Then again, she'd done it herself, hadn't she? "Mrs Harrington sounds so old!"

"Abby was asking why I always refer to you by name," Glenn said, casually picking out bits of vegetables from Tara's stir-fry, "but I've been doing it for so long now, I hardly notice it. I don't think I've ever called you Mum, have I?"

"If you do – I know you've done something wrong!" Tara said, with a playful wink at Abby, who blushed deeply.

Tara turned back to the cooker and smiled. He *had* indeed called her "Mum", and only very recently, when she'd returned from London and they'd talked some more about his situation.

"The last thing I wanted was to disappoint you, Mum," he'd said, and to her surprise, Tara had felt tears prick at the corners of her eyes. Hearing him call her that for what must have been the first and only time made her understand how truly affected he was by all this, and made her doubly resolved to help him through it whatever way she could. And by the looks of this timid little creature, he'd need it!

But gradually over dinner, Abby began to come out of herself and, judging from the calluses on her fingertips, it seemed she was as much as a computer freak as Glenn. "Abby's one of the best hackers I've ever met," Glenn enthused, his mouth open as he ate. "She kicks my ass when it comes to Linux!"

"Really," Tara said, smiling brightly and trying to conceal her worries about the sort of child these two would produce. It would either be Bill Gates or Forrest Gump!

Much later that evening, over a cup of tea at Liz's house, Tara aired her thoughts on the subject. She'd travelled home to Castlegate, leaving Glenn and Abby alone in her house to "discuss things".

"For the life of me, I can't understand how they ever got round to any funny business in the first place," she laughed, referring to Glenn and Abby. "You should have seen the two of them plonked in front of the computer when I was leaving – the house could have been burning to the ground around them and they wouldn't have a clue." She sighed. "They're such kids, really."

"They'll be fine," Liz reassured her from where she sat on the sofa, "and when they run into any problems, they'll always have you to fall back on and give them a helping hand."

"I know. Speaking of a helping hand, any word on a full-time job for Eric yet? "

Since coming clean about his employment circumstances, Eric had asked around the village and was currently keeping busy by doing some carpentry work locally. He was still working his bar shifts in Dublin, but with any luck he would soon be in a position to give those up for good.

"Not yet, unfortunately, and I think he's finally coming round to the fact that he might have to retrain. He doesn't want to stay working in Dublin anyway, and after everything that's happened recently, I don't want him to either. We need to be together as a family. But lately he's been doing a lot of work for Luke next door."

"Really?" Tara looked up.

"Yep. He's trying to give him a hand with much of the heavy work that needs doing in the house. Can you believe it? And our place practically falling asunder? The two of them are putting in a new kitchen next door at the moment. But then Luke in turn is planning to give Eric a hand with some work here so . . ." She shook her head. "I'm pleased they're getting on so well, actually. For some reason, I got the impression that Luke didn't really take to Eric initially." She frowned. "But they certainly seem fine now."

"I'm so glad you and Eric managed to work things out – and I'm especially glad that . . ." The rest of her sentence trailed off. "Well, you know . . . that none of my family was involved in it."

"Thank you," Liz said, a guilty smile on her face.

"Thanks for what?" Tara asked, reacting to the smile.

"For not vocalising my own suspicions back to me. I wouldn't have been able to handle it if you'd told me you had the same idea I had – that Eric could be the father of Emma's baby. Convincing myself that it was all in my own head was what kept me sane, so you really don't know how much I appreciate that."

Tara smiled back. "Well, the mystery has now been solved once and for all. I was going mad trying to figure who it was. Believe it or not, I'd started to wonder only recently if she might have had a bit of a thing with Dave McNamara but wouldn't say anything because of his getting engaged to someone else. And what with him being a councillor and a pillar of the community and all that."

"Interesting theory," Liz agreed, nodding thoughtfully, "but well off the mark as it turns out."

"I nearly fell down dead when she told us, Liz," Tara

went on. "I knew Emma had a thing for unavailable men, but honest to God! Still, apparently Colm is determined to give her all the support she needs, so . . ." She shook her head. She'd known that her sister had always had a bit of a soft spot for Colm Joyce – as had lots of women in this village over the years – but had no idea that it had been anything more than that. Was it because the guy – due to his ongoing confusion – was the ultimate challenge? Or did she really have true feelings for him? Poor Emma – in this case, it seemed that Colm was the one man she truly never could have. And because of this, she felt for her sister and was annoyed that Colm had messed around with her feelings like that. "Liz, can you imagine what'll it be like around here when the news finally gets out?" In the end, her poor sister had been right to keep it all a secret for as long as she could. "The gossips will have a field day!"

"I certainly don't envy her. It's tricky one to take in at all, let alone try and explain. But Emma seems a very resilient girl – when it does all come out, I'm sure she'll cope with it."

"Resilient?" Tara repeated, wryly. "That's a slightly different description to the one you used for her that night she was here, isn't it?"

Liz grimaced. "I know – I feel awful now about calling her a tramp like that. But at the time, I was so angry I *had* to lash out at someone."

"Well, Emma's a big girl and from what you were telling me, she was messing with your head anyway. She seems to like doing that." Tara had told Liz all about

Jason's telephone call to the house shortly after Glenn was born and how Emma hadn't mentioned anything about it. "She's a strange one, Liz, and as much as it pains me to admit it, it's true. While I do feel sorry for her with this whole Colm situation, there's no getting away from the fact that she really needs to grow up once and for all. I just hope that when she does have this baby, she'll stop all her silly games and start behaving like an adult."

"Well, at least the child will have two more sensible parents to rely on if Emma isn't up to the task," Liz said, unable to resist a giggle as she referred to Colm and Nicky's promise to help with the childrearing.

"Less of the sneering at my family, Liz McGrath!" Tara joked. "You've only been living in this town for barely a year, and already you're sounding like one of the natives!"

"Yep, with all these secrets and lies, I think I've just about qualified as a true Castlegater," her friend laughed. "And speaking of which, are you ever going to make the move?"

"Where? Back here?"

"Of course."

"I don't know. I've thought about it a lot lately, you know that – especially now after all this with Glenn and Abby – but I just don't know."

"I know someone who'd be happy," Liz said, her eyes dancing.

"Who?" Tara looked at her in surprise.

"Well, my favourite next-door neighbour for one. As

I've told you a thousand times before, he's always asking for you. Every time I meet him he manages to bring the conversation round to you."

Tara snorted. "He probably just wants some more mice removed."

Liz rolled her eyes. "Bloody hell, woman, can you not see something when it's staring you plain in the face?"

"What are you on about?"

"Luke's crazy about you! And I know you're a bit partial to him too – I saw you with him that night in the pub. So you'd want to get up off your backside and do something about it before someone else snaps him up. I know I would, if I were single, which I'm not of course," she added primly. "In fact, I'm very happy with my man."

"You and Natalie both then," Tara said.

Natalie had phoned her again a couple of days after her conversation with Jason.

"I'd love us to stay friends," she'd told Tara, "but I know it's not ideal. Especially not as it's getting serious with Jay and me." Then she added, almost apologetically, "He's asked me to move in with him."

"Natalie, I'm so happy for you, really I am," Tara said truthfully, "but you don't need me now. Yes, we were friends of sorts but you no longer need me to help you out with your love life. And don't apologise for that," she added quickly, before Natalie could speak. "You and Jason . . . Jay . . . are obviously very much in love, and you deserve that. You both deserve it."

"Tara, I don't know what to say," Natalie said tearfully. "I never thought something like this would happen."

"It's OK, and I'm sure we'll keep in touch and ring one another from time to time to see how we're getting on."

But of course that wouldn't happen, and sadly, they both knew it. It was a pity but, Tara thought, such was life. And she couldn't help but be reminded of Jason's comment about how the universe conspired to keep people together or apart. Maybe she shouldn't think too much more about it and instead just leave it all up to the gods.

"I'm telling you – you'd better do something about Luke," Liz was saying. "Only the other day, I saw that young Slattery one chatting him up in the greengrocer's!"

Although, on the other hand, Tara thought, smiling to herself as she thought about it, maybe this time, she should just bite the bullet and take destiny into her own hands.

Chapter 37

A week later, Tara walked up to the front door and rang the bell. Despite herself, she swallowed nervously as she heard him come out to the hallway to answer it. What the hell was she doing here? And why had she let Liz talk her into this?

"Hi there."

"Hi." When he opened his front door, Luke's blue eyes lit up, but when he looked down and saw what Tara was holding in her arms, he quickly took a step backwards. "What . . . what's that?"

"Oh, it's nothing," Tara tried to sound nonchalant. "Wow, the place is looking great!" She looked past Luke's bulky frame into the front hallway.

Eric had obviously done sterling work in the few weeks he'd been working on this place for his neighbour. The walls were freshly painted, there was a new wooden floor and skirting in place of the old worn lino and, from her vantage point, Tara could see that he'd redone some of the kitchen too.

"Well, aren't you going to invite me in? Or do I have to stand out here all day?"

"Erm, come in then." All the time trying to avert his eyes from what she was holding, Luke held back the door and allowed Tara in.

"Well!" she announced breezily. "You've certainly been busy!"

"Yes . . . erm, Tara, what *is* that?" Luke repeated, his voice quivering a little.

"Oh, this?" Tara held up the animal cage as if she'd forgotten all about it. "It's a gerbil," she told him nonchalantly.

"And what is it doing here?" Luke said, backing a little further away from her.

"Oh, silly me – I forgot to mention it. It's a present," she said, thrusting the cage at him.

Immediately Luke recoiled. "A present?"

"Yes, a housewarming present for you!"

Luke swallowed. "Erm, Tara, it's very nice of you to think of me but –"

"I thought it was the best possible gift for you."

"Ah – why?"

"Well, I know this is my territory and not yours, but surely you know the best way to overcome your fears is to face them head on?"

And by being here today, that was exactly what she herself was doing. Finally taking Liz's advice, Tara was opening herself up to the possibility of a relationship, a friendship, whatever, with Luke Cunningham.

So, it might come to nothing but wasn't it – as Liz had always insisted – wasn't it worth taking the chance? It wasn't as though she could use Glenn as an excuse any more. As of last week, he and Abby had announced they were thinking of moving in together when the baby was born, and as much as it would kill her to let him go, Tara knew she had no choice. Seventeen years on, she had to allow her son to get on with his own life, and now she, Tara, would get on with hers.

Starting today.

"Tara, I appreciate the gesture but –"

"Just let me help, OK?"

"Help with what? I'm already overrun with bloody mice. I don't need another rodent to add to my collection."

"I told you – it's not a mouse – it's a gerbil," she repeated, again thrusting the cage at him.

Then, as Luke tentatively put his hand out to take it from her, their fingers touched briefly and an unmistakeable spark of electricity passed between them.

For a long moment, the two of them stayed like that, eyes locked together, while between them in its cage, the gerbil munched innocently on a piece of lettuce.

"Tara," Luke said eventually, "did it ever cross your mind that I might not want to make friends with rodents? That I'd much rather make friends with a more agreeable and less scary species?"

"Like what?" she said, her eyes still locked on his.

"Like you," he said, moving forward, and Tara swallowed. "I think the likes of you qualifies as a species all of your own. *Genus femalus obstinatus* I think it's called."

"Me? Obstinate? Never."

"No, never in a million years," Luke said, gingerly taking the gerbil cage and setting it on the hallway table. "And don't try and play the innocent with me. Liz has told me enough about you, and I've learnt enough myself to know exactly what I'm getting into."

"Then she's probably also told you I've got a lot of baggage," Tara said, amazed that the two of them were being so frank so quickly. It felt strange, exposing herself like this, but at the same time, it felt quite . . . nice.

The first flush of attraction, the promise of more to come – Tara hadn't felt something like that in a very long time. And it was only then, standing there in front of Luke – a man she sensed wanted something to progress between them as much as she did – that she realised she missed it.

"Baggage?" Luke smiled and drew her close. Standing there in the circle of his arms, her body inches from that incredibly broad chest, his handsome face smiling down at her, Tara felt safe. She felt safe with Luke, and for the first time in ages, she gave herself up to the fact that what happened next was something she couldn't, or didn't want to, control. But she was pretty sure she knew what it was, in the same way that she was just as sure she wanted it to happen too.

"Yes, baggage," she repeated.

Luke's mouth was now only inches from her own.

"Well, knowing you," he went on, giving her a lop-sided grin, "it'll be environmentally friendly and biodegradable baggage, so I'm sure we won't have to deal with it for long."

Then, he lowered his head and kissed her softly on the lips.

THE END

ALSO AVAILABLE IN ARROW

Not What You Think

Melissa Hill

When the going gets tough, you find out who your friends really are . . .

Laura Fanning has talent to burn, a brand-new jewellery design company and a wonderful husband. Nicola Peters has independence, a job she loves and her own home. Helen Jackson has a killer wardrobe, a thriving career and a lively and engaging daughter.

But all is not as it seems. Laura's struggling to live up to her parents' impossible expectations, Nicola is coping with a life-changing event, Helen's worried that her maternal instinct has gone AWOL – and trying to cope with their problems alone is driving the three friends apart just when they need each other most.

Then into the mix comes Chloe Fallon. She's marrying gorgeous Dan Hunt and planning the wedding of the year, but little does she realise how much chaos her wedding preparations are about to cause . . .

'A warm and engaging read – perfect for the beach!' Colette Caddle

'Deserves a space in your suitcase' *Irish Independent*

ALSO AVAILABLE IN ARROW

Never Say Never

Melissa Hill

Sometimes hopes and dreams don't go according to plan – sometimes, real life gets in the way.

On a mild May evening, a group of friends on the verge of graduating speculate on what the future holds. Will Leah be a chef? Robin an accountant? And Olivia the one who holds it all together? The one thing they know is that they'll always be friends – no matter what – but they make a pact to meet up in five years, just in case fate intervenes.

Years later it's clear that life has not gone according to plan. Why is Robin in New York determined never to go back to Dublin? Why is Olivia grieving? And why does Leah feel so left out as she heads towards the big three-o?

When Robin is forced to return, they all find themselves face to face with the past – suddenly nothing can ever be the same again. And they start to realize that sometimes it's best never to say never . . .

'An absolute joy from start to finish' *Irish Independent*

arrow books

ALSO AVAILABLE IN ARROW

The Learning Curve

Melissa Nathan

Nicky Hobbs loves teaching at the local primary school. She's idolised by her class – in particular ten-year-old Oscar Samuels – but she's starting to find she'd quite like some adult adoration for a change.

Mark Samuels is a frazzled single father working all the hours God gives to provide for his beloved son, Oscar. But he's unable to see that Oscar would prefer his presence to his presents once in a while.

Ms Hobbs knows Mr Samuels is a heartless workaholic. Mr Samuels is certain Ms Hobbs is an interfering busybody. But when they finally meet they start to discover that first impressions can be deceptive. And perhaps they've both got a bit of learning to do . . .

'Tremendous fun' Jilly Cooper

arrow books

ALSO AVAILABLE IN ARROW

The Accidental Mother

Rowan Coleman

Sophie Mills has worked her Manolo Blahniks off to reach the near-top of her profession. And she's very happy with her priorities in life – her job, her neurotic cat Artemis and her passion for shoes. After all, relationships only get in the way. And as for children? She hasn't even begun to think about them yet. Until one day an unexpected visitor brings news of a strange inheritance and Sophie is suddenly, out of the blue, in sole charge of two children under the age of six. But motherhood can't be all that hard, can it?

Within twenty-four hours, her make-up is smeared all over the bathroom, Artemis has taken up residence on top of her wardrobe, and Sophie is in despair. And all her unconventional mother can suggest is Dr Roberts' *Complete Dog Training and Care Manual*.

Determined to rise to the challenge, Sophie soon realises that she'll need more than a business plan to cope with all this . . .

Praise for Rowan Coleman

'A witty, wonderful, warm-hearted read' *Company*

'Touching and thought-provoking' *B*

arrow books